Daughters of Destiny

FIONA

LINDA ANDREWS

ZUMAYA EMBRACES

2010

AUSTYN TX

FIONA
© 2011 by Linda Andrews
ISBN 978-1-936144-06-8
Cover art and design © Carol Webb

"Zumaya Embraces" and the dove colophon are trademarks of Zumaya Publications LLC, Austin TX.
http://www.zumayapublications.com/embraces.php

Library of Congress Cataloging-in-Publication Data

Andrews, Linda, 1967-
Fiona / Linda Andrews.
    p. cm. — (Daughters of destiny ; 2)
ISBN 978-1-936144-06-8 (alk. paper) — ISBN 978-1-936144-07-5 (ebk.)
1. Heiresses—Fiction. 2. Americans—England—London—Fiction. 3. Upper class—England—London—Fiction. 4.   England—Social life and customs—19th century—Fiction. I. Title.
PS3601.N55267F56 2011
813'.6—dc22
                        2011013854

To my wonderful family and friends for their support, love and guidance.

CHAPTER 1

London Docks, England
May 1892

Someone was behind her. Awareness prickled the back of her neck. Fiona Grey peered through the darkness and the thick pea-soup fog, searching the alley for a place to hide.

There. Perhaps the doorway...

Before she could move, a hand covered her mouth. The unmistakable odor of male assaulted her nose as a forearm pressed against her chest and another hand closed around her upper arm. Fiona's heart picked up tempo as the man's hard body pressed against the length of hers. She stiffened in his arms. In all her twenty-one years, she'd never been treated this way.

She twisted in his hold. How dare he!

"Shh..." Ale-scented breath hissed past her ear seconds before his hold tightened.

A moment later, her boot heels bumped over the cobblestones. Merciful heavens, where was he taking her?

Instead of anger and fear from his grip, a pleasant tingle raced through her. Most peculiar. Sure, she craved a bit of excitement, but she preferred to experience a kidnapping within the covers of a book, not in person.

The restless spirit of her dead fiancé, Milton Davis, hovered near the center of the alley. His opaque form appeared in shades of gray against the yellowish fog and glow of gaslight.

— I say, he's being a bit rough, isn't he?

Rough? The stranger's grasp exuded determination, not cruelty or punishment. Of course, given her wealth, he wouldn't want harm to befall her and risk his ransom. No, he presented only a minor annoyance. As for the other presence in the alley...

Fiona glared at her not-so-dearly departed fiancé. Did he truly think such an observation would help her? Of course she didn't precisely need his assistance. She had looked after herself for two years.

Wiggling a bit in her captor's hold, she brushed her weapons with her fingertips. The stranger held her only because she allowed it.

Milton adjusted the cuffs of his gray burial suit.

— Don't look at me like I'm infested with beetles, Fi. I did not encourage this midnight jaunt. I thought London to be a civilized place, not some godforsaken den of iniquity.

Fiona cast her gaze upwards. Milton hadn't encouraged her escape from the *Revere*, but he had urged her to walk slowly so she might see who followed her. Had he known she would be grabbed? No, she refused to believe he would endanger her life just to prove the dockyards were no place for a lady.

She wiggled. And just what manner of man was this stranger? Granted, this was her first kidnapping, but he seemed to be going about it in a rather peculiar manner. Instead of carrying her off to a waiting carriage, he appeared to be manhandling her into the very doorway she'd planned to hide in. She inhaled sharply. The scents of sea and soap filled her lungs. Alarm rippled through her—something did not ring true.

"I mean you no harm, madam." The man's breath was hot against her ear and tart with the smell of alcohol. "I must have your compliance and silence if we are to escape the docks."

Compliance and silence. This man was no common sailor. Indeed, his speech was refined, his vocabulary educated. A captain, then? Fiona struggled to fit the facts to her conclusion. In her experience running her family's shipping company, captains swaggered not skulked, and few wished to escape their beloved ships.

— Ha, I believe you owe me an apology, Fi. Milton smoothed the lapels of his burial suit. *I surmised a sailor to be the perfect guide out of this place. He wishes to escape just as much as you.*

"Mmoo uph pht." Her jaw moved against the man's palm, felt the rasp of skin against her lips. The calluses were wrong, and the hand was soft—too soft for a salt, young or old. She waited for fear to ice her skin. Instead, a sense of protection warmed her.

"Do you understand?" the stranger whispered.

"Umph." Fiona jerked her head once then stilled.

"Your complete silence, please." He gave her arm a little shake. "I can assure you those who lurk in the mist would not grant you safe passage."

Her shoulders straightened. Safe passage. So, he was no kidnapper. She fought the tendril of disappointment. Ah, well, she'd had enough adventure for one night.

Clearing her throat, she sighed then jerked her head to indicate her compliance.

"I will release you now."

His hand lifted off her mouth, but he kept it near her head. She remained still. Would he bolt down the alley if she turned to look at him? She counted to twenty. Thirty. At forty, he hadn't moved.

Milton fingered the dark spot where the cleft in his chin had been.

— *Are you well, Fi? You seem rather quiet.*

Quiet? She was silent, as requested, and stared at the wooden door in front of her face.

Fiona cleared her throat and tapped her rescuer's shoe with the toe of her boot. He remained a statue by her side. She turned slightly. He was taller than Milton had been, with a straight profile and strong chin.

"Pardon my ignorance," she whispered when he still hadn't moved, "but isn't haste a virtue at present?"

"Indeed, madam, indeed." He slid his hand down her arm and laced his fingers with her gloved ones.

Shock coursed through her. She fixated on their clasped hands. How could the press of a stranger's palm against hers seem more intimate than Milton's kisses?

"Where is your child?"

In the murky lamplight, she watched his dark brows meet in a V above his aquiline nose.

Child? Fiona glanced around her. *Milton.* He had heard her talking to Milton and thought her companion to be a child. Fortunately, Milton didn't seem to make the connection.

She stepped away from the stranger then turned to face him. Her gaze flicked over his shadowy features. She doubted he would accept her denial, so she must find another means to distract him. Fortunately, most men possessed vanity and pride.

"Is a child pivotal to your rather, um, theatrical assistance?"

He stiffened. "Theatrical assistance?"

"Lurking in the shadows, sneaking across the clearing and tossing stones in every direction." She tugged her hand from his grasp. Three fingers waved at him, one for each of his actions.

"See here, Madam, I am a..." He swallowed hard. "...an Englishman. My actions were dictated by reason not...not by a pampered Parisienne." He flicked the velvet collar of her cape.

What kind of sailor knew about fashions, Parisian or otherwise? This man was not as he seemed. Had he heard of her or her family? *Faith, Fiona, this is another country.* The Greys' membership in the First Four Hundred probably meant nothing to the English.

"Monsieur Worth designed my wardrobe, not—"

"Yet another point of honor succumbs to the folly of fashion," he growled.

"Honor!" She tried to make the connection between her cape and her honor.

He placed a finger to her lips, stilling her shout but not quelling the outrage shaking her frame.

"You agreed to keep your silence."

Her teeth clicked near his finger. She tossed her head and stepped back.

"*You* offered to guide me through this maze." She drilled his chest with her index finger.

"I cannot allow you to leave your child behind."

Child. Affronted pride would not dissuade the man from his topic. Interesting. If only she had more time to consider the puzzle he presented.

"You cannot—" She swallowed her rising voice. A close version of the truth would assuage his concerns and, more important, get her off these docks. She hoped.

"Precisely. Furthermore, I insist you collect the infant immediately." He glanced over his shoulder. "Time is of the essence."

Cursing drifted down the alley.

— *Make up something, Fi.* Milton flitted toward the voices. *I'd recognize Bosson's voice anywhere.*

Bosson. Fiona's heart kicked up-tempo. She didn't want to meet Bosson in a drawing room, let alone in a dark alley.

"Madam, please." Her rescuer plowed his fingers through his hair. His seaman's cap rolled down his back and plopped onto the ground.

"I have no child, and my traveling companion is dead." She tried to ease around the stranger's bulk, but he blocked her way.

— *But not forgotten.* Milton winked at her. *Now, urge the fellow in that direction.* He pointed the way she had been traveling before the man had grabbed her.

"Then with whom were you conversing?" Confusion thickened the man's voice.

"My companion." Fiona shifted to the other side. The man filled the doorway. How was she to urge someone that large to move in *any* direction?

— *Perhaps you should not mention me, Fi.* Milton drifted close and stuck his face near the stranger's. *His kind aren't exactly known for their intelligence.*

Fiona shook her head. Outside of her family, she had yet to meet a man who was.

The stranger cocked his head to the side.

"You just said—"

A loud banging from the direction of the railyard interrupted him.

"Sir, may I remind you that I am a *lady* standing on a decrepit dock in the wee hours of the morning? I have no baggage, unless you count the menace lurking in the shadows."

She glanced at Milton. He crossed his arms.

— *That's a fine way to treat your protector.*

Fiona resisted the urge to roll her eyes. She carried her protectors on her hip.

"Perhaps we might quibble another time?"

"Just so." The stranger offered her his hand. Warmth surrounded hers as she accepted. He tugged her out of the doorway and down the alley, taking the right lane when the path forked. "This way."

"Are you quite certain?" Fiona glanced at the buildings towering above her. "I believe I followed this path before." And ended up back where she had begun.

"I can assure you, I have my bearings."

For a while, silence reigned as they rushed down the narrow lanes. Dawn pushed back the darkness and the fog thinned, allowing her a better look at the buildings. Fiona eyed the mortar and pestle visible through the cracked paint on the building's swinging wooden sign.

"Didn't we pass the apothecary's shop before? I only ask because it appears quite familiar. And look at those golden balls." She pointed to the next placard. "I'm certain that is the same pawnshop."

His fingers tightened around hers. "Madam, I am fulfilling my part of the bargain. Do you not think you could reciprocate?"

"If you need to concentrate–"

— *Must you provoke the man, Fi?* Milton huffed. *Do you wish to arrive at your uncle's house tonight?*

How had she forgotten how sore men became when questioned?

"Very well." She pressed her lips tightly together. She would be compliant and silent.

Gradually, the crowded lanes and alleys of Wapping gave way to more modern buildings and somewhat cleaner streets. Conversation drifted out of the fog. Grunting filtered from a nearby alley. The acrid air burned her lungs. Her guide coughed.

"Commercial Road is ahead. I've a cab waiting."

Fiona nodded once, opened her mouth then shut it with a click. A group of men emerged from the mist—dockers with meaty fists swinging at their sides.

Her rescuer looped an arm around her shoulders.

Fiona resisted the urge to stiffen at his intimate liberties. The territorial move protected her from the workers' leers. Determined to help in this ruse, she leaned against his side, rested her hand on his chest. Funny, she hadn't realized how cold she was until she felt his body heat. His heart thudded against her palm. It beat almost as fast as hers. Guess he wasn't accustomed to the excitement, either.

The crooked street emptied onto a wide lane. A hansom cab wavered like a phantom in a yellow arc of light. Disappointment pulled on her, and she pushed out of his hold.

"Your coach, I believe." Relief weakened her knees. They had made it.

"'Ere now, ye didn't think the likes of you could escape us?"

Fiona pivoted. Behind her, two men stepped from the thinning fog onto the cobbled street. The smaller one tossed a knife from hand to hand. Bosson, the *Revere*'s first mate, pointed a rusted revolver at her rescuer's heart.

CHAPTER TWO

— Ha! Milton glided between the three men. See how he places himself between your person and those cads? Not that flesh would stop anything at this range. Ghostly hands measured the distance between the pistol and her rescuer's chest. *No, indeed.* Milton clapped his hands then frowned at the lack of sound. *I'll wager the bullet smashes through him and lodges in you.*

"Milton." Under her cape, Fiona set her hands on her hips. Someone must have chiseled "Rest in Peace" off his tombstone. Someone who hated her.

The stranger squared off against Bosson and his henchman. They seemed to have forgotten her altogether. She had to think, while she had time.

— Oh, right. I've sworn off betting. Arms crossed his translucent chest as he tilted his head. *Really, Fi, it's not as if I can die again.* Gray lips puckered. The pout was sharp against the yellow fog.

"Not now," Fiona hissed. Why had she ever mourned his passing? Why had she ever wanted a spirit of her own? She could have waited for Gran. Enjoyed those blissful solitary years. Unease troubled her conscience. Surely, mentioning him a time or two in passing wouldn't have caused this haunting?

— You should have heeded my advice. Hiding that telegram from your parents, haring off to England and slipping off the boat. Milton wagged an unsubstantial finger at her. *Really, Fi, you're positively reckless with your life.*

Outrage tightened her throat and immobilized her vocal cords. *She* was reckless with her life! The man had died trying to win a race! He adjusted the cuff on his best suit, but rose tinged his shadowy face. She'd talk to him about recklessness later.

"Oi thinks we'll cage these pigeons in the alley." Bosson jerked his pistol towards the narrow street.

Fear iced Fiona's spine. Would she die just as the new day dawned? Would Mam and Da remain ignorant of her fate? If only Uncle Andrew had met the boat. If only...

Scenarios swirled inside her skull. It served no purpose other than to paralyze her will.

Her fingers swept over the Colt shoved into her waistband. The pads bumped over the C-S-A carved into the grip. Too bad Da never let her practice with his gun. Now, when she needed the expertise, she was liable to shoot her rescuer rather than Bosson.

Her hand dropped to her whip, caressed the cool leather then brushed the hemp lasso. Which would be most effective against her enemy?

"The lady stays." The growl rumbled from deep between her rescuer's rigid shoulders.

"Now, why would Oi do that?" Crooked yellow teeth flashed in Bosson's sneer.

— *See, I was right.* A smug expression enveloped Milton's shadowed face. *He's a trustworthy fellow. Led you out of that hell, and now he's willing to die for you.*

Leave it to Milton to take credit for a fortuitous coincidence. No doubt he would gloat for weeks about his triumph over the shady sailors. Air hissed between her teeth, freeing her muscles of irritation. Of course, she still had to triumph over Bosson.

Fiona shoved at her rescuer's shoulder. Heat seared her palm, muscles trembled. Her view remained blocked. She stepped to the side. He shadowed her movements.

His hand shot out, closed around her hip and held her firmly behind him.

"You'll leave the lady alone to avoid bloodshed. Yours."

His answer rumbled inside Fiona's skull. Her gaze slid over his broad shoulders to the white-knuckled fists, down his muscled legs and stopped on his worn shoes. No doubt her rescuer could take Bosson in a fair fight.

But the pistol emphasized the edge held by the old salt.

Alarm thundered in her chest. Truly, any blood spilled would be his. Leading her from the river's edge was one thing, this was another. She tossed the warm velvet cape over her shoulder.

Fiona Grey took care of herself.

Her hand hovered over her cache of weapons. John Bosson was nothing compared to the obstacles she'd overcome. As soon as her Don Quixote stepped out of the way, she'd prove it.

— *Pluck to the backbone. Though I still say he's hiding something.* Transparent fingers met in a pyramid underneath Milton's pointed chin. *Look—only two days on English soil, and I already have the habits of that chap from the papers.*

That chap from the papers. Milton was no more Sherlock Holmes than she was Watson. Heaven knew she made a better detective. Too bad Milton offered nothing more than distracting commentary.

"'E's a bit nickey for a swell." Bosson tapped a tobacco-stained finger against his temple.

"Leave now, and I'll spare your life, Bosson."

Fiona blinked. Her rescuer was obviously mad to take on a pistol with fists. And just how did he know Bosson? Later. She'd think about it later.

Leaning, she peered around his shoulder. *Think, Fi. Think. You must stop him before he gets you both killed.*

Bosson's eyes narrowed to slits. "Kill me, 'e says. Open yer peelers. Oi've the barker, and me mate has the shiv."

Crimson followed the knife's progress along his rumpled companion's finger.

Milton clapped his insubstantial hands.

— I say, this is better than that shoot-out in Phoenix.

Fiona glared at him. This was nothing like the gunfight in Phoenix. There, both men had been armed…

Armed. Her hand closed around the revolver's grip. She relieved the weight pressing against her belly. Cold steel ringed her finger. With a flick of her wrist the gun spun. She caught the barrel with a slap then ran the butt of the weapon down her rescuer's arm and tapped the top of his hand.

He patted her hand.

— Give him your gun, Milton hissed in her ear.

Fiona's throat burned with a silent shout. What did he think she was doing? Trying to hold the man's hand? Wood smacked bone. Her rescuer grunted and dropped his hand from her hip. Was he ignorant of her offer or had pride stopped him from accepting the firearm?

Frustration clawed her. Men. Mr. Darwin's time would have been better spent studying the mysteries of his own gender's behavior.

"You won't get what you want." Boredom saturated the stranger's provoking statement.

Fiona sighed. Maybe the man *wanted* to die on the docks. Well, he'd rescued her, she would return the favor.

"Oi thinks oi will." Bosson sneered.

"You're very much mistaken."

— The chap's liable to talk the man to death. Don't worry, Fi. I'll give them what for. Milton spat into his palms then raised his fists. One jab than another found its mark in Bosson's stomach. Dirty fingers rubbed the first mate's belly as his frame shuddered from Death's touch.

— I did it, Fi. I did it. You saw him shudder. That was me. Milton pummeled the man a few more times. *Wait till I tell Gran. I'll bet I could knock the gun from his hand.*

Golden light infused his translucent form as he raised his fists above his head.

"Wild Bill."

She glanced at the pistol. How difficult would it be to fire? Surely, she could hit the rather large target Bosson presented.

Milton's head jerked towards her.

— Eh?

"Wild Bill," she hissed. The code from their childhood pastime penetrated his skull. Seconds ticked by until understanding lit his features.

— You want me to distract them like Brianna used to do to your parents while we hid the evidence of our shows.

Fiona jerked her head. His smoky chest puffed out.

— Right.

Fiona transferred the gun to her other hand. Steady fingers jerked on the leather thong hooked around her belt. Her whip tumbled into her right palm. She eased one step to her right. No hand rose to stop her. Another step. The men's attention was completely focused on each other. With the third step, she cleared her human barrier. She pinched the whip's handle. The lash uncoiled down her leg and lay like a rattlesnake waiting to strike.

— Ahh, the whip. Excellent choice. Milton rubbed his hands together. *I'll take the knife, you can take the gun.* He drifted into position and raised his hand. Ready.

Bosson lifted his chin. The instant his finger twitched on the trigger, Fiona flicked her wrist. The whip cracked. Metal clattered to the ground a second before the blast ripped through the fog.

"What the hell!" her rescuer cursed.

Time slowed. Bosson clutched his hand to his chest. Blood dripped through his fingers. His partner stared at the knife winking at his feet. Rage twisted Bosson's features. He lurched at her rescuer.

Fiona stepped forward, aiming the gun at his paunch.

"I wouldn't."

Bosson halted mid-step. His beady eyes trained on the shiny Colt.

"It's quite old but functions perfectly."

Bosson's adam's apple bobbed.

"Ye 'aven't the—"

"Haven't I?" Her brave words barely penetrated the pounding in her ears. *Stare him down, Fi. Just as you did that hydrophobic wolf at Gillian's ranch.* She willed her hand not to tremble.

"The territories are a violent place. Why, so far this year, three men have already expired at my feet." She forced her stiff lips into a smile. "Of course, it is only May. I have seven more months to make up the slack."

"By all means, let's add to your collection, my dear." Warm hands closed around her hand, eased the Colt from her grip. The barrel tapped Bosson's forehead and followed him as he straightened. "The Thames won't notice the extra refuse."

"Knew ye two were trouble," Bosson spat. With a vile curse, he and his crony turned on their heels and sprinted into the fog.

Victory jangled along Fiona's nerves. She had done it! Not that she'd had any doubts...

"Of all the harebrained—"

The world spun as her rescuer whirled her about. He loomed over her, his face inches from hers. His nostrils flared. White rimmed his full lips.

"Harebrained?" Fiona tossed back her shoulders, jerking out of his grip. The whip wiggled against the canvas leg of her Levi's, chased the throb from her upper arm. "You were unarmed and threatening them." Her voice rose on the last word. Warm adrenaline receded, leaving behind cold flesh, a chilling reminder of what could have happened. She cleared the hysteria from her throat. "What were you going to do? Attack them with your bare hands."

"Trust me." The words slipped between clenched white teeth. He stepped closer, forcing her to tilt her head back or stare at his adam's apple. "I am more than capable of ripping someone limb from limb."

Fiona retreated a pace. Typical male, bullying when charm failed. Well, she'd print a special edition just for his pride. No man intimidated Fiona Grey. Especially not one who gambled with his life.

"He would have shot you before you took the first step."

"*You* were more likely to shoot me than he was. Your hands shook so much I thought the earth quaked beneath your feet." Her rescuer jammed the gun into his trouser pocket. "Have you ever discharged a weapon before?"

"Once." Guilt splashed her anger. She stoked the embers, felt warmed by the rush of rage. How dare he make her feel guilty? Her quick thinking had saved his life.

"Once! And that gives you leave to wave it in front of a man?"

"It is not difficult. Point and pull the trigger."

"Point and pull..." His blunt fingers delved into his brown locks, cutting white furrows across his skull. Anger and fear warred in his brown eyes.

Fear. He had been afraid for her. His concern blanketed her, smothering her fury.

"I did attempt to hand you the pistol, but you kept patting my hand like I was some sort of faithful hound nipping at your heels."

"You tried to give me the gun?" Shock colored his question. His brows met over his nose.

"Of course. I am well aware of my limitations. The only reason I took Da's gun—"

"Your father gave you a weapon?" He crossed his arms over his chest and glared down at her.

"Not...precisely." The truth bumped against her lips. Fiona resisted the urge to chew on her fingernails. Her reasons had been sound, and the gun had proved useful.

"How *precisely* did you end up with your father's revolver?"

She raised her chin and looked him in the eye. He would not make her regret her actions. He would not.

"I took it."

"Indeed." His left eyebrow soared halfway up his forehead. "You're deucedly lucky, Miss—"

"Fi–Fiona." She cleared her throat. "Given all that has transpired..."

He nodded. "You're deucedly lucky, Miss Fiona. I doubt many experts could have knocked a gun out of a man's hand with one shot."

"Oh, but I didn't use the firearm, Mr..." Stagnant breath filled her mouth. Would he reciprocate with the use of Christian name? Her heart thudded dully in her ears.

"Hugh." He blinked then nodded once as if agreeing with a voice inside his head. "Please call me Hugh." A dimple flashed in his left cheek. "And while I beg to disagree with a lady, I distinctly heard..."

Hugh. Her rescuer's name was Hugh. And he still thought of her as a lady. Joy breezed through Fiona,curving her lips.

"Alice did sound like a shot, didn't she?"

"Alice?" Confusion furrowed his brow. "Is she your...your late companion?"

Late companion? Their first conversation rushed back to Fiona.

"Oh, no. Alice was a wretched girl at Miss Maple's Academy for Young Ladies. She did not approve of much—and of me, in particular. Mister Greenbottom had struck it rich in the mines before my father, and well, she thought that entitled her to certain privileges." Including passing judgment. Fiona shook out her fists.

"You should have seen her face when she found out that all her daddy's gold couldn't get her into New York society whereas Da's mother practically ran it." Fiona snapped her mouth shut. More information knocked against her teeth. She had already stepped so far from propriety she might have to circle the globe to get back in.

"I'm afraid I don't understand."

"When I began to practice for our Wild West show, I pretended Alice was the target. It became a code. I would tell Brianna that I wanted to play with Alice, and my sister would make certain my parents never found out about the whip. After a couple years, I just called her Alice." Fiona tugged on the lash. Finger-thick leather snaked across her palm.

— I called her Alice first, Milton huffed. *I suppose this will be just another thankless task performed by the dead.*

"You used a whip?" The words strangled in Hugh's throat. His eyes bulged in his head as they traveled over her flannel shirt, down her Levi's, flicked over her boots then whisked back to her face.

"I thought it better than the lasso. I am quite proficient in both." Unease itched her spine. She glanced over her shoulder. Nothing menacing lurked in the shadows. She turned back to her companion. A purplish cast hung over his face. Disappointment pinched her insides. The excitement must have been too much for him. "I think—"

"I bloody well doubt that." Hugh closed the distance between them in one step and jerked her cape closed, pinching the ends together with one hand. He raised his free hand and placed two fingers to his lips. An earsplitting whistle rent the air. "Good God, woman, you should have at least dressed."

"My attire is perfectly acceptable." She plucked ineffectually at the fingers. "Oh, I see—you'd both rather I slithered out a ship's window in a dress and bustle."

"You climbed out a ship's window?" A vein throbbed at Hugh's temple. The man obviously suffered from a nervous condition.

Fiona patted his hand. She'd give him one of Brianna's soothing tonics. And perhaps take something to slow her racing heart. Except the tonics were still on the ship with her trunk. Ah, well, she'd just have to use her voice. Brianna always quieted at the sound of her voice.

"Well, I couldn't very well walk across the deck while Bosson entertained his guest."

"I suppose it never occurred to you to stay put." Muscles corded his neck, like strands of rope lashing his head to his body.

Fiona's temper frayed. A nervous disposition excused only so much. She raised herself on her toes and stared into his chocolate-colored eyes.

"I waited for two *long* days."

"Proper young ladies do not—"

Hooves clomped on cobblestones. Harness jingled. Black filled Fiona's peripheral vision. She turned to stare at the hansom stopped along the curb.

"Mil...er, sir. Madam."

The carriage rocked as the burly man jumped from his perch behind the passenger's seat. The lantern in his beefy fist cast a jaundiced pall over his broken nose, pockmarked cheeks and puckered lip.

— Egad, I've spied corpses who looked less gruesome. Milton soared between the newest threat and her. *You cannot intend to go with that...that brute. I'll hail another cab, Fi.*

Two pistols winked from the brute's open coat. Beady eyes peered into the yellow mist while he fingered one revolver.

"Your carriage, milady." Hugh bowed and offered her his free hand.

— Dammit, Fi. Milton stopped in front of her, arms spread wide. Red suffused his gray body. *Don't you dare climb into that coach.*

"Perhaps this conversation would be best suited for a rapidly retreating cab." Ignoring Milton, Fiona slipped her hand in Hugh's. She'd ride with the devil to get to her uncle's house. Fortunately, a ride with Hugh promised to be much more entertaining.

CHAPTER THREE

The cab thumped in and out of a pothole. A shoulder bumped his. Hugh Gurnsey-Barrett, sixth Marquess of Kingslea, ninth Earl of Bookingham, locked his jaw. Cold brushed his exposed flesh. He hunkered further into his borrowed sailor's jacket. Awareness zapped his skin, electrified the hair on his neck and arm. For an instant, flowers perfumed the air. A heartbeat later the acrid coal smoke belching from thousands of chimneys stung his nose. The flame flickered in the lamps as another chunk of missing cobblestones personified Houseman's displeasure.

Leather creaked. Wood groaned. The small interior tilted to the left. His companion slid against his side. Her thigh flattened against his.

"Perhaps you'd prefer to drive. You have the necessary accouterments, I believe."

"My expertise resides solely as a passenger. Not that I haven't tried to drive." A smile teased her lips. Her gaze flitted to his before scampering back to admire the horse's head. "I simply don't have that magic touch."

Yet, she did seem to have bewitched him.

Bewitched. Logic railed at the fanciful notion. The lady's attraction lay in her presence, a presence that extended his adventure. Kingslea forced the sentiment from mind. There could be no other reason. He wouldn't allow it.

The lamp's golden light bathed her high forehead, pert nose and stubborn chin. Such scrutiny exercised his powers of observation and had absolutely nothing to do with a fascination for her person or her unusual accomplishments.

White satin-clad fingers tucked a strand of loose hair behind a delicate ear. They returned to her lap and clasped her black-clad ones. Mismatched gloves. Amusement rattled his control.

"Have you found yet another fault with my attire?"

Blue eyes pinned his gaze. Irritation flashed in the azure depths, tightened the delicate skin around her eyes. Guilt lashed his pleasure. This night's adventure had bruised her delicate complexion. His poorly verbalized surprise had furthered her discomfort. *Well done, Kingslea. Shall we move up to snatching candy from babes?*

Charm had never numbered among his assets. Neither did social grace. Hell, the list of his failings was endless. Parallel lines appeared on her forehead. Still, only a cad wouldn't try to make amends for his crass bumbling.

"Who could fault perfection?" The praise tripped from his lips. Perhaps he had learned a thing or two in the past five years.

Her thick lashes met then parted. Pleasure bloomed in her cheeks.

"But you are looking for something."

"Always." Restlessness prodded his relaxed muscles. He *was* always looking for something. The captain's logbook poked his belly. He had thought he had found it, yet the dawn's light revealed no solutions, only more mysteries.

First, the collector of vouchers. Now the woman.

No, not woman. Lady. An *American* lady.

"Fiona." Her name whispered across his palate. His gaze dropped to her blue-clad thigh. He'd never understood the attraction of a trim ankle, but such a well-formed limb...

His mind recalled the press of her bottom against him like a favored memory. Heat simmered in his gut. God help mankind should women ever take to wearing trousers.

"Is something amiss?" Her hand rested on his forearm.

His hand covered hers. So small and delicate, yet powerful, too. Heat seared his flesh, branding his brain with images better suited for the bedroom. His bedroom, with her black hair tumbled around her shoulders. Kingslea blinked away the images.

"A man should have some control."

"You handled the situation admirably." She squeezed his forearm. "Please don't allow your passionate nature to overset your nerves."

"Passionate nature?" He ignored the spurt of pleasure. Her personality contained as many facets as the stained glass windows in St. Paul's Cathedral did shards of color. Whereas he—he was a pane of clear lead glass. Kingslea the Cold. Bookingham the Bore. The adolescent taunts, the adult classifications.

"I can assure you, madam, I do not have a passionate nature."

"No, of course not."

His mouth opened. The words intended to disabuse her of such a foolish notion never materialized. His teeth clicked together. If she wanted to see him in such a manner...

Kingslea shrugged off his thoughts. It was the disguise—bronze skin, weathered features and ragged clothing. Sailors battled the elements every day. The rational explanation echoed in his hollow chest.

"It was very kind of your coachman to wait."

"Houseman? Kind? Such words rarely dwell in the same sentence."

Another pothole rattled the cab. Fiona braced herself against the grip but still bounced against him. He ignored the ache filling his chest as she scooted away.

"The damp and an injury had more to do with Houseman's patience than any kindness."

By rights, the valet-cum-coachman should be recovering from his gunshot wound instead of charging all over London. Unease shook Kingslea's equanimity. The bullet would have ended his life if Houseman hadn't interfered. Another errand for an anonymous debt collector. A deadly errand. Still, what could possibly connect the retrieval of personal letters and the theft of a captain's logbook?

What besides his stepmother's penchant for whist?

"Hugh." Her hand tightened on his. "Hugh?"

Kingslea shoved aside the disjointed thoughts. He would find the connection later. His gaze followed the curve of his companion's smooth cheek before settling on her eyes.

"Yes, Fiona."

"Thank you for leading me from the shipyard. I had been wandering those lanes for at least an hour without much luck." She tugged her cape close. "I shudder to think what would have happened if Bosson had found us in one of those narrow alleys."

"Bosson?" Suspicion itched Hugh's skin. How did the woman know the sailor?

"You know, the *Revere*'s first mate. His attentions had become a trifle too forward since Captain List disappeared last night. Or, more precisely, the night before last." She smoothed the thought from her forehead. "He was planning something. Something unpleasant. I thought about leaving when the captain didn't return for dinner, but Milton talked me out of it. Now, I'm glad he did." Fiona beamed at him. "Your rescue is certainly something I will tell my grandchildren."

Doubts solidified, connected divergent tracts of thought. His stepmother had been eager for him to redeem her debts. All too impatient for him to make tonight's trip. Bloody hell. The woman had baited her trap well. His folded arms contained the rage roaring to life in his breast.

"You timed your arrival perfectly. A dashing prince stepping from the mist just when I thought all was lost." Admiration blazed in her eyes.

"Hardly a prince." Bitter residue coated his tongue. Merely a second son who had the misfortune to inherit a penniless title. A title his stepmother seemed determined to auction off to the highest bidder. Preferably an American heiress with a bottomless purse. Did the Marchioness know how unconventional her earmarked daughter-in-law was? Perhaps Elspeth thought to mold her as she had worked to reform him?

"Certainly, a more noble man could not be found in all of England."

"You'd be surprised," Kingslea said dryly.

So his stepmother had decided to bring Polite Society to his door, since he refused to cross its threshold. Only one question remained—Was Fiona Grey a pawn in his stepmother's machinations, or was she party to the plot?

"London's aristocracy would be better for your admittance." Candor blazed across her features.

Hope flickered before he extinguished the flame. He had been fooled once before.

Lilly's porcelain complexion replaced Fiona's smiling face.

"Don't you see? Once the duke has his heir we can be together."

"And you will be another man's wife. Marry me, Lilly. Now, before it is too late." Raw need was in his words.

"Father would never settle for a second son. He wants a title for his money, and your brother is far too healthy."

He shook off the past.

"I dub thee Sir Hugh the Rescuer, Knight of the London Dock and Protector of its people." Fiona touched her bullwhip to his shoulder.

"I prefer to remain as I am."

She shrugged. "Just as well, I think only a queen can knight a man."

Shadows moved in the mist. Shop clerks and street vendors rushed along the sidewalks. London was awake. Awake and aware. Someone was bound to notice Fiona's arrival. Her chance of a match would narrow if someone told of her arrival with him. Not that anyone would look beyond his disguise.

But if his presence compromised her, honor would provide the means for his stepmother to get her way. A wise man would leave Fiona before the trap was sprung. Kingslea settled into the leather. This enemy required further study.

"Hugh?" She turned her large blue eyes on him.

"Yes?"

"Why are you dressed as a sailor?"

He started, shaking off his lethargy like a dog did water on his coat.

"That is what I am."

"True, your disguise is almost complete." Fiona smiled.

Coy or cunning? Kingslea scratched his chin. A day's growth of beard rasped his skin.

"I can assure you my clothes are those of a genuine sailor."

"Of that, I have no doubt." Humor snapped in her eyes. "But you have recently repaired the shoulders." Her touch danced over the stitches closing a popped seam. "This herringbone stitch is not in keeping with the long stitch used by a man of the sea."

Hugh caught her hand and dropped it into her lap. Blast! Leave it to a woman to notice something as mundane as stitching. A woman...

"Perhaps I have a wife to repair my clothing."

"Perhaps, but your hands are too soft for a sailor." She clasped his left hand between hers. Her thumb brushed the soft pads then stilled. She cleared her throat then tucked the black-clad hand behind her back.

"Of course, most sailors' coloring doesn't bleed onto their collar." She waved her white-gloved hand near the lamp, highlighting the reddish brown streaked across her gloves. "A true salt's tan covers more flesh than his shirt, whereas I'd bet your sun-kissed skin stops an inch or two under your sleeves."

The truth of her logic burned Kingslea's neck, stained his cheeks. She had ripped the disguise from his person while maintaining her own mask. Better to retreat than to find yourself at the altar. He touched his hand to his chest.

"You have found me out, madam."

She blinked once and cocked her head to the left.

"Yet I have discovered nothing." Her dichromatic palms flashed at him.

"I fear you have discerned too much." On impulse, he caught her gloved hand and raised it to his lips. Tingles raced across the sensitive flesh as gardenias and soap overwhelmed his senses. He dropped her hand and banged his fist on the roof, driving her touch from his skin. "Houseman. Stop here."

"Please, I—"

The cab halted near a towering elm.

"I have pressing business." Kingslea tossed the door open and jumped from the cab. Green and brown swirled as he pivoted. The door slammed shut as he stepped back. "Houseman will see you safely to your destination."

"At least tell me who you are."

Who he was? Who was she? Pawn or plotter? He would know once the captain's logbook was claimed.

"I am whoever I need to be." He touched his forehead and sketched a bow. "Safe journey."

"And to you as well." She raised her hand in salute than held the back of it to her cheek.

Kingslea felt her gaze on him as he picked his way through Hyde Park. Soon he would reach Speaker's Corner. Soon he would have proof of his stepmother's duplicity.

CHAPTER FOUR

Silk slipped over Fiona's cheek. Odd how the tingles racing up her arm didn't jump from her hand to her face. But then, Hugh hadn't kissed her cheek. Her tongue moistened her dry lips. Disappointment snaked through her insides before coiling in her belly.

Her gaze traveled along the path he had trod. Her chatter had chased him away. Never had she prattled on so. Never had her curiosity been so aroused. Thumb and fingers met, evening out the smear of actor's paint dying her gloves.

What had come over her? Brown eyes stared out from her memory. She had barely kept herself from brushing the lock off his forehead, caressing the dimple in his chin.

The past week's events were affecting her manners. No one in Society would believe that Fiona Grey would be dashing through London in a Worth cape and her brother's waist overalls, caressing a stranger, and giving him leave to call her by her Christian name. To everyone, she was the epitome of proper deportment, good manners and ladylike modesty.

Everyone but Hugh.

I am whatever I need to be.

His forceful statement filled her with sadness. How awful to drift through life being only what others needed one to be. If only she could help him.

"Madam?" The coachman's words interrupted her analysis.

Perhaps she would help him once she solved Uncle Andrew's problem. Fiona pulled her gaze away from the foggy park.

"Yes, Houseman."

"Perhaps we should depart. 'Tisn't safe for a lady alone."

Alone. Bleating sheep and clomping hooves filled the silence. Fiona glanced around the cab. Milton was missing as well. She shrugged. No doubt her late fiancé had swooped across the Channel to tell Gran of his heroics.

"Very well." She sighed.

"Perhaps if Miss told me which direction she wished to go?"

Leather creaked as Fiona pushed against the seat. Silk bunched around her fingers as they dove into her pocket to retrieve the telegram. She scanned the scrap of paper.

"Number One-eighteen Piccadilly."

"Very good, madam." The reins snapped over the horse's rump.

On impulse, Fiona leaned out of cab and glanced behind her. Hugh was gone, undoubtedly for good, and she had other things to concentrate on.

She smoothed the creased paper over her knees.

BRIGHID'S HELP NEEDED FOR HOUSE CLEANING STOP
MATTER IS URGENT STOP
ANDREW
118 PICCADILLY, LONDON

What matter could be so important that her uncle would interrupt her parents' holiday? He knew how much Mam and Da had suffered during the years of her sister's illness, knew how important this trip was to them all.

Matter is urgent.

"There is nothing Mam can do that I cannot." Doubt disturbed Fiona's confidence. She sucked on her bottom lip, tugged the soft flesh free of her teeth. Why hadn't Uncle Andrew met her ship when she arrived three days ago? And why had he specifically requested her mother's talents?

She tucked a wool blanket around her shoulders. She would help her uncle. After all, she had made it to England and was only minutes away from his townhouse. She would find answers to her questions as well as her uncle's. A shiver fluttered up her spine. Still...

No good ever came from talking to the dead.

CHAPTER FIVE

*Fiona stared at the white marble facade of her uncle's townhouse. Peach cur-*tains glowed in the bay windows. Gilded eyes stared back at her from the brass lion's head mounted on the door. *Thump. Thump.* The knocker resonated deep in the house like teardrops on a crypt.

"Do be sensible, Fi." The whisper teased her ears. Muscles trembled from raw emotion—elation at her safe arrival, torment at her uncle's uncharacteristic absence. Two sides of a coin flipping for control.

"No more Mr. Poe for you." She tucked an escaped curl behind her ear. He had fulfilled his purpose last night, keeping her awake until her moment of escape, but this morning was different. This morning her uncle starred in one of Mr. Poe's macabre stories.

Her gaze drifted from the shut dark-green door to the bannister. No raven cawed her uncle's name. No severed heart lay beating under the floorboards.

"It's the lack of sleep. Nothing more." *Nevermore.* The poem haunted her. She shrugged off the unease. "All will be well once I'm inside."

"Shall I wait, miss?" Houseman's voice drifted from his perch on the hansom cab. Fiona turned to the groom. The white mist swept past his cheeks, cascaded down his shirtfront. Black-shrouded servants glided across the sidewalks like shadows behind gauze.

Muscles clenched, bracing for a shudder. She'd never cared for fog. She could never shake the notion these earthbound clouds were all that remained after restless spirits finally left this plane of existence. Spectral garments abandoned by the dead. Fiona tugged her cape closer and focused on the living groom.

"No, thank you, Houseman. I am certain someone will be with me shortly."

The driver's long whip lounged against the top of the cab. The black stallion shifted his weight. Irritation smashed through Fiona's fear. She was no child to be fretted over, no maiden in need of rescue. She was an adult, and her family needed her. Shoulders straight, chin raised.

"You may leave now."

"Very well, miss." The coachman tipped his top hat and clucked at the horse. They trotted down the lane.

The words to call him back clogged her throat. Uncle Andrew needed her. Fiona turned back to the door and grabbed the brass ring. Clammy metal dampened her glove. She banged the knocker against the brass plate. Once. Twice.

Nothing stirred on the ground floor. Her gaze slid down the wall to the servants' area. Golden light spilled onto the stone steps, flicked over the wrought iron fence delineating the entrance and cast a gridwork over the hazy street. A silhouette interrupted the flow of light at intermittent intervals.

At least the servants were up, but would they answer the door at such an unfashionable hour?

Her knees buckled before she locked them and clung to the building. Cool marble sweated against her cheek. For a moment, she had actually believed...

No. No, she had not. There had been no black crepe draped over the windows, no jet wreath affixed to the door. Her aunt and uncle were alive.

So, why hadn't they come for her?

"Any number of reasons, Fi. Any number. A ship could have been lost at sea. The children could be ill." She ticked off the excuses, but the lies never persuaded her heart.

And none of her reasons explained Gibson's absence. Nothing short of dynamite could eject her uncle's stately butler from his post. Her sisters, brother and Uncle Heberon had spent endless summer days herding frogs, enacting dramatic tableaux and relating tales of certain death. Nothing worked.

Fiona tugged her watch from her shirt pocket. Of course, genteel callers did not arrive at eight in the morning. Unease slithered down her back. Uncle Andrew always left for his office at half-past. Gibson would never allow his master to rise before him. Something was amiss. Fiona worried her bottom lip as scenarios raged in her skull.

"Oh, for Heaven's sake. The silly door knocker will not supply the answer. You must get inside."

Her gaze flitted to the narrow door opening onto the Area. She could try the servant's entrance. Her feet remained still. At home, she wouldn't hesitate, but she wasn't in San Francisco. She was in England. English servants were firmly set in their proper place and, more important, determined to stick her in hers. So, here she was on the stoop, nagged by horrible thoughts, waiting for admission.

Silk fingers closed around the shiny knob. She was tired of waiting.

"And I shall finally do honor to the family name." The voice glided through the morning like oil across water, slick and sullying.

"What about Heberon?"

Fiona spun on her heel. Revulsion crawled up her spine. She knew that gloat. Her cousin was back in Town.

"That fool." A soft tick followed the scrape of boots.

The cane. How had she forgotten the cane? *He* had taken to using it after a fall. One he'd taken running away from the fury of the Grey girls. Hatred blazed through Fiona. She'd burn that cane while she was here and smash the mirror he used to admire his crooked teeth and weak chin.

"He'll be committed soon enough. And I'll inherit everything." Shadows solidified farther down the street. The wasted figure of her cousin drifted next to a husky man. Light winked from the mirror-topped cane. "Chart and those fools will have to bow to me. Piers Montague will no longer be tainted by trade. I will finally claim my birthright."

Emaciated arms swung a hand at the beefy companion's head.

"Thought your sire was a second."

Oswin. The name blew from the depth of Fiona's memory. So, her cousin still retained his old friend. Together, they weren't bright enough to outshine a candle.

"He was, you halfwit." The cane jumped in Piers's hand. He thumped the tip against Oswin's rotund torso. "I inherit the title since that buffoon Heberon can't do his duty."

Uncle Heberon was no buffoon. His mind had simply stopped growing long before his body. But then, so had Piers's.

Fiona started down the steps then stopped. She would scrub her uncle's stoop with Piers's pomaded thatch of hair.

"That's something else to thank my poor aunt for." Piers chuckled.

"Something else? You mean other than dying?"

"No, although that was precipitous. Gad, I hated wasting away in that crumbling monstrosity while that *American* played lord of the manor and dispensed a pittance for us to live on while he entertained Society and ate turtle soup."

Fiona's fists ground into her hips. An asp had fed on Uncle Andrew's generosity. She would slay the vermin then find her answers.

Her leg jumped, dispersing her impatience into the stoop. Piers would have to run a long way to gain his mother's protection.

"Then what?"

Fiona's gaze flicked to her cousin's companion. Time had not been kind to Oswin. His button eyes, upturned nose and thin mouth appeared to have been sewn too tightly to his moon face.

"The money." Piers rubbed his hands together.

"But you lost…" Oswin dabbed at the stain on his waistcoat.

"A pittance, compared to what I now control." Piers dispelled the thought with a limp wave. "With my foolish aunt dead, Heberon is guardian of the children and their money."

Oswin's forehead wrinkled. "You're going to play father?"

Piers would play tiddly winks with his teeth before anyone in her family allowed him near Melinda or Cedric. The lariat scratched Fiona's palm through her glove.

"Good God, no." Piers turned to Oswin before placing a polished shoe on the bottom step. "The brats will be shipped off to school as soon as Mother arranges it. I will merely control their fortune."

"Fortune." Oswin licked his lips.

"Hell-lo." Piers's pale blue eyes traveled insolently up her legs before languishing on her breasts. "What have we here?"

Oswin blinked up at her. "Looks like a lady."

"No *lady* calls at a bachelor's establishment." Piers strummed the trio of gold chains roped across the loose fabric of his waistcoat before tugging a shiny watch free of his puce vest. "Especially not at this hour."

"You…" Rage closed Fiona's throat.

"Yes, me." He leapt over the remaining steps and sailed across the landing. Spittle bubbled in the corner of his mouth; lust glowed in his eyes. "You see, Oswin, with money, looks and a title, the ladies line up on my doorstep." Sallow hands wrapped around her upper arms.

"Looks!" Fiona snorted. Her contempt bounced off her cousin's ballooning vanity. "I've seen handsomer wet rags."

"Careful, my sweet." Clammy lips smeared wetness across her cheek.

"You big baboon." Fiona rammed her knee into his groin, felt the give of soft flesh against her Levi's.

Alcohol-scented breath heated the side of her face. Something hard thudded against her chin, pain radiated from the point of impact. Hands shoved her backwards. Her cape trapped her bootheel. The door caught her back, slammed the air from her lungs.

Piers doubled over, cradling his abused flesh. Red suffused his face as he coughed into the banister.

"Grab her."

Fiona threw her cape over her shoulder. A foot of rope slipped through her hand. Her wrist turned, faster and faster. The lasso opened, big enough to hog-tie a man.

Oswin advanced.

"Stay where you are," she gasped, raising her arm. The widening noose clipped the bay window, bounced off the wall and knocked her hat off.

Oswin paused. His gaze traveled from Piers to Fiona before settling on her hat. Buttons popped as he bent over. Thick fingers trailed up the ostrich feather.

"Not the hat," Piers wheezed. "*Her*. Get *her*, you idiot."

Fiona's heartbeat drummed in her ear. Stiff fingers tightened the flaccid lariat. One turn. Two. The circle wobbled. *Concentrate, Fi, you can do this.*

Oswin grunted and straightened. His foot crushed the felt hat. The lasso bounced off his cheek then tumbled uselessly to the landing.

"She likes it rough." Piers staggered over to her side and clawed up her body to stand upright. "Never let it be said a gentleman didn't oblige a lady."

"You're no gentleman." Fiona slammed her knee into his groin. Again. He grunted and stumbled backward. She kicked, her boot catching him in the knee. He reeled down the steps and landed with a thump.

Pain blazed across her toes and up her shin. She'd gladly endure more to repay Piers for the insult to her family.

"You'll pay for that." Piers tugged at his neckcloth. Blood pulsed in her hand as one meaty fist captured her arm.

"If you believe that..." Fiona wrapped her hand around his index fingers. "...then you're a bigger fool than I remember." She yanked the digits backwards.

Yowling, Piers released her. She tossed his touch away. A moment later, he latched onto her wrists. Muscles burned as he tried to overpower her. She lashed out with her feet and kicked air.

"I'll give you something to remember," he hissed. "I'll take you on the doorstep, then I'll hand you over to an abbess I know who'll teach you respect for your betters."

"You'll never best me." Fiona spat on him.

Color suffused his face as the spittle trailed down his cheek. Hatred blazed in his eyes.

Fear dried her mouth. The cowboys on Gilly and Aidan's farm had taught her one more trick. A silent prayer winged its way heavenward. She filled her lungs with air, reared her head back and slammed it into his nose.

Stars exploded inside her skull.

"You bitch!" Piers flung off her hold. His hands cupped his nose; blood seeped between his fingers.

Bile burned Fiona's throat. The world swam in the tears filling her eyes. Small wonder the hands had used the violence as a last resort. It incapacitated both fighters.

She staggered back, tripped over her cape again. Her body tensed, expecting the collision with the door.

She continued to fall.

❋ ❋ ❋

"The lady knocked on the door of One-eighteen Piccadilly." Houseman stretched out on the grass under the towering elm tree. A battered bowler had replaced his top hat.

Kingslea clamped down on the frustration shredding his control. Two hours had passed since the appointed rendezvous. Two miserable hours of fending off birds and constables. Both were equally irritating.

"She arrived safely, then?"

"Aye. Well..." Houseman plucked a blade of grass from the lush lawn and chewed on the green tip. "I didn't actually see her enter the establishment."

"Why not?"

"She waved me off." Houseman's arms crossed his chest, and he glared at Kingslea. "The lady is skilled with her weapons. I thought it wise to leave."

Shock and fear rattled Kingslea's control. He leapt to his feet and shoved away from the tree.

"You left her unprotected in the middle of London?" Long strides carried him to the break in the fence. If anything happened to her...

"You forget the whip and her rope." Houseman caught up with him.

"She is a *lady*. Their delicate sensibilities—" He caught the grin spreading across Houseman's features. His hands fisted at his sides. "Is there a particular reason you're grinning like an idiot?"

"Haven't much luck with this particular favor, eh, milord?"

Milord. What knot of tangled reasoning clogged the insolent man's head. Kingslea picked at a thread waving from a popped seam. The next time his valet met a bullet, the gun might be in milord's hand.

"So, you didn't actually see her go inside?"

"Ye've your doubts about the lady?"

"Indeed, I believe her to be the worst sort of lady." Kingslea's gaze swung to Houseman. Ahh, so the groom hadn't figured everything out.

"Her?"

"Indeed." Kingslea watched as bushy black brows collided over his companion's brown eyes. "She's a huntress."

"Aye. Well, 'tis what a miss does, ain't it?" Eyeteeth winked Houseman's humor.

"True. But I believe this one to be in league with the marchioness."

"Well, that makes sense, then."

Nothing made sense. Kingslea waited until they neared the edge of the park before stopping. Houseman's penchant for keeping his thoughts to himself could be downright annoying.

"What makes sense?"

"Number One-eighteen belongs to Lord Heberon."

"Lord Heberon? I don't believe he moves in my stepmother's circles."

"Aye, well, you never know. His lordship resides with his sister, the former Lady Caroline Wickshire. She married an American." Houseman rocked back on his heels, watched a bird swoop from the tree and tipped his hat to a woman with a basket of flowers on her head.

Kingslea counted to twenty then thirty. Patience was not a virtue. Fiona smiled from his memory. Damnation, he had just quoted a woman. Only a stiff drink and several hours' sleep could blot out the memory.

"You may have heard of him. Goes by the name Andrew Grey."

"Of Grey Shipping?"

"The same."

"Bloody Hell." Kingslea pounded on his legs. Why couldn't he have been wrong for once in his miserable life?

"Aye. And there's more."

"More?" What more could there be? A special license. The banns posted in *The Times*? *He* would pick the bride, *if* he ever married.

"Course, it's not about the lady." Houseman scratched his chin. "You still want to hear it?"

"Yes," Kingslea hissed. "I want to know."

"Seems the Greys went missing four weeks past, and what with Lord Heberon's faculties being to let, the heir apparent has moved in."

"Who?"

"Piers Montague."

"Good God. No wonder the poor girl wants to marry me. Hell, I might just wed the chit to save her from that depraved creature."

Houseman's eyebrows rubbed against his hairline. Kingslea blinked. Had he really just considered marriage? No, of course he hadn't.

"Well, I can't shoot her and put her out of her misery."

"Of course not, milord."

Milord again. Amusement or arrogance. Neither was particularly desirable in a servant.

"At least you've made use of your time."

"You haven't nabbed the man?"

"No. This is beginning to look more and more like a fool's errand."

"Then why are we leaving?"

Why *was* he leaving? For a manipulative woman who wanted to purchase his title? He was not some horse to be auctioned off. He stuffed her image in a small corner of his mind.

"We're not." Kingslea spun on his heel and marched back to the Speaker's Corner. "No one even stopped to look at it?"

"Just a child."

Damnation. He lengthened his stride to a sprint. Thoughts of the woman had snatched reason from his skull.

"He slowed by the bench, but he didn't stop."

"Were you late?"

"The appointment was at seven. I arrived at six-fifty-eight."

They sprinted round the corner. The bench came into view.

"You want me to keep watch?"

"No." Kingslea's lungs burned from the exercise. "I want to catch him."

"You still think the lady's involved."

"I think our encounter with the lady exceeds the probability of coincidence."

Gravel sprayed the bench as they slid to a halt. Kingslea stiffened. A small bundle lay on top of the captain's log.

"Why would they leave the note and the book?"

Why, indeed? The crisp vellum fluttered in the breeze. The marchioness's handwriting was scrawled across the parchment. He added up the totals on the paper. Half the promised amount. Half. Red wax marred a folded scrap. He broke the seal and stared at the spidery handwriting.

"That doesn't look like your stepmother's mark." Houseman squinted at the scrawl.

"It isn't." Kingslea wadded the note into a ball and crammed it into his pocket. "It's more bloody instructions."

CHAPTER SIX

Bile soured Fiona's mouth. Her skull throbbed. White lights whirled around the cherubs flitting across the ceiling of her uncle's hall.

"I say…" Gibson's dry notes rolled around her skull like marbles in an empty bowl.

"Ged 'er, you fool." Piers's whine added an unwelcome grating noise.

Fiona hefted her weight onto her elbows. Her head bobbed on a wave of nausea.

"Shut the door and lock it." She swallowed this morning's biscuits again. "Quick."

"Now, see here." Gibson's white head turned from Piers's and Oswin's clumsy dance on the stoop to her. "This is a respectable establishment."

"Gibson." Fiona crawled backwards. Her cape's fastenings dug into her throat, choking off her air. Tingles raced around her fingers as she tugged at the steadfast clasp. Da would be proud. She had finally found the downside of well-made clothes.

"You'b pigged the wrong blace to seeg refuge." Piers glared at her from a crimson visage.

"Please."

Gibson bent closer to her. Confusion added more lines to his wrinkled face.

"Miss Fiona?"

"Yes, Gibson, it is I." She flung herself to the side as Piers gained the last step. Her foot smashed into the door, sending it crashing into its frame. The chandelier tinkled from the violence. "If you would…?"

"Indeed." The butler shot the bolt home as something collided with the door. Old bones creaked when he bent over her. "Did your father accompany you?"

"No." Fiona shook her head. The world dipped and twirled. She closed her eyes. She must get up. Uncle Andrew would not want her prostrate form to adorn his elegant entry. Her waist overalls and flannel shirt clashed with his Persian rug and Chippendale chairs.

With her hands braced on the floor near her head, she pushed herself up onto her knees. If her head didn't stop spinning she might leave something of herself behind despite her good intentions.

"Mam and Da are in Paris with Brianna."

"How is Miss Brianna?" A gnarled hand fanned the air in front of her face. "We were delighted to hear of her recovery."

"Gibson!"

The chandelier tinkled again. The shiny lock kept Piers out, but light entered around the edges of the door as the beating continued. No doubt Oswin inflicted the abuse. Her cousin was almost too refined to lift his opium pipe to his thin lips.

"Open this door! At once, I say!"

Gibson's lips curved before they settled once more in their usual impartial mask. Fiona slipped her hand into the butler's. With his help, she climbed to her feet.

"My sister is much improved. I can't say the same about Piers."

"Will your parents be here directly?" Hope shone in Gibson's pale eyes.

"Shortly. Bri does not travel well, and they feared a set back."

"Understandably so." He gingerly removed his hand from her clasp. Fiona winced at the color in the normally pale skin. "Is Mrs. Baird with you, then?"

"I'm afraid Aidan insisted Gilly remain in the territories, especially given her condition."

He sighed heavily as Fiona handed him her cloak. Was he disappointed in her clothing or her sister's absence?

"Don't worry, Gibson. I shall attend to matters until the rest of my family descends upon you."

"Yes, Miss." He swiped at a stain on the velvet fabric. "I meant no disrespect, Miss Fiona."

"And I did not perceive any." She placed her hand over his.

"You've an interesting knot on your forehead."

Gibson brushed her bangs aside and probed the wound. Tears burned Fiona's eyes despite his gentleness.

"It matches the one on the back of my head."

Long fingers slipped into her hair and grazed the knot.

"How bad is it?"

"Nothing you didn't experience as a child."

Silence settled in the hall. They both turned to look at the door.

"I suppose it is too much to hope Piers has departed?"

"Indeed, Miss. Master Montague resides here now. As do his mother and sister."

"I was afraid of that." A large grandfather clock ticked off the seconds. Two minutes later, windows rattled in her uncle's library.

"I'm surprised he didn't use the servant's entrance."

"Mr. Montague is too aware of his consequence to enter by any door other than the front."

Fiona shrugged. *She* had considered entering through the servant's area.

"Surely, the back door would not diminish his importance."

"It might not, but we shall never know. It is locked." Humor twinkled in Gibson's eyes.

"Locked."

"Why, Miss Fiona, only riffraff stumbles along at this hour of the morning. Wickham House locks its doors precisely at midnight. Lord Heberon's orders." He winked.

Fiona spirits lifted along with the corner of her mouth. Uncle Heberon's orders obviously met with the approval of the staff.

"And very sensible they are, too."

But a lock couldn't keep out the world, especially if someone in the household was determined to bring someone else in. Someone like a doctor who would lock up her gentle uncle.

"How grave are things?"

Gibson mirrored her own wince.

Poor choice of words, Fi.

"Very."

"Does Uncle Andrew know about Piers and his plans?"

"Your uncle and Miss..." Gibson's adam's apple bobbed against his collar. His eyes closed as he swayed on his feet.

"Where are they, Gibson?" Fiona propped her hopes upon the absence of mourning paraphernalia. "Piers said he...that he and Aunt Caroline..."

"They're missing." With his right hand, Gibson swept the grief from his features. "The *Sweet Wind* went down four weeks ago. The yacht wasn't far from shore. M-many survived the explosion and the surf."

Missing. Not dead. For four weeks. No one in her family had received that information. Piers must have intercepted it in his bid to steal her uncle's money.

Reeling, she looked at the butler. He seemed to be awaiting a response.

"The boiler?"

"Many assumed so, Miss, but a handful of seamen claimed differently. Well, they did until Captain Bosson told the whole story."

Revulsion pricked Fiona's skin. Surely, First Mate Bosson and Captain Bosson weren't the same man.

"Captain Bosson?"

Annoyance ticked Gibson's cheek.

"For killing the owners, that...that man was merely demoted. Mr. Bartholomew insisted the Greys..."

Fiona draped her cape over her waist overalls. At least that was one problem she could easily fix.

"Let me assure you, Gibson. Grey Shipping will no longer require Mr. Bosson's services in any capacity."

"Bless you, Miss."

Windows rattled in the back rooms.

"So, what other methods have you devised to annoy Cousin Piers? Besides the locked doors."

"Actually, your uncle insisted on such measures in the month before his death. The house was burglarized twice—March seventh then again on the eighteenth."

Twice. Fiona's thoughts whirled. Perhaps the shipwreck hadn't been an accident.

"Was anything taken?"

"Nothing of much value. They took the silver candelabra but left the silverware. Miss Carolyn's silver brush and comb set were also taken, but her jewel box remained undisturbed."

"How very odd." Thoughts died unformed. Were the burglaries the reason behind the need for someone who talked to ghosts? Unlikely—what need had a spirit for candles and combs? Another mystery to heap on top of the others. Perhaps she should have learned Hugh's address. Solving all these puzzles might require assistance.

"Perhaps Miss would like to change before breakfast." Gibson's gaze twitched over her scuffed boots before returning to a spot over her shoulder.

"I would love to change, but alas, my trunks are aboard the *Revere*."

"I will arrange for their delivery."

"Thank you, Gibson. For everything. And if you happen to hear anything more..." She waited hoping she hadn't intruded too far onto his territory.

"You'll be the first to know, Miss Fiona." He bowed and opened the door to the dining room.

The scents of fresh beeswax and silver polish greeted her. The door rolled closed behind her as memories seated themselves around the oval table. Uncle Heberon stood muttering to the silver dishes adorning the side board.

"Good morning, Uncle." Fiona plucked the silk gloves from her hands then draped the mismatched pair over the back of the leather chair.

Uncle Heberon jerked around. His hard-boiled egg crunched onto the walnut sideboard. Scrambled eggs showered the silver service. A piece of toast wobbled in his fingers before plummeting to the floor.

She stepped closer. Uncle Heberon raised his hand, dropping the bone china plate. It shattered, sending pieces across the wooden floor. Color drained from his ruddy cheeks. He flashed his palm. She stopped. Recognition flashed in his blue eyes. Fear quickly followed. What had Piers done to her uncle's simple mind?

"It's me—Fiona from America."

"I know." Wide eyes darted to the door. His hand clamped over his mouth. Fingers bit into his cheek.

"Is something wrong, Uncle?" Anger whipped through Fiona. Movement at the window snagged her attention.

Piers loped across the park outside.

She would kill him when he gained entrance. For now, she needed to remain calm. Air cooled her lungs, snatched the heat from her anger.

Uncle Heberon lifted his fingers, surrounding his lips with his cupped hand.

"I'm not supposed to talk to you," he whispered. "Gibson said."

Gibson? Confusion surged past her anger. What did the butler have to do with her uncle's behavior?

"I've just seen Gibson, Uncle."

"Yes, but did he see you?" He wrapped his arms around his waist, stretching his dark-blue morning coat taut across his broad shoulders. Gray brushed his brown hair. Her uncle would pass for any aristocrat if it weren't for the grass stains on the knees of his breeches and the innocence in his gaze.

Innocence and fear. Fiona was certain she was the cause of the latter.

"Of course Gibson saw me, Uncle." She inched closer. "He rescued me from Piers."

"Piers saw you, too?" Hope blazed in Uncle Heberon's eyes. His head inched forward, bring his chest with it.

"Ged oud ob my houze!" A stone tapped the windowsill before it slipped from his grasp. Frowning, Piers dropped to his knees and groped in the grass for another rock.

Fiona strode to the window. She waited until her cousin glanced up then tugged on the gold cord. Midnight-blue drapes fluttered over the window. Another tap sounded. She yanked on the next cord. If that nincompoop broke her uncle's window, she'd make him re-glaze it himself.

"I'm afraid I had a little disagreement with him."

"Like when we were younger." Uncle Heberon grinned.

"Like when he took your boat."

"Ohhhh!" He rubbed his hands together and bounced on the balls of his feet. "Did you do like Gilly said?"

Fiona blinked, erasing the present to delve into the past.

"Gilly?" *Two muddy girls waded in the stream behind her uncle's country manor while she wrestled with her cousin on the bank. She had stopped Piers's tattling...*

"I had forgotten my sister's advice and broke his nose again." Fiona smiled at her uncle. Humor warmed his eyes. Two more steps and she would be by his side. "Honestly, I don't think my cousin's underdeveloped chin is to blame for his behavior. I think it is his lack of spine."

Uncle Heberon's smile crumbled. His gaze dropped to the floor.

"Aunt Annabelle will blame me." His polished boot traced the grain in the oak planks.

Fiona crouched in front of him but his gaze flitted away.

"Why would she blame you for my actions?"

"Because specters can't talk or...or walk or...or give the servants instructions." Hands fisted at his side. "And they can't break noses. She'll lock me in my room again. She'll say I was bad."

A lone tear dotted his boot. He cleaned it with the sole of the other one.

"You're not bad, Uncle. You're the nicest person I've ever met."

He peered at her from between strands of fallen hair. "Truly?"

"Truly." His logic baited her attention. Ghosts. Was this the reason for the summons? To confirm Uncle Heberon's ability to see spirits? Or had Uncle Andrew foreseen his own death?

Fiona shrugged off the disquiet. Aunt and Uncle weren't dead, and she'd prove it.

She scanned the room. Where was Milton? He had never left her alone this long before.

"I am not a ghost, Uncle."

"Yes, you are." Uncle Heberon nodded once. "And I'm not supposed to talk to you."

Pain radiated up her arm as her fist collided with the table.

"Can a ghost bang on a table?"

"Yes." He nodded again. "Andy banged his knee on the washstand, and he swore, too. Caro scolded him like she does me when I take cookies before dinner."

Helplessness twitched through Fiona's muscles. Some ghosts could bang things about but that proved nothing.

"Uncle Andrew and Aunt Caroline aren't dead." Somehow, she doubted Uncle Heberon was the only one she was trying to convince.

"They are. They are. Piers told me. He said I had to listen to him. He said—"

"Piers lies," she snapped.

Uncle Heberon pulled his bottom lip into his mouth. Remorse pinned her arms to her side.

"Remember when he told you that horses talked at night? You stayed in the barn for two nights straight and didn't hear a word."

"I...I remember."

"There, you see. He was lying about that, and he's lying about Uncle Andrew and Aunt Carolyn, too."

"That's what they said, but they don't sleep in their bed or talk to Gibson or Mrs. March. And...and they don't take care of me!" He whirled around, presenting her with his back.

"I'll take care of you, Uncle."

"You can't. You're dead!" he wailed.

"Master Heb!" Gibson tossed open the door and strode into the room.

Indecision warred with Fiona. Should she tell the servant about Uncle Heberon's obsession with ghosts? Gibson would never do anything to harm his master, but in a house this size, other ears were always listening.

The butler's gaze fell upon the ruined plate.

"There's no need to fret, Master Heberon. I can get you another plate of eggs." He placed an arm around his shoulders. "Would you like that?

Lord Heberon nodded but cast a fearful gaze in her direction.

"Come now." Gibson took another plate from the sideboard and dropped a spoonful of scrambled eggs on top. "Cook's made them just the way you like." He placed a boiled egg on its stand and set both on the table. The offered chair remained vacant. "What's the matter, milord? Am I not a good keeper of secrets?"

Uncle Heberon nodded but hunched his shoulders, remaining firmly by the butler's side.

This could not continue. She must prove to her uncle that she was alive. And she must do so without revealing any trouble.

"I think my arrival has upset him, Gibson."

"Nonsense. Milord is always pleased to have your company, Miss Fiona."

Uncle Heberon jerked once and stared at Gibson.

"You see her?"

"Of course, milord." Gibson's shoulders bowed. Sixty-nine years pressed against his proud bearing. The butler had understood the strange comment. "Plain as I see you."

"You aren't dead!"

Uncle Heberon shrugged off Gibson's touch and embraced her. Strong arms crushed the air from her lungs. Hands shoved her backward as her uncle's gaze swept over her; glee lit his face.

"You feel real, but so did Caro."

"I am alive. I promise."

"Gibson would tell me if you weren't." Her uncle flung himself into his seat, kicked out the chair next to his and tugged. Fiona stumbled backward. Pain rocketed up her arm as her elbow collided with the table.

"He told me about Andy and Caro's accident." Uncle Heberon swallowed his mouthful of eggs. "Melinda and Cedric, too."

"How are my cousins?"

"Cedric likes to play soldiers with me, just like Gilly." Uncle Heberon marched his fork and knife across the table. "I even win sometimes. Melinda invites me to tea with the Ladies Fi, Bri and Gilly. I have to sit on the floor since I broke her chair. Andy promised to fix it before..."

His sadness buffeted her. Denial ricocheted inside her skull. Her aunt and uncle couldn't be dead. *But what if they are?* Would she be so cruel as to give him false hope?

"Maybe you and I can fix it together. As a surprise for Uncle Andrew," she added, forcing her doubts to bend to her will.

"May I hammer? John Coachman let me sometimes. I'm real good. I only hit my thumb once the last time."

"As long as you're careful." Fiona's gaze traveled to Gibson. He nodded in encouragement. "About Cedric and Melinda..."

How much damage had her cousin done?

"They are fine, miss. They took the news rather hard the first night, but they are doing well."

"I tell them stories like Caro." Uncle Heberon smeared strawberry jam across a piece of toast.

"I'm sure that is a great help."

"It's not as fun as listening, but Caro said I had to do it." He leaned forward and dropped his voice. "She won't allow me to sleep in the nursery anymore. She said I had to sleep in my room so they could visit me."

Gibson cleared his throat. Fear crossed his face as he set a bowl of porridge in front of her.

"Do they visit every night, Uncle?"

Heberon shoved the entire wedge of toast into his mouth. He glance at Gibson.

"It's all right, milord. Miss Fiona is here to help."

He gulped down his milk, wiped his mouth on his sleeve and swallowed.

"They've visited seven times since they died."

Fiona slid the pearl ring along her gold necklace. The engagement ring was her only tangible link to Milton. Wickham House was full of strings to bind her aunt's and uncle's spirits. That is, if they were dead.

"Have you seen them anywhere else?"

"In the nursery. They were bending over Cedric and Melinda. Piers had just arrived." Uncle Heberon frowned. "I thought they were angels."

"Have Cedric or Melinda seen them?"

"No, it was to be our secret. I wasn't supposed to tell, but I did, and now Gibson is mad at me."

"I'm certain Gibson is only concerned that Piers will find out and tattle to his mother."

"And she will think I'm bad." Uncle Heberon giggled. "Andy always called him a moldering mushroom. He was mad when he heard they moved into the house."

"We don't need any moldering mushrooms at Wickham House."

Fiona squeezed her uncle's hand. She would evict Annabelle's brood from this house but first she needed to find Uncle Andrew.

"Caro looked so sad."

"We'll cheer her up, Uncle. We will." Light glinted off the spoon twirling in Fiona's hand. "Now, eat your breakfast while we plan."

"If I may...Mr. Grey carried several documents to the Grey offices after—"

"Damn you, Gibson." Piers swaggered into the room, his stained handkerchief pressed against his swelling nose. "You are sacked. Sacked, do you hear? And forget any references. When my mother finds out about—"

"Still running to your mother, eh, cousin?" Fiona set her half-eaten toast on her plate. Adrenaline pumped through her. Her cousin's days of bullying the staff, intimidating her uncle and frightening the children were over. Greys always protected their family.

"You!" A vein wormed a path down her cousin's temple as he stomped toward her.

Fiona rose to her feet. She wouldn't need her whip or rope to cower the bully.

"You really should be more careful whom you attack."

"Gibson." Piers's eyes narrowed in his cadaverous face. "Call the watch. Have this...this person thrown out of my house."

"This isn't your house, cousin." Fiona stepped away from the table and advanced. He stepped back. "This is Lord Heberon's house. Gibson is my uncle's servant, not yours. You couldn't even inspire a dog to be faithful."

Piers's face twitched, as if teased by a memory he couldn't quite pin down. Perhaps she would help him, give him a hint about how much he had blundered.

"Bertie is fine, by-the-by. He's chasing jackrabbits on my sister's ranch."

"Bertie? The Prince of Wales?"

"No, you idiot. Bertie the border collie you beat because he wouldn't fetch a stick." Fiona snapped her fingers. *Ah, he was remembering.* "I believe I broke your nose then as well."

"And then when he stole my boat. And when he took your doll." Uncle Heberon joined in the game.

"Fiona." Cousin Piers's eyes bulged. The single thought had obviously tired of being alone and sought escape.

Uncle Heberon continued to count the times Fiona had broken Piers's nose. "And when he tattled about us climbing the oak."

"So, you remember me now?" Fiona sketched a brief curtsy.

"And when we went swimming in the stream. And then again when we were fishing—"

"That's enough, you stupid—" Piers choked under her glare. "I was always a sickly child, given to nosebleeds."

"You were a simpering bully."

"And he was mean." Uncle Heberon stuck his tongue out at Piers. Fiona resisted the urge to join him.

"Enjoy your brief victory, cousin," he gloated. "Soon you'll find yourself on the other side of the locked door. Seen any ghosts lately, milord?" Piers's lips twisted as he limped across the room.

Fiona carefully set her knife by her plate.

"If you interfere with my family again, cousin..."

Piers's step hitched before he increased his stride.

"...a cold bath won't be able to take all the pain away."

"I'll have breakfast in my room, Gibson." Piers snarled, wrenching the doors apart. "And make certain it's hot this time."

Victory drummed in Fiona's veins. She had won the first battle. Unfortunately, the campaign promised to be rather lengthy.

She turned to celebrate with Heberon. Her uncle scooted his eggs around his plate.

"Uncle?"

"I want to go to Wickinshire." Tears spilled down his cheeks. "I want it to be like it used to be."

Fiona set her hand over his. "And it will be, I promise. Now, dry your tears and go bring Melinda and Cedric down. I'm certain they would like some breakfast."

He sniffed and dropped his napkin across his plate.

"You'll save me some sausage? I haven't had any yet, and they're my favorite."

"I'm certain Gibson has them waiting."

"Just so, miss."

Uncle Heberon leapt from his chair and danced around the table.

"Wait until you see them. Caro says they've grown since she's seen them so they'd be *really* big to you."

"I'm certain they will." Her words followed her uncle through the door. He was as much a child as Melinda and Cedric. And she was responsible for them all. At least, until she found her aunt and uncle.

"We are pleased you have come, Miss Fiona." Gibson set a plate of sausages in Heberon's place and removed his dirty plate. "Mrs. Montague doesn't have Lady Caro's management style."

"How many servants have you lost?"

"None, miss. We are loyal to the master, Lady Caro, your uncle. And of course, none of us would have left the children in that lot's care." Gibson set Heberon's napkin on the table and scraped the spilled eggs onto it.

"I never doubted it, Gibson. What were you saying about the shipmaster's office?"

"Mr. Grey kept his important documents there after the burglary. I believe that is where he suspected his trouble began. Although the first break-in didn't occur until a week after they returned from Egypt. He was most upset when milady hosted the Unwrapping."

"My uncle brought back a mummy?"

"Several. Most were earmarked for the museum. The Duke of August is very generous with his finds. Your uncle agreed to transport the items gratis since the Duke agreed to lend his more prestigious finds to the museum. The museum sorted through the treasures. Alas, one specimen was rejected. They said it wasn't as well-preserved as the others. Lady Carolyn didn't want it to go to waste, so she opened it." Gibson repressed a shudder. "Quite frankly, I was happy when your uncle removed it. Corpses in the house. Milady promised never to host such a gathering again."

"Do you know what happened to it?"

"Probably sold to the apothecary. Although, I believe if a mummy possessed any medicinal value, wouldn't they have used it to save himself."

"Quite so. I will visit the shipmaster's after breakfast. Do you have any idea what Uncle Andrew believed to be the source of his troubles?"

"No, miss. However, he faithfully kept a journal in a captain's log, although he rarely went to sea." Gibson snatched the piece of toast off the floor and tossed it onto the plate. He carefully stacked a piece from the rack on top and covered the plate with a silver dome. "If that will be all, I shall have Mr. Montague's breakfast served to him. Martha should be free from her duties about now."

"Gibson."

"Yes, Miss."

"I hope I never fall out of favor with you."

"So long as my suspenders remain suspenders and not a slingshot, I daresay your meals will not require any..."

"Special preparation?"

"Precisely." Gibson winked at her and walked from the room. Footsteps pounded on the stairs. "Proper young ladies and gentlemen walk down the stairs."

"Yes, Gibson," three voices chorused.

The door burst open. Melinda and Cedric sprinted in, Uncle Heberon puffing on their heels.

CHAPTER 7

"Shoulders back. Chin up. Graceful strides." Fiona's body jerked to the com-mands like a dancer to the calls in a Virginia reel. Years of deportment lessons comforted as they constrained.

She reached the landing, exhaled an unsteady breath. A shake of her skirts released the quiver from her hands. More eyes, she reminded herself, had watched her entrance at the Huntingtons' Spring Ball. Ribald laughter swirled around her. Men's laughter. Fiona jerked the navy merino sleeves over her wrists and flicked dust off her lapel.

No one had ever treated her thus in her parent's warehouse. Indeed, all those workers were almost as courteous as a gentleman at the opera or ball. Certainly, they had stopped their hand trucks and horses but only to tip their hat.

They had never gawked.

Fiona glanced over her shoulder. Faces bloomed like flowers between crates of silk, casks of wine and boxes of sundries. Sweat from honest labor mingled with the tang of the sea, the bite of tar and the bitterness of coal. Masculine eyes noted the cut of her coat and the swish of her skirt.

The brass button at her throat slipped between her damp fingers. Her heart drummed against her ribcage. Excitement and adrenaline coursed through her. How very odd. She hadn't realized how much she'd missed her work at G&G Enterprises.

"Ye wishin' ta enter, Mum?" A man in overalls doffed his battered hat. A black-tipped paintbrush stuck out of his pocket. "Mind the letterin'. It's a bit wet." He nodded to the crisp letters of Grey Shipping marching across the pane of glass.

"Yes, thank you, I do wish to enter."

"Right angry lot, they are." The painter grabbed the brass knob in his paint-streaked hand and tugged open the door. Raised voices knocked against her, assaulted her ears. "Had ta call the Peelers, they did."

"Thank you." Fiona forced her lips into a smile, filled her lungs with courage and waded into the room.

Impatience twisted the faces of the mob surging toward three drab men. Courage and stubborness stamped the two men standing on the outside. Fear ravaged the face of the man in the middle as he stood his ground.

Uncle Andrew had been correct—Mr. Bartholomew possessed an ounce of courage. He stepped back. A bare ounce.

A man in a tidy suit shook a fistful of papers at the clerks. Her uncle's right-hand man winced, brushed ineffectively at the stain on his white shirt and backpedaled.

Two men in dark uniforms and domed hats shoved to the front. Policemen. Fiona waited. The doorman's Peelers weren't here to control the crowd; they were part of the problem.

"His isn't the first death outta this office, now, is it, sir?"

"'Ere, now. We wants to get paid. The dead 'ave no need o' money." A couple of old salts nodded.

"We're here on official business." The policemen turned to the crowd. He and his partner fingered the batons at their sides. The mob receded several paces.

"Mr. Grey and his wife had a boating accident some weeks back," Mr. Bartholomew murmured to the policemen.

"Where is Mr. Grey at present?"

"He's dead." A weasel-faced man in a stained suit clawed his way through the crowd. "And he owes me money."

"Me, as well." More bills were fanned in the air as the chorus spread around the room.

"My uncle is not dead!"

Anger, irritation and disbelief slammed into Fiona. Strings cut into her wrist when she swung her bulging purse and caught it with a chink. Ears perked at the sound of coins. She rubbed the sting from her leather-clad hand.

"Captains." Her smiled encompassed several familiar faces. Men quickly doffed their hats.

"Miss Grey?" Mr. Bartholomew scuttled around the edge of the crowd.

Her name rippled through the crowd. The connection eased the grim faces.

"Mr. Bartholomew." Fiona offered her hand. "It is nice to see you again. Although I would have preferred it to be under happier conditions."

"Yes, indeed." Limp fingers brushed hers.

"Gentlemen, I'm afraid my uncle is not here at present." Fiona's gaze touched each man, sorting them into manageable categories. This one could be charmed. Those two would be swayed by their vanity. Over and over, she nodded and smiled. Her cheeks ached. A cramp pinched her neck. The weasel and the bill fanner would be cowed by the Grey power and connections. A tiring day, but at least it would be manageable.

"I will be helming Grey Shipping until his return." She ignored the gasp of horror and consulted the watch pinned to her bodice. "Have I a full day of appointments, then, Mr. Bartholomew?"

Silence yawned. She closed her lips, hiding her grinding teeth. Really, the man was denser than a brick. Fiona caught his eye. Answer the question before all my hard work is undone.

Her reflection shone in the clerk's eyes. Small wonder the tradesmen were revolting. Unswerving loyalty aside, why did her uncle continue to employ the man?

"Appointments?" Mr. Bartholomew's adam's apple floated to the top of his throat before dropping. His head bobbed, responding to the counterweight of his large nose.

"I—I was in charge of your schedule, Miss Grey." The clerk on the right marched to her side. His coworker matched his strides. The men now bookended Mr. Bartholomew and her.

"Ah, yes, I had forgotten." Fiona smiled at the young men. At least, her uncle had hired *someone* with a functioning brain and a spine. "If you gentlemen would kindly untangle yourselves, we will take care of each of you in turn. I believe we arranged for Mr. Bartholomew to dispense funds to our captains while Mister... " She coughed into her glove. What were the men's names? She could hardly make something up.

Someone was bound to know the truth. Someone like Hugh. She forced the man from her thoughts.

"Jones, Mum," the first whispered while presenting his handkerchief.

"Black, Mum." The second offered her a cup of cold tea.

"Mister Jones will assist any tradesmen with invoices over two weeks old. Mr. Black will handle those debts incurred more recently. I promise, Grey Shipping will settle all accounts after a full reckoning." She smiled as the men formed orderly queues in front of the relieved clerks. "I thank you gentleman for your patience."

The weasel and the bill fanner hadn't budged. Fiona set her untouched mug on the table, tugged her gloves off and slapped the leather against her palm. Bullies, the both of them. She was an expert with bullies.

"Anyone requiring anything else must make an appointment with Mr. Bartholomew."

"Now, see here." The thick-necked policeman stepped forward.

"Except you two gentleman." Fiona forced the smile back in place. Irritation and curiosity tugged on her control. Obviously, the policemen weren't here with news of her uncle. So, what did business did the authorities have with Grey Shipping? "I believe the public would insist their police officers be returned to the street as quickly as possible."

"Police *constables*, Miss," the beefy man corrected, straightening his jacket. "Frazier and Smythe." He jerked his head at his companion. "At your service."

"My apologies, Constable Frazier."

Red washed over the policeman's features as she offered her hand.

"I believe my American manners are showing."

Constable Smythe cleared his throat and rammed an elbow into his companion's paunch.

"I'm afraid we'll need to speak with a company official, Miss."

"Then you may speak with me."

"Beggin' your pardon, Miss Grey, but if your uncle or—"

"I understand completely, Constable Smythe." Fiona turned on her heel and headed for her uncle's office. Men understood the authority of her uncle's mammoth desk, especially as it stood a step up from the rest of the office. *Eyes forward, Fiona.* The men would follow. She had left them no choice.

Without breaking stride, she entered the office and tossed her gloves on the mahogany surface. She eyed the high-backed leather chair. Sitting would put her at a disadvantage—smaller than the men and thus appearing weaker. By standing, she forced them to stand as well. A small display of power, one she would need. She turned to face them just as Mr. Bartholomew sidled inside.

"Miss Grey, the captains need their pay." He dropped the metal strongbox on the desk.

"One moment, please, constables." Very slowly, Fiona tugged her purse open. She peeled the denominations from the wad of bills and smoothed them flat. The pouches of coins chinked against the metal. Da always said money speaks its own language. From the way the constables watched the strongbox fill, they obviously understood exactly what it said. Money and power rested in her hands. Now, she would drive the point home.

"Mr. Essex promised to bring over the payroll." She purposely dropped the banker's name, divulging that an officer with the Bank of England waited on her convenience. "I told him three o'clock should be convenient."

"Yes, Miss." Mr. Bartholomew's knees creaked as he lugged the box from the room.

"Now, gentlemen, where were we?" Diamond earrings cut into her fingers as she untangled the bobs from her hair. "Ah, yes, I remember. I'm afraid I am the only Grey with shareholder status in London."

The constables shifted their weight from foot to foot. Perhaps she had overdone it just a tad. Money and power cut both ways, especially for a woman.

With a sigh, Fiona sank into her uncle's chair and motioned her visitors to sit. Now, she looked like a child playing at grownup. She smoothed her forehead. And her head ached. Would they never talk? She glanced at the close-mouthed men. They weren't in a hurry now, were they?

"Constables?" No response.

She couldn't very well shake their mission out of them. Fiona rested her clasped hands on the blotter. Too bad her whip and lasso remained in Uncle Andrew's townhouse.

"Perhaps if you explained the nature of your business…"

"Very well, Miss."

Constable Frazier leaned forward in his chair. Constable Smythe rolled his eyes and flipped open a small black book.

"Tuesday last the bod…er, remains of one William List was found in the area of Seven Dials. Information from one Bosson, Captain, led us to believe he, the deceased, was an employee of Grey Shipping."

Fiona blinked. Remains. Deceased. Dead. Tuesday. The day she sent the captain to her uncle's house. The day Captain List was murdered. Someone cleared their throat. She forced her thoughts to the present, focusing on Constable Smythe.

"Yes, Constable. Captain List brought me here on the *Revere*." And now he was dead.

"Very good, Miss." Constable Smythe tucked the book into his belt and rose to his feet. "If you would be so kind as to notify the next of kin as to the bod—er, remains."

Trembling arms levered Fiona from the chair. Captain List was dead. Her aunt and uncle were missing. She had sent the captain for her uncle.

"Grey Shipping will arrange for the funeral."

"Very good, Miss."

Was there another connection between her missing family and the dead sailor? She would never know unless she asked.

"Constable?"

"Yes, Miss?"

"Mrs. List will ask how he…" Fiona's tongue bumped over her dry lips. "How her husband met his end."

"He broke his neck." Constable Smythe twirled the end of his handlebar mustache. "Painless, it was. And quick."

"An accident?" Relief shook the strength from her muscles. Her bottom hit the chair with a muffled thump.

"Indeed, Miss. He most likely slipped coming out of the Landed Whale. Them steps is right narrow, and drunk as he was, well, bound to happen." The constable shrugged.

His explanation skittered across her skull. One word struck an off-note.

"Captain List was drunk?"

"Indeed, Miss. You could smell it on his clothes."

"Thank you." She nodded as the policemen settled their helmets on their heads and sauntered out the door. Captain Lisk. Drunk. The ideas chased around her brain but never connected.

"Have you news of your uncle, Miss?"

Mr. Bartholomew dropped the cashbox on the desk, nicking her finger. Blood filled the gash before plopping onto the blotter. The pain helped her focus.

"Mr. Bartholomew, did Captain List drink?"

"No, Miss." A stack of papers joined the box. "He is a Temperance man through and through."

"Was. Captain List died Tuesday."

"Never say so, Miss."

"The constables just brought the news."

"Shall I add Mrs. List to the widow's fund?"

"Please do. Grey Shipping will cover the funeral cost as well. I'll find out her wishes." But she would never relay the police's explanation. She would say the captain's death was an accident. Sailing was a dangerous business. So was unloading cargo.

Fiona glanced at Mr. Bartholomew. His lips moved. How long had the man been speaking and more important, what was he talking about?

"...glad you're here. It's the receipts, it is." He smoothed his tie over his collar. "No one's been paid for the last two weeks, and there's been muttering."

"Two weeks? I thought my uncle had been missing for three weeks."

"Four, and I..." Mr. Bartholomew straightened the neat stack of papers. "I, um, took the liberty of using the petty cash. The sailors, Miss Grey, needed their pay."

"Understandably so." She flipped open the cashbox lid. "Why didn't anyone pick up the payroll? Mr. Essex was growing concerned."

"Mr. Grey prefers to deal with the bankers himself."

"Yet *you* dispense the payroll, Mr. Bartholomew. I'm certain my uncle trusts you to pick up the funds from the bank."

"Oh, no, Miss." Mr. Bartholomew tugged on his tie again. "I wish for no authority at the bank."

"For pity's sake. It was twenty years ago. No one remembers the scandal. And you were innocent. My aunt and uncle proved it."

"It was my responsibility, miss. I was just as guilty as the duke."

The Duke of August. The late Duke, at any rate. A conniving sham of nobility who once tried to murder her uncle and compromise her aunt. That was twice in one day the duke had been mentioned. Twice after a silence of twenty years.

"I will arrange delivery of the payroll if I am to be absent. You will dispense it as usual?"

"Yes, miss."

Fiona grabbed the stack of papers off the desk before he could straighten it again.

"Are these all the invoices?"

"Only the ones we have reconciled. The most recent ones are on the bottom. The most pressing ones on top."

Numbers swam as Fiona leafed through the pages.

"So, the sharks have scented blood and are moving for their chunk of flesh before it's all gone."

"Miss Grey?"

"An unpleasant memory, Mr. Bartholomew. Nothing more. Grey Shipping has been in business for two hundred years. The company is neither floundering nor in danger of sinking." She glanced at the twitching clerk. "Well, which of our customers have stopped paying their bills?"

He ran his finger under his collar and glanced over her shoulder.

"A few have been slower to pay than usual."

"You will apprise them of the temporary change and assure them that Grey Shipping is conducting business as usual. Let them know I would hate to sell all their lovely merchandise to their competitors in order cover their debts."

"Indeed, miss." He jerked around and scurried for the door.

"Mr. Bartholomew?"

He bounced off the door frame and spun about.

"Yes, miss?"

The man had always been of nervous temperament, but today he seemed downright frantic. Was it her orders, or did he know something?

"Did my uncle mention anything unusual before his…disappearance?"

A shadow crossed his cadaverous face. The man *did* know something he wasn't telling.

"He did ask that I get new locks on the door. But that was after the break-in."

"At his house?" Fiona shoved out of her chair and strolled to the window. She thumbed through the papers while watching Mr. Bartholomew's reflection in the glass.

"No, miss. Here. Even tried to break into the safe."

Burglaries at home *and* work. A coincidence? Not likely.

"I see. Anything else?"

"I think he believed the past was coming back to haunt him."

"Haunt him?" An unusual choice of words. Too neatly aligned with her and Mam's talents. And Uncle Andrew's telegram.

"Indeed. Mr. Grey is an accomplished marksman, but they never found the duke's remains." The clerk bounced his slight weight from foot to foot.

Perhaps her uncle wasn't the only one haunted by that night twenty years ago.

"One more question, Mr. Bartholomew. Is Captain List connected to my aunt and uncle's disappearance?"

"Oh, no, Miss."

"Thank you."

The man remained attached to the doorframe. "Except…"

"Except?"

"The *Sweet Wind* was always under the command of the captain. He felt responsible for her going down. That's why he took the *Revere* to salvage her cargo and to look for your uncle and his wife."

"Why didn't Captain List sail her this last time?"

"A message came round that Mrs. List was seriously ill. Mr. Grey insisted the captain be by her side."

"Has Mrs. List recovered?"

"Indeed, Miss, the captain said her recovery was a miraculous."

Miraculous. It would be a miracle if all the coincidences were simply happenstance.

"Let's hope the news of his demise doesn't cause a relapse."

"Indeed, Miss."

"The items that were salvaged—are they still on the Revere?"

"I believe so. Of course, there were more what washed ashore, but we couldn't purchase everything back. Mostly just the personal items."

"I understand." Many people made a living off items washed ashore. Normally, she didn't mind, but everything pointed to the *Sweet Wind*'s sinking being sabotage not nature.

"If that will be all?"

"I'll need the log of the *Revere*, and I wish to terminate the services of First Mate Bosson." Bosson—who'd "found" Captain List's corpse.

"Very good, Miss."

The debauched features of the seaman poisoned her thoughts.

"Make sure you send burly men."

"Indeed, madam."

Fiona tossed the papers on the desk and shut the door. Gibson said her uncle had brought his important papers to work after the first break-in. But the offices had been ransacked. Where would be a safe place to store his journal? The safe?

One glance showed the journal wasn't on the shelves. And why would he lock up the book in the first place?

What thief would steal a captain's log?

Fiona glanced around the orderly office. The most obvious place would be the bookshelf with all the other logs. She sighed, reaching for the first book.

"Oi've a need ta put it in the master's hands." Kingslea slouched in his torn coat. Dirty fingers poked through his ripped gloves. Irritation bleached his knuckles. Better to bend the book than to snap the turkey-like neck of the pompous clerk before him.

"That's impossible." A lilac-scented handkerchief waved under his nose.

Kingslea forced his gaze to the floor.

"The owner and no other." He clutched the book closer to his chest. If a scientist ever crossed a vulture with a human, they'd end up with something like the fellow flapping around him. The man belonged in a Penny Gaff or a Wild West Show. Fiona could lasso the Birdman and...

Fiona.

Bloody hell, the woman had plagued his thoughts since he'd met her. And her scent—gardenias still perfumed his lungs.

Damn this mission.

A thousand pounds, Kingslea. A thousand pounds to return the book he'd spent all bloody night stealing. His beggar's uniform wasn't the only thing souring the air.

"Now, see here." The birdman hopped forward. "That is the property of Grey Shipping."

Grey Shipping. Could his Fiona be a Grey? Houseman had sent a telegram to inquire. Still, he wasn't likely to encounter the lady on the docks twice in one day. She would need at least that long to recover from her ordeal.

And if his whole quest had been nothing but a matrimonial trap...

Kingslea shrugged off the thought. He'd outwitted the dean at Oxford. How hard could it be to outwit two females?

"And Oi'll return it after Oi gets me reward."

"Reward?" Birdman snorted. "Extortion is more like. If you don't hand over that book, I'll call the constables."

"Them Blue Bottles ain't have no argument with the likes o' Tom Thomas."

Awareness prickled across his neck. The air hummed, enhancing the scent of gardenias. Movement caught his eyes. A woman glided across the floor. He blinked. Had she sprung from his thoughts? Dread spiraled down his back.

Or had she lassoed him as neatly as she could have snared Bosson and his rough this morning?

"Mr. Bartholomew, Mr. Thomas is only wishing to be compensated for his time, like a regular employee." Light glinted in her eyes as she smiled. "Isn't that so, Mr. Thomas?"

"Yes, Mum." Kingslea scratched his hat from his head. Was it his imagination or did she emphasize *Thomas*?

"If you be so kind as to step into my uncle's office, we'll discuss your finder's fee."

Her uncle's office. She *was* a Grey, not a poor relation. The Worth morning dress had been designed specifically for her. The navy fabric molded her high breasts, squeezed her small waist and caressed her flared hips. *Good God, what's next? A ballad dedicated to the two darts running up her rib cage? A hands-on expedition to see how to remove the dress from her back?*

One breath. Three. Five. The erotic images wouldn't cool. *Damn it, man. Her presence in this place proves her culpability.*

"Oi'll just takes me reward and leave, Mum." Reward? His reward would be leaving here before he turned into an imbecile.

"Of course, Mr. Thomas, but as these things take time..." She slipped her hand through the crook of his arm and stepped forward.

His feet carried him into the spider's lair. Damn his honor. If he wasn't a gentleman, he would have let her fall on her deceitful face.

"I thought a cup of tea might be nice." She ignored the desk and settled in a chair, motioning for him to take the one opposite her.

Very cozy. How long had the fair Fiona and his stepmother plotted together? Their scheming may have brought them together again, but he wasn't going to fall arse over teakettle for her. She wasn't that beautiful.

"Mr. Bartholomew, there doesn't seem to be a teakettle in my uncle's office."

"I'll see to it, Miss Grey."

Kingslea's gaze flicked to the birdman when he entered carrying a battered kettle. Mr. Bartholomew. He might be ignorant of the plot but that didn't make him an ally.

"Would you require anything else, miss?"

"Your clothes."

Kingslea blinked. Shock and outrage rubbed his control. No wonder the family had gone to such lengths to marry her off. The woman ordered men to strip in front of her.

"I beg your pardon?"

Laughter bubbled in his throat. Birdman should have asked more questions about his role in this farce. He reached for his tie. Kingslea's amusement died as the ends fell away. Bloody Hell. The man was actually undressing. Kingslea reached for his shirt button. If the woman wanted to see a real man he'd show her one.

"Not the ones on your back, Mr. Bartholomew." A pained expression crossed Fiona's face. "The ones you changed out of earlier."

Relief flooded the birdman's face. "Miss?"

Heat burned Kingslea's face. The sleepless night was beginning to tell. No lady would ask a man to strip for her. And Fiona Grey was a lady. A conniving lady, but a lady, nonetheless. His numb fingers fumbled with his shirt. At least, he'd only undone three buttons.

"I believe Mr. Thomas would be delighted to wear such a fine clerk's suit. You are almost his height, but not his..." Her gaze swung to his, dropped to his throat. Her pupils dilated, her lips parted.

Kingslea's hand stilled. What had he been doing? Dressing? Her pink tongue ran over her lips. Or undressing? His hands shook from the turmoil. Fingers spasmed, snapping the thread. The button slipped down his chest, bounced off his thigh and plinked to the floor.

She blinked.

"Not his size." Her shoulders trembled as she stared at the floor.

"Yes, Miss Grey."

"Thank you, Mr. Bartholomew. Kindly give me your tailor's bill for reimbursement."

The birdman nodded as he backed out of the room.

"Oi'll just leave the book."

"No." Fiona straightened her shoulders. Her chin rose, and she caught his eye despite the color in her cheeks. "No, I won't hear of it. Please, Tom Thomas, I believe you have something I want."

Want. Wanton. *Concentrate on the job, man. Find a willing woman, steer clear of the ladies.* Why did his body choose today to ignore such sound advice?

"Just the book, mum."

"A captain's logbook, I believe." Narrowed eyes focused on the leather as if to see through the binding.

"Just a book, mum."

"I—"

Birdman scampered into the room, a pile of neatly folded garments in his arms.

"Miss Grey, the clothes you requested."

"Thank you." Fiona rose and set the suit on the desk. Her index finger tapped on her lip. "Mr. Bartholomew, what do you see when you look at Mr. Thomas?"

Kingslea shoved out of his chair and hunched his shoulders. Now what was she up to?

"I'm afraid I don't understand, Miss Grey."

"What do you suppose Mr. Thomas does for a living?"

"Begs, Miss Grey. I believe he begs for pence."

Kingslea nodded. So, she had seen through his sailor's disguise. His beggar's uniform was perfect. He'd even earned thrupence on his way to the warehouse.

"Hmmm. Anything strike you as unusual?"

"Aside from his possession of the captain's book?"

"Yes, aside from that."

"No, Miss. He's a scavenger, pure and simple. Shall I have him shown off the premises?"

Kingslea locked his jaws. So, the birdman wanted him gone. The feeling was mutual. Imagine a withered shell like that thinking a woman like Fiona would actually want to see him unclothed.

"No, thank you, Mr. Bartholomew."

With a backward glare, the birdman scampered from the room. He wasn't the only one who should be going.

Kingslea tossed the book onto the desk.

"'ere's the book. Now, as to the payment..."

She walked around the desk, jerked open a drawer and chucked a bag onto the table. Coins pressed against the pouch. Judging from the size, a year's-worth of wages rubbed together inside. Was the woman crazy? Tossing around that much blunt in front of a beggar? She needed a keeper.

"Which will it be, Mr. Thomas? The clothes or the coins?"

His gaze traveled from the clothes to the bag. The money wouldn't even cover the marchioness's new dress. As for the clothes, after a few alterations they might prove useful. Still, which would a beggar pick?

"Both, mum."

"Not both." She lifted the book and flipped through the pages to the last entry. What was she looking for? He had read the thing beginning to end. There were only twelve entries. "You must choose."

Kingslea caressed the wool suit. The ink stain on the cuff. The worn and patched elbows. Little things that made a perfect disguise.

"These, Miss." He picked up the suit.

"You make a horrible beggar, Hugh." The book shut with a thud. She tossed it onto the pile on the floor.

Hugh. She knew. Blood congealed. Irritation liquefied the mass and shunted it around his body. Of course, she knew. She had helped plan the whole thing. He had almost forgotten.

He wouldn't make it easy for her. And if she thought shutting them together in this messy office would compromise her, Houseman would swear he was miles away.

"The name's Tom Thomas."

"Hugh. Tom Thomas. You are no more a humble beggar than I am your queen. Stop playing games, Hugh. You are a gentleman. Your manners give you away."

"My manners." He bloody well wasn't going to give in that easily.

"A beggar would never offer the book first. He always needs the payment in hand. Your shoulders are too straight, and you look at those you're addressing. There is nothing humble about you."

Kingslea raised his chin. Damn but the chit had a point.

"I'm new to begging."

"You took the clothes instead of money. The disguise is more important than food."

"Your Mr. Bartholomew thought your behavior out of character, not mine."

"Tell me I'm wrong."

Kingslea shrugged. Of course she knew he was a gentleman. She and his mother had arranged this little meeting.

"I cannot."

She smoothed her hands over her face.

"So, you needed to be a beggar this afternoon. You fooled Mr. Bartholomew. Did Bosson believe you were a sailor, too? You thought he was after you this morning, didn't you? And I thought..." Her voice cracked. Her jaw slid back and forth. "Never mind what I thought. How did you acquire Captain List's book, Hugh?"

"Found it."

Her cheeks paled. "Found it? On his dead body? Or was he alive when you...when you...?"

Dead. The captain was dead? If this was an elaborate matrimonial plan, why was the captain dead?

"I have come to the conclusion that most only see the surface truth. Indeed, rarely does someone trouble enough to look at the heart of the matter. Did you happen to 'find' my uncle's *log* as well?"

Kingslea shook his head. She knew he had caught onto her plans. That was why she was conjuring up another intrigue. He wasn't such a fool.

"I'd better go." His feet didn't budge.

"Wait." Desperation blazed in her blue eyes. "Who do you work for? Whatever he's paying you, I'll double it. I need my uncle's book, Hugh. I need..."

His body throbbed. She spoke of needs when it was she who conjured this hunger inside him. His control snapped. No more beggar. No more sailor. She asked for Hugh. She could deal with the consequences. He stalked across the room.

"If you're tired of games, madam, then you should not have instigated such a farce."

Her eyes widened, but she didn't retreat.

"I didn't—"

"You did. What am I worth?" He backed her against the wall, boxing her in place. "A bag of money? Those diamonds winking from your ears? What?"

She tilted her head to look at him. "Anything, I'll give you anything, just..."

"Anything?" Her skirt brushed his thighs. Madness. Her feigned innocence had been pushed him to the brink of madness.

"Name your price." Her gaze dropped to his lips. A siren luring the unsuspecting to their doom.

"You, Fiona. I want you, damn it." He pushed away from her, stormed across the room and threw open the door.

CHAPTER EIGHT

Men: the missing link between women and apes. Fiona gathered her crackling hair in her fist and twisted the waist-long locks. Mr. Darwin was too close to see the truth.

"He thought we wouldn't recognize him." Her blue eyes supervised her hands coiling the hair ropes into a bun. Her fingers walked over the vanity, snatched up a hairpin and plunged it into her hair. Metal scratched her scalp. "How could anyone believe a little dirt and a few ragged clothes would provide an adequate disguise?"

She flicked open her jewelry box and selected a short strand of pearls. The cool rounds clinked together as she threaded them through her hair.

"The man's logic is completely devoid of reason. We simply offered him a job."

Buy him?

Thick cream cooled her fingers. She returned the top to the jar and rubbed the lotion on her chest and shoulders. The scent of gardenias wafted from her skin. She eyed her reflection in the mirror.

"I never wanted to buy him, I simply wanted to lease him for a while." Doubt flashed in her reflection's eyes. "Lease his services, not his..."

Broad shoulders edged the thoughts from her skull.

You, Fiona. I want you.

Hugh's words heated her skin like an August breeze in the Arizona Territories. Hot. Sultry. Tingles raced along her arms. Her knees trembled, and fluttering tickled her stomach.

Her hand stilled on the rise of her breast. The silk camisole felt rough against her flesh. The woman in the mirror had flushed cheeks and over-bright eyes. Was this desire?

"What do you know of desire?" Silk lacings cut into her fingers as she tightened her corset. "Not one blessed thing. But you do know illness."

Brianna's wan face filled her memory. Fiona shook her head to clear the thoughts.

"Tis symptoms of an illness. Nothing more."

Damnation. Hugh's parting curse, aimed more at himself than at her. Yet, his word had scored her bones.

"He is obviously succumbing to the same malady. It may very well be contagious." Contagious. She must see him again, just to be certain whatever was happening to her wasn't fatal. "And how will you manage to find one man among the millions who live in London?"

Her reflection remained mute.

He had found her twice. But then she hadn't needed his help. Men sensed when a woman needed assistance, and it triggered a run-and-hide reflex. Her gaze fell on the train of a skirt disappearing into the wall behind her. Even Milton had vanished.

So, how *had* Hugh found her? He possessed her name, whereas she...

"Hugh could very well be his Christian name, but Tom Thomas—that is obviously a pseudonym."

Fiona twined her gold chain through her fingers and lifted it off her neck. She placed a kiss on her engagement ring before dropping the jewelry into her silk purse. Perhaps he would find her again. Anticipation and anger wrestled within her.

"Oh, bother. You'll be tied to the house, sewing, balancing the household accounts, dealing with the servants, until he deigns to call on you."

Call on me.

Hugh/Tom Thomas would hardly walk up the front step and knock on her door. Fiona slouched against the vanity and propped up her chin. A sigh dropped her shoulders.

"So, you never lay eyes on the man again. You haven't exactly lost the love of your life."

Love of her life. Milton had been the love of her life. And she had lost him. Hugh's face sailed across her consciousness. The two men's faces spun through her memories—one body, two heads. A seraph of confusion.

"You've dwelt too long in the man's world, Fi. Love Hugh. Utter nonsense."

— Miss me, love?

Milton's semi-opaque face superimposed itself over her reflection. Fiona's heart slammed into her throat.

"Jesus, Mary and Joseph."

For one brief, insane moment she had seen her life so entwined with his their existence was inseparable. As they had been in life.

— Tut. Tut. What would Gran say? Translucent hands waved through the gilt edging as he swam the rest of the way out of the wall.

"Who do you think taught me?" Ribbon tickled her shoulder. "Good gracious."

She had forgotten her state of undress.

A low whistle slipped from his lips.

— I always thought you looked lovely in your clothes, but this... Phantom arms crossed his smoky chest.

Fiona slipped off the stool and yanked her dinner dress off the bed, brandishing it in front of her.

"For heaven's sake, Milton, I am in the middle of dressing for dinner."

— Would you have acted thus after we married. He spun about and dashed to the window.

"We were never married, Milton." The coral silk slipped over her head. Milton's question circled her thoughts. Would she have been so modest? Thoughts of Hugh had accompanied her toilette, yet with Milton...

They are not the same, Fi. You can control your thoughts, whereas Milton...

"Where have you been?" She slipped her arms through the small sleeves.

— Don't know. He stuck his hand through the window. A roosting pigeon flapped away. Cold fogged the glass. *Wasn't here. Wasn't there. Wasn't anywhere. Just endless darkness everywhere I turned.*

"The Nothingness." Fiona began slipping the buttons through their holes.

— Are you almost finished, Fi? This staring out the window is deucedly lacking.

"Just the buttons. You may turn around, though. Gran always craved company whenever she returned."

— How's that?

"When Gran expends too much energy, she slips into the Nothingness. The place between two worlds. She assures me it is very different from Purgatory."

— So, if I help you again... Milton floated across the room. He reclined on the bed, his hands tucked beneath his head. *...I'll return to the Nothingness?*

"Most likely." Fiona smoothed the buttoned placket and stepped into her slippers. "I missed you."

— I know. He smiled at the ceiling. *I heard you calling me. Your voice led me back into this world, Fi.*

"Are you sorry you returned?" She stopped by the bed. Her gloves lay across the coverlet, empty hands reaching for what could have been.

— Anything is better than the Nothingness. He sat up and drifted closer to the fire. *Is this new dress for me? Payment for my suffering.*

Guilt trounced her calm. Hugh had taken up residence inside her skull, dictating her actions. Thoughts of Milton intruded only when she touched his ring. And she had called him back.

"I thought you preferred me in blue, Milton." Fiona smoothed the pink silk.

—*I've changed my mind*, he sniffed. *I much prefer you in…in this color.*

"It's coral," Fiona's hand hovered over his arm.

— *Ouch.* He soared across the room, rubbing his arm. *Geez, Fi, you know how much it burns when you touch me.*

"Sorry." Feeling needled the cold from her hand. *Penance, Fi?* "I just grabbed the dress. The maid, Milly or Tilly, unpacked my things. The wardrobe was packed, so I reached in and pulled this one out. No conscious thought."

Hush, Fi. Only liars explained so much. She smoothed the pearl choker.

"Aunt Annabelle insisted I accompany them to dinner."

— *Well, you must eat.* Long fingers steepled beneath Milton's chin. He tilted his head to the right. *When was the last time you attended a dinner party?*

"The Hudsons the night before you…" *Died.* Fiona inhaled a shaky breath and her stomach cramped. In her obsession with Hugh, she'd forgotten.

— *You haven't been since, have you?*

Guilt lashed her. How could she have forgotten, for even a moment, about the night Milton died?

"I was in mourning."

— *I've been gone almost two years, Fi.* Milton and his words drifted on the draft.

"After your accident, Brianna's sickness worsened and…" Fiona forced the balls of blood-spotted handkerchiefs from her mind. Her sister's recovery was almost assured. "We didn't think she would survive. Dinner parties and balls seemed like a waste of what precious time we had left."

Milton crossed his arms.

— *Your sister's health has been improving for the last four months.*

"I attended Gilly's wedding reception and the round of dinners, parties and balls."

— *And you stuck by your sister's side.* Milton scowled. *You never danced. Not once. When we would attend, I had to drag you off the floor to eat.*

He had. Fiona rearranged the bottles on her vanity. But that seemed a lifetime ago.

"Things are different now."

— *You barely talked to anyone. I was a trifle jealous at the swarm of men you attracted, like moths to the spark of your wit.*

"I'm not the same person I was." And she didn't really miss being a debutante, concerned about parties and impressions and talking about nothing. Cotton rubbed her palm as she chased the wrinkles from the coverlet. "Neither of us is."

— *I'm dead, Fi. I stopped changing almost two years ago, but you…you stopped living.*

Stopped living. The accusation drew blood.

"I get up every morning, dress and eat breakfast."

— *Then climb into your carriage and dash off to the pier.*

"Mam and Da are occupied with Brianna. Investigating any chance for a cure."

— *You speak more to those sailors on the pier than to any eligible bachelors.*

"My family needs me." Fear snaked over her flesh. *But will they need you when you get home? Brianna will be cured. Mam and Da can take over the business once more.* Wasn't her brother running G&G Enterprises in her absence?

She straightened the cut-glass bottles on the vanity into a line of two.

"Eventually, I'll enter society again."

— *With ink stains on your fingers and a deplorable habit of being unfashionably late.* Milton's lips curled.

Fiona quickly donned her gloves.

"I like helping Da with the business." She liked talking about something, accomplishing something rather than yattering on about nothing.

— *You belong in your own home, Fi, not in some dark office, rubbing shoulders with the dregs of society.*

Irritation jerked her shoulders straight. Milton had always hated her work. Anything that took her attention away from him.

"My work is not keeping me now," she snapped.

— *I just feel responsible for your unhappiness.*

Responsible? Without physical boundaries, the man's ego had swelled to enormous proportions. When they were courting, she had enjoyed his outrageous statements, but this...

Fiona snatched her purse and fan from the vanity and yanked her shawl off the bed.

"Aunt Caroline and Uncle Andrew are missing and presumed dead. Aunt Annabelle and that toad Piers want to lock up Uncle Heberon and cart Melinda and Cedric off to a boarding school. Someone is spreading malicious lies about Grey Shipping. Where, precisely, does your burden of guilt fit?"

— *I only meant that you should be managing your own house, not your doddering uncle's, and tending your own children, not worrying over someone else's. If I hadn't taken that bet, you would have those things by now. You would be happy. Settled.*

A slew of babies chaining her to a house. One that reflected her husband's position in San Francisco society. Had her fiancé's death provided a release of not just his spirit but hers as well? She slammed the door on her thoughts. There would be time for introspection later. She had a job to do now.

"Does this mean you aren't willing to help me, Milton?"

— *Your wish is my command.* He bowed and drifted to her side.

"Look around the house. See if you can find any..." Fiona swallowed the hesitation. She was in charge. Her family depended on her. "Any trace of my aunt and uncle."

— You think they're dead, then?

Dead. Her heart rejected the weight.

"I don't know." Doubt slipped past her lips. "They certainly wouldn't have left Uncle Heberon and their children to the mercy of Aunt Annabelle if they could prevent it."

He nodded, spun about and headed for the nearest wall.

— Anything else?

"Yes. Find out if Uncle Heberon can see you."

— Heberon. Which one is he?

"I'll point him out." Fiona settled her hand on the doorknob.

— Is he going to dinner as well?

"No, Piers doesn't allow him outside."

— Cousin Piers? Milton jerked around.

"The same."

— Can I accompany you to dinner?

"I'd be delighted, but remember the rules." She tugged open the door and strode into the hallway.

— Right. Yes or no questions only.

"Gibson said we're to gather in the drawing room. Ready?"

Milton nodded as they reached the first-floor landing. She dried her palms on the wool shawl and cleansed her lungs with one deep breath. The enemy lay behind the parted mahogany doors. Voices buffeted the stillness.

"...to get a husband, of course. Why else does any American heiress darken our shores."

Piers's disdain soured the air. Fiona stopped. They were unaware of her presence. Such an opportunity was not to be missed. She crept closer to the door; the oriental rug silenced her steps.

Milton soared to the door and stuck his head through the wood.

— I say, he's a nasty little fellow. Can see why you avoid him. Husband-hunting? He laughed. *He doesn't know you very well does he, Fi?*

"Is that what she told you, Piers?" Aunt Annabelle sharp notes shredded the tranquility.

"Not in so many words."

— Pompous popinjay. Look at him strut around. If I weren't dead, I'd teach him a lesson.

"I could tell by the way she was looking at me, Mama. An earl would be a catch for a nobody from America."

"She'll need all her money to land a husband." A young woman's voice slithered into the hall. Fiona smiled. Cousin Edwina's smiles were as false as paste jewelry and about as useful. "Did you see her clothes and her hair?"

Clucking filled the air. "And I am almost positive she powdered her face. I don't think we should have anything to do with her. Do let's cut her, Mama."

— *Why on Earth do you wish to help these vipers, Fi?* Milton hovered half-inside the door.

I don't, she mouthed. Her family never had much to do with this branch of the family tree, especially after she'd turned twelve.

— *Then can I have a bit of fun? Please, Fi. Gran has taught me some tricks.*

"Really, Edwina, how could we possibly cut her? She lives in our house."

"Then, let's toss her out. She can stay at an hotel like the rest of the Americans."

Fiona glanced at Milton. Red tinged his transparent form. The Montagues needed to be taught a lesson.

"Be my guest."

Milton rubbed his hands together before disappearing through the door.

"We can't do anything until that imbecile is locked away."

"And let us not forget the money. She is liable to take the children with her. Do shut the window, Piers, dear. There seems to be a draft."

"Ring for the servant, mother. That is what they are paid for, is it not?"

"Very well, pull the sash, Edwina. Maybe that worthless butler will rouse our unwanted guest."

Fiona stepped closer, peering over the door hinge and into the room.

"I don't see how she can take those brats. I'm head of the household."

He reached for his brandy glass. Milton moved it out of his reach. Piers frowned at the snifter then lurched after it.

"This is England, after all."

"Unfortunately, Piers, her father is legally their guardian. After all, they are his brother's children."

"So, then, what are we to do with her?" Piers raised his glass to his lips. Milton tapped the bottom, and brandy splashed his chin.

Fiona clamped her hand over her mouth and choked on her giggle.

"Do be careful, Piers." Aunt Annabelle rubbed her neck as Milton trailed his fingers across the exposed flesh. "Where is that servant? Ring the bell again, Edwina."

Her cousin shuffled across the small field of vision.

"We shall find dear Fiona a husband, of course."

"What!" Silk swished as Edwina slid to a halt in front of her mother. Anger smeared red on her pale cheeks. "Mama, you cannot mean it. This is my year. You promised me."

"You shall have your lord, Edwina dear. Your dear cousin's portion will undoubtedly attract many suitors. And you shall have your pick of them. After all, money can't hide her age."

Fiona blinked. Her age? She was twenty-one, not thirty. Why, at home, she could have any number of men.

"Do you mean it, Mama?"

"Naturally, my dear. For a small fee, my sister will provide entree to the most select doors. Every eligible lord will be presented to you *before* your cousin."

"That's all very well for my dear sister." Yellow teeth flashed in Piers's gaunt face. "How, precisely, does that stop her from taking the Grey money? I told you the banker refused to give me any, didn't I, Mama? Said I wasn't authorized to withdraw funds. Even after I dragged those brats along to prove I was their guardian."

"Don't worry, Piers." Aunt Annabelle patted a curl Milton had tugged from her hair. His tongue stuck out of his mouth as he worked on removing a pin. "We'll have the man fired once we leak word of the Greys' unfortunate demise."

"And when will that be, Mama?" Piers whined. "I am tired of waiting."

"After the season, of course." Another lock joined the first across Aunt Annabelle's shoulder. "Mourning would be a trifle inconvenient at the moment."

"And how am I to pay my debts until then?"

"On your expectations, of course. Edwina, dear, come and fix your mother's hair. Why on earth did we hire that maid? My hair is already falling down, and we haven't even departed."

Edwina picked up the pins at her mother's feet and dutifully rearranged the fallen tresses.

"Expectations? That fool Heberon will live forever."

"Perhaps, but I was speaking of your nuptials."

Fiona stepped back. Piers was engaged? Who was the unfortunate woman?

"My what!" Piers dropped his glass. The sifter hovered in the air for a heartbeat before floating carefully to the floor.

"Surely, you've heard the rumors. Your marriage with Fiona has been arranged since birth. Her father is only allowing her this season as an indulgence. American girls are quite spoiled."

"You want me to marry *her*?"

Thoughts sloshed in Fiona's head. Marry Piers? She would rather die. Milton hovered near Piers's elbow, his head cocked to the side. Milton might be her past but that didn't make Piers her future.

"Well, her person does come wrapped up in all that delicious money, dear. Lock her up at Edgewood afterwards. A wife takes a vow of obedience."

"Obedience." Piers rubbed his hands together. "And I'll be lord and master. She's not likely to agree to it."

Obviously, Piers wasn't completely obtuse. She'd have a legion of dead fiancés before she married him.

"Who says she'll be given a choice?"

CHAPTER 9

Fiona's stomach lurched.

"Gibson." Hair cushioning her palm, she smoothed the ends flat. Her heart slowed to a normal tempo. "You startled me."

"It is the servant's job to listen at doors, Miss Fi." Amusement wiggled the wrinkles bracketing his mouth.

"Did you hear?" She swallowed the building outrage. "That...that foul..."

"I expected it, Miss." Gibson snapped his wrists, and the cape in his hands billowed around her. The breeze from her cape brushed her heated cheeks.

"Well, I certainly didn't. To think anyone would imagine I would marry that...that..." Her mind fumbled for an appropriate description. Nothing she concocted seemed vile enough. Silk cooled her shoulders.

— *Milk-sucking serpent?* Milton supplied.

"Thank you." Rage shook her limbs. Fingers tumbled over the pleats in her bodice. Where was her whip? She'd teach that milk-sucking serpent about obedience.

"The odds are not in your favor, Miss Fi." Gibson buttoned her cape, gnarled fingers grazed her chin.

"Not at the moment, Gibson, but they will be." She tossed open her fan. Waves of air cooled her thoughts. Her whip and lariat would take care of Piers but the others . . .

— *Guess a dead fiancé is only can only do so much good, eh, Fi.* Milton scratched his neck then adjusted his cuffs.

Fiancé. She needed a fiancé. Hugh's face shimmered in her memory. A fiancé would always be close. She slapped the fan shut. Such a man would naturally help her to find her aunt and uncle.

"Servants can only do so much, Miss."

"I will not marry that...that..."

— *I should say not.* Milton puffed up his chest. *Imagine that...that...*

"Milk-sucking serpent."

— *Precisely. Imagine that milk-sucking serpent thinking he could take my place. But, Fi, maybe you should look about for a husband. You are here, after all.*

"You think I should marry?"

"It is expected, Miss." Gibson stepped through Milton, shivered then tugged his coat closer. "You've sacrificed several years already caring for your sister."

"Sacrificed?" Her actions had cost her nothing. Indeed, she was closer to her parents, sisters and brother than to most of her friends.

— *See, Fi. I'm not the only one who thinks so.* Milton patted Gibson's bald pate. The butler slapped his head. *I like him.*

"May I remind you that I am here to find Uncle Andrew and Aunt Caroline, not a husband?"

"Indeed, Miss." Gibson squared his bent shoulders and brushed at an invisible spot on her shoulder. "But you must guard against ardent would-be grooms."

— *That's right, and while you're doing that I'll find you a husband. Someone tall. With a firm hand.* Milton ticked off his list.

"I will find a gentleman ally on my own." And she knew the perfect candidate. Doubt shook her conviction. He had made it clear he was opposed to helping search for her family. How would he react to posing as her lover?

"The temptation might prove too strong."

"Nonsense, Gibson." He wouldn't need to kiss her. Of course, a quick peck or two might go far to convincing her matchmaking aunt they were serious. "I know it is only acting."

"I was talking about the gentleman, Miss."

Fiona cleared her throat. "As was I, Gibson."

— *Indeed. You're taking my idea much better than I thought.* Milton smoothed his hair. *Well, I suppose almost two years of mourning is sufficient to recover.*

"A *pretend* fiancé should buy me sufficient time, don't you think?" Fiona watched the blackness fade from Milton's form. She had enough problems to solve. She could do without a self-pitying dead fiancé.

— *Still, you should marry, Fi. I'll have to approve of him, you know. I feel a certain responsibility.*

Milton was responsible. Responsible for making her head throb.

"Thank you, Gibson, I believe I am ready now."

"Don't thank me, Miss Fi." The butler opened the door the rest of the way. "I feel as if I am leading the lamb to slaughter."

"Do we have room in the smokehouse for three Montagues?" she whispered, sweeping into the drawing room. "Aunt Annabelle." Fiona kissed the air beside her aunt's cold cheek and turned to her cousin. Age had some advantages, chief among them a sharply honed tongue. "My, Edwina, look at the young lady you've become. With your hair up and your skirts down, you could almost pass for *seventeen*."

"Edwina is eighteen this year, Fiona."

"Really." Fiona circled her cousin. Once, they'd had a chance at becoming friends. Now, the armies had been drafted, and Edwina was on the wrong side. "And she looks so fresh in her charming dress."

"I make my debut this year. I have already been presented to the queen."

Fiona kept her lips still. They had waited precisely one minute before pulling rank. Did they truly think mentioning royalty would cow a Republican?

"And how is Queen Victoria? We chatted for practically fifteen minutes during my presentation. I believe she had a fondness for Aunt Caroline's mother."

Edwina's cheeks flushed. Her jaw slid back and forth before she found her voice.

"Her Majesty enjoys good health."

"Aren't you going to say hello, Fiona?" Piers's voice oozed across the room. Fiona unclenched her fists.

"Hello, Piers. Sorry for the...oversight." She bounced on the balls of her feet, reminding him of her two-inch advantage over his own modest height. Anger reduced his lips to a slash in his face.

"May we leave now?" Edwina's whine deflated Piers's building anger. "We wouldn't want to keep Aunt Elspeth waiting."

"I don't believe you've had the honor of meeting my sister, Fiona." Aunt Annabelle set her hand on Piers's arm. White flashed on her knuckles before she sauntered towards the door. Piers winced and rubbed his arm. "I'm certain if you bring out your best manners, we might persuade her to help us with your search."

"My search?" Fiona fell into step beside her cousin.

"Oh, yes, Piers informed me of your mission. You were very fortunate he stumbled across you this morning. Noblemen are very sensitive about any hint of scandal."

"Indeed, *cousin*, you wouldn't want a gentleman to marry you only for your dowry." Edwina smirked.

"I couldn't imagine anything worse." Fiona nodded. Did they plan to spread unsavory rumors about her? That would hardly force her to accept his finger let alone his hand.

— He's worse. Milton shot through Piers. Her cousin wrapped his arms around his slight frame to stop from shivering.

"Piers, do assist Fiona into the carriage while I find that...Oh, Gibson. Where are our cloaks? I distinctly told you to have them—"

"Madam." Gibson held out the cloaks.

Fiona drifted out the door. A slight drizzle dampened her cheeks. She nodded to the burly footman.

"Really, Americans are so lax in their attitudes." Her aunt jostled her shoulder as she strode past. "Servants overstepping their bounds. Young girls running about unescorted." She placed her hand in the footman's and looked back over her shoulder. "Don't worry dear, we'll keep your indiscretion in the family. It would positively ruin your marriage chances."

— If I were a betting man... Milton slipped into the carriage, icing over the windows. *I'd say your indiscretion would be common knowledge before we gain entry to her sister's house.*

Fiona climbed aboard the brougham. It might be the one bet Milton ever won.

❋ ❋ ❋

"The black necktie, Houseman." Kingslea adjusted the starched collar of his shirt. Eight sets of eyes surveyed his progress from the splintered mirror.

"You're not attending the marchioness's dinner party this evening, milord?" The valet frowned at the white scrap of cloth draped over his hand before turning a questioning gaze to Kingslea's spider-eyed reflection.

"I am dining at my club." Firm. Determined. He straightened his spine. Away from here. Away from her. No doubt, Fiona would attend his stepmother's little party. He intended to heed this afternoon's warning.

Desire and will warred whenever Miss Grey was present.

Houseman tossed the white necktie over his shoulder, pulled open the split wardrobe door and selected a black one from the nail.

"So, you've learned all you need about this morning's work?"

"I've learned enough." A large lump pressed Kingslea's throat. Clumsy fingers tried to coax a bow from the knot.

"'Ere now." Houseman seized the tie and loosened the fabric. "Betty won't like to reheat her iron."

"Betty?"

"The maid. And don't change the subject."

"I wasn't aware we were having a conversation." His valet tugged on the tie. Fabric cut across Kingslea's throat. Air stopped mid-swallow. "Good God, man. Are you trying to dress me or kill me?"

Houseman's eyes narrowed under his bushy brows. "Aye, milord."

Kingslea wedged a finger between his collar and neck. Air flowed easily in and out of his lungs.

"My Fiona is Miss Grey, niece of Andrew Grey, proprietor of Grey Shipping. Undoubtedly wealthy and looking to purchase a destitute aristocrat for a husband." He flashed his palms at the waterstained ceiling. Peeling wallpaper fluttered as he dropped his fists to his side.

The corners of Houseman's lips twitched upwards before he suppressed the exuberant display of emotion.

"*Your* Fiona is the middle daughter of Everett and Brighid Grey, brother and sister-in-law to Mr. Andrew Grey. The Greys reside in San Francisco, although they have strong connections to New York society. What need has a woman to cross the Atlantic when she already has a ring?"

"She's married." Shock gutted him. Fiona was taken. The truth echoed in his hollow chest. There was no elaborate plan to trap him. No invitation in her ripe lips. Hell, her uncanny deductions could simply have been exercise, an escape from boredom. His gaze fell on his white necktie. All the more reason to avoid temptation.

"The bloke died in a carriage accident, two years back." Houseman lifted the black coat from the patched coverlet and held it open.

"She's a widow then?" Kingslea shrugged into his jacket. A widow. Perhaps he could discover if her lips fulfilled their promise after all.

"Mr. Davis met his end before he spoke his vows."

"Then she is still a maid." Back to his original hypothesis. Disappointment warred with elation. Fiona was untouched. And untouchable. Kingslea retrieved his gloves from the bed. A long night of dining and drinking at his club awaited him.

"Aye, a *troubled* maid." Houseman retrieved a brush from the cracked marble bed stand. Coarse hair scratched Kingslea's felt hat.

"Troubled?" Kingslea pried the headgear from his valet's hand. Not that he was interested in Fiona's troubles. He was simply making conversation. "What trouble could a wealthy heiress have? A bad case of woe over an absence of admirers? With her looks, not to mention her fortune, she won't complain for too long."

"Doubt they'd need armed guards to keep a gentleman away." The valet lifted the door back into the wardrobe and picked up the dirt- and makeup-stained towel crumpled on the floor.

"You underestimate the lady's charms." Kingslea fished his valet's words from his memory. He had missed something important. "Armed guards?"

"Aye, milord. Three prowl the house at night, plus a detective stands on the corner. The house has been burgled twice. The same as the offices. All a month or so afore the lady's arrival. Talk is, the uncle summoned help just prior to his disappearance."

"He asked for help from his niece?" Granted, Fiona seemed capable, but she was still a woman. And much too young to have a fiancé nearly two years deceased. How young did Americans marry off their daughters?

"They are an unusual lot, the Grey sisters. The staff keeps mum on them. Odd that they spent every other summer in England yet roused no gossip."

Dinner at the club, Kingslea. Her troubles prove nothing. His conviction wavered.

"Money quiets most scandals."

"There is something more. I feel it."

"Perhaps you feel a longing to return to your Molly." Longing. As a simple farmer, he had hoped to have what his valet and wife shared. As a destitute earl...

He shrugged off his thoughts. He might still find a modicum of affection. But first, he had to find his sister a husband. One willing to support a mother-in-law.

Houseman crossed his arms over his chest. "Or maybe I spied Sullied's man skulking about in the Grey's stable, asking questions."

Sullied—his nickname for the offensive Duke of August. Clarity beamed through Kingslea's murky logic. He rubbed the star-shaped scar on his hand.

"The Duke of August was making inquiries about Fiona?" Fiona needed protection. Sullied would deny her curiosity, crush her sense of humor.

"Seemed right interested in her and her fortune."

"Lilly and her pounds weren't enough for the cretin?" Lilly. At least he no longer felt as if someone had ripped out his heart through his chest at the mention of her name.

"There also seems to be some connection between the missing Greys and the late duke."

"Houseman?" Kingslea jerked on the end of his tie. He would help Miss Grey but only until another debt had to be repaid.

"Yes, milord."

"My white tie." *And the attraction*, his conscience nagged? Such a trifle barely warranted mentioning.

"And if this is all a clever ruse to purchase your noble person?"

Gardenias teased his senses. Fiona's memory stepped into the room. The curve of her neck. The light touch on his arm. Heat snatched the breath from his lungs.

"Then I will simply name a price Miss Grey isn't willing to pay."

CHAPTER 10

I've seen less haggling over mining shares, Fi. *Milton shot across the room to* hover by Piers's elbow. An enameled box trembled in her cousin's hand. His wild-eyed gaze darted around the room as he flipped open the top.

— *I am rather enjoying this.* Milton tapped the bottom of the snuff box. White powder burst into the air before raining down on her cousin's black lapel. Eyes bulging, he kicked the embroidered fire screen. Metal scraped the marble fireplace.

Fiona smoothed her skirt. Perspiration dampened her gloves, darkened the chiffon fabric, casting depth to the embroidered daisies cascading from her hip. She was the only person not enjoying herself. Self-pity agitated her control. Two years of disuse had rusted her social skills. Outnumbered. Outflanked.

Out of place.

Oswin's meaty fist seized the falling screen and set it right. Piers's shoulders rolled as his companion brushed at the stained fabric. Flesh slapped flesh. Oswin held his hand to his chest; hurt tugged on the corners of his mouth.

No need for a lifeline, Fi. You've simply overestimated your dormant abilities. She balanced the ivory fan on her knees then shifted to the right. The cushion bulged next to her thigh. Six against one would be halved once she found an ally. Memories of Hugh flipped through her mind like colors in a kaleidoscope.

"I think that would be more than sufficient recompense for my patronage." Elspeth Gurnsey-Barrett, Fifth Marchioness of Bookingham, flipped open her fan and cooled her dimpled cheeks. Tendrils of gray-streaked hair fluttered in the breeze.

One thousand pounds for entree into British society. Worth every penny if it helped Fiona find her aunt and uncle. She could endure any humiliation for her family. She was the patient one.

— *I don't think this was a very good idea, Fi.* Milton ran his fingers across the back of her aunt's neck. She adjusted her shawl. *I refuse to consider either of those two for your husband.*

A groan fisted in Fiona chest. *Seven against one.*

Milton had rattled on practically nonstop about finding her a husband. A chipped Dresden shepherdess beckoned. How unfortunate the porcelain figurine would sail right through her traitorous fiancé. Of course, the crystal bowls tumbling over the end table would be heavier. Fingers walked over her lap before she caught them. Alas, smashing things would accomplish nothing.

— *I'm beginning to see why you've not allowed anyone to court you. I was an amazingly good choice.*

Her hands became a study of pink and white in her lap. Pain burned her shoulder blades. Of course, such an outlet would undoubtedly lift her spirits. Her sister would certainly approve.

"She's a bit older than most." Aunt Annabelle sowed the seeds of failure with a malicious smile. "That may limit her choices."

Piers wasn't a choice. He was a death sentence. His own. Smile, Fi. Fiona shored up her sagging smile. Gilly would have told them in no uncertain terms what she thought of their condescension.

And she would have punctuated each insult with smashing china.

Too bad they didn't know how lucky they are.

Fiona's lips stuck to her dry teeth. Her cheeks throbbed. Two years' tuition at Miss Pittman's School for Young Ladies had been money well spent. Sure, her needlepoint might be a knot of confusion, her watercolors might resemble a discarded artist's palette, but Fiona Grey's smile was worthy of any masquerade mask.

And almost as stiff.

"A mature gentleman may see that as an advantage."

Color blotted her aunt's cheeks at the marchioness's backhanded defense.

"You don't think most will find it hard to retrain her in the correct ways?"

— *Retrain?* Fury tinted Milton's wavering form with purple. *They talk as if you are a horse or dog.*

They would not talk about a horse or dog in such an offensive manner. Envy squeezed Fiona's chest. *Animals can kick and bite.* A lady did not hear, see or say anything offensive. Society constrained her more than a tightly laced corset. A smile was a poor weapon at best, but it was the only one available to her at the moment.

But moments quickly pass.

And *her* time would come.

"I am certain *some* may find her...colonialisms charming." Aunt Annabelle's hand flopped over her wrist. "Of course, they will not do for a duke..."

Colonialisms? The ache spread over Fiona's jaw and gripped the base of her skull. If ever she needed a reason not to join the English ranks, these four harpies and two dolts had supplied it. First, the matrons shredded her reputation with their catty remarks. Then the two schoolgirls gnawed on the remnants like pack hounds with a discarded soup bone. As for the men...

Fiona dismissed her thoughts. Maybe, if she smiled broadly enough, her cheeks will flip over her ears and block out their conversation.

"The prince is rather fond of them, I believe."

Them. Americans. She might as well be a butterfly pinned to the wall. Dissected. Examined. No doubt they would ask her to open wide if her smile didn't already reveal her back molars.

— *I say, Fi. What if your face freezes in that death grimace?* Milton tapped the seashells threading a path through the obstacle course of photographs frowning from atop the grand piano.

Death grimace? Death would be a release. She must endure this trial. Fiona straightened. At least her spine hadn't snapped. Her fingers brushed a leafy fern escaping a gilt cage. She would repay her aunt's kindness. London was a cosmopolitan city. Surely, some merchant sold snakes.

"The pink is almost becoming on her." Aunt Annabelle smoothed the goosebumps from her flesh.

Poisonous asps. One for everyone.

— *She's jealous, Fi.* Milton's tongue stuck out of the corner of his mouth as he concentrated on the clasp of her aunt's necklace. *I know you're becoming, and I'm dead.*

Her gaze flitted to Milton. Killing them wasn't such a grand idea. They could very well haunt her for eternity.

"It isn't even a proper ballgown, Mama," hissed Cousin Edwina.

Of course, there were always ways to deal with wayward spirits. Gran said exorcised spirits endured terrible agony.

"Monsieur Worth's creations flatter practically everyone." A pout ruined Lady Melody Gurnsey-Barrett's full lips.

But would a Catholic exorcism work on their Protestant souls?

— *Women really aren't the fairer sex, Fi.* Milton tugged on his ear. *A man may punch you in the face, but he'd never launch such a cowardly attack. Unless he weren't a man at all.*

"True. Too true." Her aunt clucked. "Is your son not joining us tonight?"

"Kingslea *had* promised..." Disappointment twisted the marchioness's features. "Well, he promises too many things. This room was barely done in time for our arrival, and the ballroom is still in chaos. He claimed to have forgotten his sister's debut, but we've been here two weeks and he has yet to get the repairmen to finish. In fact, he lets them have off Sunday following half a day on Saturday. Have you ever heard such a thing?"

Aunt Annabelle patted her sister's hand. "We are fortunate that our townhouse needs only a little redecorating."

Somewhere deep in the house a clock bonged eight times. An hour had passed since their arrival. Fiona's stomach rumbled its displeasure. Would they ever serve dinner?

Lady Kingslea freed her hand.

"You are also fortunate that your Piers is such a devoted son."

"Yes," Aunt Annabelle preened, "but you mustn't blame yourself for Lord Bookingham's failure. You hadn't a hand in raising him."

"True. True." Lady Bookingham rose and shook out her skirts. "Things were so much better when Edward was alive. He understood what was due his station. Why, we're practically reduced to wearing rags."

Rags? Fiona covered her snort with a discreet cough. Her hostess's yellow-and-blue velvet dress was a copy of the Worth gown her sister had ordered this spring from Paris.

"There, there." Aunt Annabelle strolled to her sister's side. "Matters can't be as hopeless as that. With a well-placed flower and perhaps some lace, your dress will be quite passable for a matron."

Fiona choked on her laughter. Compliments were not in her aunt's nature.

"Really, Fiona, stop that incessant hacking," Aunt Annabelle snapped.

Lady Bookingham straightened into a study of lines—compressed lips, narrowed eyes and squared shoulders. "You are too kind, Sister."

"As for Kingslea, Piers will have a word with him. They are almost of the same station, after all."

"Such a devoted son." The marchioness's sarcasm sailed over her aunt's head.

The drawing room door slid open. Three men sauntered inside.

"Devoted son?" A broad-shouldered man stepped forward and bowed to her hostess. "Lady Bookingham, you honor me."

Fiona blinked. Those blue eyes. Those dimples. Blood roared in her ears. Hugh stood in the door way. Her Hugh, in gentleman's clothing. Fear clawed up her spine. Impersonating nobility used to be a crime. Was it still? She stumbled forward on wooden legs then caught herself on the back of the lumpy sofa. The crisp fabric slipcover bunched under her fists.

"I hope you haven't held dinner too long." He bowed over the marchioness's hand then moved on to her aunt's. Pleasure had thawed the shock from the sisters' faces. "It took me a bit longer than expected to round up enough escorts for such lovely ladies."

"All that matters is your safe arrival." Lady Bookingham cooed.

Fiona blinked. He wasn't impersonating anyone. Her Hugh was the much maligned Marquess of Kingslea. No. Not her Hugh.

She swept a critical eye over her surroundings—the threadbare carpet, the chipped statuettes and lumps under the slipcovers. Caution tempered her happiness. The carefully masked decay could mean only one thing—a light or empty purse. Dread solidified in her throat. She swallowed the lump. No wonder Lady Kingslea had jumped at the chance to sponsor a rich American.

She, too, had a groom already picked out.

— *These three are much more suitable.* Milton circled the trio of men like yesterday's cigar smoke.

There would be no ally for her. Fiona stepped away from the sofa, forced her fingers to uncurl. Just another determined suitor to be thwarted.

A suitor she'd spent time alone with. Unchaperoned time. One word from him, and her reputation would be ruined. Panic huffed in her ears. Three deep breaths calmed her racing heart. *Leave. Now.* Rusty legs responded to her brain's urgent command.

I'm not for sale.

Hugh's vow soared in her mind as he blocked her exit. Panic smashed her focus. Her muscles twitched from the rush of adrenaline. She stepped to the left then right. He shadowed her movements. Trapped. Nonsense, she simply had to step back, skirt the couch and…

Her gaze left his crooked bow tie, tripped over the cleft in his chin and settled on his twisted grin.

And listen to him claim the prize—her dowry.

Challenge lifted his left eyebrow. "I see another English rose has bloomed in my humble drawing room."

His lips moved. Seconds passed before she processed his words. English? He wasn't going to betray her?

"I'm afraid I'm American," she hedged. Perhaps, he was simply toying with her.

"Fiona," The marchioness's lace sleeves brushed Fiona's exposed upper arm. "Allow me to present my son, the Sixth Marquess of Bookingham, ninth Earl of Kingslea. Kingslea, this is Miss Fiona Grey. She arrived yesterday on her uncle's ship."

"Delighted." Fiona forced the reply through her stiff smile.

"Really?" Kingslea raised her hand to his lips. Heat seared her fingers through her gloves. Electricity teased the hair on her arms. Wariness guarded the amusement dancing in his eyes. "I thought you just said you were afraid."

— *Familiar chap, isn't he?* Milton tapped his index finger to his chin. *And his clothes are not of the first cut. In fact, I'd wager they're almost as old as my burial suit.* Phantom arms crossed over his translucent belly. *He won't do. No. Not at all.*

"Kingslea!" Hugh's smile stiffened in the face of Lady Kingslea's glare. "Pay my…my son no heed, Miss Grey. His sense of humor is an acquired taste."

From the contortions of her ladyship's lips, she had yet to cultivate the appetite.

"Then there are no dragons or demons I might slay that will lessen your fear, Miss Grey?"

"Kingslea!" The hiss whistled by Fiona as the marchioness flapped her arms like a drenched hen.

Fiona tugged her hand free of his grasp. Air chilled the skin despite the satin. She clasped her hand before it could return to Hugh's hold. A poor substitute, at best.

"I'm afraid one cannot slay an American accent or colonial manners—they are simply for the stouthearted to endure."

"Endure." The marchioness's eyeteeth winked in her sharp smile. "Nonsense, my dear."

Fiona's arm burned from the peeress's grip. She shoved Fiona's arm toward Hugh.

"Your manner is quite quaint and, um, charming."

Fiona's body lurched after her reddened arm. *What's next? A ribbon?* Annoyance sucked Aunt Annabelle's lips from her face.

"Forgive my manners." Hugh avoided the collision with a quick backward step. "Ladies, may I present Lord Alveston and Baron Winthrop. Alveston, Winthrop, you remember Lady Bookingham and her sister Mrs. Montague. Miss Montague is making her debut with my sister."

Fiona stumbled to the left as the younger ladies flocked closer, like birds to a child with bread crumbs.

— *That one isn't bad.* Milton swept through the girls and peered into Lord Alveston's face. *Rather aristocratic nose, his brow isn't too low. Not bad at all, though his face lacks a chin.*

"Baron Winthrop." Edwina shoved her hand in the pudgy man's face.

"I believe I'm supposed to be delighted." He place a kiss an inch above the proffered hand and lowered it to her side.

— *This one has two chins.* Milton swept to Fiona's side. *Do you think he stole it from Alveston?*

"Milton," she growled.

— *It was a yes-or-no question, Fi.* Milton sniffed and stepped through a landscape painting.

"Actually, it's Lord Kingslea." Hugh appeared at her side. His blunt fingers caressed the permanent folds of the Dresden? shepherdess's gown. "Or Kingslea, if you prefer."

She preferred Hugh. A sigh bowed her shoulders. *Time to stop wishing on stars, Fi.*

"I think 'milord' covers your confusing use of titles."

"Except for Winthrop." The figurine thumped to a stop in the middle of a lace doily. "He's a baron. Properly addressed as sir."

Another lesson for the ignorant. Fiona snapped open her fan. The others she could understand—they didn't know her, but Hugh...

She shook her head. Lord Bookingham was not the same man she had met twice today.

"It may surprise you that many men in America are addressed as 'sir' as a sign of respect."

— *One less with me gone.* Milton peered into Hugh's face. *You know, this fellow looks familiar. Fi, you're not even paying attention to me.*

"Of course, you'll be Lady Winthrop and your children, or at least your oldest son, will inherit the title. He's not a bad choice for husband."

— *You can't really be listening to him. I know you better, and I say none of these are fit to take my place.*

"A husband?" Fiona's hair tickled her neck from the breeze her fan whipped up. The last time the Earth had seen such a pairing was when Noah built his Ark.

— *Fi?*

Hugh's face changed from ashen to healthy as Milton waved a hand in front of her face.

— *Well, I'm not going to stand here and be ignored. I'm going to check out the rest of the house. One of us must focus on finding your family.*

"Of course, your heart may already be set on Alveston." Hugh tucked his hands under his arms and rocked back on his heels. "He is an earl. You would been a countess and a lady."

Why was he being so accommodating about presenting her with suitors? Unless...

Fiona slapped her fan closed. Her palm stung. He did not consider her refined enough to be his wife.

"One must always strive to be a lady."

His head snapped up. Blue eyes bored into hers.

"Forgive me, have I insulted you in some way?"

Rage exploded inside her skull like a photographer's flash powder.

"You and every one of your unfortunate countrymen and women have heaped insults upon my head since I stepped off the boat."

"I—"

"Contrary to what you may think, I am already a lady. I don't need a title to prove it."

Hugh's smile fell short of his eyes. "Does this mean you are not seeking a husband?"

"I am seeking—"

"Ah, Bunsen." Lady Kingslea raised her voice. "I hope your presence means dinner is finally ready?"

The butler straightened. "Indeed, my lady."

"Miss Grey, if I may be so bold?" Hugh set her hand on his left arm then covered her fingers with his right hand.

"I—" She should pull free of his grasp, end this farce and...

And what, Fi? The question ricocheted inside her skull. She had stepped into her uncle's shoes by way of Grey Shipping's clerks—their vendors had not wanted to deal with a mere woman. Men ran business. Men ran investigations. Women's only outlets were solely through good works and society.

And society loved to gossip.

"Thank you." Fiona nodded. Hugh would no longer distract from her purpose. Especially now she knew where she stood with him. Not that it mattered. She never wanted to be *his* wife, anyway.

Piers stepped in front of Hugh. "I promised to escort my cousin in."

From the corner of Fiona's eye, she saw her aunt nod. Aunt Annabelle hated competition. No one knew Hugh had decided not to chase the dowry prize. No one but her and him. Fiona felt her smile soften. A calculated pursuit of Hugh would definitely irritate her aunt, cousin and the superior lord himself. Perhaps this evening could prove amusing after all.

She stepped closer to Hugh. The soft wool suit sleeve tickled her upper arm.

"Have you met my cousin Piers Montague, my lord?"

Hugh drew himself to his full six-foot height and gazed down his aquiline nose at her cousin.

"Indeed, I have."

Piers inched closer to her. Sour sweat and sweet opium poisoned the air. Clammy fingers plucked at her hold. Her knuckle popped as he pried her index finger from Hugh's arm.

"Is it customary in England to take a lady in to dinner one piece at a time?" She stepped forward, grinding the heel of her shoe into the nearest boot.

Hugh hissed.

"I am certain his lordship doesn't wish to spend the evening listening to the details of your condition." Piers' hand sawed back and forth as he tried to get a hold on her next finger.

Condition? What scheme had her cousin's drugged mind concocted?

"I'm sure I don't know what you mean."

"Come now, cousin. We're all family here. There is no need to hide your condition."

"What condition would that be, Montague?" Hugh forced the words through his closed smile. His hand slid over hers as he cocked his head.

Astonishment seared Fiona. Hugh wouldn't actually believe she suffered from a condition, would he? Why not? He believed she was seeking a husband.

"Your actions might be rewarded sooner if you stood on his foot." A slight inclination of the head accompanied Hugh's whisper.

"Sorry." Fiona eased her foot onto her cousin's boot. She shifted her weight. Piers yelped and stepped backwards. With a yank, he jerked his foot free. Her teeth rattled in her locked smile.

Hugh pushed her gently to the left and stepped around her cousin.

"Make certain you try Mrs. MacGregor's ham thimbales." Hugh nodded to the butler as they neared the drawing room door. "They are one of her many specialties."

"That sounds—"

Something shoved against her shoulder. Her shoulder jostled Hugh's. Piers limped in front of her, spun about and stopped.

"As I was saying, Fiona suffers from weak nerves. Runs in the family, you know. Causes erratic behavior."

Nerves. He had the audacity to speak of her faults when even she knew his behavior was outside the bounds of propriety. Fiona's free hand dropped to her waist. If she had her whip, she'd show him nerves.

"I do not believe *my* behavior is causing comment, Piers."

"Perhaps you had best escort your mother in to dinner, Mister Montague." Hugh voice was even as he flicked an imaginary speck of lint from his jacket. "Your nerves may support each others."

"Really, Fiona, if you weren't so *American* you would know that there is an accepted order in the dinner procession."

"There is no procession, Piers." Fiona jerked her head toward the couples behind her. "You are holding it up."

"No need to stand on ceremony, nephew." With a swish of velvet, Lady Kingslea materialized at their side. She hooked her arm through Piers'. "It is just family tonight."

"Which is all the more reason to teach dear Fiona the proper manners now." Aunt Annabelle huffed to a stop. "No one need witness her unfortunate blunderings."

"Imagine a peer of the realm reduced to a mere no one." Hugh winked at Fiona. Masculine chuckles sounded behind her.

Embarrassment burned her cheeks. She had forgotten their audience. What was happening to her? Gilly was the temperamental one. Fiona was the obedient daughter—well-behaved and well-liked by society. Except this society barely tolerated her presence.

"I'm certain I meant no offense, my lord." Aunt Annabelle glared at Fiona.

Perhaps it wasn't her time spent in the office or her hibernation these last two years that caused her unusual behavior. Perhaps it was *them*. Piers. Edwina. Aunt Annabelle. And Hugh.

"Then why don't you apologize to Miss Grey?"

Shock coursed through Fiona. Apologize? Why was he trying to reenter her good graces?

"I beg your pardon?" Aunt Annabelle pressed her hand against her heaving bosom.

"Miss Grey's manners have been impeccable during our brief acquaintance," Hugh advised her.

"Yes, well." Piers cleared his throat and adjusted his cuffs. Gold swirled around the diamonds winking at his wrists.

Fiona blinked. Piers was wearing Uncle Andrew's cufflinks.

"That is because I spent this morning tutoring her in the proper deportment of an earl's wife. None of that havey-cavey business of running around London without an escort or chaperone."

Piers had commandeered her uncle's personal items, his fortune and his house. Had her cousin also stolen his life?

"You—"

"Oh, dear." Piers winced as he scratched his nose. "Don't worry, Fiona, dear, I'm certain word of your indiscretion will not leave the *family*." With a grin curdling his lips, his gaze swung to Lord Alveston and Baron Winthrop.

Fiona rolled the tension from her shoulders. If she didn't find an ally soon she would need an alibi *and* a priest.

"I am certain I could arrange for a distasteful repayment should any unfortunate gossip enter society."

Her cousin paled under Hugh's threat.

"How very thoughtful of you, my lord," Aunt Annabelle purred.

Too thoughtful, Fiona thought. Still, she needed an ally. And what better one than a confirmed bachelor? Not that she was interested in his future eligibility. Her breath hitched in her lungs. *Really, Fi, you should know better than to lace your corsets when you're angry.*

"Hu—" She coughed the intimacy off her tongue. "Pardon me, Lord Bookingham."

"Yes, Miss Grey."

"I promise not to bore you with talk of disease if you would kindly lead us to dinner."

"But..." Piers whined.

"Your wish is my command." Her aunt and cousin parted before Hugh's stare.

CHAPTER 11

Fiona had picked him.

Kingslea straightened in his chair. He had been right to attend. Only at home could he eat asparagus soup as creamy and warm. With a nod, the butler and maid cleared the soup bowls from the table. Crystal bit into his fingers as he raised his wine glass. The tang of pepper complimented the fruity alcohol sweetening his palate. He had made the right choice, but how could he accomplish his goal?

"Your chef is quite extraordinary." Fiona dabbed her lips with the burgundy napkin.

Such a ripe mouth would also be missing from his clubs. Kingslea gulped his wine. Alcohol burned his gut but seemed cool compared to the heat searing his flesh. What price would he pay for a taste?

"My mother has been searching this age for a dish so savory."

Savory. Kingslea groaned and finished his wine. How could food be so provocative? No, it wasn't the food but the company. Fiona sighed and moaned with every spoonful. The damn woman could seduce a monk by reciting a meteorological report.

And she had chosen him.

Bunsen lifted the empty bowl from her stack of plates. "Thank you."

"One does not thank the help, Fiona." Piers thwacked at a lump of asparagus floating in his soup. "In fact, society does not acknowledge them at all."

"I—"

"Except, perhaps, to rebuke them for bringing one cold soup." Pier's thin lips curled. He dropped the spoon into his broth and wiped his hands. Creamy liquid splashed the olive tablecloth. "They live to serve their betters. Thanks is redundant."

Bunsen's shoulders straightened as he slowly removed Piers's bowl. Kingslea set his glass down with a clunk. Cold soup. Steam still danced above his stepmother's bowl and misted the spoon sticking out of the soup tureen. The posturing little prig was no one's better.

"My soup was delightfully warm." Fiona smiled at her cousin.

"As was mine," Lord Alveston seconded. Heads bobbed around the table.

The butler slowed as he passed Kingslea's chair. A thin skin stretched across the soup. The soup *was* cold. How the devil had Montague managed such a feat? And why? The man hadn't exhausted material to complain about.

"Of course, you have been rather busy." Fiona helped herself to a portion of salmon then streaked the delicate flesh with sunny hollandaise sauce. "I'm certain no one would mind if you focused on dissecting your meal instead of the olive walls, the health of the ferns or the luster of the walnut wainscoting."

Montague shoved a pinch of snuff up his nose, dusted his fingers on his lapel then scraped a large portion of fish on his plate. Next, he drowned the salmon in sauce.

"A properly reared young lady takes an interest in her partner's preferences, cousin."

As Kingslea watched, the vapor wafting from Montague's fork thinned then stopped. The imprint of five slim fingers appeared in the sauce. A palm appeared next like an invisible hand was playing in Montague's food. Kingslea blinked. Curdles replaced the phantom hand.

"You are not my dinner partner, cousin." Fiona chuckled as Montague forced the bite of food around his large adam's apple. Her steaming forkful danced in the air before she swallowed it.

The salmon dried out on Kingslea's tongue. Aye, Fiona had chosen him. He set his fork across his plate. But then, she had a limited selection from which to choose.

"Is your dinner not to your liking, my lord?"

Even his stepmother would have chosen him over Montague the mushroom.

"My lord?" Concern furrowed Fiona's forehead.

Kingslea blinked. Fiona's hand inched closer to his. His arm twitched with the need to flip over his hand, to let hers walk into his grasp, and to press his naked flesh against hers. Damnation. Houseman always swore his curiosity would get the better of him.

"P—Pardon me, I wasn't quite attending." His valet had never prophesied that it would drive him mad.

"Understandable, given the nature of Piers's soliloquy." She tilted her head to the left. "Has his instruction cooled your appetite?"

Cooled. An odd choice of words, given the circumstances. Odd. He was the odd man, imagining mysteries where none existed just to be next to her.

"Not at all." Kingslea picked up his fork and knife. "Although his presence is another matter entirely."

"I think his poor appetite is his past returning to haunt him." She popped another piece of fish in her mouth and chuckled.

"More likely a draft." An icy breeze blew on his neck. Kingslea glanced over his shoulder. No one was there. Unease rippled down his spine. "Do you believe in spirits, Miss Grey?"

Color tinged Fiona's cheeks. Pearly white teeth bit her bottom lip.

"Of course, my lord." Her hand trembled as she raised her wine glass. "And yours are some of the finest I've tasted."

She took one gulp than another until her cheeks bulged.

Good God. He was talking about ghosts. How had he became so side-tracked? She lowered her glass. Kingslea blinked. Her damn smile had tangled his thoughts in knots. Well, it stopped here. She would answer his questions. He'd offered her two choices for a husband. It was time she told him which one had piqued her interest. His stomach churned, pulverizing his dinner.

"Of course my dear cousin believes in spirits." The grating voice came from his left. "Her fancies are just one of the things she and my brother have an understanding about."

Kingslea considered his neighbor. Miss Edwina Montague had her brother's pointed nose, sour lips and darting eyes. She also possessed a spare twenty pounds. Dimpled hands picked at a slice of roasted chicken.

"An understanding, you say?" Was the schoolgirl attempting to warn him away from Fiona?

"Oh, yes. They spent practically every summer together growing up and..." She peeked at him from under her lashes. "...growing closer."

Kingslea twirled his fork. The chit had actually batted her eyes at him. Fiona coughed. Was she jealous of the clumsy flirting or outraged by the insinuation?

"Would you care for some more wine, Miss Grey?"

"No." She set her hand on her chest. "Thank you."

"As I was saying..." Edwina shot a glare across the table. "...my dear cousin and brother were childhood playmates. Mother wouldn't allow me outside, as I was much too young then, but Fiona and Piers were inseparable."

"Indeed." Kingslea's gaze drifted from Miss Montague's pouting face to Fiona's smooth cheeks. There could not be a large age gap between the two, yet Fiona had been engaged more than two years ago. Engaged to another man. He straightened his napkin in his lap then rubbed a spot of tarnish from his spoon.

"My cousin exaggerates the, um, closeness of Piers and myself. A folly of her youth, I'm afraid." Fiona's forced laughter grated on his ears. "My sisters and I spent our summers roaming Uncle Heberon's country seat. The Montagues only spent a fortnight with us before dashing off to another estate."

"Those were the days." Montague reclined in his seat, twisting his napkin around his index finger. "Remember the picnics by the stream? The boating excursions…"

"I remember my pet snake, you calling us savages and then running to your mother for protection." Fiona nodded as Bunsen removed her empty plate then flashed her teeth at her cousin. "Sammy the snake and I had many adventures that summer."

Montague shuddered upright. His flat gaze landed on Fiona.

"Right until his timely demise at the end of a garden tool."

"You—" Fiona's hand closed around her knife. Rage bleached her knuckles as she lifted it from the table.

Good God, would she eviscerate her cousin at dinner? Kingslea's hand walked across the table. Not that Montague didn't deserve to be punished for harming something of Fiona's.

"Milton." The growl slipped out between her teeth. Her hand hovered in the air. Muscles roped her forearm.

Kingslea straightened. Who was Milton?

"More salmon, Miss?" Bunsen appeared on her left. A shudder rippled through his bent frame. Montague cowered behind the older man.

"No. Thank you." Fiona opened her hand. The knife clattered against the others next to her plate. Her arm floated gracefully after it. "I was hoping for something with a little less backbone."

Wine burned Kingslea's nose. Less backbone than Montague? That pretty much ruled out all vertebrates. Kingslea coughed the chuckles from his throat. He should not laugh. A side dish of murder was not on the menu. Neither was insanity.

"My cousin does get attached to the most peculiar creatures," Edwina wheezed, reaching for her glass of water. "Once, she asked aunt if she could keep—"

"Not the crystal." At Fiona's cry, Kingslea's gaze flew to her goblets. They stood straight as the Queen's Guards guarding Buckingham Palace. Her cousin's presented a different picture.

Edwina's water glass clunked against her wine glass. They toppled into the sherry glass. Liquid splashed against the silver base of the fruit stand. Bunsen rushed forward. A handy towel blotted at the spill while Mary the maid replaced the glasses with fresh.

Crimson stained Edwina's cheeks. She glared across the table.

"I never touched the glasses, Lord Kingslea."

"Pay it no heed, Miss Montague. The servants will soon set everything to rights."

"Did anything break?" A blush bloomed in Fiona's cheeks.

"No." Was she embarrassed because her cousin hadn't claimed responsibility for the accident? And why would she deny her part in the mishap? Both he and Fiona had seen her reach for the glass. Kingslea's gaze drifted along the table. Between the Elspeth centerpiece, the large bowls overflowing with fruit and the compotiers displaying their delicate cakes, Fiona would not have been able to see her cousin's hands.

So, how had she known about the disaster?

Another mystery to add to the list. A list that would never shorten unless he took control of the situation. Now, before Fiona distracted him again.

"Your brother didn't seem to be very understanding about Sammy, Miss Montague. In fact, he seems to have taken the snake's existence as a personal affront."

"That was my opinion also, my lord." Fiona beamed at him. "I thought if only Piers would spend time with him, perhaps further his acquaintance with Sammy..."

"You placed the serpent in my bed!"

"Well, where else would I put him?" Fiona helped herself to a ham timbale and spooned cucumber sauce over top. "Piers was a sickly child. He spent practically the entire fortnight in his room. Fortunately, dear Edwina kept him company."

Kingslea added a spoonful of peas to his plate. He had lost control of the conversation again. No. He shook his head. He had lost his illusions of control. Bunsen looked at him before walking past with the carrots. Damn, the woman had cost him his favorite side dish. Now he would have to get some from the sideboard. He stifled his annoyance.

"I was not a sickly child." Montague stuffed a forkful of ham into his mouth then quickly gulped his wine.

"You mentioned an uncle Heberon, Miss Grey?"

"Yes. He is Aunt Caroline's brother."

"Doddering old fool." Piers muttered to his peas.

Fiona nodded once. Montague's snuffbox emptied its paltry contents down his shirt front.

"Uncle Heberon is a very special gentleman." Her smiled brightened. "He lives with Aunt Carolyn and Uncle Andrew."

"Is that Andrew Grey of Grey Shipping?"

The skin between her eyes puckered. "Have you had business dealings with my uncle, then?"

"Alas, no." Was she baiting him about the captain's logbook? Hoping he would reveal knowledge she wanted. She would just have to wait, as he had waited. "My condolences on your loss, Miss Grey. I heard your uncle's ship went down some weeks ago."

She shoved her half-eaten entree to the side and scrunched the napkin in her lap.

"Your condolences are unnecessary, my lord. Aunt and Uncle are not dead."

"Then I look forward to meeting your aunt at Lord Saunders's ball. You are planning to attend, aren't you?"

"Yes." Fiona shook her head. "No. I mean—"

"You must forgive my cousin's stumbling, my lord." Montague's smile oozed across the table like coal smoke polluting the blue sky. "Naturally, we attend the Saunders's ball. It promises to be a delightful start to a propitious season."

Kingslea winced as his knife scritched against the Royal Doulton china. The moldering mushroom knew as much about manners as a sparkling pane of glass knew of deception.

"So, will your aunt be attending, Miss Grey? She is sponsoring your Season, is she not?"

"Oh, no, Mama has volunteered. As has your mother, my lord." Edwina sidled into the conversation. "We shall be quite the cozy trio, Melody, myself and, of course, dear cousin Fiona."

A greenish hue colored dear cousin Fiona's face. Had she swallowed a bug, or was her cousin's simpering ruining her appetite as it did his? Kingslea pushed his peas to a corner and laid his silverware across his plate.

"I'm certain they shall find their generosity amply rewarded."

"That is certainly true." Fiona's mumble crept across the table.

"Did you say something, Miss Grey?" So, she preferred her value measured in something other than pound notes. Of course, she might still wish to purchase a husband. It was imperative he find out, especially with Sullied lurking about like a shark in bloody water.

"The trauma of the shipwreck was too much for Aunt Carolyn." Fiona carefully set her fork on the side of her plate. Kingslea saw her fingers cross before she slid them into her lap. "Uncle Andrew insisted she recuperate instead of joining in the whirl of the Season."

She was a dreadful liar. Not only had she stared over his right shoulder the entire time she had spun her tale but she had also straightened her knives and forks twice. God had finally decided to smile on him.

"How fortuitous their demise didn't delay your Season."

"Oh, dear Fiona's Season has already been delayed two times." Edwina cut off a bite of ham. Her fork swung in the air, reaching for height as she made her points. "First there was the death of her betrothed, and then her sister's unfortunate illness."

"Your sister is ill?"

"Was, my lord. Mam and Da—"

"Mother and Father, Fiona." Montague interrupted. "Spare us the trappings of your unfortunate Irish ancestry." A violent shudder ripped through his wasted frame. Skeletal fingers tugged on the edges of his coat.

Kingslea relaxed his fist then tapped hers. Her gaze swung to his. After a small shake of his head, anger melted from her blue eyes. One more disruption by the sniveling snuff addict, and Fiona and her knife would wait until Kingslea had dissected the mushroom.

"Mam and Da…" Fiona's irises traveled to the corner of her eyes. Blue tinged Montague's lips, and his teeth chattered. A smirk lifted her lips. "…took Brianna to the Territories. Another month or so, and her recovery should be complete."

One mystery solved. She came to London because her parents had been occupied with their daughter's recovery. Fiona arranged her forks so their tips formed a straight line; then her nimble fingers smoothed the napkin in her lap. She had omitted something. Something important. Was it her uncle's summoning telegram or…?

An absurd notion splashed in Kingslea's brain.

Or had she never informed her parents of the telegram?

The certainty weighted his gut. She was here alone and defenseless. The image of her lasso and whip flashed in his skull. Not completely defenseless, but certainly outnumbered.

"Are you and your sister close?"

"They're twins," Edwina volunteered. "Although you would never know it to look at them. Mother says all Irish births are like that. Only their brother resembles Uncle Everett, and that is merely in passing."

Fiona stilled in her chair. Her restless fingers lay motionless in her lap. Chalk would have added color to her complexion. Her lips moved, but no sound disturbed the air. Moments passed before his brain interpreted her message.

Do something.

Warmth exploded in his chest. So, she had recognized him for an ally.

"I have known English ladies who have given birth to twins, one son and one daughter. I'm certain you will accept that such offspring look nothing alike."

"Well, I—"

"Precisely." Kingslea's head began to throb. No wonder he eschewed society. Catty remarks, clawing for attention and whining voices. If Edwina Montague was a wheel, his coachman would have drowned her in oil. "It must be a relief to have your sister healthy, especially as you seem to be shadowed by death."

"P—pardon, my lord?" Fiona centered her dessert plate then traced the circumference with her index finger.

Now what had he said? Hadn't he changed the subject?

"Naturally, I assumed your companion was deceased." She lined up her glasses. What more could the woman want? Unless…

Suspicion knocked the breath from his body. Did she think he was going to expose their morning meeting?

"Montague did mention your solitary arrival."

She swallowed hard and nodded. Her fingers rested by her plate.

"Yes, my traveling companion is also dead."

"But she was of no relation." Edwina chased a pea around her plate before spearing it on the tines of her fork. "Just someone hired for an escort."

"No." Fiona cleared her throat. Loss pinched her eyes, tightened her mouth. "No relation."

Kingslea's heart stumbled across several beats. To have such an affection for another being...to be the object of Fiona's affection...

His gaze traveled down the table and locked with Lady Bookingham's cold one. His stepmother pursed her lips and jerked her head in Fiona's direction.

"Yet you feel her loss keenly."

Bunsen appeared with dishes of mousse au chocolat. Fiona nodded and selected a large serving from the tray. A smile flirted with her lips.

"Not as much as you might think."

Kingslea blinked. "Pardon."

"At times, I can almost feel Mil—um, my late companion's presence."

"You must strive to overcome your sentimentality, Fiona. Do you mourn last year's dresses?" Piers huffed. "No, of course not. Your companion would have been discharged soon after your arrival. Her death means you can buy another shawl or pair of gloves. A savings of both time and money. Firing servants can be rather unpleasant."

Montague's glass dish scraped his plate. Within seconds, the clear crystal had fogged.

Improbable notions teased Kingslea's reason. The draft over Montague's place at the table seemed to increase almost in proportion to his attacks on Fiona's manners.

"You must have been close for the attachment to linger."

"Yes."

"We've all felt loss." Edwina bounced in her chair, her eyes watching the dessert's progress around the table. "When I turned sixteen, my favorite hunter had to be put down. I cried for days until Father bought me a new one."

Disgust left a bitter taste in Kingslea's mouth. Could Miss Montague truly think the loss of a horse on par with the loss of a dear friend? Of course, she could. The Montagues would turn on each other like rabid hyenas if it suited their needs. At least the chit had left him an opening.

"And are you seeking a replacement companion, Miss Grey?"

"At Fiona's age..." Edwina sucked the chocolate from her spoon. "...she requires something a little more permanent."

"Entering the Season seemed the quickest way to find—" Like a sudden hailstorm, apples and oranges rained down on the table. The fruit bowl emptied before his eyes. Apples, oranges, pears and figs—the treelike formation slid like snow down a mountain

Every piece headed for Fiona.

Glasses clunked. Plates scratched. Silverware clanked together. Her hands flew over the table, trying in vain to stop the avalanche.

"Well, ladies." His stepmother rose at the end of the table. "Perhaps we should take our coffee in the drawing room."

"A novel idea, sister." Aunt Annabelle glowed in triumph.

Fiona rose with the others, a cornucopia of fruit balanced in her arms.

"Really, Fiona. You look like a peasant girl coming to the big city to hawk her family's produce."

With a flick of her wrist a bruised pear rolled into Fiona's palm. "You didn't eat much, cousin. Perhaps a nice piece of fruit will appease your appetite."

Montague backpedaled to the door, hiding his face behind his hands.

"You wouldn't."

"I'll take those, Miss." Bunsen held a platter out to Fiona.

"Thank you...Bunsen, isn't it?"

"Yes, Miss."

Fiona leaned over the platter. Her bounty rolled down her arms and onto the dish.

"I wasn't going to throw it. It would have been a waste of good fruit."

Bunsen's lips twitched. "Yes, Miss."

"Not that I would have missed." Fiona leaned closer to the butler. "I've had years of practice." With one last look at the fruit, she sighed and draped her napkin over her ruined place setting. "I am sorry for the mess. Bedeviling my relations was one thing, making extra work for the staff is another entirely."

"Very good, Miss."

Kingslea bounced on the balls of his feet. He wished she would stop conversing with Bunsen. After all, *he* was her dinner companion. She should be talking to him.

"Miss Grey?"

She paused at the end of the table.

"Yes, my lord."

"You never did answer my question." Impatience twitched though him. "What are you hoping to find?"

Her gaze drifted from Alveston to Winthrop then settled on the tinkling chandelier. She shook her head.

"Why, I hope to find what I'm looking for."

Kingslea stopped gritting his teeth. "And what is that, precisely?"

"A family." She shrugged then turned and strolled through the door. "My family."

CHAPTER 12

Kingslea leaned back in his chair, swirled his brandy. The nutty aroma tempted his palate but his friends' opinions ruled his appetite. Eight. Nine. The scent of gardenias lingered. Fiona's perfume. Ten.

"Well, what's your opinion?"

Winthrop cleaned the ice cream off his spoon then set it beside his dish.

"Melody has grown into a fine young woman. She generously offered me her pudding." Pudgy fingers dipped into a bowl of water. Slices of lemon surfed on the waves. "Shouldn't have much trouble marrying her off. Specially with the dowry you've managed to amass."

"Thanks to you." Kingslea toasted his friend before swallowing his brandy. Alcohol scalded his throat, burned his eyes. Why was his friend rattling on about his sister when it was their opinion of Fiona he wanted? Needed. Couldn't they see the mystery she presented?

"You did the work." Winthrop snatched a petit four from the tray on the table and popped it into his mouth. "I just made a few suggestions"

"Very prosperous suggestions."

Bunsen appeared at Kingslea's elbow, an open walnut humidor in his hands. The scent of tobacco wafted from the fat cigars rolling within, over-powering the remnants of gardenias.

"No, thank you, Bunsen."

"Very good, sir." The butler clicked the top shut, strolled to the other side of the table and offered one to Alveston.

"Kingslea is well-informed regarding his sister's prospects." Lord Alveston rolled a cigar between his thumb and index finger, dragged it beneath his nose then nodded. "He's talking about Miss Grey, you nodcock."

"Oh, well…" Winthrop smacked his lips. His fingers wiggled over the selection of cakes before settling on a pink-and-white one. "Why didn't you say so? Can't be expected to know—there *were* four women present."

"Five women. Why on Earth did you invite *him*?"

Bunsen handed Alveston a cutter for his cigar then stuck a match.

"You know Winthrop can't see anything if food is present."

"Damn fine chef, Kingslea has." Winthrop brushed the crumbs from his jacket and smiled. "Would steal her away if we weren't such friends."

True friends. They were worth more money than he'd spend in four lifetimes trying to sate Winthrop's bottomless appetite.

"You know why, Alveston. Winthrop can procure information from a rock."

"And here I thought you invited us to discuss the fair Fiona." Alveston stroked his mustache, like a cat cleaning his whiskers after eating a canary.

Kingslea's canary. Warmth imbued his arms. How could he have forgotten what a rake Alveston was? The fair Fiona. Why had he never noticed the change in his friend's voice when he spoke of the fairer sex? A spider would spin a lifetime before producing that much silk.

"*Miss* Grey is—"

"Pardon the interruption, milord, but the lady forgot her gloves." Bunsen lifted a pair of long white gloves off the table. "If you don't require anything else, I shall return them to her."

"No!" Kingslea's shout resonated in his ears. Logic demanded the gloves be returned to their owner. Something more powerful demanded a trace of her remain.

"As you wish, milord." Bunsen carefully draped the gloves over Kingslea's hand.

"No need to trouble yourself, Bunsen. I'll return them when we rejoin the ladies." Silk caressed his fingers. Her skin would be smoother, more supple to the touch. Warm and…

"Will there be anything else, milord?"

The butler's smirk cooled Kingslea's thoughts. What on Earth had gotten into Bunsen? The man had rarely smiled for four years, and now, he was grinning like a baboon with a bunch of bananas.

"Yes. Bring me a bowl of soup. Hot, very hot."

Bunsen blinked once. Twice. His features slipped into their normal neutral mask.

"Anything else, milord? I believe Cook still has a slice of pigeon pie."

"Just the soup." The palm of her glove slipped into his hand. Limp fingers drooped over the side. Not quite the same as holding her hand.

Someone cleared his throat.

"Winthrop, you want something else?"

"I'll just finish these delightful pastries, shall I?" The baron dragged the half-empty serving dish before him.

"Are you certain it is the same woman you met?" Smokey words tripped from Alveston's lips. "She's not at all like you described her. Meek. Timid. That oaf Montague pounced on her every move, and she never brandished rope let alone a pistol."

"I think a revolver might clash with her gown," Kingslea noted dryly.

"Worth. All the Americans have them. Only ones who can afford his price. Rolling in the blunt, the Greys are." Winthrop swallowed his cheek-full of pastry. "You think I've the Midas touch that family practically invented it. Grey Shipping almost went broke fifteen years ago."

"How's that?" Kingslea warmed his brandy between his palms. Houseman's information hadn't included such a tidbit, but then, his valet had inquired about more recent events.

"Outdated ships, swindling clerks, bad weather, lost ships." Winthrop swallowed the rest of his wine. "Real streak of bad luck."

"What saved the company?"

"Not what—who." Winthrop popped the last bite of his pastry into his mouth and chewed.

"Good God, man." Alveston pounded the table. Cigar ashes punctuated his exasperation. "You bore us with business prattle day in and day out, yet when we want to listen you're too busy eating."

Winthrop ran his tongue over his teeth and sucked at the recently liberated bits of food.

"Who turned Grey Shipping into a success?" Kingslea wrapped Fiona's gloves around his hand. Tingles raced over his fingers. Silk ripped. Better to buy Fiona a new pair of gloves than to throttle his friend.

"Rumor has it the younger brother—Evan?"

"Everett."

"Right, Everett gets the credit. Not quite his style. It's said he did some havey-cavey business during their little skirmish over there in the sixties. His reputed talents might account for some of his successes, but not all."

"So, he got lucky with a few investments." Unease itched Kingslea's back. Winthrop's business acumen was nothing short of phenomenal. In another life, he'd have been burned at the stake. To think someone had even better fortune...

"*I'm* lucky; *he's* phenomenal. The things Grey shipping undertook..." Awe slackened Winthrop's jaw. "They were three steps ahead at every turn. Knew what was going to happen before anyone else. Captains stayed in port an extra day or left with half a load, beating storms that sank ships, delayed arrivals to markets. Their half-full load commanded prices equal to a full cargo."

"If not Everett, then who?"

"His wife. Was her idea to start G-and-G Enterprises. G-and-G provided the capital to refit the ships, buy merchandise, everything. She sent telegrams across the Atlantic, a couple clerks got very rich letting Grey Shipping's competitors peek at those messages before delivery." Winthrop shook his head. "Marry Miss Grey, and you wouldn't have to go on your quests anymore. Neither will your great-grandchildren."

"American heiresses are not exactly a novelty during the Season."

"The Greys are obscenely wealthy, even for Americans." Winthrop selected another tart from the tray. "Mining, cattle, shipping, oil, that Edison fellow—you name it, they own a part of it."

Obscenely wealthy. The description poisoned Kingslea's thoughts. A fissure raced up the side of his snifter. He carefully set the cracked glass on the table. Fiona's wealth was not her most attractive attribute. Neither were her blue eyes, her flowery scent or her trim figure. He was interested only in the mystery she presented. And the link she was between him and the person collecting his stepmother's vouchers.

"I like my diversions."

"She's richer than Lilly ever was. Oughta make the woman green with envy."

Kingslea's muscles froze, a moment ripped out of time. Funny. After five years of haunting him, Lilly's memory hadn't joined him for dinner. Yet the women were both wealthy, Americans and beautiful.

Alveston bounced in his seat.

"Wha'd you do that for?" Winthrop dropped his sweet and clasped his shin.

"It's fine. The comparison between Fiona and..." *Lilly*, his brain finished. His tongue curled, strangling her name. "She was bound to come up."

Winthrop picked up his tart and shifted his legs to the left.

"That's right. Lilly's old news, and you owe me ten pounds." He pointed a finger at Alveston.

A blush broke over the lord's face while he scrutinized his cigar.

"Why does Alveston owe you ten pounds?"

"Lost the bet." Winthrop frowned at the empty dish then blotted the crumbs with his finger. "Fair is fair. You didn't mention Lilly once."

Dread froze the food in Kingslea's gut.

"Why would I mention Lilly? Her marriage to Sullied was over five years ago. And her annulment was last year's gossip."

Invisible communication passed between his friends. Alveston sighed, scratched his head and finally looked into Kingslea's eyes.

"She's back in town for the Season."

Lilly was in London. His stomach jumped, knocking a beat from his heart.

"Thought you knew. She's to be at the Saunders' ball."

"No. I didn't know." Odd how his voice reached his ears but he hadn't felt the words tumble from his lips. Numb. He was numb. His brain screeched to a halt. Over her. He was over Lilly. Kingslea dragged his fists across the table and plopped them in his lap. The callow youth she had duped was gone.

If he helped Fiona enter society, he would meet Lilly. Face-to-face. Shaking hands filled another snifter with brandy. One gulp burned his tongue, stung his lips. His lids drifted over his watery eyes. Lilly. Fiona's face smiled at him from his memory.

Lilly's hold had been broken. Fiona's face was proof that his logic and reason had tamed his foolish emotions.

"Your soup, sir."

Soup. Thoughts bobbed in his skull like bits of asparagus in the broth.

"Yes, what were you going to do with the soup, Kingslea?"

"Another experiment, no doubt." Concern crumpled Alveston's forehead. "As long as I needn't ingest anything, I'll help."

"The soup, sir." Bunsen bent to place it on the table.

Fragmented thoughts touched and reformed. The answer to Montague's frosted food. Kingslea would solve this one mystery then move on to Fiona's dilemma. Heat seared his fingertips as he picked up the bowl and stood.

"We joining the women?" Winthrop caressed a pear.

"Not yet." Kingslea set the bowl in Montague's vacant spot. Steam danced above the bowl. He claimed his seat and stared at the bowl.

"What are you expecting to happen?" Alveston glanced from the bowl to him and back again.

"The soup should cool."

"Yes, I believe that happens when food is removed from heat."

Kingslea glared at his friend. "Montague's food cooled very quickly."

Bunsen poked the bowl. "The draft appears to be gone, milord."

"So it does." Fiona was also gone. Coincidence? Logic dictated it be so yet instinct told him his logic was flawed.

"Will you pursue Miss Grey?" The tip of Alveston's cigar glowed red.

"Now who's the nodcock?" Winthrop smiled, a benevolent garden gnome watching over struggling spring bulbs. "We were the bait in his experiment—er, the rats in his trap. No, that's not right."

"*Were* we part of an experiment?"

"You agreed to help." Kingslea shifted in his seat. He hadn't deceived his friends...exactly. He had asked them to distract his stepmother and her guests. He just hadn't told them the whole scenario.

"You offered us up as husband material to Miss Grey, didn't you?" Alveston stabbed out his cigar.

"It is why most American heiresses grace our shores, is it not?" Winthrop's gaze drifted to the still-steaming soup.

"Fiona's not seeking a husband." Kingslea's voice was steady, a reflection of his conviction. "She looking for her family."

"Need a husband for that." Winthrop pushed out of his seat and padded around the table.

"At least, *ladies* do." Alveston smirked.

"Fiona is a lady," Kingslea ground out. "And she is not seeking a husband." Hadn't he given her two very good candidates? She hadn't shown the slightest interest in either. So, what had her cryptic comment meant?

"Your logic is murkier than usual, my friend." Alveston smirked.

First Bunsen, now Alveston. Another baboon had left the jungle to gather around his dinner table. A baboon that found fault with his logic.

"This from a man who only passed his courses because I wrote his papers."

"Ho-ho." Alveston picked up his bent cigar. He snapped it in two and plucked a match from the match safe. "So, your reasoning is sound, is it?"

"It is."

Alveston puffed on his cigar until the end once more glowed.

"Then why did a marquess invite a lowly but well-off baron and earl to dine?"

Winthrop's spoon slowed as it passed through the soup. "If your lady is seeking a husband, your circumstances and title make you a much more suitable...candidate. After all, Lilly never noticed anyone but you until Sullied came along."

"Bloody hell." He was such a fool. First Lilly, now Fiona. How many times could a man fall for the same tricks? Believe the same lies? No. Not the same. He wasn't in love with Fiona.

He would never fall in love again, especially with a mercenary American.

"You should have picked a poor duke or two to feed instead of your inferiors." Alveston bowed his head.

"No need." Kingslea knocked his snifter against the table. Glass crackled. Brandy beaded along the crack. "Sullied's already been spotted sniffing around."

"Thought Miss Grey didn't make her bow until tonight?" Winthrop finished the soup and rested his hands across his bulging stomach. "Wasn't cool in the slightest. Don't know what Montague was complaining about."

"Montague complains about everything." Alveston rested his elbows on the table. "You've seen them together, Sullied and Miss Grey?"

"No." Kingslea put a hand up to ward off his friend's questions. "Houseman told me the duke's man has been sniffing around."

"He would know." Winthrop nodded, "Servants always know, usually before the lord and lady."

"Tut-tut, one does not talk to servants." Alveston whined, a perfect imitation of Montague.

"Don't be an ass." With a flick of his wrist, Kingslea's napkin sailed across the table and smacked his friend in the face.

"Sullied's interest may be more business than personal."

"Marriage *is* business, nothing personal about it." The knowledge was bitter on Kingslea's tongue.

"Grey Shipping has been transporting Sullied's trinkets and baubles. The man's got pharaoh sickness, always digging up something and ferrying it back here."

"Which makes an alliance with a Grey heiress all the more profitable." And likely. Kingslea ignored the jab of disappointment. He wasn't interested in marrying Fiona.

Silence joined the men at the table.

Alveston ground out his cigar and checked his watch.

"Lady Kingslea been gambling again?"

"Undoubtedly. Why do you ask?"

"You interested in wedding Miss Grey?"

"No."

"But you are interested in annoying Sullied, maybe luring his intended victim away?" Alveston crossed his arms over his chest.

Revenge. The idea had merit. If he could inflict half the pain he had felt at Lilly's desertion…

But the duke loved no one but himself. And Fiona was innocent. Regardless of what anyone might think, he still had his honor.

"I think she needs help."

"With that family, I don't doubt it."

"Piers was behaving oddly, even for him." Alveston rubbed his chin.

"Thinks he has a claim on the girl," Winthrop declared. "That understanding business. Warning you, he was."

"Fiona will not marry that sniveling whelp," Kingslea scoffed.

"Was he wearing paint?"

"Covering up his black eyes, I've no doubt." Was that Fiona's work, Kingslea wondered?

"How do you know?"

"Saw him last night." The sour features had glowed in the smoky haze of the gaming hell. Not that he had been looking for Montague. His search for the *Revere*'s captain had led him to the place. "His nose was smaller."

"Didn't know you were such close friends."

"He was in a gaming hell, I was looking for someone."

"Rumor has it he's been dropping a monkey everywhere he goes." Winthrop stood again and brushed the crumbs from his chest.

"Where'd he get the blunt?" Alveston asked.

"His expectations."

"Then he *is* engaged to Miss Grey."

"No." Winthrop took his seat again. "With Miss Grey's aunt and uncle's mysterious disappearance, he should have access to their sizable fortune." He frowned at them. "Or he would have had, until Miss Grey's arrival. I hear the man got rather nasty when the banker refused to allow him to withdraw funds."

"All the more reason for *the* man to marry her." Alveston's left eyebrow arched. "Even if she isn't willing."

"I'm going to help her find her family." Odd, Kingslea thought. It almost seemed as if his mouth had reached that conclusion before his brain.

"And why we're going to help you." Alveston smiled. "Who knows, maybe we'll even annoy Sullied."

"Milord." The butler squeezed into the room and smoothed his ruffled hair.

"Yes, Bunsen."

"The Montagues are leaving, milord."

"Good riddance, I say." Alveston brushed at his sleeve.

"They are taking Miss Grey with them, my lord."

"What!" Kingslea's chair crashed to the floor. Ten strides carried him to the dining room door. He shoved Bunsen aside. The hallway was empty. He turned to the staircase and took the steps two at a time. Muscles burned along his legs. His chest heaved. He strode across the landing. His stepmother lounged in her chair, stabbing a piece of linen.

"Really, Kingslea." The marchioness tossed her stitchery to the ground and rose to her feet. "Did you have to linger over your brandy?"

"As host—"

"Host!" Her screeching couldn't blister his calloused hide. "You always hide behind your role when it's convenient. Your brother never would have allowed that leech to charm a woman he was interested in. Your brother—"

Twenty years of unfavorable comparison plucked at Kingslea's control.

"My brother is dead, madam." Anger throbbed in his low voice. "He has been dead for these last three years."

"How cruel of you to remind me." His stepmother turned her back on him. "Can't you see I still grieve the loss of my son."

Her son. Lady Kingslea had never acknowledge a relationship with Kinglee. At least not until he inherited the title upon his brother's untimely death. She'd thought he'd prove useful to her and her aspirations. He'd have happily have done it if only to maintain his peaceful existence. Alas, that was not to be. Their lavish lifestyle had brought the estate to the brink of ruin. Now, he could barely keep her in silk. As for her debts, those he'd paid off with his hands, like a common laborer.

The marchioness straightened her spine and spun about to face him. "Why won't you do your duty? If not for me, then for your sister?"

"Would it make you happy if I went after Miss Grey?" The words slipped out before Kingslea could stop them. He was eight-and-twenty, sixteen years older than when he had foolishly presented his new stepmother with a spurned offering of wilted flowers.

"Yes," she hissed. "Which is exactly why you won't."

Regret and longing wrestled along the periphery of his control.

"Do you know where they went?"

"The Saunders' ball." Her speculative gaze raked him from head to toe.

The Saunders' ball. Kingslea nodded. The same function Lilly was attending. His mouth dried and his heart pounded. Could he face her again? In front of Society? Yes. He shook off his doubts. Fiona needed his help and his protection.

He pivoted on his heel. Alveston and Winthrop lounged in the doorway.

"Gentleman."

Both nodded and preceded him down the stairs. Bunsen held three cloaks in his hands.

"Wh-where are you going?" The marchioness leaned over the banister.

Kingslea shoved his buttons in their respective holes. He could not tell her. He could...

The consequences and benefits seesawed on the scales in his mind. If she thought he was interested in Fiona, she might make his life a little less hellish. He might even convince her to abstain from gambling for a bit. Yes, this little intrigue might provide more benefits than just an appeased sense of curiosity.

"The Saunders' ball."

CHAPTER 13

— **You must apply yourself, Fi.** *Milton was a gray smudge near the pris*tine crown molding of the Saunders's ballroom. *There are scores of eligible men here.*

The ache spread across Fiona's knuckles. Cramped fingers straightened. The damp handkerchief plopped onto her dance card. *Open. Close. Open. Close.* Piers's scrawl slithered over the page. The idiot had claimed four dances. He obviously wasn't accustomed to using his brain. They had forced her into the Grand March. She would die before yielding three more dances. She dipped her handkerchief in her lemonade and scrubbed the paper.

"Work. Please God, work." The page crinkled from the dampness. Bits of paper rolled, fading the pencil stain. "Thank heavens."

If only she could erase her cousin as easily.

— *Aren't you almost finished?* Milton dropped behind her velvet chair and peered over her shoulder. *Perhaps you should just leave the last one. Three dances have already ended, and you're still at work.*

"Milton." Fiona's fingers twitched. How many suitors had he selected since their arrival? Ten. Eleven. More. She had stopped counting at nine, and that was a waltz and a quadrille ago. She might have to have him exorcised to get some peace.

— *You could at least make some effort, Fi.* Suffering pulled his features into an upside down U.

"I'm looking for my aunt and uncle, not a spouse." The whisper of violins, the piping of flutes and the toot of horns drifted through the fern shielding her position. "Besides, you know Da's rule."

— *I'm certain he wouldn't disinherit you.* Milton tapped his chin twice. *And, in order for you to marry without his presence, you must first purloin a groom.*

"I'm beginning to think it was a mistake to come here at all." Fiona peered through the green screen. Vibrant waspwaisted ladies tumbled over a canvas, subdued by the innocence of youth and punctuated by somberly clad escorts. Diamond, rubies, emeralds and sapphires twinkled like galaxies orbiting fleshy necks and white wrists.

How many people had she met? Four—no, five—before Piers had claimed her for the first dance. Two had asked her cousin for introductions.

Introductions that were refused.

"None of these people even know Aunt or Uncle." Air washed over Fiona's face as she fanned her dance card dry. "I would have accomplished more either at home or at the office. Melinda and Cedric are certainly more entertaining."

Milton sat on top of the plant and crossed his arms over his chest.

— *You're simply fuming because the Montagues whisked you away from that Kingston fellow.*

"I wanted to ask Kingslea for his assistance."

Aunt Annabelle was intent on limiting her introductions. Her cousins had fallen in behind the plan, like buzzards feasting on fresh kill. She needed an ally, and Hugh was perfect. He had entree into society and wasn't above mingling with those most in this room considered their inferiors.

Hugh. Even her sighs sounded like his name.

"Who knows when I'll see him next."

— *What do we need him for?* Milton pouted. *We can find your aunt and uncle by ourselves.*

"We could." Fiona set her glass by her foot and tested her dance card. Still damp. "But London is quite different from San Francisco. We need a guide and..."

Piers drifted by with Oswin.

"And I think my interest in Hugh will irritate my cousin."

— *Wasn't my pestering him at dinner enough?* Milton said, adjusting his cuffs.

"You were wonderful, Milton." Cold needled her hand as it passed through his arm. "I just think someone living would be a better deterrent to his more, uh, amorous plans. And then there are the fortune hunters. I think Hugh's title is sufficient to persuade other, lesser nobles to try elsewhere. At least, that's what he seems to think."

— *You don't like him, do you, Fi?* Milton's face bloomed above the fern. The tips of the leaves curled. *I mean, he's okay, but let's face it.* He surveyed his fingertips. *He's definitely not me.*

White flashed on Fiona's lids as she flattened her palms against her eyes. Her ex-fiancé's reasoning had become almost as unsound as his form.

"Milton, if he were you, he'd be dead."

— Why is it that you have oodles of sympathy for fallen women, beggars and drunken sailors, but you haven't an ounce of compassion for the dead? He turned his back on her, his legs fading away.

Pressure built in her temples and drained into the center of her forehead. First, he complained about her lack of interest in a man, then her willingness to enlist Kingslea and now her lack of compassion. What was next? The clothes he helped pick out?

"Maybe because I know too many restless spirits."

— Ha! He spun about and pointed a wispy finger at her. *So, you admit it.*

"To what…" She rubbed the throbbing. "…did I admit, precisely?"

— That you spend too much time with the dead. That's a big step, Fi. He flitted behind her and shooed her towards the dance floor. *Now you can stop hiding behind a potted palm and spend some time with the living.*

"I have one more signature to go." Fiona eyed her cousin's loopy handwriting. Too bad she couldn't change the P to an H. The IE looked enough like a U, the GH would be simple enough. A yellow drop clung to her fingers as she dabbed at the card. "You know, lemonade doesn't work as well as I thought it would. Yet lemon juice is the main ingredient in my ink-removal concoction."

— Yes, well, I think…

Milton shot to the ceiling. His body quivered like smoke from a lit cigarette.

— Him. I think you should talk to him. Yes, broad shoulders. And tall. His dark hair has just a touch of gray. Experience, you know. He's well-dressed. And… he's walking away from that little mushroom Edwina. Fi, do look up. You're going to miss him.

"Go away."

"But I just arrived."

The deep baritone rumbled into her sanctuary. Her heart bumped against her breastbone. Muscles contracted. Pain rattled up her shin as her toe collided with her crystal punch glass. Lemonade splashed the fabric wrapped around the plant stand.

The voice was familiar but lacked the sleepiness of Hugh's. Fiona glanced up. Cold brown eyes gazed down a straight nose at her.

Hugh's friend. Names wrestled in her memory. None seemed to fit the contemptuous lord. Or was he the baron?

"I'm sorry, Lord, er, Sir…"

"Lord Alveston, at your service." He bowed, a mockery of civility. "I am a friend of Lord Kingslea, as is Baron Winthrop."

"Yes." Fiona blotted her spilled drink with her damp handkerchief while her dangling dance card brushed her arm. "You joined us for dinner at his house."

Alveston plucked his handkerchief from his pocket and snapped it at her.

"Tell me, is it an American custom to drown your dance card in warm lemonade?"

Fiona bent closer to the spill. How long had he been watching her? *Confound it, Milton. You were supposed to be keep watch.* Color left her knuckles as she wrung her handkerchief over the pot. He'd been too busy evaluating men as husband material to prevent people from observing her conversing with the air.

White waved in her peripheral vision. Lord Alveston did not like her. His handkerchief was not a flag of truce. Indeed, it was nothing more than a ploy to lull her into a false sense of security. Fiona squared her shoulders and rose to her feet.

"I believe the proper custom is to deny liquid to any paper, hence the name parchment." She ignored his clean cloth and stuffed her damp one in her purse.

"We call it vellum in England." His left eyebrow arched as he neatly folded his handkerchief then returned it to his pocket.

— *Vellum.* Milton drifted through the wall and ran his fingers along Lord Alveston's nape. *Ever notice how pompous the English sound. Vellum. Lord Snootface Vellum at your service.* He bowed. *Have I explained how the universe revolves around my esteemed person?*

Laughter bubbled in her throat. This was the Milton she remembered, overflowing with irreverent wit to cheer her.

"Yes, of course. Lord Vellum, um, Alveston." Fiona sucked her lips between her teeth. She would never have restrained her laughter if she was at her desk. Alone with her numbers. Safe, reliable numbers.

"Are you free for this dance?" His brows met above his nose, suspicion narrowed his eyes.

— *Do dance with him, Fi. It's a country dance. If that performance you gave with Piers is any indication, time has not improved your grace. Please, Fi.* Milton clapped. *Please. Ol' Lord Vellum will have bloodied toes. Vel...lum.* Milton flicked his finger over Lord Alveston's chest, emphasizing the syllables.

"I—"

"Fiona, dear." Edwina swatted aside the fern and pressed against his lordship's side. She jumped as the plant swatted her back. "Lord Alveston, it is ever so nice to see you again."

Frustration whittled at Fiona's control. Why had these two sought out her company? They obviously didn't like her. She choked on her groan. Maybe his lordship will take Edwina's bludgeoning hints and partner her in a dance.

"Miss Montague." He inclined his head a fraction in her cousin's direction. "Miss Grey, perhaps we should take our places." He crooked his arm in her direction.

— Go ahead, Fi. Milton poked Edwina's shoulder. Her cousin absently batted at the fern. *Stomp his toes into a jelly.* He scratched his head. *No, wine. Yes, they stomp grapes to make wine.*

"She can't." Edwina planted her stout frame in front of them. "Piers is looking for you, cousin. This *is* his dance, after all." She wrapped her pudgy hands around Fiona's wrists and tugged. "I hope you understand, my lord. A gentleman's prior claim should always be honored."

— Gentleman? Milton plucked a feather from Edwina's hair. *She* is *talking about Piers, isn't she?*

Lord Alveston rested his hand over Fiona's, firmly returning her hand to his arm.

"Yet I don't see your brother claiming the prize, Miss Montague."

Edwina tugged harder. Fiona felt air under her palm. Tingles ran up to her elbow then trickled down to her fingers. Good heavens, she would think twice before she participated in any more taffy pulls.

With a yank, she freed her hand.

"I'm certain your brother appreciates your interest, Edwina. Dear." Silk slipped against silk as Fiona pushed her glove back over her elbow. "But he only wrote his name in for the first dance."

"No, he didn't." Edwina ground her fists into her hips. Her breasts jiggled like frothy syllabub over her bodice. "I saw him write it in four places."

"Four?" Scorn seared Lord Alveston's deep voice. "Really, Miss Montague, you must be mistaken." He pinched the point of her handkerchief then picked lint from his lapel. "To dance *four* times is tantamount to a proposal, not to mention the epitome of bad taste."

"Yes, well." Edwina cleared her throat. "Perhaps it was only three."

— Nicely done. Milton applauded. *I suppose there is a use for pomposity after all.*

"Yet Miss Grey is certain his signature appears only once."

"You know as well as I, my lord, that an American education can't compare to the British in terms of excellence."

"Are you saying Miss Grey can't count to four?"

— She is. I'd wager little Miss Frumpet can't count to eleven with her shoes on. Milton stepped through Edwina. Her cousin shivered but held her ground. *I say, she's a cold-hearted wench.* He rolled up his sleeves. *Well, I'll roast in the fires of perdition before I'll allow her to insult you again, Fi.*

"Miss Grey can count—and hear—perfectly well, thank you."

"Then show us your dance card, cousin dear."

Fiona slapped open her dance card. Her palm stung but not as much as if she'd dragged it across her cousin's smug face. Four names appeared on the lines, Piers's only once. At least, if one did not look too closely.

She snapped the book closed. "I believe even a person educated by Britain's tutors can count to one."

"But..." Edwina clawed after the book. Fiona gathered the train of her dress, draping the silk over her dance card.

"I shall claim my dance now, even though it is half over." Lord Alveston glowered at Edwina until she stepped back. "Miss Montague."

— *Not bad for an Englishman.* Milton looked left then right. *I'm going to search for your future husband, Fi. I think I saw him over there.*

Fiona followed Lord Alveston onto the dance floor. They took their place among a half-formed set. His hands were not as strong as Hugh's, his shoulders not as broad.

"I had a bitch like her once. Whelped the most amazing hunting dogs you've ever seen but bit the hand of anyone who tried to feed her. Had to put her down after she attacked one of the tenant's children."

"I believe the authorities would frown on such action in my cousin's case."

"You know, Miss Grey, I could like you."

They parted, and she found herself facing another man. Hair matted his knuckles. Sweat beaded in the muttonchops bracketing his jowls. He wheezed sour beets as they performed the steps.

Hugh had smelled of fresh bread. His hands had been smooth, as had his jaw. Fiona curtsied in parting. How very odd. She had never noticed a man's toilette before.

Lord Alveston bowed then clasped her hand.

"You're not going to allow yourself to like me, are you, my lord?"

"No." A quick turn then they promenaded forward.

"You are a good friend to Lord Kingslea."

"Hmmm." He spared her a glance before turning his gaze straight ahead. "A good friend wouldn't allow him to embark on this madness he's set his mind to."

A spurt of adrenaline punched two beats from her heart. Hugh had spent last night on the docks, and this morning he had been at the shipping office. Reason told her something governed his actions—something other than boredom.

"Is he in danger?" She forced the words from her tight throat.

"I believe so."

"If there is anything I can do..."

"Your kind has done enough."

Pain burned her neck as he jerked her forward.

"My kind? Do you mean Americans?"

"I mean indulged American heiresses hunting titles."

"I can assure you—"

"No, let me assure you, Miss Grey." Lord Alveston wrested her to a stop before the echo of music faded. "You may think that your cousins are vile and low, but should you prove as treacherous as Lilly..." He dragged an unsteady breath past his thin lips. "...you will discover just how vile and low I can sink."

"Lilly?" Fiona shrugged off his warning and focused on the tidbit of information. Lilly. Treacherous Lilly. Who was she? More important, what had she done to Hugh?

"Heed my warning, Miss Grey. Accept Kingslea's help with your husband hunt if you must but don't raise his expectations."

At the edge of the dance floor, he shrugged off her hand. Fiona blinked. The world had gone mad. Truly, utterly mad.

"Hugh is going to help me find a husband""

"That is what you are after, isn't it?"

"No. I'm looking for my family."

"Actually, my dear…" Lord Alveston's smile would have graced a swaying cobra. "…I believe your family is looking for you."

"Fiona." Piers winced as he limped toward her. His sister pounded along at his side. "Edwina tells me I neglected to sign your card for the supper dance."

"Are you certain you feel well enough to dance, cousin?" Fiona taunted. She had deliberately stepped on his toes, yet he had demanded more dances. How much plainer could she be? As for the supper dance, for him to take her in would lend credence to their bogus understanding.

He rubbed his nose and sniffed. Snuff flakes decorated his jacket. Edwina elbowed him in the side, and he lurched for Fiona's card. Greed and drugs fueled his courage and masked his pain.

"This time will be different." His bloodshot eyes narrowed. Menace bubbled in the spit flying from his mouth.

She stepped back. Warm hands closed around her shoulders. The nutty fragrance of brandy overpowered the sour sweat, clashing perfumes and bitter disappointments cloying the air.

Hugh.

"Alas, you'll have to wait in line, Montague. Miss Grey has promised me the supper dance."

"No, you can't." White rimmed Piers's thin lips. "Fiona and I have an understanding."

Hugh stepped around her, placed her hand on his arm then gently squeezed her fingers. Pleasure tripped over anger, resentment and panic and raced to the fore of the sensations buffeting her.

"You could have saved yourself a little embarrassment if you hadn't exited with such…haste."

"Fiona insisted we stop at home." Edwina shouldered her brother out of the way. Her fan flapped coyly in front of her face. "The poor dear is always forgetting something."

"Yet, if I'm not mistaken, your brother has changed his jacket and replenished his snuffbox."

"Spilled some sherry," Piers mumbled as he stuffed the ornate box into his trouser pocket.

"My card, my lord."

Piers stumbled forward, lunging for the card. Hugh slipped the strings off Fiona's wrist and held it out of her cousin's reach.

"Thank you, Miss Grey." He opened the dance card and tilted it in the light. The corner of his mouth twitched.

"I'm afraid you're too late, Lord Kingslea. As you can clearly see, I've already claimed the supper dance."

"On the contrary, it says 'Saved for L. K.' Yes, it is quite distinct, isn't it, Alveston?" Hugh shoved the dance card under his friend's nose.

Air stilled in Fiona's lungs. The scales of judgment seesawed in Lord Alveston's eyes. Would he concur with his friend, or would he save him by tossing her to her cousin's mercies?

"Quite. Saved for L. K. Of course, the lemonade has bleached it just the slightest bit."

"Lemonade?" Kingslea glanced from his friend to her then peered closer at the dance card.

They *knew* of her duplicity. Embarrassment burned Fiona's cheeks. But would they give her away? No. It would reflect poorly on them if they changed their story now.

"I'm afraid I spilled a little on my card."

"Then we are lucky I came along when I did." Hugh scrawled his name across the poorly erased signatures. "Of course, it helps that I had reserved an earlier dance."

Piers bobbed around Hugh's shoulder then oozed between him and Lord Alveston.

"I see you have this dance free, cousin." He reached for the card.

Hugh snapped it closed and slid it back on Fiona's wrist.

"On the contrary, since Miss Grey spilled her lemonade, we must get her another one immediately." He swept his index finger down his nose and nodded once. "Dancing can parch one so."

"Thank you, my lord."

"Perhaps, I—" Piers limped after them.

"Ah, Montague," Hugh's other friend from the party stepped from the crowd. "I wonder if I could have a word with you." Baron Winthrop stepped in front of him, dragging Melody before Edwina. "There is an investment I'm considering I wanted your opinion on..."

Piers speared her with one last look but stayed put. Undoubtedly, Hugh had choreographed the entire scene. He would be a perfect partner.

"Thank you for you timely rescue."

"You are quite welcome."

The crowd parted in a hush of whispers before them. Fiona shrugged off the clandestine looks. Let them gossip. She would not miss this opportunity to talk with Hugh, enlist his help.

"Lemonade was perhaps not the best choice to erase his signature." He nodded to a cluster of men at the bottom of the staircase and turned her toward the punch table at the back of the hall.

"It was the only thing I had on hand." She smiled at his clean jaw. Why wouldn't he look at her? Doubts buzzed in her mind. Had she misinterpreted his intentions? Was he here to help or simply mock her? He must help her. He would help her. "If I had known I would need it, I can assure you I would have bought my own erasure receipt."

"Have you a need to erase many suitors' names?"

"Oh, no. I'm afraid my bookkeeping isn't as neat as it could be." Fiona stopped, knowing manners would force him to follow suit. Instead of looking at her, he scanned the crowd. "Da likens my writing to hieroglyphs on my better days and crab tracks in the sand on my worse. Uncle Andrew said I should patent my concoction and sell it. Apparently, I'm not the only clerk with the need to erase ink."

"You keep books for your father's company?" He handed her a cup of punch then secured one of his own. He continued to survey the crowd squeezing in the narrow space.

Why was he pretending he didn't know? He had found her at Grey Shipping this morning, poring over the accounts.

Something thumped against her back. A plum-colored turban landed on top of her glass. Kingslea lifted the hat from her cup and nodded at their audience.

"Oh, thank you, dear boy." A severe-looking woman snatched the headpiece from his hands. She settled the mass on her white hair then turned back to her companions. "Rather clumsy of my maid not to secure it properly."

A gossip. Fiona recognized her ilk. Every society bred them.

Fortunately, Hugh recognized her kind as well. Enough to protect her reputation in his own way.

"Um, I..." Warmth filled her belly, just as embarrassment burned her cheeks. Perhaps Milton was right. She had been out of society too long. "I manage my father's household accounts, and well, I tend to get ink all over my hands. My aunt is the same way. Heaven help me if gloves ever go out of fashion." She flashed the backs of her gloves at her audience.

"You must be very close to your family." Hugh removed her glass from her hand and set it on the sideboard.

"Yes." Fiona slipped her hand through his arm. Muscles rippled under her palm. Deceptively strong. *Deceptive*, her mind corrected. *A very desirable trait for a partner.* Ideas fomented inside her skull. "Very."

✲ ✲ ✲

"Curious." He led her through the crowd and out onto the balcony. A handful of other couples lingered amongst the pots of bushes and flowers.

Fiona glanced over her shoulder. The trio of eavesdroppers lingered at the door. All the women needed was a cauldron, and they could be Shakespeare's witches. Fiona walked to the end of the balcony. Wrought iron spikes slipped under her gloves.

"How so?"

"I would have thought you would be with your aunt and uncle while they recover from their experience."

"I—"

Hugh placed his hands over hers.

"Please, Miss Grey."

She glanced up.

He stared down at her, amusement and exasperation simmering in his eyes.

"Don't bother concocting a fairytale."

"How did you know?"

"You are a horrible liar." With a soft tug, he freed her hands from the wrought iron railing. His blue eyes peered into hers. "Your hands give you away—the bigger the lie the more they work."

Very slowly, he raised each one to his lips. Electricity hummed in her veins. Fiona resisted the temptation to fan herself.

"I would like to help you on your mission."

Her mission. Reason parted the lazy sensations floating through her. What was the matter with her? Hot one minute, cold the next. Fluttery stomach then gooey insides. She must not yield to whatever sickness was threatening until she had found Aunt and Uncle. And for that, she would need Hugh's help.

Hugh wanted to help.

"Lord Alveston said you would help me find a husband." Odd. No one considered her good enough to wed him. Anger seized control of her voice. "Have you one picked out one for me? Has he broad shoulders and just a touch of gray in his hair? And let's not forget his teeth. I must insist on a spouse with all his teeth."

"Enough," rumbled from Hugh's chest. He held up his hand then wiped the smile from his mouth. "May I speak frankly, Miss Grey?"

"Please do."

"Earlier, you said you were looking for your family." He leaned closer to her, blocking out their audience, reducing her world to only him. "It is my belief that you are really looking for your aunt and uncle. Am I right?" Triumph twinkled in his eye.

"Why should I trust you?" Fiona forced false doubts into words. She trusted him. The acknowledgment lifted her spirits. "Shareholders have lost faith in businesses for less."

"Perhaps you shouldn't, but I may be able to help." His thumb traced lazy circles on the soft flesh between her thumb and index finger. "You must admit I have a unique ability to assume various roles."

"Yes, your disguises are nearly perfect."

"Nearly?" Humor crinkled the corner of his eyes.

"*I* recognized you."

"Indeed."

"And in exchange for your help, I suppose you wish a little reimbursement for expenses."

"Another withdrawal from the Bank of Grey?" Hugh shook his head. "No, Fiona. It isn't your money that interests me."

Her heart tripped over a beat. "Then what?"

"The adventure. The battle of wits." He rubbed the star-shaped scar on his hand while he examined the foliage behind her head.

"You are not the best of liars either, my lord."

His lips quirked as if his smile was rusty.

"There is a small personal matter I believe overlaps with your inquiries." His gaze locked with hers. Truth darkened his eyes. "Indeed, our meetings were directly related to this matter."

"And will you tell me what this matter is?"

"I fear that would betray a confidence."

Disappointment tossed her swallow of punch in her stomach. He didn't trust *her*.

"I see."

"Do you?" His gaze intensified, as if to peer inside her skull and determine her thoughts.

What she offered so freely, he required be earned. Was Lilly the cause of his suspicion? Was he comparing them? Fiona straightened her shoulders. Lilly, schmilly. He offered his assistance. His feelings for treacherous love didn't matter. Not one bit.

"Well, I must admit there are places we could go together that I cannot go alone."

"Do we have an agreement, then?"

"There is one small problem."

Confusion wrinkled his forehead. "Is there?"

"We will have to spend a rather large quantity of time together."

He nodded; his thumb worried the cleft in his chin. "Yes, I've believe that might be necessary."

For an intelligent man, he was not making the right connections. Fiona took a deep breath. She would simply have to spell it out for him.

"Some might mistake you for a suitor."

He recoiled. His hands fisted at his sides.

"You have a point."

"I'm certain no one will think any worse of me. After all, most already consider me a title-hunting heiress. But..." She placed her hands on his. "I don't want them thinking of you as a fortune hunter."

"Me?" His eyes widened. "You're worried about *my* reputation?"

"You are doing me...my family...a very big favor."

"Miss Grey, I can assure you, society has called me worse things than a fortune hunter."

His pain squeezed her heart. *Your* plan, Fi. Stick with your plan.

"We could turn such gossip to our advantage."

He stepped closer.

"Piers and his shenanigans are interfering with my inquiries. And I think your mother's—"

"Stepmother."

"Stepmother's matchmaking may be a bit tiring. If everyone thought the banns were on the horizon..."

"Then we might both purchase some peace." Hugh rubbed the scar on his hand. "What will happen to your reputation when an announcement is not forthcoming?"

"'I'll be in America." The thought didn't cheer her as it ought. "Believe it or not, I've been called worse things than a jilt."

"You will never be called unkind things on my account."

"Partners?" Fiona offered her hand.

"Partners in curiosity and, unless my ears deceive me, in this waltz."

He escorted her to the ballroom as the violins struck the first chord.

"What do you know of my aunt and uncle's disappearance?" she asked him.

"Their ship sank not too far from shore. Everyone else survived but them. I also know there have been several burglaries both at Grey Shipping and at your house."

"You are remarkably well informed."

"As I said, there are some strange overlaps between my business and yours." He shrugged. "Partners should be helpful."

"You seem to know more than anyone here about Aunt and Uncle."

"I don't believe your family attended many social functions." He frowned into the crowd then turned his attention to her. "They stayed with the political set rather than with the Ton."

"There is one man I am anxious to meet. I wonder if you could procure an introduction for me."

"That shouldn't be terribly hard to arrange. Who do you wish to meet?"

"The Duke of August."

Pain rocketed up her shin as he stepped on her foot.

CHAPTER 14

The Duke of August.

A plague on Kingslea's existence. A horseman trampling his garden. Pumping blood pulsed in his chest.

The lilting waltz changed nationalities as the clock turned back five years.

"Mother insists that I meet him." Lilly's golden eyes sparked with mischief before sliding away from his gaze to peer into the crowd.

"You haven't told your mother about my proposal." His statement struck a jarring note, fouled the rhythm of his feet.

Full red lips moved. One. Two. Three. One. She nodded, shaking the tight smile from her face.

"I haven't had time. This is Mama's first season as well." Lilly's alabaster brow wrinkled as he missed yet another step.

One. Two. Three. She silently urged him into the proper cadence. Proper. Everything about Lilly was proper from her demure gown out to her pearl-handled fan and down to her satin slippers. She was even the proper height. A full head shorter than his own modest height. His hands flexed. He would protect Lilly.

"Will you tell her?" He inclined his head, the only liberty permitted in her rigid stance.

"Of course." She sighed

"Then why meet Sullied."

"Sullied?" Lilly shivered, honeyed locks trembling from the tight knot perched atop her head. "Is that the duke's nickname?"

"It is what we call him." Foreboding rolled like thunder in his skull. Instead of being put off by the nickname, she seemed intrigued.

"What can meeting one duke matter?" Annoyance flashed in her eyes. She tossed back her head and stepped an inch farther away. "You know my heart belongs to you, Mr. Gurnsey-Barrett."

Gurnsey-Barrett. He had given her leave to address him by his Christian name. She never had.

"Hugh. Hugh?"

Gardenias teased his nose. A plump hip cushioned his palm. Firm breasts brushed his chest. Lilly had never permitted him to hold her this closely. Kingslea slammed into the present. Fiona was his partner now. Fiona wanted to meet Sullied.

He filled his lungs with air. Despite the nonchalance of her question, he knew that meeting the Duke of August mattered.

To them both.

"Indeed, my lord, your valet's skill is to be complimented. Seldom have I observed such a close shave without even the hint of a nick." Dilated pupils reduced her blue irises to a thin azure ring. Fiona cleared her throat. Her eyebrows wiggled. "My eyesight is quite good, my lord."

Obviously, she had continued the conversation while his years had melted away. His mind blanked at the possibilities. What reply could he give? *Compliment her.*

"And your eyes are quite lovely."

Her sigh washed over him. Lemonade and disappointment.

"I needn't such a close view."

"Oh. Quite." Kingslea set her the proper distance away. Cold air filled the vacated space. "I apologize."

"For attempting to stuff me into your shirt or for stepping on my toes?"

"I stepped on your toes?"

"Twice."

"Then I apologize for both offenses."

"Only one apology is necessary. Your cologne is rather pleasant." She beamed at him. "Clean and somewhat...masculine. G-and-G could make a tidy profit listing it in our catalog." She wrinkled her nose as another man whisked past. His odor lingered after he and his partner twirled by. "Of course, it wouldn't have the same effect when used to mask poor hygiene."

Pain zipped up his shin as she stepped on his toe. Red suffused her grimacing face.

"Sorry. I'm not a very graceful dancer. I normally have to count. One, two, three. One, two —"

"You're doing fine."

Lilly had counted to help him keep time. Whereas Fiona...

Logic rattled to a halt. Fiona liked his cologne.

"I don't use cologne." The thought slipped off his tongue.

"Are you certain?"

"Yes."

"Oh, well. Guess the deal's off." Her hand spasmed on his shoulder. "I can hardly stuff *you* in a bottle."

"For which I am eternally grateful." His teasing fell flat. What had you expected, old man? What use was flattery to logic and reason? None. It wasn't as if he was courting her. They were partners.

Nothing more.

They completed a circle of the dance floor before she found her voice.

"You haven't answered my question."

Hope withered. Her bizarre comment about his nonexistent cologne had not suffocated her desire to meet Sullied.

"Haven't I?" The question now became why he had wanted it to?

"No." Her blue eyes locked with his. Steel girded her resolve. "Will you introduce me to the Duke of August?"

He would. There was no reason not to. After all, the duke had been seen making inquiries about her. Better to know what mischief he intended. Logic churned out the list of reasons.

"No."

"Why not?"

Why not? Because his brain had lost control of his vocal cords. In fact, his whole body seems to be in the throes of rebellion. Armed with logic, he attempted to quash the mutiny. Fiona wasn't Lilly. He wasn't in love with Fiona. There was absolutely no reason not to introduce her to the Duke of August. His brain sent the message to his vocal cords.

"Because..."

Blond hair bobbed on the periphery of his vision. Dread skittered down his spine. The duke hovered on the edge of the dance floor. His pale-blue eyes raked Kingslea before settling on Fiona's bare shoulders. A quick turn placed him between Sullied's leer and Fiona's innocence.

"He's not here."

"Then tonight really was a waste of time." Disappointment weighted her voice.

Stagnant blood pooled in his chest. Such selfish behavior benefited no one, and it had harmed Fiona. Hadn't he promised not to hurt her?

"Is it very important that you meet him?"

"His name has come up twice since my arrival."

"A coincidence?" He knew it was not, but the attempt to comfort stemmed from someplace other than his brain. He would discover where later. When he could face the answer.

"That's precisely what I wish to discover." For a heartbeat, she leaned closer. "He had some business with my uncle the day they sailed. Maybe he saw something. Maybe..."

Maybe he sabotaged something. The idea exploded in Kingslea's skull like Chinese fireworks. If Sullied was guilty of scuttling a ship, society would shun him. He almost smiled as he spied his nemesis.

"He's here." And *he* was back in control.

"I thought..."

"He just arrived." The lie tripped from his tongue. He ignored the stab of remorse. No harm had been done. Besides, he could hardly be responsible for the actions of his rebellious body.

"Where?" She rose on her toes and peered over his shoulder.

"The tall fop on the edge of the dancers, by the marble pillar." He spun her a half-turn. "I believe he is talking to Miss Montague."

Her gaze impaled him. "You don't like him?"

"What's not to like?" He shrugged off the tension knotting his shoulders. Her eyes narrowed. "Michelangelo's David made flesh. Women swoon and salivate." He swallowed the bitterness.

"I thought that was just Edwina."

"No."

Her gaze probed his soul.

"Have you never wondered why men also carry a handkerchief? It is to comfort the ladies when such an Adonis chooses another."

"And you will introduce me despite your loathing of the man?"

She still had to lay eyes on "the man." See the truth for herself. Was she toying with him? The way Lilly had right up until her wedding day?

"No."

"Then—"

"If I were to introduce you, it would arouse suspicion." His mouth gushed balderdash while logic fished for a reasonable explanation. "Not a wise course of action, given his association with your missing relatives."

"Uncle ferried his treasures, I don't really believe..."

His treasures. Sullied's priceless treasures. The sale of which had kept him financially solvent after his annulment. How would he benefit from sinking the ship? That was the mystery. A mystery Kingslea intended to solve.

"You should consider him. Scuttling a ship requires money and connections. Sullied has both."

"Then why would he beg an introduction to me?"

"He will. I guarantee it."

Interest sparked in her eyes.

"Of course, it may take a bit of acting on your part."

"Acting?"

Fiona's condition on their partnership hummed in his body. An improbable idea buoyed by logic. His plan was bound to work.

"I believe it is time to begin." He maneuvered around a rotund couple wheezing through the steps and hooked her arm through his.

"Why are we leaving the dance floor?" Excitement danced in her eyes.

His body answered with a flush of heat. She trusted him. Of course, she might not once she learned his plan could blemish her reputation.

"One does not make love to a woman in the open."

"Make love?" She tripped on the carpet.

His hand slipped around her waist. Awareness coursed through him. Talk of love had effected him. His touch helped her regain her balance, nothing more.

"You agreed my appearing to press suit was a necessary part of the our partnership." He helped her into a seat behind a large plant.

"Yes, but how..." She scooted closer to the wall.

"First things first." He slipped her dance card off her wrist then balanced the paper on his knee and began to write. "Mortis should have been a lord, but Peterson would never be anything better than a baron." He slanted the bogus signature to the right.

A gloved finger pointed to the illegible scrawl next to a polka.

"Who is that?"

"That is Graf von Momfried."

"Hugh, why are you volunteering your friends to dance with me?"

"They're not my friends." The signature streaked across the page.

Fiona snatched the dance card and pressed it to her chest.

"Perhaps you had better explain."

"Indeed." He reached for the book. She smacked his hand with it. Tingles raced up his arm. "Montague wishes to dance with you. I cannot claim all your dances, so..."

"So, you've filled my card with fictitious characters." She flipped open the book and peered at the names.

"Yes. No." Talking to the top of her head was unproductive. He slid his finger under her chin and turned her face to his. "The men are real, just not their titles."

"And they won't mind dancing with me?"

The question tumbled through his mind. His reasoning was sound. Perhaps it was the explanation.

"I doubt they dance anymore. Mortis, Peterson and Momfried were professors from my youth. When last I saw them, they still had most of their teeth."

"Well, then, they deserve two dances apiece." A smile curved her lips. "Thank you. I never would have thought to write in my own partners."

"The trick is to remember to change your handwriting." Kingslea traced her cheek. Her skin was smoother than he'd thought. And those tiny wisps curling around her face were rather attractive. "Sullied will insist he meet you when he finds out about my interest in you." He leaned closer.

"Pretend interest." The tip of her tongue slid over her dry lip. Such luscious lips, and red like ripe strawberries.

"Hmmm. Relax, Fiona." He shifted his weight slightly. The delicate chiffon skirt fluttered against his thigh. "Ahh, I detect a slight draft. If you shiver just so..."

"I—"

"There you are!" Winthrop shoved their green screen out of the way.

"Allow me to escort you back to your family, Miss Grey." Alveston stepped in front of Kingslea and tugged Fiona from her seat.

Damnation. He knew Alveston was a snake but to steal his woman right in front of him? And they were supposed to be friends.

Winthrop thumped him on the chest and shook his head. Dammit. Couldn't they see he had the situation under control?

"I—"

"Remember this song, Kingslea?" Alveston shot a concerned look over his shoulder.

The man should be concerned. A couple decades earlier, and it would have been pistols at dawn. Interrupting a man...

"It's as if the past is just around the corner." Alveston whisked Fiona into the crowd.

"Remove yourself from my path, Winthrop, or I'll—"

"Ahh, Mr. Gurnsey-Barrett." Lilly materialized from behind Winthrop. "Or should I say Lord Kingslea."

CHAPTER 15

"Have you forgotten my warning, Miss Grey?" Lord Alveston's *threat streamed* by her ear, like a shark's fin slicing through a calm sea.

"No." Fiona tugged on her arm. His grip tightened. Her arm would be bruised tomorrow. She could admire his loyalty to Hugh more if the restraining noble were across the room

"Yet you continue to encourage Kingslea's attentions."

Heads turned. Lord Alveston steered her through the parting waves of humanity, a rudder to her ship.

"He is a man grown." She jerked to a stop. Vibrant colors bled onto a white canvas as he spun her about.

"He is my friend." Eyeteeth flashed in Lord Alveston's smile. "Make no mistake, Miss Grey, I—"

"No, my lord." Red rimmed her vision. Anger closed her throat, squeezing her words. "I have had enough of your threats and insults."

"My warnings—"

"Are unnecessary." Fiona wrenched out of his grip. Blank faces turned in their direction. Rumors hissed and sputtered. She ignored her audience. She had tolerated Lord Alveston's overbearing concern, but she would not tolerate violence against her person. "If you continue your attacks, I will treat you as I would any other cad."

His eyes narrowed as he raked her from head to foot.

"I see no whip or firearm."

"I need neither to inflict pain where a man is most vulnerable."

Several bystanders gasped. Lord Alveston smirked.

"Not a very appropriate threat for a *lady*."

"Those who will act do not threaten, my lord."

"It seems as if Kingslea has assessed at least one of your traits correctly, Miss Grey."

Pleasure warmed her. Hugh had talked about her to his friends.

"Perhaps you should take your concerns directly to him."

"*He* has lost perspective." The bitter cold in Lord Alveston's voice thawed to a mere chill. Hostility melted from his eyes, curiosity and reluctant admiration took its place.

"You're mad, sir." Fiona retreated a step. A teasing lord was more suspect than an angry one. At least most men spoke the truth when in the throes of anger.

"Not mad, Miss Grey." Lord Alveston smiled. "Livid."

"You are deliberately misinterpreting my comments." Her traitorous face smiled back. Not that she trusted Lord Alveston. He might be a steadfast friend to Hugh, but he thought such kinship made them natural enemies. For all she knew, he had simply changed tactics. Or as her grandmother always said, "attracting bees with honey rather than vinegar." Despite his abrupt truce, she still wouldn't mind if a chandelier crashed down on his head.

"Ahh, Alveston." The lazy drawl shored up her crumbling defenses.

— *That's him, Fi.* Milton slipped between her and Lord Alveston. *Isn't he something? Reminds me of a statue I saw once.*

A statue. Odd how Hugh seemed to haunt her almost as much as Milton. Fiona caught her tongue between her teeth. Not that she'd object to a bit of statuary close by—she'd certainly break it over someone's head. Especially since she had her choice of targets.

— *You're not looking, Fi.* Milton waved his hand in front of her face. *He's to the left.*

She ignored him. Any breaking of eye contact now, and the officious lord would think he had won.

— *That's still straight. This is left.* Milton scratched his head. *Watch me. I'll move left, and your eyes can follow. Do co-operate, Fi.*

She'd cooperate with the priest when he sent Milton to the other side. Until then, she'd had enough of men. If they weren't insulting her, they were procuring her a husband. She allowed the full force of her irritation to blaze in her eyes.

Lord Alveston arched his left eyebrow and broke eye contact. The slight smile froze on his lips as he turned to the newcomer.

"Alveston?" The drawl drifted over her shoulder.

"Your..." His adam's apple bobbed as if he'd just swallowed a large insect. "Grace."

She'd faced down her opponent. Victory thrilled through her, danced out her fingers and toes. Da would be proud. Her whoop of triumph lodged in her throat. Too bad crowing was considered ill-mannered. She followed Lord Alveston's lead and turned to Milton's hand-picked suitor.

"Your Grace." The man's large chest swelled. "Next you'll be calling me duke." Sharp teeth shredded his forced laughter. "No need for ceremony between old school chums. What was that delightful nickname you dubbed me?"

"There were so many it is hard to remember."

Lord Alveston clearly hated the man. Fiona agreed. There was something off-putting about him. A shiver rattled her teeth. He was the thing that slithered in a darkened room.

— *His clothes are off the first cut and the finest cloth.* Milton fluttered around the man, pointing out his attributes like a salesman to a reluctant customer. *No patched apparel, like that Kingston fellow. And this chap has powerful shoulders. He'll take good care of you, Fi.*

Fiona smoothed the curls at the nape of her neck. Take care of her? She took care of herself, and her family as well. Had she changed so much since Milton's death? Her gaze swept over the newcomer's broad shoulders. She preferred Hugh's shoulders, and his presence. She scanned the ballroom. Where was he?

— *Many of the women compare him to Hercules or whoever that Greek fellow was.*

She nodded as her gaze swung back to the man. He posed like a Greek statue. And like many in the pantheon, he accepted the world as his altar and expected the lowly humans to worship him.

"Well, if you are here then Gurnsey-Barrett must also be present."

The crowd shifted. Her heart stilled. Hugh was with another woman, leaning over her cleavage as if searching for a lost guinea. Jealousy slammed into Fiona. How could he convince anyone he was courting her if he was busy leering over that woman's profligate bosoms?

"He's Lord Kingslea now." Lord Alveston stiffened.

Her attention shifted to Lord Alveston. Even he had noticed Hugh's devotion to the woman's attributes.

"Indeed." The newcomer brushed a smudge off his coat.

— *Lord Snootface isn't as bright as these sputtering candles.* Milton flicked Lord Alveston on the ear. *Your future husband is begging an introduction, and Snootface is pretending you're not there.*

For once, she and Lord Alveston agreed on something. In fact, he had done her a favor by not introducing them. She could slip into the crowd without causing affront. She inched backwards. Milton would be hurt by her retreat. Another step toward freedom. She would blame Lord Alveston. Indeed, Milton's bedeviling might be the perfect revenge.

— *Perhaps you should let him know you aren't averse to the introduction, Fi?* Milton's touch sowed goosebumps up her arm.

"Yes, I thought I spied him earlier." The man's gaze swung to her. His gloved fingers fondled the chunky gold chain draped across his vest. "Of course, he was dancing, so naturally, I thought I had been mistaken."

— *I know that look, Fi,* Milton gloated. *He's taken with you. Very taken. Now all we need is Snootface to introduce you.*

Fiona froze. She was also familiar with the look on the man's face. He was comparing her to a mental standard, deciding which pieces of her to change to better suit his taste.

Lord Alveston looked from her to their company than back again. She shook her head. A smile warped his lips.

"Miss Grey, allow me to introduce the Duke of August." Alveston closed the distance between them, set his hand on the small of her back and pushed her forward. "Your Grace, this is Miss Grey."

"Your Grace." Fiona ground her heel into Alveston's toes as she curtsied. The man was horrible. He knew she hadn't wanted to meet the man, yet he had introduced her to...

The Duke of August.

Fate was laughing at her. The duke was supposed to be a kind, elderly gentleman, not this...man who look as if, should one tug too hard on his glove, his skin would slough off and reveal a vile creature underneath.

"Miss Grey." The duke sketched a brief bow, "It is, indeed, an honor."

For her. She heard his voice in her head. Sullied. Hugh's name fit. *Hugh.* Her gaze skipped around the room. Where had he gone? And where was the tart? Had they slipped behind another fern? Was he kissing her? Kissing her the way his eyes had promised he would kiss *her*?

— *Say something, Fi.* Milton huffed in her ear.

Her tongue stilled in her head. She didn't want to talk to the duke. She wanted to see Hugh. Make certain he wasn't making love to another woman. To that woman.

"May I have the pleasure of dancing this polka with you, Miss Grey?"

Dance? Fiona crushed her irritation into a manageable size. How dare Hugh be dancing with that woman when he was supposed to be searching for her aunt and uncle. Guilt assailed her. *She* was supposed to be searching for Aunt Caroline and Uncle Andrew.

"I'm sorry, Your Grace." Tingles raced across Fiona's palm as she slapped open her dance card. Hugh's handwriting marched across the pages. His plans held merit. Her full dance card meant she could stay by his side and make certain he focused on their adventure and not that Jezebel in a red dress. "I've promised this dance to Mr. Monfried."

"Monfried?" The duke frowned down at her. "I don't believe I've had the pleasure of his acquaintance."

— *Who's this Monfried fellow, Fi?* Milton shoved his elbow into Lord Alveston's gut and hovered in front of her. *Can't be all that honorable. You shouldn't dance with anyone I haven't met. These functions are swimming with all sorts of unsavory characters.* He glared at Hugh's friend.

Lord Alveston shivered. He stepped back and peered over her shoulder.

"Monfried? Peterson? Mortis?" His eyes narrowed as he inspected their slots. Confusion furrowed his forehead then fled from his face. "I am glad to see your dance card has dried, Miss Grey."

— *Your dance card is full!* Milton crossed his arms over his chest. *Really, Fi. What use is my guidance if you insist on filling your dance card with unacceptable gentleman?*

"Everyone has been most welcoming." Dread slithered down her spine as Lord Alveston shifted away from her. He recognized the names. Fiona smoothed her skirt. Could he expose her without revealing Hugh's part in the deception?

"I am too late." Disbelief colored the duke's voice. "I should have know such a beautiful lady would not sit out any dances." The orchestra picked up tempo for the polka. "Such an inattentive partner is unworthy of you, Miss Grey. The music has begun, yet he has not claimed your hand."

— *He has a point, Fi.* Milton nodded. *The laggard couldn't blame you if you accepted another partner in his stead.*

An insult is much easier to shrug off than an unwanted partner's touch. Fiona slipped on her smile.

"That is my fault, gentlemen. I promised to meet him by the stairs." She gathered her chiffon skirt in her hand. "If you gentlemen will excuse me, I believe I should find Mr. Monfried."

"No need, Miss Grey." Lord Alveston stopped her withdrawal with a staying hand. "In the rush of introductions, I forgot my duty as messenger."

"Messenger?" Fiona's tongue swelled from lack of moisture. He would hand her to the devil to protect Hugh.

"Yes." Lord Alveston rocked back on his heels and beamed at her. "Monfried had to leave. His sister twisted her ankle and required his assistance." He chuckled as he expanded the joke to include the duke. "You remember Julia Monfried, don't you, Your Grace? She made her bow some years back. Never took. Had a face like a horse and a laugh to match."

"Yes," the Duke of August agreed, "of course. One could never forget that laugh."

Lord Alveston chuckled. "The amazing August luck holds—yet another lady becomes free to enjoy your illustrious company."

— *I say, Fi.* Milton rubbed his hands together. *That could be a sign from fate. You could marry the Duke of August and become a duchess. That has to be somewhere high in the peerage, don't you know.*

She could also run screaming across the ballroom and smash through the glass windows at the other end. *Focus, Fi. Remember why you're here.* Hot air filled her lungs. She'd come to find information about her aunt and uncle.

Hugh's deep-throated chuckle jangled along her nerves. *He* was obviously too engrossed in that woman's assets to be of use. She would find them herself.

"Shall we, Miss Grey?" The Duke of August pointed his crooked elbow at her.

"How could I refuse?" Fiona tossed back her shoulders. Dancing with His Grace was not a setback, it was a step in the right direction. She set her hand on his arm and followed him onto the dance floor. Indeed, she owed Lord Alveston for his part in the introduction.

— *Refuse?* Milton floated next to her. *Really, Fi, a little thanks would be more appropriate after all my hard work.*

She nodded. Yes, she would thank Lord Alveston by informing Edwina of the man's interest.

"Are you and Lord Alveston well acquainted." Or had the man used opportunity to pawn one person he detests off onto the other?

"We both attended Charter House."

— *You're doing great, Fi,* Milton cheered. *I'm going to keep that pesky cousin of yours occupied. That fellow is coarse enough to interrupt. Be nice, Fi. He is your future husband.* With that parting threat, he dropped through the floor.

Fiona slipped her hand into the duke's, her social mask firmly in place. A shiver shook her locked muscles. A polka—at least she had been spared a waltz. Still, the duke's touch was as lively as a dead fish. And half as welcome.

"Of course, we weren't at the same level."

"I see." Longing filled her. Why couldn't British dances have callers? Anything was better than this. She tried to go right, and he went left.

"Of course you do." He wrestled the lead from her and forced her into a turn. "Americans are very adept as sifting the gold from the dross."

Forget the steps, Fi. Focus on your inquiries. Heaven knows you don't want a repeat performance. Gold and dross. It was obvious which the duke considered himself to be.

From the corner of her eye, she spied Hugh taking to the floor with that woman. Who was she? It was obvious she wasn't part of his search. His interest in her seemed base.

"Then you are older than Lord Kingslea."

"In truth, I barely remember the man." They stumbled around a laughing couple. "I had to make a few discreet inquiries so that I might make your acquaintance."

"Why trouble yourself over an American?" Their dancing did not reflect well on either of them. It was clear His Grace was his favorite own topic.

Sweat beaded his forehead as he dragged her around another couple.

"Your beauty, wit and name are on everyone's lips."

As was the size of her fortune. Hugh had said Sullied was rich and powerful, so what motivated him?

"I'm flattered."

"Naturally." He pursed his lips and tugged his boot out from under her foot. "Grey. Grey. I believe we may have mutual acquaintances. Do you perchance know Andrew Grey of Grey Shipping?"

If her name and dowry were, indeed, a topic of conversation then so was her connection to Grey Shipping. She had not been out of society so long she had forgotten how quickly the tiniest tidbit spread.

"He is my uncle." Why had he feigned ignorance? Sullied obviously had something to gain. Otherwise, why bring another gentleman into their conversation, even if it was only his name?

Hugh danced past them. That woman had her head thrown back, offering her white throat to him as she assaulted the rest of the dancers with her annoying laughter. What could Hugh have said to make her laugh with abandon? And why hadn't he shared the joke with her?

"Those worthy of acquaintance in London are very few in number."

She would discover Sullied's reasons after she found out what his business was with Uncle Andrew.

"You are, indeed, a member of a select group, my lord."

"Your Grace."

"Your Grace." She aped his correction. "You are the first gentlemen I've met this evening who is acquainted with my aunt and uncle." Fiona held her breath, hoping he would list others who fell into the same category.

"It is important to cultivate the best acquaintances."

Or those who helped buoy one's own good opinion of oneself. The man probably wouldn't notice a battle exploding around him unless the combatants dirtied his shoes. Still, she had to try. Her family was counting on her.

"I'm am certain the Saunders' are honored to be among that number."

Sullied remain mute. A groan lodged in her throat. The Saunders's had evinced no recognition of her name when she met them at the door, but she had hoped...

"I will tell my uncle you treasure his friendship."

"Treasure." Interest sharpened his eyes. "An odd choice of words. Has your uncle spoken of me and my little hobby?" The duke smacked his lips.

Too bad she hadn't gotten any answers—she would have taken pleasure in informing His Grace of his place in the grand scheme of things. She corralled her frustration. Until then, she needed to keep him talking.

"Not in any detail."

"I have taken an interest in Egypt."

He peered into her eyes. Fiona kept her arms locked in the proper position. She would not fidget, nor would she smooth her dress. She was a person, not some long-buried artifact to be scrutinized.

"The strength and agility required of a true archaeologist suits my abilities and temperament. Regardless of what you might read in the papers, treasures are not found on every dig. Sometimes there are only mummies, papyrus—that is a paper, of sorts—and the occasional statue, usually pocked and abused by time." He spun her across the floor, his eyes glazed as if he were staring across the desert. "I have been more successful than most. Most don't realize that patience is often a more valuable asset than money."

"How fascinating." And how could she bring his lecture back to her family and his connection with them? *Think, Fi. This dance must end eventually.*

"Pitting oneself against the cunning of the ancients, mind and body, is invigorating." He focused on her again. "The priests of ancient Egypt were quite clever with traps, tricks and false rooms."

"You must find the challenge highly rewarding."

"I have rescued many treasures." His Grace preened.

"You must have many less fortunate amateur Egyptologists clamoring for a peek at your collection."

"Only the rarest and most beautiful of items are worthy of keeping."

Fiona blinked. Was he *flirting* with her? Her skin squirmed over her skeleton. She must be mistaken. Please, God, let her be mistaken.

"And the rest?"

"There are always collectors with less-discriminating tastes." His gaze slid over her shoulder. His eyes narrowed as he followed a couple.

Hugh and that woman danced past. Fiona tripped over her skirt. Wasn't it enough that he was enjoying another woman's company. Did he have to throw it in her face?

"Those who don't mind the castoffs of their superiors."

Fiona forced her attention back to Sullied. She had never wanted Hugh's help. She didn't need Hugh. The duke knew something, and she must find a way to get him to part with that information.

"I wasn't aware of my uncle's interest in Egypt." She was equally certain he would have mentioned such a ghoulish interest in the dead, especially given her family's connection with the other side. On the other hand, that could explain his summoning of Mam.

"Your uncle is a very cosmopolitan man. I suppose that comes from the nature of his business. Shipping, you know."

Arrogant. Opinionated. Her insulting description kept time with the jaunty music. Wouldn't *his* haughtiness be surprised should he learn she was one of her uncle's partners?

"I convinced him to hold an unwrapping some months back. Naturally, we used one of my own mummies."

"That was very generous of you, Your Grace." She squelched her frustration. He had finally returned to a topic of interest. "I've never been to an unwrapping. Is it as sad a crush as this ball?"

"The mummy was worthy of little else." He smiled down at her. "The only thing interesting was an amusing little trinket found amongst the wrappings."

He wasn't going to answer her question. Either her aunt and uncle's friends weren't worthy of his notice, or he had a more sinister reason for keeping mum. She must continue her role of interested partner. Doubtless, she would need to question him more later.

"Is that common? To wrap valuables with the dead."

"For the nobles and some high priests." His gaze dropped to her neck then darted to each of her wrists. "Did your aunt show you the bauble before…?"

"No." He was interested in the jewelry? Perhaps he would trade information for it. "No, I don't believe she had."

"You'd recognize it if you'd seen it. The hieroglyphs are quite distinct."

"Hieroglyphs?"

"Writings of the pharaohs." He studied her closely. "My watch fob is engraved with those that spell my name."

"Can you read hieroglyphs, Your Grace?"

"Hieroglyphs. Greek. Latin. French. German." He shrugged.

She was being dismissed. So, he wanted the jewelry her aunt had unwrapped. Enough to scuttle a ship for?

"You are quite accomplished, Your Grace."

"As befits one of my station." Boredom weighted his voice.

It was nice that *he* now thought their dance had gone on too long.

"I am certain you are a fine example of dukedom."

"Would you be interested in viewing my collection, Miss Grey?"

Fiona blinked. The man must possess two minds—dismissing her one minute then inviting her out the next.

"Are you hosting an exhibition, Your Grace?" And how many of her aunt and uncle's acquaintances would be there?

"No." He frowned at her. "My collection on loan to the British Museum. Everyone can benefit from the mastery of the ancients."

"In what way?" At least, her voice held none of her disappointment.

"Why, their medicine and healing arts are far superior to ours, as evidenced by their preservation of their dead." His gaze swung to her. "Do you know, many believe their priests knew the secrets to immortality? Indeed, some theorize one priest actually became a god."

"Immortality?"

"Fairy tales, of course." He turned her once than stopped. The music had finally ended.

"Thank you for the dance, Your Grace."

"It was an honor." He walked her to the edge of the dance floor. "Shall I procure us some lemonade, or perhaps you prefer negus?"

"No, thank you. I believe I see my next partner." Fiona stiffened. Hugh was two couples in front of them. That woman clung to his side like a well-tailored coat.

"A word of caution, Miss Grey." The Duke of August stopped on the edge of the dance floor.

"Have no fear, Your Grace, I am not seeking immortality." Nor anything to do with Egyptology. She would ask Gibson who was at the unwrapping. If she hadn't been so distracted by thoughts of Hugh, she might have thought of asking the butler sooner.

"I refer to a more immediate threat."

"A threat?" She listened with half an ear. Gibson might know where to find her uncle's log. She would ask the butler when she got home.

As if on cue, a clock struck midnight. Tomorrow would be better.

"Gurnsey-Barrett, or whatever he calls himself now, is not to be trusted."

"He isn't?" Gurnsey-Barrett. Her attention riveted on His Grace. The man was talking about Hugh.

"Definitely not. He's destitute, Miss Grey." The Duke of August caught her hand and patted it. "He clings to respectability only because well-meaning friends refuse to cut him."

Hugh's hatred of Sullied ran both ways. Interesting, but of no relevance to her inquiries.

"Whatever has he done, Your Grace?" The question slipped past her intentions.

"I tell you this only for your protection, Miss Grey, and because I feel a certain responsibility to watch over you in your uncle's absence."

"How very gracious of you."

"A nobleman's burden, Miss Grey."

Fiona's gaze settled on Lord Alveston. She doubted there was anything noble about the duke's *on dit*. More likely, his confidence concerned revenge more than interest in her welfare. She understood revenge.

"Perhaps if you told me of his crime."

"The worst, Miss Grey." Sullied leaned close, his stale breath washing over her shoulder. "He ripped a mother away from her babes and lured a woman away from her husband."

Shock rooted Fiona to the spot. Whatever she had expected, it certainly wasn't that.

"I see the disbelief on your face, my dear." The duke's sigh caressed her bare shoulder. "I know it is true. You see, it is *my* wife he stole."

Without another word the Duke of August disappeared into the crowd.

— *Well, isn't he perfect, Fi?* Milton flitted to her side. *I can tell by the look on your face that he is. Now, all we have to do is—*

"Fiona, dear." Piers broke through a row of dancers preparing for the quadrille.

— *What will it take to get through to the man?* Red tinged Milton's opaque body.

"Mama is looking for you, cousin dear." Piers glared at a cluster of gentleman looking in her direction. "Come along." His hand closed around her upper arm, and he dragged her forward.

— *Don't go, Fi. You can still dance with His Grace.*

Fiona spotted Hugh in the crowd. He still had his limpet. An ache started in her chest, one that rivaled the agony needling her feet. She had no reason to stay.

CHAPTER 16

"Our dancing brings back so many pleasant memories." Red rosebuds eyed him from a nest of green leaves circling her upswept hair. Delicate feathers quivered around Lilly Lawson's creamy shoulders. A few vibrated free of their stitches and splattered his jacket with a fleet of white spiders.

"Indeed." The warm scent of roses rusted the chains of logic and reason. Raw emotion surged, rattling caged memories. Had she ever danced this close? Her feather bodice swept his chest. Petals, soft and dewy, kissed his chin.

"Garden parties, croquet on the lawn, Ascot and the Henley Regatta." Her sigh washed over him, as thick and sweet as fresh cream.

Freed of their confinement, memories bobbed into the present. Warmth filled his limbs. Stolen kisses behind the hedge, a quick press of uncovered flesh, fervent vows thick with passion and lapping at their future. Snippets of happier times crowded his vision.

"Your beauty made the stars weep with jealousy."

"Such sweet words made you my most particular beau." Her eyes shimmered with kept tears. White teeth glistened behind parted full lips.

Air froze in his lungs, locking him in a time ripe with promise. How could he have forgotten the ecstasy of falling in love, the inferno of desire? Why had he ever wanted to? Callous reason dashed the languid memories.

Lilly had married another.

Loved another.

Kingslea blinked. The Saunders's ballroom came into focus with blinding clarity, decadence and overindulgence spoiling the freshness of youth. Time had gifted him with a modicum of wisdom. He simply needed to keep hold of it while in the siren's company.

"I do not remember you holding your tongue for so long." Amber eyes gazed up at him from between lush black lashes fanning over white skin just beginning to crease with age.

"Time has changed many things."

"But not all." Her chin lifted. The necklace of emeralds and amethysts undulated over her full breasts. For an instant, her forehead rested against his chin.

His mind registered the softness of her skin, the heat created from the contact. Yet his heartbeat remained steady, his hands dry and his stomach settled. So long as the whirlpool of emotions stayed five years distant, he could remain in control.

"Your dancing skills have improved greatly, Lord Kingslea." Her smile wavered then widened.

"Thank you." Her praise grated. He had mastered the intricate steps by necessity, not to please her. A dancing bachelor was welcomed everywhere, especially in the homes of those who conducted business over dinner.

He turned to avoid the hedges concealing the orchestra. Of course, most in this crowd shunned the taint of business even as they coveted its money.

"You make me exceedingly curious to discover what other talents you have cultivated while I was away."

Away? Kingslea covered his stumble with a quick half-turn. Is that how society terms an unpleasant union? Away. Yet she had not been out of society. Indeed, the newspapers reported Her Grace's attendance at this ball and that dinner. He knew. *The Times* articles never woke him from his living nightmare.

"Have I shocked you, my lord?" She grinned at him.

Was she so confident of his reaction and her attributes? Kingslea grimaced as memories fluttered through his mind. Certainly, nothing in their past would shake her conviction. Flattery was potent, addicting and distracting.

A couple jostled his elbow.

"Sorry," the red-faced youth muttered as he maneuver his glowering partner a step away.

Kingslea nodded. He glanced at the eager faces turned in his direction. While the ballroom was not excessively large, there were not enough dancers to justify the crush near his person.

Suspicion crowded his vision. Had Lilly chosen him as a partner for the attention it garnered or to renew their acquaintance? There was but one way to discover the truth. He allowed a smile as his gaze roamed over her face.

"Forgive me, Miss Lawson. I had forgotten how beautiful you were."

"Were?" Anger tightened the corners of her eyes, sharpened the curve of her smile.

Achievement jangled Kingslea's nerves. Vanity—a weapon sharper than a surgeon's scalpel—was her Achilles' heel. He reined in his elation. An effective instrument provided he used it judiciously and remained unbewitched by the illusion. Lilly was the one who needed to be placed under the spell. A spell his poor word choice had nearly broken. The gems twinkling at her neck provided him with inspiration.

"Where once you were an amethyst, now you are a diamond."

She straightened in his arms, her lips softening into a smirk. Her forehead nuzzled his neck. Only an heiress would consider comparison to a worthless sparkling stone a compliment.

Throaty laughter rumbled near his shoulder. His gut clenched. Bitterness flooded his tongue. Fiona. His gaze found her two couples away on another man's arm. She had wasted little time in gaining an introduction to Sullied. Kingslea executed a quick turn, keeping them in sight. He had interrogated many people—never once had he batted his eyes or leaned in so close.

"You flatter me. Amethysts, diamonds. Is that how you see me, as a jewel to be treasured?"

Fiona's chuckle tugged on his ears. What the devil did the woman find so amusing? The duke was dull, boring, not to mention downright irritating.

"Mr. Gurnsey-Barrett?" Lilly's voice cracked.

Kingslea dragged his gaze away from Fiona. He would remind her of their bargain after this infernal dance ended. Lilly's pouting lips caught his attention. Meanwhile, he would uphold his end.

"It has been an age since anyone has addressed me so..." He deepened his voice. "...intimately."

A giggle rippled past Lilly's lips.

"I sincerely hope you don't hold my blunder against me, my lord. Dancing with you has transported me to an earlier time."

"Of course, my dear, of course." Kingslea nodded to a passing couple. How many other reminders would she slap him with? More important, when would she realize her attempts at intimacy left him cold?

"I see the duke did not waste much time in courting a replacement." A brown eyebrow hooked above her eye. "I wonder who she could be?"

Bells clanged inside Kingslea's skull. Lilly's interest in Fiona was poison. He tried to execute a quarter-turn. Lilly kept her arm straight, refusing his lead. Since wrestling her around the dance floor was unacceptable, he would need another way to bring her off-topic. Boredom had worked before...

"How's that, my dear?"

"I was speaking of the duke's dance partner." Lilly's eyes narrowed. "She looks familiar."

"Does she?" Her question quivered with danger. If he held his tongue, and she discovered he had danced with Fiona... What could Lilly want with him? If he knew the answer, he could draft the safest reply.

"Do you know her?"

Did she? Unease slithered through Kingslea's belly. He would ponder the implications of revelation later. Now, he had to answer Lilly's question.

"I believe she is an American, perhaps you know her from home?"

Lilly smiled patronizingly. "It is a rather large country. Father wouldn't allow us to socialize with any but those of our own class." She locked her arms, marching him around the dance floor, shadowing Fiona and Sullied. Her gaze scampered away from his. "Still, you may be right."

Change the subject, man. His mind groped for an idea. Lilly's clothes? They would exhaust that topic within two minutes. Her horse? She hated to ride. The voyage to London? Had she ever left? *Think man, think.* Light dawned. *Her.* Lilly was her own favorite topic.

"I wonder..." she began.

"Your appearance has caused quite a stir tonight." Kingslea jerked his head toward the crowd. Eyes followed their progress across the oak planks. Fans fluttered with the breeze of flapping jaws. "I do believe your name is on everyone's lips."

"*We*, my lord." Lilly squared her shoulders. Her hand clenched his arm. "*We* are causing quite a few comments and speculation." The chill in her eyes thawed as she turned her gaze on him. "No doubt they are commenting on your reentry into society as well as my triumphant return."

His reentry? Annoyance itched Kingslea's back. Obviously, she had not bothered to keep herself informed of *his* doings.

"Surely, they don't think the two are connected."

"Society may be much taken with rumor and innuendo but sometimes smoldering embers exist beneath billowing smoke." Her fingers crawled up his arm, rested on his shoulder.

Muddled faculties. The woman actually believed he had returned for her. He searched the crowded. Apparently, others supported her hypothesis. Eyes darted from Lilly to him, back and forth like observers of lawn tennis. The past pressed against him. Distant dreams spun gossamer threads, binding his will to resist.

He shrugged, snapping the ties.

"My sister makes her come-out this season." A smile trimmed his grinding teeth. "I'm certain those endowed with reason will make the connection."

"Of course, of course." Lilly patted his shoulder.

Bloody hell. Now, the woman treated him like a cosseted lap dog. He pivoted. Lilly's skirt billowed then slapped their red-faced shadow. Kingslea jerked his head in acknowledgment. Conniving woman—she deserved to be abandoned in the middle of the floor.

Too bad he was too much of a gentleman to do it.

"And how is dear Melanie?" Lilly's forehead creased.

"*Melody* is quite well." Two more couples twirled between him and freedom.

"She is quite young, isn't she?" A bead of perspiration slid down Lilly's temple. Her eyes widened as they measured the distance between her person and the pillars of wallflowers.

"She turned eighteen last autumn."

"Eighteen—such a young and foolish age." Fabric banded his arm. Lilly stepped backwards.

His jacket slipped across his shoulders. His throat throbbed from the press of his tie. Infernal enigmas—she planned to strip him of his jacket if he tried to leave. He followed her lead.

"I am certain you will protect her from the follies that I endured." She released his sleeve as they neared the center of the dancing.

"I was certain your mother exonerated you of any imprudence when she spoke at your annulment." Kingslea glared at the dancers. Too many couples twirled between him and freedom.

"Yes, she did, didn't she?" Lilly smacked her lips.

Fiona swung into view, blue eyes blazing in his direction. Her voice filled his head. Why was he dancing with Lilly? Nothing connected her to the missing Greys. Nothing at all. As for the jacket...

Kingslea shrugged. While it might be his newest, it was still last year's style. Indeed, it engendered no special affection.

His feet slowed. A gap appeared in the crowd. He would give Lilly one chance to leave the floor on his arm. If she balked, he would leave in his shirt sleeves.

"Grey."

"Pardon?" Habit allowed his feet to keep time with the music.

"I do believe she is Miss Grey." Lilly stared at the couple moving a few feet beyond her left elbow. "Of course, she was ahead of me at the academy." Lilly smoothed his jacket. "No. No, I must be mistaken. That particular Grey possessed a shocking mass of red hair. She was always arousing trouble. She was expelled several years ago. Rumor had it that she joined the circus."

"Hard to imagine the daughter of a respectable family causing such a scandal."

"Undoubtedly. Still it could be one of the younger Greys. They had three daughters."

"Had?" He should leave, follow his planned course of action. His feet refused to obey.

"The one is surely deceased by now."

"Dead?" Fiona's past was not his concern. Unless it shed light on her aunt and uncle's disappearance.

"Yes. Consumption." Lilly smiled. "Mother says Mr. Grey married beneath his station. Breeding will tell. The lower orders possess a disposition favored by the wasting disease."

Lower orders? Piers had alluded to Fiona's mother's Irish ancestry. Curiosity sparked to life. Perhaps the Greys' disappearance was related to Ireland. Bloody Sunday was not so very long ago.

"She doesn't look dead to me."

"I'm certain Lady Saunders is not in the habit of inviting corpses to her balls." Lilly pursed her lips. "She must be the other Grey—Faith...or Felicia. Then again, perhaps Grey isn't the correct surname. She was engaged. What was his name?"

Davis. Milton Davis. The name bubbled to the surface of Kingslea's brain.

"I'm certain I don't know."

Lilly peered into his eyes. "Of course not. He's dead as well."

"Your Miss Grey seems surrounded by death."

"She withdrew from society immediately afterwards." Lilly leaned closer. "Probably more from the scandal than heartfelt loss."

"Scandal." *Not your business, old man.* His mouth followed orders from someplace other than his brain.

"It was quite delicious." Lilly shivered. "His carriage overturned. He was racing. The winner was to receive an unimpeded chance at courtship of Miss Amy Maystone. She was a very well-known actress at the time."

"I see." Once more his mouth and mind parted company. How could any man prefer the charms of an actress to Miss Grey?

"Her father belongs to New York society. I wonder why she is here?"

"Perhaps she is hunting a title."

"Oh, darling, that is so passé." Lilly patted his arm.

Focus on the steps, man. One-two-three. You are not a pet. Turn. You can endure Lilly for a couple more minutes. One-two-three.

"Very few American heiresses bother anymore. Father says it is because the English are so very unlike American husbands. Why, the English husband has no wish to work at all."

Another Father-based lecture.

"Perhaps she is not Miss Grey at all."

"I'm positive—she is the drab Grey. Drab. Gray." Lilly chuckled.

Kingslea forced a smile. Fiona was a study in contrasts. Black hair. White skin.

"I was really quite amazed when I learned it was the other one struck down. Twins, you know. Nothing alike." Lilly whispered her secret. "The other was well-liked, but this one...I remember the other girls talking about her. The teachers held her up as the model of proper behavior." Lilly clucked her tongue. "What would the girls say—Finicky Fiona dancing with a divorced man? Imagine the scandal that would cause."

"I believe your marriage was annulled."

"Yes. Yes." Lilly waved away his words. "Fiona Grey. All that money could explain the duke's willingness to overlook her unfortunate parentage. After all, his little hobby is quite expensive."

The Duke of August needed money? How the devil did one spend half a million pounds in five years? But Lilly would know—she had been the man's wife.

"I was under the impression there was a tidy profit to be made from ransacking the tombs of the dead."

"That's what he tells everyone." Lilly peered up at him. "Father says his boastful nature is due to his title."

"Indeed."

"Not that you suffer from the same affliction." She patted his arm again. "Father thinks that being the second son spared you the burden."

"Undoubtedly." Then again, Lilly might not know anything her father hadn't told her.

"Come, I haven't insulted you. Pray tell me I haven't." She rested her forehead against his chin. "I meant that as the sincerest compliment. Father certainly takes your interest in business as proof of your superiority." Lilly eased away. Her brown eyes pleaded with his. "Father says you're almost American. That is the highest compliment he has ever given any of my suitors."

"A high compliment to anyone except a peer of the British Empire."

"Father doesn't hold your noble blood against you. He says you have earned your own nobility." Her gaze drifted across the crowd. "Wealthy American men are made according to Darwin's rules. Only the fittest survive. Father said that your investments have proven quite..." Lilly cleared her throat and turned her attention back to him. "Forgive me, my lord. I forgot that one isn't to speak of business."

"No, indeed. I am quite eager to discover your father's opinion." His sarcasm fell short of its mark.

"Father has taken it upon himself to guide me. He wasn't at all approving of the duke."

"Yet you married him."

"Mama had convinced him I was set on marrying a duke, but we both know my heart was given to another." Tears shimmered in her eyes.

The cynic seized Kingslea's thoughts. Mayhap Lilly refused to cry because she possessed only one set of tears.

"Do we?"

The moisture evaporated.

"It seems the duke isn't the only one interested in poor Miss Grey."

"As you've noted, American heiress seem to be in short supply this season. I am certain there are quite a few who could use the infusion of...new blood."

"The English have such a quaint manner of phrasing unpalatable topics." Lilly's glare targeted Fiona. "Perhaps I should renew an old acquaintance."

Fiona and Lilly. Friends. His mind batted aside the notion. Any disagreement would gird Lilly's determination.

"Perhaps you should."

Her gaze raked his face. "Forgive me, my lord, if I bored you with the details of my past."

Her past was dangerous territory. And Fiona's was...

Focus. Lilly might yet reveal a motive for Sullied's interest in the Greys.

"It is your future that interests me." The lie was tart on Kingslea's tongue.

A blush bloomed in Lilly's cheeks. "I was proper like her once, you know. Of course you know—you were with me. Had I not been so proper we would be happy now. And this scandal wouldn't have fallen on both our names."

His gaze slipped across the bobbing heads and settled on Fiona.

"Perhaps I should warn her of the duke's interest."

"It is only a dance."

"Yes, only a dance." Lilly sighed. "Every time you used to pencil your name in next to a dance, I knew we would be sitting out. We were quite cozy behind..." Her gaze flew across the room. She impaled the greenery before glaring at him. "The very corner where I found you."

Anger hummed, vibrated the feathers on her dress. Kingslea tensed. If memory served, she became very unreasonable when irate.

"There are many such places here," he hedged.

"Oh, I am quite certain. For an entire Season you always led me to the corner farthest from the stairway. I—" She gasped. Anger, like clown's rouge, dotted her cheeks. "I thought for certain it was a sign of your forgiveness."

"Did you expect we could pick up where we left off?" He stopped two beats ahead of the music.

"Well, certainly not where we left off. Some things have changed." She nodded to a couple strolling past then crammed her hand between his arm and side. He slowed her march to a discreet saunter. "I am not the foolish, naive, proper miss that I was. Time has been a cruel teacher, but I have proven an apt pupil." Rage glittered in her eyes.

"I believe we had the same teacher."

"I know exactly what I want, my lord." She smiled at him. "And this time, I won't allow anyone to block my path." With that, Lilly picked up her train and stormed away.

Kingslea adjusted his sleeves. Had she just threatened him? She had no hold over him. Their little dance had proven that.

Unless...unless, her father was collecting the marchioness's IOUs. A clever means to acquiring a title without a large dowry.

Yet, Lilly already possessed a title.

Through marriage. A marriage she had dissolved. And Dear Father Lawson doted on his daughter. But what connected them to the Greys? He knew of only one way to discover it.

He would have to charm his way back into Lilly's favor.

CHAPTER 17

— I say, Fi. *Milton charged through the door and halted at the foot of the* brass bedstead. *Ever since my banishment to the nothingness, I haven't near the fondness for walking through walls I once possessed.* Dark gray blindfolded his eyes.

"I'm dressed, Milton." Fiona tightened the velvet sash of her blue dressing gown. Why did he bother covering his eyes? If she could see through his entire being, certainly he could see though his fingers.

His hand dropped to his side.

— Have you no sympathy at all for my plight? Food has no taste, cigar smoke possesses more substance, and horses...Well, they only like the dead safely nailed in coffins. He crossed his arms over his chest. *Walking through walls is one of the few benefits of being deceased.*

Fiona tossed the last hairpin onto her dressing table. It pinged against the marble top before rolling to a halt next to the mirror. Jet hair tumbled down her back. Pain needled her scalp.

"Don't the rats keep you company?"

— Rats? He darted to the bed. Legs tucked under his body, he glared at the walls.

"Can't you hear them scrambling around at night, scratching at the walls, biting and fighting each other as vermin do?" Metal cooled her palm. Fiona slid her brush across the vanity. Bristles scratched the top.

Milton's eyes widened; he clasped his legs to his chest, hovering a good foot above the mattress.

Poor Milton. Death hadn't killed his fear of rats. Guilt trampled her amusement. She was usually more understanding.

"That was my brush scratching, not a pack of ravenous rodents." Fiona dragged the brush across her scalp. Pleasure crackled across her brain as the brush stroked electricity from her long locks. Her eyes drifted closed. Tension released her shoulders.

— *You've a rather uncivil temperament, this evening,* Milton huffed. *I did warn you not to go with him, didn't I?*

Fiona's eyes opened with her shaky exhale. With his hands cradling his head and his ankles crossed, Milton relaxed above her coverlet. Of course, her dearly departed's omniscience didn't usually accompany throbbing feet, pulsing ribs or a pounding head.

"What would you have me do?" Twenty-one. Twenty-two. Warmth teased her shoulder before jerking away. One hundred brush strokes. An eternity. "Run shrieking across the dance floor?"

— *Certainly, Piers has elicited a similar response from many a maiden.* Milton rolled onto his side. His fingers eased over the chiffon flounce of her discarded dress. *You were certainly very fetching this evening. I am glad your mother insisted no mourning colors in your new wardrobe.*

Thirty-nine. New wardrobe. Forty. Throbbing feet. Forty-one. Pulsing ribs. Forty-two. Her new wardrobe didn't fit. Had her measurements changed? Wouldn't her old clothes pinch if they had? Her hand stilled. Bristles quivered in expectation.

"Do you think I embarrassed them tonight?"

— *Embarrassed? Them?* Milton blinked and sat up. Red swirled within his darkening frame. *They are embarrassment personified.*

"I don't think I fit my clothes." Her brush clattered to the vanity, punctuating her worst fear. She knew something had been different since her bow three years ago. At first, she'd attributed it to the passage of time, but now doubt gnawed at her. Trembling fingers slipped between rattling china bottles before tugging a silk ribbon from under a jar of hand cream.

— *Not fit? I was positively damp with the drool engendered by your finery.*

"You mistake my meaning." Fiona gathered her wayward tresses. The jagged tips brushed her thigh. Hair tickled her hand, drew her scalp into tiny pyramids. The ribbon slipped along the ponytail before gliding to a stop at the base of her skull.

— *There was bound to be a period of adjustment, Fi.* Milton stationed himself near her shoulder and peered at his smudged reflection. *After all, they are foreigners.*

"This is England, Milton." The cut glass stopper bit into her fingers. "They are English."

— *Precisely.*

Lavender toilet water splashed into her palm.

"There was no awkwardness the last time." Faceless admirers swam from the depths of memory. They had swarmed around her and her sisters like bees in a flower garden.

"Much has changed since last time."

Fiona's reflection scowled at her. When had that started? Certainly, balancing the accounts could be vexing but scowling...

"You mean *I've* changed."

— *No. I mean many things have changed. You forget, I died later that year. Brianna fell ill and is now almost fully recovered.* Milton stroked his chin. *You're still the same. Obedient. Dutiful. Graceful. You sailed halfway around the world to help your parents, didn't you? How many daughters would forgo the bustle of society to assist her uncle in England?*

Fiona busied herself with her knotted sash. Forgo society. She had never thought to enter it this season. As for her parents, they needed to help Brianna. It was why she had kept the telegram a secret. To protect her family. Deception tainted her noble ambition. She straightened the cut glass bottles on her dressing table tray.

Had she another reason for sailing to London?

— *Come, now, tell Milton what is really bothering you.* He patted the bed. *It's that Kingston fellow, isn't it?*

"Kingslea." The earl's visage grinned at her from another's embrace. The rug bubbled as Fiona shoved her chair back. Not that she gave a fig if he carried on a flirtation with the whole of London. She flopped onto the bed. Her concern lay with finding her aunt and uncle. "I don't see what *he* has to do with anything."

— *Of course not.* Milton's smoky index finger jumped from one square of the single Irish Chain quilt to the next. *I must admit to a bit of envy myself. To hold a lady that close, feel her skirt brush your thigh like a lover's touch...* A deep sigh blew him onto his back. *Any woman could get the blood pumping, but a lady, especially one as breathtaking as she is...*

Breathtaking? Obviously, death had effected the man's taste in ladies. That strumpet was too flashy by half. Fists pushed Fiona onto her side.

"You don't have any blood, Milton. Nor breath for her or any other *ordinary*-looking woman to steal."

But Hugh did.

Hugh also possessed a crooked smile, a perfectly centered cleft in his chin and strong hands. Not to mention an inclination to flirtation. Hair twisted around her index finger. A man wasn't that polished unless he practiced. Frequently. Fiona swallowed the bitterness invading her mouth.

— *Ordinary,* Milton scoffed. *Cascading honey hair, flashing brown eyes and an island of golden skin.* He stroked Fiona's quilt, flicked the white yarn tying down the squares.

Annoyance shimmered through her. The man's fondling of her coverlet was becoming an obsession.

"Hair. Eyes. Skin. Most ladies possess them."

— *Right.* He sighed, caught her eye then cleared his throat. *Quite...ordinary.*

"I would have had a better time searching for my uncle's journal."

— *I bet Kingston wouldn't.* Milton smiled.

"Milton."

— *Don't worry, Fi.* He winked at her. *Her family probably bundled her off in a carriage, too. I doubt the plaster on these walls clings as deliciously, er, I mean, closely. Scandalous, really.*

"My aunt's behavior or that woman's?"

— *Um, your aunt's, naturally.* Milton adjusted his cuffs. *I wonder how long they had that cab waiting. Piers didn't even let you collect your cape before shoving you inside and slamming the door behind you.*

"They even made me pay the fare." Embarrassment scalded Fiona's cheeks. She'd seen garbage chucked out of the house with more tenderness. Perhaps her humiliating exit was her cousin's revenge for this morning's tussle. Pain lightninged across her skull as she touched her bruised forehead.

— *I'd bet a monkey Edwina wears your cloak home.* His eyes twinkled. *What do you say, Fi?*

"I'm not in the mood to lose."

— *Just as well. Money's not much use to me now.*

Fiona dragged a pillow under her head. Feathers poked her cheek, crackled in her ear.

"Did you learn anything useful tonight?"

— *Eh?* Milton stared at the spirit washing her face at Fiona's washstand.

"Milton." She prayed her whisper reached only Milton's ear.

— *I found your future husband, didn't I? Tell me, what do you think of that August fellow. He's a duke, you know. Apparently, they're a rather rare breed, especially the unmarried ones.*

Fiona rolled onto her back. Lush white pineapples streaked her ceiling. Her aunt's choice of ceiling decoration was a safer topic than her opinion of the duke. "I was referring to my aunt and uncle."

— *Old news, my dear.* Milton stretched out beside her. *Today's juicy* on dit *concerned a scandalous lover's triangle. It seems that a certain American miss was wildly in love with an English lord, though heaven knows why, and—*

"And that has nothing to do with my aunt and uncle's disappearance."

— *I thought I was being extremely helpful.*

"I know, Milton. I know." Fiona forced a yawn. "I believe I should retire now. It has been an exhausting day."

— *You can't fool me, Fi.* He sat up, his hands resting on his hips. *You plan to sit there and brood.*

"I am not a hen sitting on a clutch of eggs, Milton." Fiona tossed her pillow. It sailed clear through him. "It is called sleep. Mortals do it. Once you're dead, I suppose you have no need of it."

— *My dear Fi, resting in peace is highly overrated.* He kicked ineffectively at the pillow. *Besides, when all of eternity is before you, why not enjoy it?*

Fiona yanked down her blankets. Cool air wafted over her cheeks.

"Kindly refrain from enjoying it in the children's, servants' or Uncle Heberon's presence." Her slippers thumped to the floor.

— *They're all asleep anyway.* Milton drifted over to the mirror. *You never did answer my question about the duke.*

"Didn't I?" A shudder rattled up her frame. The sheets were cold and damp. Embers glowed in her fireplace. Another inconvenience of her early return. Maybe she should have Milton ice her aunt's bed.

— *You know perfectly well that you did not.* He smoothed his hair and adjusted his tie. *What did you think of him, Fi?*

What did she think? Sullied was not Hugh.

"He danced tolerably well."

Milton spun on his heel.

— *Danced tolerably well? That's it? Not dashingly handsome, plump of purse, or a veritable fountain of conversational wit?* He dragged his hand through his hair. *For heaven's sake, Fi, both of you are considerably interested in the dead.*

"He desecrates tombs!"

— *Yes, well, he turns a tidy profit.*

"Are you offering me compensation for our conversation, Milton?" After turning off the gas to the wall lamps, Fiona retrieved her pillow from the end of the bed and slapped it into place. She had nothing in common with the arrogant aristocrat.

— *No, of course not.*

"Helping the departed cut the ties binding them to the earthly plane is not the same as raiding their graves and pilfering their things." She smashed a second pillow on top of the first.

— *I am beginning to think you don't want my help in finding a husband.* Red swirled in his gray.

"Milton." Flesh slipped under her fingers as they circled her temples. "I need your help to find Uncle Andrew and Aunt Caroline."

— *And the other?*

"Please, Milton." Fiona slid her crossed fingers under her knees. Please God, let her vague answer pacify his pride.

— *All right.*

Unease twitched through Fiona. Pink still tinged his form. Pink meant anger, and anger fueled the ability to shatter statues, twist sheets and create mayhem.

"What are you going to do?"

— *I'm going downstairs.* His sigh restored his normal color. *There is a gathering of old souls. They promised music.* He waved his hand. *Probably some dead medieval minstrel plucking a lute or a lyre. Definitely no waltzing.*

"Maybe you could teach them."

— *Perhaps.* He tapped his chin. *There is a lady who died quite tragically. She might find comfort in learning something new. The dead seem to stagnate.*

"I'm positive waltzing is just the thing."

— *Do you wish me to remain, Fi?* His gaze washed over her. *I will stay if you wish it.*

"No, Milton." Fiona turned down the lamp on her nightstand, leaving a pleasant glow in the dark room. "Go, please. Enjoy your eternity."

— *You're not going to sulk, are you, Fi? I'm certain that woman was nothing more than a passing fancy.*

That woman. Fiona suppressed the memory, punched the lumps out of her pillow and closed her eyes.

"Goodnight, Milton."

— *Goodnight, Fi.* He stepped through the door.

"Oh, what's the use."

One hundred and fifty pineapples striped her ceiling. Three hundred twenty-one fleecy ewes had leapt over the fence in her mind. Sleep hadn't dogged the heels of monotony.

Fiona shoved aside her blankets and kicked her legs free. The wool rug sucked at her feet. Cold air swirled around her ankles.

"I may as well make some progress toward finding answers."

Sulfur stung her nose as she struck a match. Glass scratched metal as she lifted the globe from the gas sconce. The teardrop flame dipped at the end of the matchstick.

"No point in waking the rest of the house." The fire died with a soft whoosh. "Where should I start?"

Her gaze swept the room, easily distinguishing the ripe edges of the washstand, the sturdy angles of the wardrobe and the dainty curves of the dressing table. Her ghostly reflection wavered in the mirror.

"You might stop talking to yourself."

Her uncle's rooms seemed the most logical place. Chilled wood slicked across her bare feet as she padded across the room. The glass knob molded her palm as she eased into the hall. Blue buttons glowed at the top of the gas jets. Her hand hovered near the globe. It would serve her aunt right to return to a dark house.

Except that the servants would pay for Fiona's mischief. Her fingertips drummed her nightgown. Disappointment weighted her heart. There would be other opportunities for revenge. She tiptoed past Aunt Caroline's bedroom.

Aunt Annabelle slept in there now.

Outrage battered Fiona's bones. It didn't matter. Aunt Caroline always slept with Uncle Andrew. She pushed open her uncle's bedroom door.

Tobacco, cinnamon and sandalwood complimented the softness of roses. Memories stormed her—fairytales at bedtime, picnics on the lawn and music composed of laughter.

They couldn't be dead. They just couldn't.

Her knees wobbled then buckled. The impact with the floor rattled out her skull. Teeth sank into the fleshy part of her hand, a poor imitation of the pain shredding her insides. Keening scratched her throat. Hot tears scalded her cheeks. Her spine bumped against the door. Ten. Twenty. Thirty times. Anger bundled the grief. Useless grief.

She dried her nose on her sleeve. Tears dampened the back of her hand. Emotional turbulence had controlled her since she set foot on English soil.

Fiona clawed up the door and swayed on her feet.

"I would know if they were dead." A deep breath cleansed the doubt from her lungs. "I would know. And I don't." She padded to the bed. "So, they can't be dead."

The Persian rug muffled her footsteps. The cuff of her aunt's dressing gown nestled in her palm. A framed daguerreotype stared across the green-and-blue coverlet at her.

"I will find you." Her palms bumped over her hips. The dampness made patches of cotton translucent. "But first, I need that journal. Where have you hidden it?"

The sepia likenesses remained mute.

"Right. Methodical and thorough, as Da would say." Fiona turned to her right, lit the wall sconce and started her search.

The painting of the storm-tossed clipper ship hid seamless green wallpaper. Her cheeks heated at the stacks of unmentionables filling the drawers of the wardrobe. Crisp sheets of vellum filled the drawers of the desk. Uncle Andrew's mahogany pipe rested atop Aunt Caroline's rose-embroidered tidy.

Thirty minutes later, Fiona dropped onto the bed.

"Look on the bright side, Fi. Now you know they *can't* be dead. Your prayers would have certainly conveyed them into this world."

Fatigue weighted her limbs. Her eyes drifted closed. Her fingers closed around the velvet collar of her uncle's smoking jacket. She snuggled under the garment's flaccid embrace. The scent of his special tobacco and soap filled her lungs.

Creak.

Adrenaline gushed through her. Her heart stilled in her breast. Someone was in the hall. A sliver of the room appeared in the spaces between her eyelashes. The doorknob turned.

Run. Hide. Indecision locked her body in place. Now she knew how spiders felt when she lit the lamp.

The door eased open.

"Caro? Andy?" Uncle Heberon's whisper preceded his slouched form.

"Uncle Heberon?" The name creaked through her tight throat.

"Oh, hello, Fi. I thought Caro had returned." His slippered feet tiptoed across the carpet. The bed dipped as he took a seat next to her. "Caro tells the best stories. I've been writing them down." Spidery words crawled across the papers he shuffled in his ink-stained hands. "She tells them to me, and I tell them to Melody and Cedric. My sister never runs out of daring tales. She's been telling them ever since I can remember." Brown eyes blinked at Fiona. "Do you know any stories?"

"I know a few."

Uncle Heberon's shoulders drooped. "Andy knows only a few as well." He folded the papers and stuffed them into his pocket. "He met real pirates once. He said they exchanged cannon fire, and when they boarded…" His bounce undulated across the bed. "Well, Caro made him change the ending. He's told it four times, and every time it ends differently."

"Those are the best kinds of stories." Fiona tossed her ponytail over her shoulder.

"Yeah. He tells me stories when Caro needs to rest." Uncle Heberon's forehead creased. "Did you have a bad dream? I can read you Caro's story." His fingers slipped into his pocket.

"I was almost asleep when you came in."

"Oh." His shoulders drooped.

"Perhaps I could hear it tomorrow night when you read it to Cedric and Melody."

A smile brightened his face. "Yes. That would be fun." He shuffled the papers again. His eyes skipped over the pages. "I guess it's not fair for you to hear it first."

"I wouldn't want to accidentally reveal the ending."

Paper crinkled as he molded the pages to his chest.

"No. No, that wouldn't be very nice at all." He slid the papers into his pocket and compacted them with his fist. "After the accident, I slept in here. I prayed every night, just like Caro taught me, for them to return. And you know what?" he whispered, leaning closer to her.

"What?"

"They returned on the third night."

Fiona plucked at the wrinkle in the coverlet. Uncle Heberon's explanation made sense. Hadn't Milton returned at the behest of her own prayers? So, why hadn't they visited *her*?

"Do they appear every time you pray?"

"No. I didn't pray tonight, and they came."

"They were here?" Shock and suspicion rippled through her. Milton hadn't said anything about meeting her aunt and uncle. Was he punishing her for the rejection of his self-appointed replacement?

"Tonight?"

"Yes, they were sorry they missed you but hoped you had a good time." He scrunched up his face. "Did you, Fi? Did you have a nice time?"

A nice time? Hugh stepped onto the stage of her thoughts. A dancing, laughing and entertaining Hugh. Yes, she had enjoyed herself until...

Dark clouds blotted out his face, sucked the warmth from the memories. Until that woman appeared.

"Yes, Uncle."

"You're home awfully early." Distrust bubbled the flesh between his eyebrows. "Surely you did not lack for partners. Caro had many partners before she married Andy. She would come home and tell me story after story about her suitors."

"My dance card was full," Fiona answered truthfully. Filled by one man. The same man who filled her thoughts.

"Then why did you return so soon?" Uncle Heberon crossed his arms over his chest. "Caro never returned until daybreak."

"Aunt Annabelle thought I was having too much fun." The truth sounded acid to Fiona's ears. "She had Piers stuff me in a hack and ordered the driver to ferry me home."

"Probably no one would look at that horse-faced Edwina with you around." Uncle Heberon grabbed the pillow and hugged it close. "I would have danced with you."

"You would have been my most dashing partner."

A blush seeped down his neck. Fiona slipped her hand in his. His callused touch was reassuring. Envy twitched through her. Uncle Heberon's world was in black and white, whereas the shadows had completely obliterated the contrast in hers.

Responsibility pressed against her.

"Uncle, the next time you see Uncle Andrew, do you think you could ask him where he keeps his journal? It is a most vexing dilemma. I have searched the whole room and have yet to discover it."

"I did ask, Fi." Uncle Heberon scooted closer to her. "I remembered what Gibson had said at breakfast, so I asked." Pride glowed in his eyes.

"That was very clever of you, Uncle. I had quite forgotten Gibson's advice." Adrenaline quickened the tempo of her heart. "And did Uncle Andrew tell you where the journal was?"

Heberon's head bobbed. "If you remove the bottom left drawer from his desk and lift the drawer guide, you'll find the journal in a secret compartment."

"Which desk?" Fiona glared at the writing desk shoved into the corner of the room. Those spindly legs could hold no secret compartment.

"The one in his library."

Of course—the library. How silly of her not to think of it before.

"Thanks, Uncle."

His stubbled cheek scratched her lips.

"Andy says he doesn't think it will be of much use but that you might as well have a peek."

Fiona slid off the bed. "That was very kind of him."

"Fi." Uncle Heberon slid off the bed, too, wrapping his hands around the belt of his robe. His slippered toe traced the anchor design woven into the carpet.

"What is it, Uncle?"

"Caro asked that you look at something for her. She thinks it might be involved somehow. Andy doesn't think it worth sinking a ship, but..."

Could it be the duke's bauble? Fiona forced air in and out of her lungs.

"What is it?"

"A necklace they found."

Victory danced beyond her grasp. Uncle Andrew could be correct. Coincidence might be the only link between the ship's sinking and the jewelry.

"Was it with anything?"

"It was buried in a dead man. He was wrapped like a present," Uncle Heberon shuffled towards the door. "Though why anyone would want a pile of moldy bones—"

A wrapped dead man. Hugh would certainly be interested in this turn of events. She would send a message round to him tomorrow.

"You mean a mummy?" Fiona blew out the light next to the dressing table.

"No, Fi." Heberon opened the door. "Not a mummy, it was a man."

Fiona cleared her throat. "Where is the necklace now?"

"Andy said it would be next to the journal."

"Thanks, Uncle." Turning off the gas, she blew out the last light.

"Will you retrieve them tonight?"

"I thought..." Wheels creaked. Muffled voices slipped rose from below. Aunt Annabelle had returned.

"Aunt Annabelle." Uncle Heberon's eyes widened. "She gets very cross if I stay up late."

"She won't find out." Fiona eased the door shut and tiptoed down the hall. Heberon slouched by her side.

"Are you certain?" He eased open his door and slipped inside.

"Just climb into bed and close your eyes. She'll believe you're asleep."

"'Night, Fi."

"Goodnight, Uncle." Fiona waited outside his door. The rustling of cloth stopped at twenty-two sheep. Whining drifted up the staircase.

Poor Gibson. Listening to her aunt's diatribe in the middle of the night. As soon as Uncle Andrew and Aunt Caroline returned, she would request they give him a week off to recover.

Satisfied, she turned on her heel and tiptoed to her room. Easing the door shut, she sighed. Not that she cared if her aunt found her out of bed. She tossed her dressing gown across the foot of the bed. She simply didn't want to disturb the rest of the household.

After turning off the wall sconces, Fiona reached for her blanket. Her shaking hand hovered at the edge of her coverlet.

Someone had been in her room.

Someone had made her bed.

Her gaze darted around the room before she dropped to her knees and checked under the bed. No one was here now. She dragged herself to her feet. A white square of paper stared at her from the center of her pillow.

Fear buzzed inside her skull, dried her mouth. *It's just a piece of paper, Fi.* She swallowed hard. *Paper can't hurt you.* She poked the folds open as if expecting it would snap at her. Waves of black ink flowed across the paper. She blinked, and the words came into focus.

Death is the reward of the curious.

CHAPTER 18

Fiona sat up in bed. The sheet cascaded down her heaving chest. Cold air snatched the sleep from her body. Her heart fluttered against her breast while her breath rasped in her ear.

What had so violently rousted her from sweet slumber's embrace?

Possibilities careened inside her skull, only to be dismissed more quickly than unfit suitors. She peered into the darkness. Fatigue burned her eyes and spilled lassitude in her limbs. Shadows stagnated in the corners.

"Milton." Her hoarse whisper scratched free of her tight throat and disappeared into the darkness. She cleared her throat. "Milll-ton."

The night answered with silence. Panic cracked her control. If Milton hadn't woken her then who…? The servants?

Her gaze drifted to the window. Rivulets snaked down the pane while the London Particular wrapped the house tighter than spun sugar around a cone. She shook her head. The servants wouldn't be awake yet.

Her aunt, then, or perhaps Piers. Had they tried her door again and found it locked?

Fiona's gaze darted to the black face of the Louis XIV clock. Indecision paralyzed her. If she struck a match, they would know she was awake. Yet if she remained in the dark, she would also remain ignorant of the time.

The grandfather clock tolled four times. Each bong resonated through the house, a perfect imitation of a monk's funerary chant.

"Hardly an appropriate thought, Fi." She wrapped her arms around her chest, stopped the trembling from shaking her apart.

Four a.m. Much too late for her aunt or her cousins to be prowling the house.

Then who?

The anonymous writer? Had he returned to fulfill his threat?

Anger crashed through the numbing fear. She was not as helpless as others of her class, but her strength did not rival a man's. Fiona raked the key off her nightstand. The note crinkled in her palm.

"It couldn't be the threat's author, Fi. How could he slip past Uncle Andrew's guards?"

Logic relaxed her knotted shoulders. Where had the guards been earlier? Granted, the fog might keep even the most diligent guard in ignorance, but to brazen an entry twice. Unless...

Cold pricked the back of her neck.

Unless he had never departed.

Uncle Andrew's journal.

"Botheration." Oh, why had Aunt Annabelle returned so precipitously? To ruin Fiona's evening, naturally. Her aunt's lifelong alliance with mischief would not be abandoned even for the ball of the season.

"Screw your courage to the sticking point, Fi. You must retrieve that journal." Her limbs remained uncooperative. "Everyone depends upon you."

Her legs twitched. She shoved aside the warm blankets and scooted to the edge of the bed. The thick carpet squished against her toes. She balanced her weight on the balls of her feet then stepped forward.

Skeletal fingers slid up her foot and closed around her ankle. She kicked at the restraint, overbalanced and toppled forward with a scream trapped in her throat. Pain rattled from the epicenter of her elbows. Sweet metal exploded in her mouth. She flopped onto her back, slashed the air with the teeth of the key. Her foot thumped against the side of the bed. Her captor clawed at her free foot while tightening his hold. She kicked air, swung her leg back and bashed her heel against the floor

Where was he? Hiding under the bed?

"Coward," she spat. Adrenaline pumped strength into her thin arms. She jerked upright, wrapped them around her captured leg and threw her body backwards.

Shades of gray swirled together as she tumbled heels over head across the carpet. Something rapped her skull. Stars blinked in her vision.

Free. She was free. Yet, her leg was still caught. Had she yanked his arm from the socket? Good—then she had a weapon she could beat him with. She plucked at the fingers. They sawed back and forth across her ankle.

Fiona froze. No moans of agony. No puddles of blood. She traced the fingers to their source.

"How perfectly delicious, Fi. You've been snared by your own whip."

Nimble fingers loosened the leather strap.

"Good thing Milton didn't witnessed your battle." She grasped the whip and crawled to her bed. "He would never stop laughing."

Exhaustion shoved aside the waning adrenaline. She clawed onto the top of her bed, plopped her weapon on the spare pillow and dragged her blankets around her shoulders.

"Look on the bright side, Fi. The journal is safe."

The feather pillow cupped her head. Her eyes drift closed.

"Your whip can't read." Her giggle warmed her pillow.

Thump.

Bump.

Thud.

"Jesus, Mary and Joseph." Gran's favorite curse filled Fiona's mouth. Her fingers closed around whip, key and note.

"Milton?" She tossed aside her blankets and toed into her slippers. Sulfur stung her nose as she struck a match and touched it to the lamp's wick. "Death certainly hasn't improved your hearing. Keep it down, I said. Have a little compassion for the living."

Shoulders drooping, she pushed aside the blankets and slipped out of bed. Cold damp air swirled around her ankles. Warm smooth cotton nightgown lapped at her heels.

"Rest in peace." Her snort tossed the candlelight around the room. "Undoubtedly, the benediction would be better served carved on his forehead than his tombstone."

Metal scraped as she unlocked her door. The hinges protested the disturbance.

"This had better not became a nightly ritual, Milton. England may be Protestant, but I'm certain I can find a Catholic Priest somewhere."

Milton and Hugh. Living or dead, men were nothing but a bother. The whip thumped against her nightdress as she shuffled down the hall. The banister cut into her belly as she peered into the stairwell. Green light spilled from the ballroom.

Did she really wish to disturb them? Did she really want them to discover her abilities?

"I most certainly do not. Let them enjoy their dance. I seem to be the only one disturbed by it."

Fiona turned to go then stopped. Golden light stretched across the marble entrance hall. The spirits were not the only ones up to mischief this evening.

Could it be the missing guards? She had not told them about the note. They needed to know.

Fiona winced as the second stair creaked. The fourth answered. A shadow blocked a patch of light escaping from under the door.

What if it weren't the guards in the library?

Uncle Andrew's journal was. Unless the intruder had found it. She had to protect that book. The answer to the mystery lay in its pages.

She padded across the first-floor landing and paused at the top of the stairs. There were the stilted tones of a medieval accent mixed with a touch of French, while Milton's voice competed in volume with a jumble of Latin.

Should she disturb their dance? Enlist their help?

Her hands slipped over the glossy newel post. If the library's occupant proved to be the guards, she would have four—no, five—more shades to plague her. And if it wasn't then one scream would bring Milton to her assistance.

A puff of breath extinguished her lamp. The carpet runner muffled her footfalls. She padded across the landing and pressed her ear to the door. The smooth wood echoed her breathing. The light was gone. Had her visitor departed with it? She wouldn't know until she opened the door.

Fiona set the lamp on the hall table and clasped the glass knob. The latch eased back with a snick. The door eased open on well-oiled hinges. Thank Heavens Gibson ran his staff efficiently.

She slipped inside and slid the door closed.

The open window framed a man's wiry silhouette. She crept forward. Her lariat quivered as she slackened her grip. Closer. Just a little closer, and she would have him. She cleared the hulking shape of the couch. Two more steps.

Her toe popped as it collided with the claw-foot of the end table. She swallowed her cry and stopped. Her lungs burned from the stagnant air. *Please, God. Don't let him have heard.*

The man paused then dove through the window. Bushes rustled. Fog seeped inside the room like wisps of smoke.

She had lost him. Disappointment whimpered against her locked teeth.

Another shadow moved to the window.

Two. There had been two intruders. Buzzing filled her ears. She skated across the carpet, avoiding other hazards. What if there were more? Her lariat could handle one but two or three? Why hadn't she brought Da's gun?

She turned the rope's end in her hand. Round, like the barrel of a gun. It just might work. Besides, help was only a scream away. She closed the space between them and pressed the tip of the rope into his back.

"Cease your struggles, or you'll meet your maker with a few perforations He hadn't designed."

CHAPTER 19

Kingslea froze, locking his grip. Something round and hard pressed against his back. *A gun*, his brain crackled at the connection of word and sensation. A gun made messy holes in one's skin. He jerked forward. Curses fouled his mouth. The windowsill cut into his belly, hindering his breathing.

The fabric in his fist jerked taut, twisted then flattened. His body spasmed with each contortion.

"Hold still, I say."

Pressure increased against his spine while frenzy tainted his captive's movement. Seams popped. Fog blotted his face like wet cotton. Bones ground together as he reeled in the miscreant with his own coat tails. *Steady, old man. A few more turns of the wrist, and Fiona will have her answers.*

His arms burned. The coat slackened then jerked taunt. Fabric ripped. Empty sleeves slapped the side of the townhouse.

The London Particular swallowed the man and his identity. Frustration whistled through his teeth. His gaze traveled towards the invisible heavens. Three more minutes, and Fiona would have no reason to endure Sullied's attentions.

He braced his arms next to his torso. Damp wood sucked at his palms.

"Bloody Hell."

"I hardly see the need for profanity, sir."

I hardly see the need...

Muscles bunched, strained the sleeves of his evening jacket. Sarcasm wrapped in a proper package. Awareness pumped through him. Fiona. Her dress brushed the back of his thighs as her scent of gardenias teased his nose. The woman had made a mockery of his plans. Again.

"Well, I certainly do." He pushed against the sill and stepped back into the room.

"Slowly. Don't make any sudden moves. And...and put your hands up. Where I can see them." Her voice trembled.

Hugh froze as the pressure returned to his spine. She was afraid of him. Was it possible she didn't know who he was? How could that be?

"This gun has a hair trigger. If...if I am startled, it will go off." Her breath came in fast gasps. "At this range, a blind man with a peg leg couldn't miss."

Blind, he could understand, but peg-legged? Hugh shook his head. He would sort out her confusing threats later. Now, he intended to collect a little interest on the trouble she had wrought—ruining his plans at the dock, helping the thief to escape and cheerfully allowing another man's embrace.

"Put your hands up."

Hugh dropped the jacket and obeyed. He would allow her to keep her illusions of control for the moment. If he remember correctly, the desk was at the farthest end of the library. There were three chairs, two couches and at least six toe-mashing tables on this side. Not to mention countless knick-knacks, books and plants.

"Did you and your larcenous cohort find the book?"

Now what was she blathering on about? Book? They were in a room filled with bloody books. That was the problem. There wasn't a soft spot for her to land and the couches were too far away.

"Answer me." She prodded him with the muzzle of her pistol.

"Dunno," he ground out. "We was interrupted, like."

His boot traced the carpet. Blessed are those with money to spend on thick carpets and a platoon of fat pillows. Not a bad landing, provided her pistol didn't discharge. He shifted his weight onto the ball of his foot.

"Who do you work for?" She emphasized each word with a jab.

Look on the bright side, old boy, at least you know where the gun is.

"You."

Kingslea pivoted about, captured her wrist and aimed the barrel of the gun at the fireplace. His free hand wrapped around her waist, flattening her against him as he hurled his weight backwards. Air whooshed out of his lungs upon impact. Nausea squeezed his stomach.

The corner of the pillow jabbed his cheek.

Damnation. He had misjudged the distance. Just as he had erred in his assessment of his opponent. Fiona wiggled in his grasp like a hooked worm. Pain racketed up his leg as her heel struck his shin.

"Let me go. Let me go, I say." Fingernails raked the back of his hand.

Pride sauntered into his muddled mind. Any other woman would have surrendered to hysterics but not his Fiona. His fingers manacled her free wrist and dragged it away from the gun. His knuckles rapped on the carpet. The impact shook the pistol free from her grasp.

"Be still, woman, or you'll do yourself an injury."

"You're the only one in harm's way."

Stars exploded in front of his eyes as the back of her skull collided with his nose. Warmth trickled down his cheeks. The tang of metal teased his palette. In the instant his hold relaxed, she rolled away and clambered to her feet.

"Fiona!"

"Stay away from me."

She darted toward the door, her white dress billowing behind her like angel's wings. Nausea fomented distrust in his stomach. Bile burned his tongue as he staggered to his feet and half jumped, half fell over the couch. His body groaned at the abuse, but at least he reached the door just as she did. His shoulder exploded with heat upon collision with the door.

"It's me, Fiona."

"I know who you are." She yanked on the immovable door before ramming her elbow into his gut.

Any other time and he might have enjoyed her fire. Any other time his lungs wouldn't be burning from missed breaths, and his bones wouldn't be bruised from her foul temper. He spun her about, pinned her hands between her lush breasts and sandwiched her between his length and the door.

"You're a lying, thieving bas—"

"Uh-huh." He rested his index finger against her supple lips. "Is that any way to talk about your partner?"

"You are no partner of mine, sirrah." She straightened in his hold.

Frustration rattled his composure. Could she really not recognize him?

"It's Hugh, Fiona." Tension remained coiled in her body. He tried again. "You remember—the Earl of Kingslea? We sat not more than six hours ago in the Saunders' ballroom and—"

"I know *what* you are." She growled and jerked her body to the right. Her eyes glittered in the darkened room.

Unease slithered in his belly. Was he really the cold fiend everyone painted him? Letting his pride egg him into a tussle, a tussle that had unhinged her delicate feminine mind.

"What I am is—"

"A lying, thieving ba—"

"Miss Grey," Kingslea growled. Insult him she could, but slandering his dead mother's memory he would not allow.

"Baboon." Her fists thumped his chest. The movement jiggled her ripe breasts, teasing the nipples to a peak. Heat flooded his groin. Good God, she wore nothing but a nightgown. A thin barrier that tempted more than it tempered.

The distance between man and beast seemed much closer than allowed by Darwin's dispassionate theories.

"Perhaps we should discuss this on the sofa." With plenty of frigid air and pillows between them.

Kingslea forced his feet to move. His traitorous fingers walked up her arm and found a home between her fingers.

"There is nothing to discuss."

"I disagree." Another step backwards. The distance between them lengthened. She might not follow his lead, but she hadn't tugged free of his grasp.

"That is because you are a disagreeable specimen."

Another step. Their arms were perpendicular to their bodies. Still she resisted his guidance. Kingslea had an unpleasant inkling he was losing a silent argument.

"I believe an explanation may be in order."

"Pray do begin whenever you are ready." With a toss of her head, she marched forward until she walked by his side.

"Me?" How natural it felt to have her rub shoulders with him.

"Yes, you." She tugged her hands free.

His empty fingers clawed at cold air. Sulfur bit the air as a match flared to light. The flame kissed her smooth cheeks, reflected off her eyes. She would be beautiful at sunrise, breathtaking at sunset, and irresistible every second in between.

"What can I say?" The latest intrigue had driven him insane. Only dementia explained this maelstrom of emotion, this rejection of control.

"This is my uncle's house." She settled on the couch, draped her nightgown over her legs and folded her hands demurely in her lap. Light filtered threw the cotton, highlighted the turn of her hip and the curve of her breast.

"So it is." Kingslea snatched up the nearest pillow. Velvet dried his damp fingers. How the devil was a man to concentrate when temptation took a seat next to him? He tossed the cushion onto her lap. She caught it to her chest, covering the silhouette of her charms. Logic trickled into brain, restoring a modicum of control. He unstuck his tongue from the roof of his mouth.

"I am waiting." Fiona turned and stuffed the pillow behind her back. Jet-black hair cascaded over her shoulder, shadowed her high breasts and lay across her lap.

Muddling mysteries. Kingslea shifted. He would have a word with his tailor, his trousers seem to have shrunk. Had the woman no sense of modesty? Even a lady had to realize the reaction such a picture effected. He thumped on the couch behind him. A pillow cushioned his hand. He tossed it into her lap.

"Your silence implicates you." She frowned at the pillow, scooted forward and set it behind her.

Better implicated by silence then damned by erotic thoughts. Her knees bumped his. Electricity shot along his nerves, contracting muscles. He bounded closer to the arm of the couch, whacked his elbow as a reward. He rubbed the throb from his flesh. A gold tassel caught his eye. Another pillow.

"Hugh."

He jerked it off the chair and thrust it at her.

"I do not require another cushion." She shoved it back at him. "I require answers."

"For propriety's sake, Fiona." Kingslea pressed the pillow into her lap and held it in place. "Keep the deuced pillow."

She glanced at the cuffs of her nightgown and fiddled with the buttons at her throat. Her chin rose as she turned to him. She blinked then hugged the fabric shield closer.

"My ball gown concealed much less."

Kingslea choked on a groan. Did she honestly believe he needed another reminder of her bare shoulders, the sway of her wispy skirt with every movement? His hand migrated down his face. He shoved off the couch. Distance was good. The reflection in the windowpane snagged his attention. Of course, it would be ever so much better if she stopped haunting him.

"I am not so easily evicted from the topic at hand."

Neither were his thoughts. Kingslea walked around the desk and sat in the chair. Scent of tobacco wafted from the leather upholstery. A solid slab of oak separated them.

"Neither am I."

"Then do start your exposition." Fiona lifted the candle from the end table and sauntered toward him. "And do stop hiding in the shadows." She outlined the edge of the desk. "Unless, of course, you mean to tell me a fie-fie anecdote."

"You don't trust me to tell the truth?" Trust. A empty word bandied among the *Ton*, yet he wanted, needed her to trust him.

"I trusted you enough not to yell for the guards when you attacked me."

"Hardly proof of faith."

"I caught you rifling my uncle's library. For that alone I could yell for the footmen." She set the candle on the desktop and crossed her arms.

"You don't know, do you?" Kingslea leaned forward. If she thought help was just a yelp away, why had she and her pistol ventured into the library?

"Pray do enlighten me."

"Where is your pistol?" He shot out of his chair. They'd wrestled over by the window, so the gun couldn't be far. He peered closer. An odd shape stretched across the carpet. He lifted the candlestick off the desk and held it in the direction of the window. Light seeped across the floor.

Fiona's whip. He had known she was armed, but what was a whip compared to a gun? He turned back to his companion, who had lined up the inkwell with the pen stand.

"Fiona?" Foreboding pricked his neck.

"Yes, Hugh?" She dusted the shiny oak desktop with her ruffled cuffs.

"Where is your gun, Fiona?"

"Why should I answer your questions?" Her fingers walked to the humidor before she shoved them under her arms. "You have yet to answer a single one of mine."

"I pledge to answer your queries if you answer mine." Kingslea set the candlestick on the desk, crossed his arms and glared back at her.

"Ladies first?"

"Agreed."

"What did you hope to discover in my uncle's house?"

"Not what, who. Your visitor entered about half-past midnight."

Her eyes narrowed. "Why didn't you alert the guards?"

"Because that nincompoop known as your cousin dismissed the footmen right after he sent the watch at the corner home."

Fear was like ice on his skin. Fiona had been alone, unprotected in the house with an intruder. He would not have waited so long to enter if he had known. Bloody hell, why hadn't the woman stayed longer at the ball? Alone with Sullied or alone with a thief. Purgatory lay in such a choice.

"Piers dismissed them?" Disbelief colored her voice.

"Indeed."

"But why? He may not value my skin, but he positively dotes on his own."

"Perhaps you are mistaken. Your fiancé returned at one a.m."

"You are mistaken. Piers is not my fiancé, and my aunt returned at two a.m. The clocked tolled upon her return."

"He was here for a short period. I nearly collided with him on the sidewalk."

"You were following him?"

"I was..." Insane with rage when she disappeared along with Sullied. Of course, he would turn over his estates to his stepmother before he admitted to any such thing. "...concerned."

Terrified Sullied would turn her against him. Had he? Fiona certainly didn't seem glad to see him.

"Concerned?"

Kingslea stiffened from the frost in her tone. "For your safety."

"My safety?" She snorted. "*I* was not in any danger of being swallowed by that...that woman's decolletage. Of course, you may have encountered difficulties seeing around such a clinging vine."

Woman. Clinging vine. Elation lifted the corners of Kingslea's mouth. Fiona was jealous. That would account for her ill temper.

"I—"

"Don't fob me off with some Banbury Tale. We both know my aunt and uncle do not socialize with the likes of her, er, um, I mean, tonight's society."

"Li—" He snapped the familiarity off. "Miss Lawson was providing valuable insight into Sullied's business ventures."

"Insight." Fiona glared at him. "Such a novel description."

Kingslea caught her hand and flattened it against his chest. His heart battered his breast as if to jump into her palm.

"Sullied's dabbling with the ancients isn't as profitable as he would have us believe. His creditors are one step away from his door."

"You sound deliciously pleased with that tidbit." She stepped closer to him, touching her toes to his boots.

"I am." He smiled at her. His heart floated on a cloud of gardenias.

"You don't like him much." Her gaze unfocused as she looked in his eyes.

Why had he never noticed the shards of silver in her indigo eyes? His thumb traced her jaw, reveled in the smoothness of her skin.

"Where is your father's gun, Fiona?"

"You have it." Her nimble finger danced over his tie before skipping over the nape of his neck. "All I had was the whip."

His heart squeezed to a stop. She had confronted a stranger without any chance of assistance with nothing but a whip. He didn't know whether to throttle her or congratulate her on her cleverness. He settled for the next best thing.

Kingslea's heartbeat started the moment his lips settled over hers. Warm, soft and welcoming. His tongue glided over the smooth surface before nibbling on her bottom lip. Her mouth opened, and his tongue invaded. Sweet like honey and filled with all the promise of a lifetime of Christmases. She swallowed his groan and offered it back to him.

He left the heaven of her mouth and tasted her neck. Her shoulder blades filled his palms, but his body craved more. They inched to her sides, reveled in the soft press of her breasts before sliding down to cup her buttocks.

"Hugh."

Losing himself in the melody of her sigh, he lifted her onto the desk. His neck trembled with her laughter, quivered with her kisses. Cotton bulged from his fist. A trim ankle winked at him.

Kingslea's teeth clicked shut as something hit the back of his head.

CHAPTER 20

"I am simply saying there are better ways to knock sense into a man." King-slea's gaze traveled around the room as his heartbeat settled into a somewhat normal rhythm. Colors appeared brighter, edges sharper. Daylight would explain the phenomenon, yet a single candle lit the room.

"It was a pillow, not a cricket bat." Fiona aligned the blotter with the edge of the desk for the third time. She hadn't looked at him since he'd broken off their kiss. Kiss. An inadequate word to describe the sensations exploding within his body when his lips touched hers.

"And I did not throw it."

Her full bottom lip disappeared into her mouth only to be returned through the press of pearly white teeth. She had scraped off his kiss. Oak slipped under his palms. Had she compared his kiss with her late fiancé's and found it wanting? White bleached his knuckles. Better to throttle the desk than her pretty neck.

"I hardly think the pillow flung itself off the couch."

She plucked a strand of brown hair from between her fingers and tucked it into her fist.

"Then would you believe a jealous ghost hurled it at your head?"

"A jealous ghost?" Undoubtedly her fiancé. Kingslea tugged on his sleeves, straightened the point of the handkerchief in his pocket. So, she had been thinking of him while they kissed, whereas he had thought of...of nothing but her—her taste, her scent.

"It makes as much sense as my arms stretching across the room, plucking a pillow from the divan and tossing it at your head."

"Nothing so preternatural. The chair next to you has two pillows."

She stretched out her arm toward the seat. The pillows remained a good two feet from the tips of her fingers. She couldn't have hit him.

He sighed and raised his hand until he cupped her smooth hand.

"If my attentions are so abhorrent, you have only to say so." Not that he would apologize for kissing her. His gaze dropped to her lips, swollen from the attention he had administered only minutes ago. Undoubtedly, memory had embellished the sensation of their touch. He leaned closer, felt the heat of her skin. Noted the rise and fall of her chest.

Perhaps he should kiss her again. If only to prove his memory wasn't failing him.

Her grip on his hand tightened. Pleasure rippled through him. He had given her every opportunity.

"I've had a communication of sorts from my uncle."

Kingslea stopped. Frustration gripped his body as reality swept the heat from his skin. Her uncle. He had offered to find her family, not deflower her. He forced his feet to step back.

"They're alive." And he was no longer needed. *Look on the bright side, old man—neither is that jackanapes Sullied.*

"Not quite." Fiona milked her fingers. She caught his glance then sat on them. "Uncle Heberon said they really didn't mix in society. Their diversions tended to be of a more political nature."

"That concurs with my findings." She spoke the truth, yet instinct screamed that she had omitted some detail.

"Yes, well." Shoving away from the desk, she rearranged the pillows on the chair. "My uncle left us some help. I know where he keeps his journal."

Which uncle? Heberon or Grey? Kingslea smoothed the wrinkles from his forehead.

"Grey kept a journal?"

"Don't tell me you didn't know?" She stopped folding the knit throw and draped it on the back of the chair. "That *is* why you were on the ship, wasn't it? To steal his captain's log?" Her fists settled on her hips. "I bet your mysterious employer sent you here to steal it." She beamed at him. "Yes, that makes sense. And he made you return Bosson's diary because it was the wrong captain's log."

Damnation. Her reasoning appeared sounder than his.

"No one sent me here, Fiona. I came because I saw someone enter your house."

"And you followed them in?" She crossed her arms over her chest and inched closer to the desk.

"You don't believe me?" He had to make her trust him. Only, why did he demand she give him what he refused to grant her? Because his life might depend on it. The woman was remarkably gifted with unearthing weapons aimed at putting a period to his existence.

His gaze bounced wildly around the room. A crumpled mound lay on the floor. The jacket. Kingslea strode toward his salvation.

"I want to," she told him.

He kicked the garment into his hands.

"You can." He stalked across the room, shaking it in her direction. "This came from the *real* thief. The thief I was attempting to apprehend when you threatened me with a deadly puncture." Smooth wool brushed his palm. He dipped his hand into the pocket. Damp silk lining stuck to his hand. "Nothing. No crumpled paper. Not even a pence. Our thief is obviously not an amateur."

"How do you know?"

"There's nothing incriminating in his pockets. Nothing to link him to his crime. Even the jacket was probably purchased from the ragman." Kingslea tossed the jacket onto the chair. So far, his assistance was about as helpful as a spilled honey at a picnic. "No clue to the wearer's identity. He's very clever."

Fiona glanced at the jacket. Her fingers smoothed the label.

"Jean Pierre Boudin."

"Hmmm?" If only he had captured the bugger.

"The tailor is Boudin." Gold silk winked at him from the lining. "He's my uncle's tailor. His *Parisian* tailor."

What was she talking about?

"Your uncle broke into his own library?"

"Not unless he shrank in the sea." She shoved open the lapels. Her fingers punctuated her points with excited jabs. "These are water-stained. And see these seams?"

"Yes." He moved the candle closer.

"This jacket's been altered."

It was only natural she would notice such things—she was a woman. Her cleverness soothed his ego more than his pithy thoughts. Careful, old boy. You can't change all your thoughts at once.

"The chap was rather slight. I imagine if we find the tailor who's responsible for the sewing…"

She shook her head. "Any dressmaker or wife could have altered this."

Her assessment was correct. Again.

"Well, at least it proves my story."

"Yes, well…"

"I wonder if Sullied employs any footmen this slight."

"I believe you're allowing your dislike of the duke to influence your theories."

His gut knotted. She was defending Sullied.

"My valet spied the duke's men lurking about just this morning."

"Indeed."

He refused to argue with her. She would discover the veracity of his words just as he had acknowledged the accuracy of her conclusions.

"You said your uncle left us a journal?" With any luck it would reveal the duke's black heart.

"It's here." She crouched in front of the desk and pulled out the bottom drawer.

"I might have to reevaluate my judgment of the thief if he couldn't find a book in a drawer."

"It's not *in* the drawer." Fiona gritted her teeth and tugged harder. "It's under it."

Under it? That was decidedly more clever, though not what he would have expected from a man of Grey's reputation.

"Allow me." Kingslea eased around her hands and tugged. The drawer came free with the splintering of wood. Oak knocked pain into his shins.

Fiona shoved the drawer onto his foot and lifted something from the base. She stuffed the plank under the desk. Blackness gaped back at him.

"It's more than a necklace." She stared at the hole.

After all her prattling about the journal, he thought she would have dived in after it. Perhaps she was afraid something was in the cubbyhole with the book. Something with multiple legs.

"Allow me." He balanced his weight on the balls of his feet and leaned forward.

"No. Don't!" Color fled her cheeks.

"I can assure you I am more than capable of dealing with whatever is inside."

"Take only the book. Don't touch the box."

Box? He saw nothing. How could she see a box? He reached again. Her slap stung his hand.

"Use the light." The candle's flame sputtered as she yanked it off the desk. In the other she held the false bottom, like a cook ready to slap the lid on a flaming kettle. "Okay, only the journal. Touch only the journal."

He grunted. He may not have picked up that many clues, but he was no simpleton. Leather rubbed against his fingers. Cold pricked his skin, teased the hair on his arms upright. He lifted the book and freed it from its hiding spot.

She shoved the bottom into place then snatched the book from his hand.

"Put the drawer back."

"Aye, aye, captain." He slid the drawer back. Muscles protested as he straightened. Perhaps he was getting too old for his adventures.

She stood next to him, tapping her toe.

"The couch, I think. Then I won't have to crane over your neck as you read."

"You wish me to read it?'

"Yes. Aloud, of course—I don't wish to miss anything." She handed him the book.

"As you wish." He offered her his arm. After she accepted, they set off for the sofa.

February 2nd H came in today. The windbag blustered as usual. Shorted one bolt of silk, barrel of wine and three cases of tins of milk. Refused to honor bill. Sixth confrontation since Jan 5. Made it clear this was the last credit from G. S.

"Who is H?"

"Undoubtedly a merchant. It will be easy enough to discover his identity. I'll simply cross-check the amount credited with his name."

"Do you know how much a bolt of silk, a barrel of wine and three cases of tinned milk cost?"

"Roughly. I've been keeping G-and-G's accounts for several years now."

"You don't seem too concerned."

"The less a businessman pays for his goods, the more he profits. Some are so reluctant to compensate us that we require payment before the merchandise is unloaded."

"And here I thought piracy was dead."

"The pirates are dead—long live the pirates."

February 4th Cart upset. £ 1,000 lost to crowd. Sweep responsible eluded watch. Third time in New Year. Deliberate? B wants to hire guards. Neither same route nor same driver.

February 5th D.of August blew in like ill wind. Refused to honor waybill. Claims two sarcophagi and one chest mislaid. B contacted museum. All pieces arrived and accounted for. Only such occurrence this month.

"Only such occurrence this month?" Kingslea stroked his chin. "Do you suppose he refers to Sullied's visit or to an intact shipment?"

"One would hope he means the duke's call." She leaned closer to him. "Not that merchandise doesn't 'fall' off the wagons some days. But an everyday occurrence—well, that would signal something else entirely."

"Something else? Someone doing a bit of shopping gratis, perhaps?"

"Unscrupulous folks help themselves to anything they can grab when the wagon slows or stops due to traffic. I hardly think that sufficient motive for scuttling a ship, let alone attempted murder."

"Three full wagons valued at a thousand pounds apiece. Men have been killed for less than three thousand pounds." Gardenias teased his senses. Her arm brushed his. And what would he do for one more kiss?

February 6th August offered mummy in lieu of apology. What need have I of a corpse? C insists on hosting an unwrapping.

February 8th Amazed by the turnout for an unknown corpse. If only the blighters could muster a fraction of that sympathy for the living and destitute. Still, rallied support for bill.

February 9th Dinner out. C claims items in boudoir rearranged. Sapphire bracelet lost, clasp faulty. Everything else looks undisturbed, but then, we rarely venture into her room.

Her room. Her bedroom. As if his erotic thoughts needed anymore stimulation. Kingslea cleared his throat and turned the page.

February 11th Hancock in today. Personally checked shipments. Want wagoneers to double-check shipments. B reluctant—must pay literate drivers more. Note from Piers demanding an increase in his allowance. May be related to toughs' visit at office today. Drop word to jewelers to keep watch for bracelet. Talk to moneylenders.

"He seems to suspect Piers's involvement."

Fiona shrugged. "That makes no sense."

"Piers is next in line for the title, is he not?" Kingslea latched onto the one thought that didn't involve naked flesh.

"Yes, but—"

"If Piers is in heavy with the cent-percenters he may not want to wait while nature runs its course. Heberon would be easy enough to outwit, but not Grey. My guess is your uncle stood in the way of title, land and money. Three very powerful motives."

"Except the title comes only with The Willows, which Aunt Annabelle and her spawn have bled dry and are anxious to escape."

One estate for a title as old as Hebron's? He was missing something. Again. He had to break out of this rut. Perhaps Fiona put some opiate in her perfume. Opium dulled one's wits.

"What about the three estates in the country, the townhouse in London and Bath plus the castles in Scotland and Ireland? The oldest male usually inherits the property."

"They belong to Aunt Caro."

"Weren't they entailed?"

Fiona shook her head. "Aunt Caro's father broke it when he realized how, um, special Uncle Heberon is."

"Does the land revert to him should she predecease him?"

"I think it passes to the children, not that uncle would ever want for anything." She smiled at him and leaned closer. "Uncle Andrew would not allow it."

Her eyes were really the most amazing color. *Stick to the topic, man.*

"But your uncle isn't here to prevent it. Does Montague know?"

"If he didn't, he does now. The banks wouldn't allow him to withdraw funds this morning."

"So, before your arrival, Piers had control of everything."

"Da wouldn't—"

He held up his hand, silencing her.

"Who's to say your father would discover the truth until Montague had drained the estate? With the older Greys missing but not dead, and your uncle, niece and nephew under Montague's control, who would contact your father?"

"Gibson might."

"Let us not forget that Montague released the guards and returned to this house while everyone else was out. Anything could have happened to you, Fiona." He clasped her hand. Warm, soft and beautifully alive. "Given the past mischief, the police constables wouldn't have considered him a suspect."

"That might explain how the note came to be on my pillow."

"Note? What note?" Anxiety sharpened his voice.

She winced and nibbled on her bottom lip.

"Just a little something I found when I returned from searching my uncle's room."

A ragged breath steadied his nerves, trimmed his voice to a low shout.

"What did the note say?"

"Something about rewarding the curious."

Her fingers folded her nightgown into four neat pleats. He stopped the fifth by setting his hand on hers.

"Rewarding the curious with what? And don't feign ignorance. I can see the truth in your eyes."

"Death." She cleared her throat and looked at him. Fear flashed in her eyes. "'Death is the reward of the curious.'"

"Bloody hell." If he killed Piers now, he could plead insanity. Alveston and Winthrop would no doubt vouch for his erratic behavior. A lifetime in an asylum versus Fiona's safety. A bargain, really. "Do not tell me there is no need for swearing."

"Just read, please."

February 12 C agrees to frank Edwina's season. H wants
them in to reside at hotel. A simple stroke of brilliance that.

February 13 Balanced books. Twenty-two discrepancies. B discharged two wagoneers, saw them pinching items from shipment. More disturbances at house. Hired three footman. C sleeping fitful. Children starting at shadows. 4th night C & M slept in our bed. H snoring on the divan. C urging me to send for B.

"Why would he send for Bartholomew?"

"I think this B stands for my mother—Brighid. The telegram I received was dated three days later."

"Your aunt and mother are very close?"

Fiona smoothed the waterlogged pages of the journal.

"They were fast friends from the moment they met."

She evaded his question with an answer.

"So, your aunt wanted your mother's companionship, and your uncle thought an extra warrior in the house wouldn't hurt."

Instead of cheering her, his casually offered remark weighted the corners of her mouth.

"Warrior?"

"Tell me, Fiona, what weapon does your mother wield so adroitly."

"Mam doesn't approve of weapons."

"No guns or whips?"

"Nor knives or arrows." The tightness around her eyes eased, a testament to her closeness with her family. "She's afraid weapons can be easily parted from their owner." Fiona leaned closer, as if to whisper a confidence. "And that's not even mentioning the strictures on overconfidence she preaches every Monday. Mam believes true survival depends on awareness of things around you. What might and might not be used in an emergency."

"So, your father trained you?"

"Oh, no. On this, Da sided with Mam. Grandmama blamed his abhorrence of guns on the War. Mam said a skillet had prevailed where a pistol had failed."

"A skillet?"

"Yes, but one doesn't decorate with skillets. Fortunately, andirons are in almost every room, needlepoint bags with their sharp accoutrements and, if all else fails, fountain pens."

His gaze traveled to the desk. The woman could take on an army with the knickknacks his stepmother collected.

"Good God."

"*He* is, but not all men are. A lady needs to protect herself and her reputation."

"You graced Montague's countenance with a black eye." He couldn't help the grin.

"My cousin is frightfully pale. I simply thought a little color might help."

Kingslea swallowed his laughter. The relatively unmolested state of his person attested to some level of trust between them.

February 14 B handled discrepancy with Hottstedder shipment. New clerk hired. Friendly with wagoneers. Too familiar? Some drivers counting boxes before departing.

February 15 two larcenous entries, at home and at office. Bills of lading destroyed. Books ripped apart. Ghosts don't break glass, though E might disagree. C happy I sent for E & B.

"E is your father."

"Yes, Everett Grey."

"Does he have any experience in this sort of thing?"

"Of course not. What need of ghosts for merchandising?"

Ghosts. That was the second time she had mentioned spirits.

"I hardly think there is a preternatural cause behind the mischief."

"Then we agree." She nodded. "Uncle Andrew sent for Mam to comfort Aunt Caroline, and for Da to help catch the living villains terrorizing his family."

February 16 Removing family to the country. Returning mummy to Egypt. Sweet Wind sails tomorrow.

"When did the ship go down?"

"The night of the seventeenth."

"Why weren't his children and brother-in-law on board?"

"Melody can't tolerate the sea, and Uncle Heberon fears sea monsters. He will only travel by rail."

"Brilliance in simplicity." He would have liked Fiona's family. "Your uncle's phobia undoubtedly saved three lives."

Muffled voices drifted in the window. Yellow light pushed against the fog.

"I believe that is my cue to exit." Kingslea stalked toward the window.

"Surely, you can use the door."

"I have found that butlers are most particular in how they leave things. Yours will undoubtedly note any disturbance in the hall, and questions will arise. The window is the safest course." He straddled the sill, not the most comfortable position under normal circumstances. Downright unmanning, given Fiona's proximity.

"Be safe."

"Keep your door locked." Fabric ripped as the hinge sliced through his sleeve. Such trouble for an adventure. He slid the rest of the way out the window.

Grass squished under his feet. The hedge clawed at his back. Yet, he would have endured so much more for another kiss.

"Do you think Piers will try to harm me?" Fiona leaned out the window. Her hand rested on the window latch. Black hair spilled over her shoulder. The lady of the manor waiting for her knight errant to return.

Didn't all knights require a token, a remembrance for their quest?

"I wouldn't wish to flee to the continent with a murderess." He grabbed her chin and slanted his mouth across hers.

His memory had not done their kiss justice. Kingslea pulled back before the heat consumed them both. Roses bloomed in her cheeks. A smile teased her lips.

"No matter how justified your actions." He pivoted about, sidled through the hedge and loped toward his house. Running would have been undignified.

CHAPTER 21

— **For pity's sake, Fi.** *Milton strolled through the cane chair opposite her uncle's desk*, folded his arms and glared down at her. Aren't you finished with those wretched accounts yet?

"I would be finished more quickly if you would cease interrupting me every ten minutes inquiring if I have finished." Fiona rubbed her burning eyes and reshuffled the stack of invoices. Cramped numbers streaked the overlarge pages. Neat and legible, they stubbornly balanced every time. Something was definitely wrong. "Why don't you scare some horses?"

— *You're confusing me with Gran,* he sniffed.

She tossed her pen down. Ink dotted the pages. Tension knotted her shoulders. Her palm flattened her nose as her hand reshaped her face. She had added the columns twice, compared the entries against the invoices. Everything tallied, yet nothing made sense. Maybe she needed a fresh pair of eyes. Hugh's brown eyes...

Fiona ran her tongue over her dry lips. Thoughts of Hugh interrupted her almost as often as Milton.

"I'm certain somewhere nearby the men are gambling with their hard-earned wages."

— *It isn't as entertaining as it once was.* Milton jabbed at the inkwell, prodding it across her desk until it bumped against her blotter. *I always know the roll of the dice, the turn of a card.*

With a sigh, she picked up the inkwell and set it next to the kerosene lamp.

"Surely, there are other spirits wandering the docks."

— *Have you seen them?* Milton wrapped his arms around his chest. *Disreputable, not to mention downright frightening, and those are the friendly ones. Apparently, there is this headless fellow had his severed head mounted on a pike.*

Well, dead or no, he can't bring himself to put it back on his shoulders, so he walks around thumping the staff on the ground with every step.

"Milton." Fiona held up her hand. Headless ghosts and skewered heads. She needed silence. Blessed peaceful silence. "I am unable to concentrate while you talk. If I am unable to concentrate, then I will never finish."

Milton drummed his fingers on his arm.

— Admit it, Fi. You're scared. That's why you're here tallying the same numbers over and over again.

"Scared? That's preposterous. When have you ever seen me afraid?"

— When I kissed you right after you accepted my proposal. When you discovered that Brianna was coughing blood. He bent across the desk so low his face was level with hers. *You're frightened every time you realize you're not in control.*

"Of course I was afraid when Brianna's handkerchiefs were spotted. She was dying, Milton. My sister was dying." Fiona snatched her pen off the desk and rolled it between her thumb and index finger.

— The dead are not lost to you, Fi.

"That is cold comfort."

— Today we would have celebrated two years of wedded bliss. Two years. He poked the same number of fingers at her. *You would have thrown a party that everyone would have bartered with the devil to be invited to. Your parents would have had a miniature you to bounce on their knee and with whom they could break every rule of etiquette.* He frowned down at her. *Today, you have nothing. You just stopped, Fi. You stopped living. This has become your tomb.*

Fiona shifted in her chair. An anniversary. A celebration of an event that never was—her wedding. A vision of domestic tranquility flashed before her eyes. Hugh stood as husband. Hugh made her feel jealousy, confusion, joy, anger. Myriad emotions thundered inside her skull. Hugh made her feel alive.

Milton was wrong.

She was alive. Painfully alive.

She focused on the balance sheets. For a while, Hugh had managed to make her forget the guilt.

"This is an office, Milton, not a tomb."

— I fail to see why you must balance the books at all. Isn't that what those crows are for?

"They are clerks, Milton. Clerks, not crows."

— Clerks. Crows. They all resemble each other, except that Bartholomew fellow. He's more like a vulture. Swooping and picking. They don't like him much, Fi. Milton hovered at the edge of the desk and fiddled with his cuffs. *Not that I expected much devotion, but at that other place everyone seems to rub along tolerably well.*

That other place. Longing washed over her. At home, her presence was accepted and welcomed. Not so here. Men practically shrank from her presence, conversations ceased. It was almost as if they were afraid of her. Had they heard of her gift? Did they fear she would bring the graveyard with her?

"That's because almost everyone has been at G-and-G Enterprises for a year or more. I understand that Uncle's two clerks have been employed for less than six months."

— And that your uncle hired that Black fellow, and The Vulture hired the other. He's a bit of a pariah, Black is.

"Mr. Bartholomew has been in my uncle's employ for seventeen years." Papers slipped through Fiona's fingers. She tucked the straightened pile under her arm. Maybe she should return to the townhouse. Maybe Hugh would call. "Uncle trusts him implicitly."

— You are finished, then?

And if Hugh avoided her? If he dropped her completely because of one simple breathtaking kiss. Trembling fingers thumbed through the ledger. There were three more months to wade through. Three months that might yield a clue to her uncle's disappearance. Duty, not fear of life, kept her here.

"No, Milton. I told you I—"

— Have to double-check all the entries for the last five months. His head bobbed with each word, a puppet parroting his master's movements.

Irritation flashed through her. Fiona set the pen on the open book.

"If you know..." She forced the words through her teeth. "...then why do you keep asking?"

— If you had planned to review months' worth of bookkeeping, then why didn't you rise earlier? Milton tapped his cheek. *You slept till well past noon, Fi. I don't remember you sleeping so late, not even when we courted.*

Fiona cleared her throat, removed the bundle under her arm and studied the top page. She hadn't wanted to wake, hadn't wanted to leave that world slumber had created.

"I was tired from the journey."

Letters and numbers blurred as she shuffled the papers. To sleep, knowing such vivid dreams awaited, knowing Hugh waited. She filled the ache in her gut with a lungful of cool air.

"It was a long voyage."

— I was worried, I can tell you. Deep shadows marred Milton's forehead. *You were up all night sulking, weren't you? Such petulance stains the complexion, and you still have that unfocused look about you.*

"Unfocused look?" Why was Milton pretending ignorance? He had to have seen her in Hugh's embrace, had to have tossed the pillow at Hugh's back. Yet he continued to gloss over the lovemaking as if it never happened.

— Yes. As if you would ever prefer Morpheus's world to this one.

"I did have quite pleasant dreams." Fiona's cheeks tingled. She remembered Hugh kissing her lips, her neck, her shoulders. The silkiness of his hair, the scratch of his unshaved chin. Cool air washed over her face as she fanned herself with the invoices. Thank heaven she had never been inclined to blush.

— *That's it, Fi. That is precisely the look.* Milton's touch chilled her brow. *Maybe you're coming down with a fever. All that fresh air you insisted on taking on the ship, and then that midnight promenade. You know, Fi, consumption runs in families. Didn't your sister first manifest symptoms while you vacationed in London?*

"I do not have consumption, Milton."

— *Yet you exhibit all the evidence of illness—bright, unfocused gaze, flushed cheeks, and a nervous disposition.* His narrow-eyed gaze raked her from head to toe. *Either you're succumbing to a fatal illness, or you're in love.*

Love. Her heart stopped. Could she be in love with Hugh? No. She knew love. She had loved Milton, knew the warm comfort of his presence. With Hugh, the heat blazed like an inferno, and comfort...

She shrugged. Comfort proved as elusive as moonbeams.

— *Is it love, Fi? After only one meeting?*

She shook her head. One meeting? She had met Hugh three times and relived each encounter dozens more.

"I'm distracted, Milton. I find much is weighing on my mind."

— *Good. You can finish this tomorrow.* He rubbed his hands together. *There is still time for you to change and fix your hair in that becoming way you did last night.* He snapped his fingers. *You could cut a few of the roses the duke sent and put them in your hair. It's quarter till the hour. By the time you're ready, you won't have missed much.*

Missed. Missing. *That's it!* Nothing was missing. It was obvious. She plopped onto the chair. Leather sighed in welcome.

"I am not leaving yet, Milton." How could Grey Shipping have three months without a single crate, can or barrel going missing?

— *This is about that Kingston chap, isn't it?* Milton's fist punched through the papers. *He's a fortune hunter, Fi. I've seen that hungry look before.*

Fiona tugged the papers off the desk and leaned back in her uncle's chair. The instant she managed to banish Hugh's image, Milton brought him up. A deliberate distraction, one designed to make her quit work and return home.

"Kingslea looked well-fed to me." Victory hummed in her veins. This morning's work would reveal a few answers. She yanked open the desk drawer, grabbed her purse and slapped it on the desk. The invoices ruffled in the breeze.

— *Not for food. He's hungry for money. Your money.*

"It always comes down to money." She tugged out Uncle Andrew's journal and flipped open the pages. January 21st. Her index finger found a two and a one in the ledger. The cramped numbers lacked her uncle's fluid grace.

— *Have you found something, then?*

"Yes. This isn't my uncle's handwriting. He always kept the books. He didn't even trust Bartholomew to do it. The clerks copied and invoiced, but they never entered the final amounts—only Uncle did that."

— *Perhaps the records were with your uncle when he...*

"Perhaps, but that doesn't explain the losses."

— *What losses?*

"Exactly. According to both the invoices and the ledger, Grey Shipping hasn't suffered a single loss in five months. Not one. Yet Uncle Andrew said several shopkeepers complained about missing items in February alone. I found none."

— *So, he made a mistake. It has been known to happen.* Milton shrugged. *Do you remember in September when you were off by two dollars? You stayed up all night recalculating the figures until you found it.*

"Yes, Milton, I remember. But we are not talking about two dollars. The Duke of August chartered an entire ship to bring his cargo home. That manifest doesn't even appear in the stack. Nor in the month before or after."

— *The Duke of August? Why didn't you say so?* Milton dashed to the door. The hem of her coat fluttered. *There's not a moment to lose, Fi. You need to rush home and change. When the duke calls on you, casually invite him to take tea then...* Milton wagged a finger at her. *No. He might not like his future bride behaving like a common cleric, so—*

"Clerk, Milton. A cleric is a minister of the church."

— *Just so. He might take exception to your, um, well, this.* Milton drifted closer. *Fi, you didn't mention your, um, hobby while he twirled you about the dance floor, did you?*

Her hobby. She had always thought Milton hadn't believed she could converse with the dead. Of course, he had always said he believed her, yet...

"My hobby? Are you referring to my seashell collection or my butterfly collection?"

— *I am referring to this.* He opened his arms wide.

"Ah. You are wondering if I told the duke that my dead fiancé has chosen him as the man to take his place."

— *Good God, that sounds as if I want the man's life.* Pink tinged Milton's smoky form.

"Then you shall be relieved to know I didn't mention you once."

— *Yes, well.* His fists settled on his hips. *I'm talking about* this *hobby.* He soundlessly stamped his boot. *This...this unnatural interest you have in men's business.*

Men's business. This conversation had repeated even before his death.

"I own a share of this company, Milton. Do you condemn a farmer for taking an interest in his fields?"

— *That's different.*

"Why? Because I am a woman. You laughed at my interest in math and protested Da's teaching us some of the defensive arts. I thought it was jealousy, but now—"

— Fiona Anne Grey, dismount your suffragette soapbox at once. The flame sputtered in its globe as he sailed across the room to confront her. *You will have a husband who accepts these peculiar inclinations of yours. But you must allow him time to adjust to his wife's superior prowess with such matters.*

"Superior prowess." Flattery. Milton had rarely resorted to flattery with her. They had known each other too long. He wanted something. But what?

— Does he know of your business interests?

"He knew of my connection to Grey Shipping. It was the reason he sought an introduction."

— Only one of many reasons, Fi. Of that I am certain. Milton patted her shoulder then drifted towards the door. *How did you know he chartered a ship? It is hardly small talk, and quite frankly, a little too pedestrian a topic for one in his lofty position.*

"He mentioned his acquaintance with Uncle Andrew while impressing upon me his interest in all things Egyptian." A shudder rippled through Fiona. The duke had wanted that necklace. Aunt Caro had been right to want it returned. Buried with those it helped. Damn. One thing at a time, Fi.

"Uncle Andrew's journal mentioned the exact dates as well as discrepancies in the bookkeeping and an unusually high volume of missing freight."

— So, you found it, then? Your uncle's diary.

"Uncle Heberon told me where to find it. Apparently, they visited while we were at the ball."

— I don't trust this, Fi. Milton set his elbow on his folded arm and propped his chin in his hand. *I've talked to the other shades. Not one of them has noticed visitors flitting about the place.*

"Aunt Caro and Uncle Andrew are not dead." Fiona straightened the papers.

— Yet, your daffy uncle sees their ghosts. Fi, how many mortals do you know that can walk through walls?

She rubbed the ache from her chest.

"I'm certain there is an explanation. There has to be another explanation, Milton." She scraped her uncle's journal into the desk drawer, buried it under a pile of invoices and slammed it closed. After locking it, she pocketed the iron key. "How many restless spirits do you know that I can't see?"

— Yet, you must accept that they are dead. I can hardly see one of your family leaving their children alone so long.

Pain zipped up her arm as she gathered February and January's invoices from the desk. Blood oozed from the paper cut and stained the neat papers. The chair creaked as she rose to her feet.

"I'm going to ask Mr. Bartholomew about the duke's invoice."

— *Ha.* Milton's hands rested on his hips as he floated beside her. *You always change the subject when you know I'm right.*

"Milton." The brass doorknob cooled Fiona's palm. Her aunt and uncle couldn't be dead. As soon as she knew the reason the *Sweet Wind* had gone down, she would find them.

— *Yes, Fi?* Milton paused with his right side in the wall.

"Stop fogging the windows."

Except for the creaking of the door hinges, silence blanketed the room. A trio of men plunked their cups onto the stove and sidled out the door. Two others cast furtive looks in her direction before continuing their mumbling. Milton had been correct about one thing.

The men were definitely afraid.

There wasn't enough time to reassure them. Fiona nodded to the remaining cluster. They jumped apart and bolted out the door.

Milton placed his hand upon his chest.

— *Upon my mother's grave, Fi, I did nothing.*

"Your mother is not dead."

"It is the sentiment."

"Did you need me for something, Miss Grey?" A young clerk traced the edge of his lapel with one hand as he strode across the floor, tapping the pen in his other against his trouser leg.

"Actually, I am looking for Mr. Bartholomew."

"He's stepped out, Miss." The pen stilled as the man tossed a glance over his shoulder. "Perhaps I could be of some assistance regarding the invoices."

"That's very kind Mr...Black, isn't it?"

"Yes, Miss."

— *He's a bit intense, Fi.* Milton circled the clerk. *I don't trust him. See how his eyes shift?* He drifted closer. *I do believe there is a bit of perspiration on his lip.*

"The invoices match the books perfectly."

"They do?" Mr. Black smoothed hair then adjusted his bow tie. "Of course they do, Mr. Bartholomew is very careful with them."

"Mr. Bartholomew has been keeping the accounts since my uncle's accident?"

"I believe he reconstructed them after the *Sweet Wind* sank."

— *He's not looking at you, Fi.* Milton tapped his chin. *He's lying. You're a liar, aren't you?*

"I am looking for the manifest for the Duke of August's February shipment. Would you happen to know where it is?"

"Mr. Bartholomew keeps them in his office. He reviews all the invoices before he enters them into the ledger."

"Thank you." Fiona headed toward the office. Cramps seized her stomach. Bartholomew kept the books. The books that failed to deduct items she knew to be missing. Seventeen years of trust wasted.

She flattened her hand against the door and pushed. Burnt tobacco, liver-wurst and strong tea perfumed the tidy office. Stacks of papers paralleled the edges of the desk. Two silver-trimmed fountain pens poked the air next to a half-empty inkwell. A pristine silk tophat perched above an ebony frock coat.

— *What is it, Fi?*

"How am I to tell Uncle Andrew?"

— *Tell him what? That his vulture is obsessively tidy?*

"That he's been skimming money, Milton. What else explains the missing invoices and unreported losses?"

— *How can* not *reporting something that is there gain him money?*

"I don't know."

Milton drifted near the coat tree.

— *He certainly isn't purchasing new clothes. This coat is two years out of date, and there's a button missing.* He poked the broken thread. *Shall we search his office?*

Search his office. She should. Uncle would not like it if she accused a man without proof. Especially Mr. Bartholomew. Her hand settled on the pull of the top drawer.

"Uh, Miss Grey?"

Fiona started. Her knuckles rapped the edge of the desk. Pain ricocheted up her arm. The clerk stood in the doorway; his narrow-eyed gaze traveled down her arm to the desk. He knew what she had been about to do. Had Bar-tholomew left him behind to spy on her?

"Yes, Mr. Black?" She gathered all the papers into a pile and scooped them into her arms. Metal etched a scratch into her arm. She shook the pile. A square-tipped letter opener tumbled onto the blotter.

"There is a gentleman here." Mr. Black glanced over his shoulder. "He says you've been expecting him."

Milton glanced from her to the door.

— *It could be the duke. Quick, Fi, drop the papers and try to look feminine.*

Feminine? Fiona swallowed her outrage. Too bad she didn't dare blister the air in front of witnesses.

"Did he leave a card?"

"No, Miss."

"I see."

She juggled the pile. A few slips of paper fluttered from her grasp. Mr. Black scampered forward, picked them up and placed them on top of the load.

"Shall I show him out?"

Cramped writing caught her eye. *One crate tins—5 pounds; bolt of cotton—6 £ 2s 3d; twenty plugs tobacco—1 £ 11d; one barrel—*

"Miss Grey?"

Could these be the missing items? All were small enough for a thief to carry off. Yet why would Bartholomew keep them on a separate list?

"No. I'll see him."

"Very good, Miss."

Fiona walked out of Bartholomew's office. A broad-shouldered man stood near the window, tapping his silk hat against his pinstriped trousers. Her heart squeezed to a stop.

"Sir."

He turned at Mr. Black's salutation. A black-headed pin winked at her from the folds of his jet tie.

"Miss Grey will see you now."

"Hugh."

CHAPTER 22

"Miss Grey." Hugh stalked forward. The contours of his jacket snuggled his lean hips with each stride. "I apologize for reporting to work so late." His warm hands slipped around hers.

Naked flesh pressed naked flesh. Electrical currents zipped through her faster than the copper wires at home. If his touch spoke of decadence in the daylight, what would happen if he should kiss her with the sun shining? Fiona's gaze dropped to his lips. Full. Parted. Expectant.

"Say you forgive me?" Deviltry flashed in his eyes before he raised her hand and placed a kiss on it.

Pleasure paralyzed her tongue, curled her toes in her boots. "Ummm."

"Did I hear correctly, sir?" Bartholomew glided into the room. "You are reporting for work at..." He pinched open the watch at his waist, whisked a cloth across the shiny glass then snapped it closed. "...at four in the afternoon?"

Hugh opened his own frock coat and palmed his watch. For a brief instant, the image of gunfighters at twenty paces flashed inside Fiona's skull.

"Perhaps you should wind your timepiece, sir." Hugh's right eyebrow arched. "I have seven past the hour."

— *Cheeky fellow.* Milton inched closer. *I say, Fi. He looks remarkably like that Kingston fellow.*

"I know." Three pairs of eyes turned to her. Fiona cleared her throat. "We are fortunate to have you with us at any time."

"Miss Grey." Mr. Bartholomew placed himself squarely between her and Hugh. Color stained his cheeks. Irritation blazed in his eyes before he dropped his gaze to the floor. "May I speak with you?"

"Of course, Mr. Bartholomew." Fiona nodded.

"In Mr. Grey's office?"

"Oh, don't mind me." Hugh shook his head at her. So, he didn't trust Mr. Bartholomew, either. What had he and Milton seen in the homely man that she didn't?

"Of course." Hugh's eyebrows wiggled. A vein throbbed in his neck. He didn't want her alone with Mr. Bartholomew.

— Don't worry, I'll keep an eye on the blighter. Milton flicked Hugh's ear. *It will take more than a change of clothes to get past me, Fi.*

"It is nice to have you here." Fiona squeezed Hugh's hand before turning away. Confronting her uncle's manager would be less unsettling with help a shout away. Not that she would require Hugh's assistance, Da had taught her how lethal ordinary things could prove.

Still, she thought as she glanced over her shoulder, it was nice to have an ally.

Mr. Bartholomew quietly shut the door, cleared his throat and looked up at her from under his bushy eyebrows.

"Miss Grey, we at Grey Shipping have a protocol for the hiring of clerks."

Protocol. Fiona swallowed her outrage. To think a thief would deliver lectures on propriety.

"I know, Mr. Bartholomew, I helped draft the procedure." Mr. Bartholomew was a thief, she reminded herself. Disbelief coursed through her. *What more proof do you require, Fi? A signed confession?*

"Yes, well..." He wrapped a knobby claw around his throat. "With the circumstances surrounding your uncle's... um..."

"Disappearance?" The ledger would convince a jury. Fiona rubbed her uncle's blotter. Then why wasn't it enough for her?

"Yes. I—" He straightened his shoulders and managed to meet her eyes. "I feel that employees need a certain continuity. Should you feel that an additional clerk is a necessity, I would be more than happy to place an advertisement."

"That is very kind of you Mr. Bartholomew, but Mr., um..." Fiona forced a cough from her throat while her brain groped for a name. Gold buttons winked at her from her cuffs. "Mr. Buttons is my father's man of affairs."

Satisfaction rippled through her as the manager's adam's apple. She dropped the invoices on her desk.

"Given the nature of my uncle's disappearance, the board felt Mr. Buttons's presence might prove useful."

"Then he's not a clerk." Mr. Bartholomew's eyes widened. His jaw moved up and down then stilled.

"No, Mr. Buttons is not a clerk." Her gaze dropped to the papers now littering her desk. The invoices from Bartholomew's office. She ran her finger down the list of items. The manager's gaze followed her motion like a cobra swaying to music. Was this a list of the missing items? But why weren't they recorded in the ledger?

"Are those papers from my desk?" His fingers crawled across the blotter, spiders invading a house.

"Yes." She splayed her fingers over the pile. "I needed to find the Duke of August's manifest."

"I had thought your uncle resolved that problem before his disappearance."

"So, you know of the duke's shipment?"

"Oh, yes, Miss." Mr. Bartholomew puffed out his chest. "His Grace prefers Grey Shipping above all others."

"Yet, according to the ledger, His Grace hasn't shipped anything with us all year."

Mr. Bartholomew's fingers nibbled at the stack of papers. On impulse, Fiona tossed the ledger onto the desk. A handful of invoices fluttered to the floor.

"The ledger?" He jerked back, and his fingers crawled over themselves in front of his sunken belly.

"Yes. Every shipment, purchase, sale and loss is supposed to be recorded by date in this book, Mr. Bartholomew."

"Everything?" He licked his lips, "I didn't know, Miss Grey. Your uncle never taught me how to record." The manager blinked then cleared his throat. "I thought this was the correct manner. Invoices and sales here. Thefts..." He dropped his gaze to the book, opened it and turned to halfway through the pages. "...and other losses here. Wages and cargo in the back." He tapped the Duke of August's name. "I have filed them according to their order in the book. When you asked for the invoices, I naturally assumed..."

"Perfectly understandable, given the circumstances." Fiona smiled at the losses tallied on the page. Mr. Bartholomew was innocent; Uncle's faith was justified.

"I hope you have not spent all morning looking for them."

"It's nothing." Relief weakened her knees. She sank onto the seat. "You have done a wonderful job keeping the accounts."

"Thank you, Miss. Then you will not require these." He scooped up the invoices and hugged them to his chest.

"Well, since that matter is cleared up, I find I have time to enter these myself."

"But...but they are not in order." He tugged a handful free. "Please allow me to set them in order for you. It is my job—"

"Don't worry, Mr. Bartholomew, your reputation can stand a little disorder." Fiona plucked the invoices out of his grip. "In fact, I think you should take the rest of the day off."

"Miss?"

"Go home, or to the theater."

Gray crept under Mr. Bartholomew's skin. His shoulders drooped.

"Mr. Buttons is replacing me, then?"

"Heavens, no, Mr. Bartholomew. You are irreplaceable." Fiona patted his hand then tugged the invoices from his grip. How could she ever have thought such frail hands would be capable of such villainy? "I simply wish to thank you for all you've done while Uncle Andrew was indisposed. You've shouldered this burden too long—let us carry the load for a while."

"But..." He gazed at her from under his eyebrows. "Miss Grey, I would feel remiss in my duties, if I allowed—"

"Nonsense." She waved his objections away and strode toward the door. "You deserve it."

The doorknob turned under her hand. She stumbled forward as the door swung open. Strong hands closed around her shoulders, steadying her.

"I hope my arrival hasn't discomforted you." Hugh straightened her like he was posing a doll. "You took longer than expected. I thought you might require my assistance." He kneaded her shoulders. "Did you?"

"Yes, I mean, no." Fiona felt a grin lift her lips. How long had it been since someone looked out for her?

— I say, Fi. Are you quite certain you are not feeling ill? Milton waved his hand in front of her face.

Fiona forced the smile from her face. Milton looked out for her welfare. Numbers blurred as she thumbed through the stack of invoices. Why did that suddenly seem inadequate?

She shook her head to clear the confusion. "Your arrival has been most fortuitous."

"How may I be of service?" Hugh glanced at Bartholomew and arched an eyebrow.

— There, Fi, now you're looking more the thing. Milton drifted closer to Bartholomew. *Did you get Beakboy to confess his villainy?*

Fiona rolled her eyes and returned to the desk. Men. They were always convinced they were correct. Paper slipped through her hands as she tapped the invoices against the desktop. How would they feel when a mere woman proved them wrong?

She forced her features into a placid expression. Not that she took pleasure in such a task. "Marsh Mercantile" marched across the top sheet. Darn. The list of missing items must have blown off her desk. She would have to retrieve it. She spun on her heel. Two pieces of paper lay on the office floor.

— I think they want you to introduce them, Fi.

She froze mid-step.

"Yes, of course. Mr. Bartholomew, this is Mister..." A draft scooted the papers closer to the bookcases. If they slipped under the shelves it would take her the rest of the day to recover them.

"Book—" Hugh's baritone cut into her contemplations.

"Bookbuttons." Fiona slapped the invoices against his chest. "But Father calls him Buttons. Mr. Buttons."

Hugh gave a small nod. His fingers brushed hers as he caught the papers. He juggled the papers in one hand and thrust his free one at her uncle's manager.

"I have heard a great deal about you, Mr. Bartholomew."

"Yes, well." Bartholomew offered his limp hand then quickly tugged it free. "Perhaps, I should see where Mr. Black has gone to." He sidled toward his office, clutching his reddened hand to his chest.

Fiona's skull throbbed. Disappointment weighted her gut. Why had Hugh mangled the man's hand?

"I thought you were going to take the rest of the day off, Mr. Bartholomew." She deliberately stepped on Hugh's foot as she strode after the manager. He grunted and stepped backwards.

— *That's it, Fi. Grind his toes to a jelly.* Milton shook his fist at Hugh. *We don't need his kind of help.*

"Yes. Yes, of course." Mr. Bartholomew shuffled into his office. "I'll just retrieve my coat and leave, shall I?"

— *Doing it a bit brown, old man.* Milton glared at him. *He acts like you kicked his best hunting dog, Fi.*

"I'll expect you at the usual time tomorrow."

— *Tomorrow?* Red suffused Milton's cloudy form. *Why are you allowing that thief back in here?*

"Yes, Miss Grey." Mr. Bartholomew shrugged into his coat and trod across the room. "Goodnight, then."

"Goodnight, Mr. Bartholomew." The door snicked closed after his bent frame.

— *I'll make certain the miscreant leaves.* Milton darted through the wall.

"Bookbuttons?"

A clammy breeze brushed her cheeks as Hugh waved the stack of invoices at her. Fiona grabbed them out of his hands. Men's pride. It was almost enough to make her forget she'd been happy to see him. A sigh released her shoulders. Then she had to go and look at him.

A dimple winked in Hugh's cheek. Dimples. Milton said that God gave some people too much flesh on their face, and he had to stop it from dripping over their lips. Milton didn't have dimples.

"You were supposed to be Mr. Buttons." She emphasized the last word.

"You stammered. I thought you needed assistance in finding a name for me."

Irritant. Annoyance. She had plenty of names for him. Lover? Her heart thumped. Distraction. A very big, handsome distraction. *Focus, Fi. Remember why you are here.*

"I had already named you, which you would have known if you hadn't tried to rescue me again."

He kicked the office door shut, folded his arms across his chest and leaned against the wall.

"We could have gotten our story straight in the coach, had you waited for me."

"I didn't know you would be coming." Fiona cleared the whine from her throat. She had spent exactly twenty-three minutes watching the pendulum swing in her uncle's grandfather clock. Twenty-three endless minutes. White flashed on her lids as she dragged her thumb and finger across her eyes. How could she have waited another three hours to see if he would call? If he would kiss her hand. If he would kiss *her*.

She shook her head, knocking aside such foolishness.

"I have work to do." Organizing these invoices. She shuffled the invoices then plucked one out. *May tenth follows the ninth, Fi.*

"We settled this last night." Hugh tugged the pile from her grip and tossed them on the desk.

Settled. Last night. Last night he had settled his lips over hers and...

White caught her eye. The list. She slipped around him and picked up the paper. Shelley's Emporium. What had happened to the list? Perhaps it had been the other piece of paper. She knelt on the floor.

"Have you found anything?"

Even with a lamp, she doubted if she could find the list under the bookcases. Maybe Milton could push it out for her. Of course, he had disappeared when she wanted him.

"Aside from Mr. Bartholomew's unorthodox bookkeeping, I have uncovered nothing suspicious."

"So, how have you spent your morning?" Hugh held out his hand.

Fiona rocked back onto the balls of her feet. To accept or not to accept. Had she ever faced such a quandary? Her fingers bit into the bookshelf. She pulled herself to her feet. He was a distraction. His touch...

She swallowed the lump in her throat. "I don't need another stricture, Mr. Bookbuttons."

"Just Buttons, if you please." Hugh frowned down at her and clenched his empty hand. "I believe that is what your dear father calls me."

"Why Book?"

"Bookingham, actually. One of my titles." His thumb worried a nick on his chin. "When lying, it is best to cling as tightly to the truth as possible."

"How many titles do you have?"

He shrugged. "Enough."

"So, Hugh is...?"

"My Christian name."

Warmth pulsed through her. His given name. He had told her the truth.

"I see. What about Tom Thomas?"

"Hugh Thomas Gurnsey-Barrett, Sixth Marquess of Kingslea, Ninth Earl of Bookingham, Baron Proffitt, etcetera, etcetera, etcetera." He bowed low. "Now that we have been properly introduced, perhaps we could return to the business at hand. Who is the pesky villain who has been making a profit from Grey Shipping?"

"I believe that would be the Greys. Mr. Bartholomew is completely innocent. I think I will recommend that Uncle teach him proper bookkeeping so that such confusion does not arise again."

Hugh stuck his hands in his pockets. His eyebrows formed a V over the bridge of his nose. Did he doubt her?

Fiona unburied the ledger and flipped open the pages.

"Income. Losses. Miscellaneous."

"So it would appear."

"So it is."

"I believe you."

"Then why are you giving me that look." She crossed her arms and glared back at him.

"My apologies." He removed his hands from his pockets and smoothed his jacket. "You know these things better than I. If you say everything is in the proper order then I believe you."

"Oh." Chagrin heated her cheeks. He hadn't looked as if he believed her. The last time someone had looked at her that way, Milton had put a rat in his pocket. Fiona froze. Milton had disappeared after being alone with Hugh. "The suit looks good."

"My housekeeper stayed up all night making the alterations."

"She did a wonderful job." She stepped forward. Hugh straightened away from the wall and eased to the right. No unsightly bulging pockets, spreading inkstains.

"I doubt Mr. Bartholomew recognized it." Fiona took another step forward.

"Speaking of Bartholomew, what on earth did you say to him?" Hugh moved farther right, shadowing her movements, keeping the same distance between them. "He looked at me as if I were Beelzebub himself."

"I told him the board sent you to investigate Uncle Andrew's disappearance." Why was he avoiding her?

"Was that wise?"

Wise. Perhaps Milton had split a scam in Hugh's skintight trousers.

"How much do you know about clerking?"

"Good point." Hugh dropped into the cane chair. "Do you trust the man?"

Trust Bartholomew?

"Uncle Andrew trusted him with his life." She'd had the same confidence until this morning. Although everything had been explained, she found the doubts still lingered. " Mr. Bartholomew always alluded to a debt of honor he owed Uncle."

"Honor, eh. Any idea what that entailed?"

Blackmail, theft and coercion. Mr. Bartholomew had been a pawn of the current Duke of August's father. Wrongly accused then as he had been now.

"I—"

"Sir!" Mr. Black's shout rattled the window in her office door. "If you would..."

"I insist on speaking to Mr. Grey personally." Heavy footsteps thumped the wooden floor.

Hugh pushed out of his chair and reached for the doorknob.

"Perhaps we had best see the cause of such a ruckus."

"It does appear as if Mr. Black needs rescuing." Fiona sailed through the open door.

A corpulent man with a purple face reared back at the sight of her.

"Who the blazes are you," he wheezed.

"Sir, may I remind you there is a lady present." Mr. Black tossed her a wide-eyed look and tried to wedge himself between her and the newcomer.

"Demmed females." The man shoved Black out of his way. "Yer kind have no place in business."

Fiona sighed as his gaze bounced off her and landed on Hugh. How could she have forgotten the blustering windbags? A dull ache pulsed across her forehead. Before, she had used his kind to vent her grief. Now...

"Where is Mr. Grey?" Pain rattled down her arm as his meaty fist collided with her shoulder. "I demand to see Mr. Grey."

"Good sir." Fiona planted her feet shoulders'-width apart. He wasn't going to shove her aside so easily again. "If you would simply..."

The hand dropped, and he sidled around her.

"You, there." The wood planks under his feet groaned. "Where is your employer?"

"Mister..." Fiona turned, following his progress.

"Stop interrupting, woman." His girth undulated to a stop. Button eyes peered at her from folds of flesh. "Egads, no place is sacred. Why aren't you at home, eh, gel?" Fermented breath washed over her. "Not enough babies, I'd wager. Your good wife needs plenty more babies." A sausage-thick finger thumped Hugh on the chest. "Babies are the answer. Keep her out of trouble and in her proper place."

Babies. Hugh's babies, nestled under her heart. Fiona wrapped an arm around her flat stomach. Flat. Empty. Anger drowned the sense of loss.

"Now, see here."

"He's right, darling." Hugh winked as he placed his arm around her shoulders. "Your beautiful presence is distracting us poor men,"

Betrayal whipped through her. Hugh wanted a partner—so long as he was in charge.

"You..."

"Why don't you wait for me in my office, dearest?" Warm lips pressed against her temple. Her treacherous feet carried her toward her uncle's office. "After I see to Mister..."

"Higgenbottom."

"After I see to Mr. Higgenbottom, we can discuss those other matters." Hugh nodded to their audience.

"I think—"

"And I agree completely. A spot of tea would do very nicely, dearest."

They cleared the doorjamb.

"You want me to make tea?"

"I want you to find out why your uncle's ship sank." Hugh glanced over his shoulder. "Only you can know if something is missing, Fiona. If I attend this small matter you will be free to do a little more digging."

Pleasure spurted through her. Hugh *did* believe in her.

"You realize your rescue has cost me Mr. Black's faith in my abilities."

"You'll bring him around." Hugh squeezed her hand and backed toward the door. "Don't worry if there aren't any sandwiches. I'm certain Mr. Black can dig up a tin of biscuits."

Biscuits. Sandwiches. Fiona stared at the silhouettes moving on the other side of the opaque window. She'd pour his tea in his lap.

"Now, Mr. Higgenbottom, how might I help you today."

Fiona strode to the open door.

"You can't help me—only Mr. Grey can."

The wooden jamb bit into her palm. Of course, if she were lucky Mr. Higgenbottom would be worse than a lapfull of scalding tea.

"Mr. Higgenbottom, I am Mr. Bookbuttons, Mr. Grey's man of affairs." Hugh extended his hand and winced as it was swallowed by the other's. "He has charged me to act in his stead while his wife recovers from her accident."

"Demned women." Beady eyes flicked to her. "You, there!"

Fiona jumped at the bark.

"In the office, like your husband commanded. Take a vow of obedience, they do."

She stepped back into the office. Laughter tickled her palm.

"Of course, they always forget that one."

"Er..." Hugh coughed. "Quite. How might I help you?"

"My usual driver didn't deliver the shipment."

"Was anything missing?"

"Here, now, that's not the point. I trust Crabbe. Not any of the others. Always dropping something and dunning me for it."

A giggle tickled Fiona's ears. She'd gladly allow Hugh to serve all the Mr. Higgenbottoms in the world. She had work to do.

"All right, Uncle, why did the Sweet Wind sink?" Her gaze skimmed the bookshelves. Someone had straightened the books in her absence. "Mr. Bartholomew definitely needs a vacation. I remember his wife loved the sea."

Her fingers bumped over the years of captain's logs. Something skittered across the floor. She froze. A white square of paper lay against the base of the bookshelves.

Fear soured her mouth.

The last time she had found a folded scrap of paper, it had contained a threat.

CHAPTER 23

Fiona's hand trembled as she reached for the note. She curled her fingers; the bite of her nails burned her palm. Paper can't hurt you, Fi. She flung open her fists and glanced over her shoulder. Male voices drifted in the open door.

You need not open the note. Hugh is a call away.

Coward.

She squared her shoulders. Fiona Grey was no coward. Her fingers closed around her uncle's letter opener. Cool silver weighted her palm. The tip poked the paper. It scooted a couple of inches across the wood plank.

"For pity's sake, Fi. It's not alive." Air inflated her constricted lungs. Paper crinkled between her index finger and thumb. She tossed the note. It arced through the air to land on top of the invoices heaped on her desk.

Pushing to her feet, she walked to the desk.

"Now all you have to do is open it."

She plucked a fountain pen from the drawer. With a hard rubber barrel in one hand and a silver letter opener in the other, she prodded the note open.

IOU £500
E.R.

Laughter barked past her lips. Her knees trembled. It wasn't a threat at all. It was an IOU. An IOU? Questions buzzed in her head.

Why would Mr. Bartholomew have an IOU?

Unless...

She yanked open the bottom drawer, hoisted out the strongbox and twisted the combination lock. The oversized bills stared up at her. Her fingers flew over the stiff money. Her brain tallied the numbers once. Twice. Every penny was accounted for.

Dropping the lid, she tucked the box back in the drawer. Her uncle's leather chair welcomed her weight. What was the IOU for?

"I hope your Mr. Bookbuttons doesn't run screaming from his post." Black strode into the room, looked at the mess on her desk and stacked his contribution in the corner. "Mr. Higgenbottom strained Mr. Grey's patience more than once. Demands partial credit for every dented tin."

Indecision flipped through her. Should she mention the debt, or wait until Mr. Bartholomew returned? She picked up the scrap of paper and tapped it on the desk. It could be a personal debt. Nothing whatsoever to do with business.

"Mr. Black, do you know why there is an IOU mixed in with the invoices?" If it was a personal matter, she had neatly evaded mentioning names. And if it wasn't...

She shrugged off the doubts. If it wasn't, then maybe the clerk would know to what it pertained.

"Hmmm." Confusion furrowed his forehead as he stared at the note. He started to shake his head, paused then nodded. "Yes, yes, of course."

— *He's coming, Fi.* Milton shot up through the floor, breezed a shiver through Mr. Black and stuck his face through the window glass.

"Mr. Black?"

"E.R—it must be Mr. Richard, Miss Grey." Black rubbed his hands together. His purple fingernails warmed to pink. "Mr. Richard's account has been allowed to lapse since his wife required extra care. Consumption, don't you know. Mr. Grey has generously allowed his shipments to proceed as usual so that he might attend her without suffering the loss of his business as well."

Fiona nodded. That sounded exactly like her uncle. He had even offered to run G&G Enterprises when Brianna's surrender to her illness became inevitable.

"Who is minding his shop?"

"His sons, Miss. The Richards are good for it. The Mister's been in tighter straights than this, and he's always recovered." Mr. Black pinned his gaze on her. "Do you wish to rescind his credit?"

"No." She forced her lips into a smile. "I don't think that will be necessary."

"Shall I return this to Mr. Bartholomew's office?" Mr. Black's hands stretched toward the note.

"No, thank you."

"Very good, Miss." He bowed, turned on his heel and marched out the door.

— *Fi.* Milton darted in front of her, waving his hands. *Fi, didn't you hear me? The duke is here.*

"Ah, Mr. Bartles." The Duke of August's petulance oozed through the open door.

Breath froze in her lungs. Hugh. She must warn Hugh. The duke could expose them all. Fiona dashed to the door; ideas stormed her, wrestled for dominance.

"Please tell Mr. Grey that the Duke of August wishes a word."

"Of course, Your Grace." Mr. Black cast a questioning glance in her direction. Fiona nodded and walked forward.

"Miss Grey." The duke started then sketched a brief bow.

"What a delightful surprise, Your Grace."

"This is most fortuitous. Your devotion to your uncle does you credit." His hand slithered around hers. "There isn't many a lady who would take time out of her shopping to grace her uncle with her presence."

"I am an unusual lady, Your Grace." Relief bowed her shoulders. Hugh had obviously stepped out with Mr. Higgenbottom. But how long would they be gone—and how to warn him? Her gaze slid to Milton. Her ex-fiancé would be more likely to expose Hugh than to protect him from exposure.

— *Behave, Fi.* Milton glared at her. *Or you won't get a good night's sleep for a week. I promise you.*

The duke peered over her shoulder before returning his gaze to her.

"I see your uncle has stepped out."

Fiona sighed. Another lie. However was she to keep track of them? Perhaps she should follow her uncle's example and keep a journal.

— *Talk to him, Fi,* Milton prompted.

"Uncle was about to see me home but was called away on urgent business." It would be no good confessing to a priest. She was thoroughly unrepentant. She had to protect Hugh. He was here on her account, which made him her responsibility. Her falsehoods were positively bedeviled by good intentions—and Milton.

— *That's good, Fi. Now, ask him to tea or...* Milton circled her. *I know— mention the ball you plan to attend this evening then he'll ask for a dance and—*

And maybe she would see a priest after all. Milton was afraid of churches.

"It seems I have become quite stranded."

"Allow me to escort you." The duke offered his arm.

— *Very clever. Although you should try to get him to commit to one dance whilst you are tucked in his carriage. A waltz would be best, although—*

"That is very kind." Fiona turned her back on her personal shade and set her bare hand on the duke's arm. Soft flesh and wool cushioned her palm. "Are you quite certain I am not interrupting your business?"

"Never allow thoughts of business to concern you, my dear." He patted her hand. Her skin itched from the contact. "If I may confess, I used that as an excuse to apprise your uncle of my intentions."

— *Ha!* Milton wagged a finger at her. *I knew his presence was more than simple coincidence. He's courting you, Fi.*

"Your intentions?" Fiona suppressed a shudder. The man's grimace showed more teeth than a rotting corpse. Corpse. Why must the dead plague her?

"Yes, I know. But I find that I have developed quite a taste for the fresh American lady." His Grace opened the door and motioned her out. "Quite different from our delicate British flowers. Positively brimming with passion, always ready for an adventure." His thick tongue strolled across his bottom lip.

Fiona's jaw throbbed. Did the man practice cloaking insults in compliments, or was he simply gifted? Too bad more men didn't say what they meant. *Men like Hugh*, her conscience teased. He had better appreciated her sacrifice.

"It is so remarkable that you noticed."

— *Fiona Anne Grey, your tongue is sharper than your whip.* Red tinged Milton's smudged form.

"I notice many things, my dear." The duke set his hat on his head and gave it a sharp tap. "I noticed you were not at home for my call. Indeed, I was most perturbed, even a touch jealous." He smirked down at her as they descended the steps. "You see, I was practically convinced you had been seduced by an…" He cleared his throat. "…an undesirable person."

— *Now, Fi. I'm certain he has nothing but the utmost respect for your uncle.* Milton wrung his hands.

Splinters from the wooden stair railing bit into her skin. That was definitely an insult. She stopped two steps from the bottom landing. Once they were outside, she would send him on his way. Alone.

"Oh, Mr. Bookbuttons." Mr. Black's hail shattered her plans.

Hugh saunter into view. Tall. Proud. Honorable. She'd started on this path; she'd travel it to the end. She had endured insufferable prigs before.

"My uncle wouldn't allow any undesirable persons into his house, Your Grace."

"Naturally, Miss Grey. Naturally." He smoothed his moustache, smoothed the transition of whiskers into his sideburns.

— *There's that Kingston fellow, Fi.* Milton hovered over a pile of crates. *You should let him see you.*

Fiona's heart slammed in her chest. They neared the crates where Hugh stood talking. If the duke turned his head he would certainly spy him. How could she divert His Grace's attention?

Stumble.

Her feet obeyed the command. The short stagger carried them past the point of danger.

— *Ha. You did that on purpose.* Milton floated a foot in front of them. *So, did you like having his arms around you?*

"Are you quite all right, my dear?"

"Yes," Fiona forced the brightness from her smile. It wouldn't do for the duke to drown in the same conclusion Milton had. "The roses you sent were quite lovely."

"Yet they pale next to your beauty."

"You are too kind." And his flattery stank more than an unclean stable. Fiona winced, knowing his inflated opinion of himself would attribute her reaction to the weak sunlight rather than his person.

"Would you allow me one further kindness?"

Her gaze traveled to the sluggish river. Hugh had said the river wouldn't mind another contribution of rubbish. However, she sincerely doubted His Grace would ask her to chuck him in the fetid water.

"After all of your indulgence, how could I possibly refuse?" Very easily, she just had to think of something that would pacify Milton. She liked to sleep.

A hansom cab lumbered to a halt next to them.

"At yer service, Gov'nor."

Fiona blinked. What was Houseman doing here? He had brought Hugh. And he would also dutifully report anything she said to Sullied. God certainly took pity on fools.

— *Don't worry, Fi. I don't expect an answer. The dead are accustomed to being ignored.* Milton pouted.

The duke handed her into the carriage.

"Sorry for the conveyance, my dear. I had thought to be longer so I sent the coach home. This is not the safest area for one's prized cattle."

"I understand."

"Of course, you do." The cab door closed with a thud. He pounded on the roof with his gold-topped walking cane, and they jolted forward. "As I was saying, my collection is on the way to Piccadilly. Please allow me to offer you a private tour."

"How positively delicious, Your Grace." The lie burned Fiona's throat. The carriage bumped in and out of a pothole. "But I am afraid I have been gone far longer than expected. My aunt will be worried."

— *Worried?* Milton scolded. *That woman doesn't worry about anyone but herself.*

"Perhaps another day?"

"Quite right, Miss Grey." The duke consulted his timepiece. "Tomorrow would be better. I shall call around two."

Fiona collapsed against the seat. She had been granted a reprieve until two tomorrow. Unless an emergency occurred at half-past one.

CHAPTER 24

"You will see to it personally?"

"Yes." Kingslea nodded. How many times had he assured the man? Four? Doubt wrinkled the shopkeeper's sweating forehead. "Of course." Five.

"You're a good man, Bookbuttons."

Higgenbottom slammed one meaty fist into Kingslea's shoulder. Pain zigged across his shoulder blades, milked tingles from his fingertips.

"I'll make it clear to Bartholomew that there should be no changes to your route." Kingslea pumped the man's hand and forced his grimace into a smile. His surreptitious audience wouldn't see any weakness. Navy fabric fluttered in his peripheral vision. Fiona. Lead plummeted to the bottom of his belly.

Sullied.

Had she palmed him off on the blustery Higgenbottom to further her interest in the duke?

"Ah, jealousy." Higgenbottom compounded his assault on Kingslea's back by grinding the small bones of his hand together. "Go up there and pacify the missus. What with the way she looks at you, your lady wife shouldn't be too hard to woo."

Lady. Wife. Fiona. His. Kingslea nodded to the corpulent man and spun on his heel. He was a reasonable man. A civilized man. He forced open his fists. She could have made her unhappiness known in a far more productive manner than flirting with Sullied.

"Another baby or two wouldn't hurt, either, eh?"

Higgenbottom's bark of laughter hounded Kingslea through the corridor. Stacked crates intermittently blocked his view of his quarry.

A baby or two wouldn't slow Fiona's pace. She would do what she wanted. Hell, he'd even help. A growl rumbled from his chest. But he positively drew the line at her clinging to another man tighter than a barnacle to a ship's bow.

"Mr. Bartholomew has made many changes."

A man stepped from an alcove of boxes. Kingslea's boots skidded in a puddle. Pain burned up his thighs as his feet went in opposite directions. His elbow slammed into a crate. Finding his balance, he glared at the latest impediment. Were the fates conspiring against him?

"Eh?" He searched for a name. Blank? No. Black.

"Mr. Bartholomew has made many changes." The clerk's chin bobbed. He glanced over his shoulder. "That's why you are here, isn't it?" He lowered his voice. "To investigate."

Damn Fiona. Her faithful Bartholomew had all the discretion of a social-climbing mama.

"I'm just a clerk." Kingslea transferred his weight to the balls of his feet. His gaze skimmed the slight man. And speaking of Fiona, where had Sullied taken her? Mr. Black's head obstructed his line of sight. "Like you."

"Is that why Miss Grey allowed you to call her *wife*?"

Irritation itched Kingslea's skin. The little clerk had overstepped his mark. Fiona was not his concern.

"I am here to help."

"Oh, aye. The lady who faced down a room full of angry sailors, captains and dockers yesterday needed protection from a lone windbag today."

Sailors, captains and dockers. Pride swelled Kingslea's chest. His Fiona was a fine, capable lady. Maybe a bit too capable. He stroked his smooth jaw.

"Say your conclusions are correct." Her explanation seemed the most logical. Perhaps he could turn the situation to his advantage. "If I'm not an ordinary clerk then what would I be looking for?"

"Black." A rough-looking man with bent features cracked his scraped knuckles and glowered at Kingslea. "Thought Bartholomew had you working upstairs today."

"Yes. Yes."

The clerk dismissed the menacing words with a wave of his hand. The man was either a fool, or this confrontation was staged solely for Kingslea's benefit.

"He'll return to his post after we finish our conversation." Kingslea matched the rough's glare. He remained rooted, a tableaux of intimidation.

Black leaned forward and straightened a crooked crate.

"Look for what you can't see," he muttered.

Wood bit into Kingslea's hand as he helped align the crate's corners.

"If I can't see it, then how will I find it?"

"Black."

A quartet of thugs added their intimidation to the first man's. He silenced them with a one-eyed glare, puffed out his chest and continued his demands.

"The boss means fer his instructions to be forced, er, followed, even when 's not 'ere."

"Because you're in a position to," Black concluded to Kingslea then tapped the crate again and plunged through the crowd. The men escorted him to the stairs and resumed their original posts.

Kingslea shoved another stack of crates. His muscles shook with stored adrenaline. That had been as illuminating as a street lamp in a thick fog. What the hell was he supposed to do now?

Look for something he couldn't see, because he was in a position to?

He adjusted the cuffs of his suit. Was enigma-spewing part of a clerk's training? Perhaps the cryptic message was for the benefit of their audience. Fiona would know. Fiona, who had left on the arm of Sullied.

How dare she sneak out of here right in front of his eyes? They were supposed to be partners. Kingslea trudged up the stairs. Well, he would live up to his end of their bargain.

Silence blanketed the office. Wood creaked in the corner. The bent-featured thug leaned against the wall, picking his nails with a thin knife.

Black hunched farther over his desk as his pen scratched furiously across the sheet of paper. Kingslea strode into Fiona's office. Where should he start? His gaze rested on the stack of papers. That was as good a place as any. After all, he was searching for something that wasn't there.

He plucked a handful off the stack. Higgenbottom's name caught his eye. Yards of silk, pounds of tea, casks of spices, bolts of cotton—

"Mr. Bookbuttons?" Black scratched on the door.

Had the man come to explain himself then?

"Just Buttons."

"Mr. Wells wishes to speak to someone in charge."

Kingslea ignored the stab of disappointment. He had always loved a challenge before, so what was different about this time? Fiona. Her name whispered across his conscience. Leave it to the woman to disturb him even when she wasn't here.

"Very well." He followed Black out the door. Paper crinkled in his fist. Hell, the invoices. He glared at the papers. He could hardly return them to the office. The thin man with the twitching nose was already looking at him suspiciously. He folded them neatly, tucked them into his jacket pocket and held out his hand. "Mr. Wells, I presume?"

❋ ❋ ❋

"What shall I do with these, milord?" Houseman clutched papers in his hand.

Kingslea stifled a groan. He had forgotten about the invoices. That explained his irrational need to see Fiona. Ignoring the chiding doubts, he smoothed the white cravat at his throat.

"Set them near my gloves."

"You are taking them to the ball?"

"They are the property of Grey Shipping. I am certain Miss Grey will notice their absence." Absent. Missing. What's not there. An entire afternoon wasted, solving other people's problems. Had Fiona made any progress?

"The fancy dresses, the mounds of food and music are certain to remind Miss Grey of scraps of paper filled with crooked lines of numbers."

Sullied's sulky face polluted his thoughts. Progress in their investigation, that is, not with her courtship of a title. He jerked his shoulders forward, pulling the evening coat from his valet's hands. *How could she prefer Sullied to...me?* He ignored his reflection's eyes. Not that he was interested in marriage.

"And you are quite certain she will be at the Graham-Russells'?"

"Yes, milord." Houseman whisked the wire brush over the evening coat then cleaned the collected lint from the bristles. "Shall I repeat it another three times?"

"I don't wish to haul sensitive documents all over London." He tugged on his worn cuffs. Perhaps he should purchase another evening suit. If Fiona insisted on spending her time in society furthering her inquiries, honor demanded he accompany her. Not that he could afford anything as elegant as Worth, but his tailor produced quality work for a fraction of the normal price.

"Oh, aye." Houseman busied himself picking up discarded clothing. "The price one pays for watered silk and the amount one charges the nobs is liable to cause palpitations in the ballroom."

Supple leather sheathed Kingslea's fingers. Uppity servants. Good God, now he sounded like his stepmother.

"She actually said she was going to the Graham-Russells' ball."

"Yes, milord."

"Kindly do not take that tone with me, Houseman. I am not a simpleton."

"Of course..." Houseman caught Kingslea's eye in the mirror. "...not, milord."

"Heroic rescue of inattentiveness, Houseman." He stepped into his waiting boots, "I find the entire thing highly suspicious."

"The Graham-Russells are not acceptable, milord?" Houseman tugged and smoothed Kingslea's immaculate attire as he circled.

"You are not attending, man." He shrugged into his overcoat. "It is Miss Grey's behavior that I find questionable. Are you quite certain she recognized you on the box?"

"Though she did not address me by name, I believe the Miss to be quite perceptive."

"Did she acknowledge you in any way?"

"She paused briefly before alighting." With one last swipe at the overcoat, Houseman turned his attention to retrieving the top hat from its place of honor.

Yes, his Fiona would have recognized Houseman. And she was just woman enough to use the coachman/valet's presence to her advantage.

"Just as I thought."

"Milord?"

Kingslea opened his bedroom door and strode into the hall.

"I have no doubt, Miss Grey deliberately misstated her true intentions. She knew you would report any information back to me." She knew he would listen. Kingslea pivoted, narrowly missed colliding with his valet, and marched back into his bedroom. How had the blasted woman gotten into his head? He shrugged out of his overcoat. More important, how was he to get her out?

"You're not going to the ball?" Houseman growled as he scooped up the discarded coat.

"I'm not a fool, no matter what Fiona may think." Kingslea's fingers fumbled with the buttons of his waistcoat. "She is not going to be at the Graham-Russells' but she wants me there, like a hound following a false scent."

"Are you not assisting the lady in her search?"

"Of course. I gave my word, didn't I?"

Houseman scratched his head. "Then why would the Miss deceive you?"

Because she hadn't liked his handling the Higgenbottom incident, or because she hadn't liked being thought of as his wife? Disappointment muffled his heartbeats. Houseman cleared his throat. Expectation weighted the air, pressed Kingslea to speak.

"She was a bit...ruffled when last we parted. The lady doesn't appreciate being protected."

"How very inconvenient for you, milord." Houseman smiled.

He buttoned his waistcoat. Mary would never forgive him if he rearranged her husband's face—ugly, smirking face though it was.

"That is only the beginning. Doubtless, I shall spend my evening dashing hither and yon looking for her."

"So, you will escort your sister and, er, the other to the Graham-Russells?"

"Yes, although I shall undoubtedly find her at another function, aflame with pretty indignation."

"Then you and Sullied..." Houseman spat into the wash basin then drew his hand across his mouth. "...will be in the same company."

"How's that?"

"She told the duke they attended the Graham-Russells' ball."

"Did she?" Kingslea shrugged back into his overcoat. Had he underestimated her? Heaven knew she was unlike any other lady of his acquaintance. Perhaps she really *had* wanted him to know where she would be this evening. What better place to announce her interest in Sullied?

Would his heart again be trod upon by the dancing masses?

His heart?

For such an injury to occur, he needed to love Fiona.

Love Fiona.

Absolutely.

Not.

Absolutely not. He nodded. His brain was finally functioning properly. He liked Fiona, but then, he liked Houseman's wife Mary.

"Aye, she did."

It meant absolutely nothing. He smoothed his mussed hair. Nothing. He was a man in control of his life.

"Where did they go?" His teeth captured his tongue. Copper exploded in his mouth. His life may be under control, but his body seemed to have rebelled.

"To the museum, milord."

"And did he impress her with his glittering collection?" Kingslea straightened his shoulders. It was better to know now, in the privacy of his bedroom, than to be disappointed in front of an audience.

"If those were his intentions they died unborn in the cab. The horses stood for a full eight minutes afore he bundled her out." Houseman followed him out into the corridor.

"Bundled her out?"

"Aye. 'Twas a right peculiar shade of green, she was." Houseman pressed the top hat into Kingslea's hands. "The dead aren't to her liking, I'm thinking. His lordship appeared most upset when he handed her into the carriage."

"Did he see her home?"

"Oh, aye."

Kingslea paused at the top of the landing. Why was Houseman suddenly so close-mouthed? Had the bounder kissed Fiona? Hell, that would have been the first thing out of Houseman's mouth. His valet wanted the Duke of August planted six feet under almost as much as he did.

"What happened when they arrived?"

"He walked her to the door."

"He didn't enter?"

"No."

"Because you were watching?" Old doubts stirred in Kingslea.

"Neither saints nor angels tread in a woman's mind, milord."

"Almost as dangerous a territory as her pride," he agreed.

"Ye'll be apologizing, then, milord."

Kingslea nodded then caught himself and shook his head.

"Apologize? I've done nothing wrong."

"Me Mary tells me that sometimes it ain't what you've done so much as what you've failed to do." Houseman winked. "A lady's pride needs almost as much protecting as her person, and with a lady of Miss Grey's skills, it just might need a bit more."

"Indeed, Houseman. Indeed." Kingslea mentally kicked himself in the posterior. How had he not seen it before? Every man at Grey Shipping would deny her the chance to use her considerable skills if she wasn't a relation of the owners. And he had gone willy-nilly along with them.

She had handled angry sailors, captains and merchants.

Black's words tormented him.

"I believe I shall practice my apology in the carriage."

"Very good, milord."

"Ah, Lord Kingslea, bless yer heart, yer still about." Corsets creaked and keys jingled as his housekeeper glided up the stairs to meet him.

"Is there something I may do for you, Mrs. Proust?"

"Bless you, milord, no." Her papery hands fluttered around her ample bosom before diving into her apron pockets. "The tailor sent this round." She pressed a folded scrap of paper into his hands. "Said he found it in the pocket of your jacket and thought it might be important."

> Your performance has been most disappointing thus far. Perhaps your marked interest in Miss Grey can be of use. Escort her to the function of her choice for the nights of 1st and 2nd June. Give the guards and servants the night off.

Anger blazed through him. Fiona was in danger. Paper crunched in his fist. The anonymous note writer had better enjoy his last few days on this earth.

"He apologized for not returning it with the suit, milord." The housekeeper shrank into her wrinkled flesh and retreated a few steps.

"Thank you, Mrs. Proust." Kingslea filled his lungs, willed the anger to ease its grip. He had four days to plan. Four days to remove Fiona and her family from harm's way. "I trust you and the rest of the staff will enjoy your evening off."

Gnarled fingers clutched at her chest. Relief eased the pull on her mouth, but fear retained its grip on her shoulders. Irritation sparked anger's tinder. Even after five years in his employ, Mrs. Proust still expected a beating whenever he became displeased. Too bad he couldn't disinter her former employer and kill him all over again.

"Very good, milord." Red stained her fingertips as she wound her apron around her hands. "Thank you, milord." She bobbed a quick curtsey and fled down the staircase.

"Another note?" Houseman brushed Kingslea's shoulder.

Another demand. He dropped the paper into his valet's hands.

"Was my clerk's disguise ever out of your sight?"

"Indeed. I left it in the cab, in the stables." Anger throbbed in Houseman's ruddy jaw. "You wanted more information about the lady."

"Damnation."

"Aye." Houseman neatly folded the crumpled paper. "The Graham-Russells' or one-eighteen Piccadilly?"

"Neither." Courses of action swirled inside Kingslea's skull.

"Neither?"

"Find out if the Greys have acquired anything recently. That might point out our walking corpse."

"Corpse."

"If he harms Fiona…"

"Aye, well, I'll line up the disposal crew."

"Give me something, Houseman." He winced as pleasant conversation drifted out of the drawing room. "Anything."

"I'll not fail you."

Kingslea shoved open the tall mahogany doors, caught sight of his sister sitting by the fire. The golden light flattered her straight nose and the curve of her slender neck. So very different from a skinny waif with muddy toes and an injured woodland creature tucked in her apron. When had she grown up?

"Melody."

For an instant, mischief sparkled in her clear lavender eyes. Coolness quickly took its place.

"Lord Kingslea."

Loss punched him in the gut. His stepmother wasn't completely to blame for the distance. He remembered shoving aside his sister's offers of comfort. Perhaps it wasn't too late. Perhaps he might yet regain Melody's affections.

"You look especially lovely this evening."

She blushed and shrugged off his compliment.

"Sir Winthrop has been telling the most delightful tale of your school days."

"Has he?" Kingslea's gaze slid to his old friend. He wasn't the only one to notice the change in his sister, then.

"Did you really release toads into the larder?" Melody regarded Winthrop from under her lashes.

Winthrop caught Kingslea's eye, cleared his throat and pawed his cravat. Embarrassment stained his round cheeks.

Kingslea adjusted his cuffs. Perhaps he had left his sister in his trusted friend's care too long.

"I was never *accused* of any such thing."

"Sullied took the blame." Lord Alveston rocked back on his heels, grinning as he inspected the marble fireplace. Was that relief in his eyes?

"However did you manage that?" She spared him an admiring glance but focused on Winthrop.

"His noble brow is almost as low as his intelligence," Winthrop whispered.

While Kingslea himself seemed to have developed a blind spot. He would need to keep an eye on his friend.

"Really, Kingslea?" His stepmother sashayed into the drawing room. Overripe roses clouded the air. "Have you no respect for your betters?"

"Only when I find them, Madam." Kingslea raised his glass of sherry then downed the contents in one swallow.

"Melody, stop giggling." His stepmother's command turned the cool air brittle. "It is most unbecoming to a lady."

Vibrancy melted from his sister's countenance like snow before the summer sun.

Kingslea stepped between his sister and stepmother.

"A house should be filled with genuine laughter."

"Yes, Mama." Melody arranged the folds of her skirt.

"Mother," Elspeth snapped. She tugged on the bell pull. Fabric ripped. "Can no one in this house use the proper titles? Wherever could you have learned such vulgar familiarity?"

"I believe that would be my cue." Winthrop and Alveston flanked him. "Perhaps if you had thought of your daughter instead of your own pleasure for the first thirteen years of her life, she might not have been corrupted by my offensive person."

"And if your brother had had the decency to live, I might not be subject to it now."

"You needn't be any longer." Kingslea let his anger slip. Power warmed him. "Melody, I believe you can make your mother's regrets to the Graham-Russells."

"You wouldn't dare." For once the color in Elspeth's cheeks had a natural origin.

"Perhaps, I should..." Melody's gaze wavered. Pearly teeth bit into her bottom lip.

"Enjoy yourself, despite your mama's debilitating headache." Kingslea nodded.

Winthrop offered his arm to Melody and escorted her out the door.

"Bunsen, I'm afraid my stepmother will be staying home tonight."

"I most certainly—"

Kingslea overrode her protest. "Please advise the staff that this changes nothing, and they are still to take the evening off."

"You...you barbarian." His stepmother picked up a Dresden shepherdess.

"Break that, madam, and the funds to replace it will come out of your dress allowance."

"I hate you." She set the figurine on the table and flopped onto the couch. "I wish you had died instead of your brother."

For the first time, her words lacked their sting.

"Tsk-tsk. How many times must you repeat the same tired statement?"

"Until it comes to pass." She glared at him. "Your cousin Edward is ever so much more manageable."

"Goodnight, madam." Kingslea shut the door quietly behind him.

She had just presented him with an unsavory possibility. These never-ending errands might be a way to help cousin Edward succeed to the title.

CHAPTER 25

— **I say, Fi, our hostess must be pleased.** *Milton's face beamed at her from the* creamy walls.

"It is a crush." Fiona tossed a smile at the apologetic man who'd jabbed her in the side. Another bruise. She swallowed the groan scratching her throat. The elegantly dressed mob surged toward the dining room, carrying her along like a rock tumbling in a silk-and-wool stream.

"Terribly so," her abuser agreed before turning his attention back to his whey-faced companion.

— *I fail to see why the English are known for their manners.* Milton scowled. *It was perfectly obvious that you weren't speaking to him.*

Fiona slipped between the potted palms. For her sake, it had better not be obvious. If word went round that she talked to herself, Piers and Aunt Annabelle would gleefully pack her off to the asylum.

The hum of violin strings danced down the stairs in three-quarter time. A waltz strummed the steps from her feet.

Where was Hugh?

She craned her neck to peer up the stairs. Edwina clung to the arm of a lanky gentleman. Poor Lancelot. He had shambled up to Fiona hopeful of renewing their past acquaintance and had been fettered by Edwina's salivating interest. A pained expression scrunched his face as he pried her cousin's fingers from his arm. Guilt flopped in Fiona's stomach. Someone really should rescue him and his ten thousand pounds.

She batted a flat leaf out of her face. Edwina's grating laughter screeched down the staircase. Fiona pressed farther under the staircase. There was a fine line between self-preservation and cowardice.

Her gaze swept over the studied boredom of the swells, the damp enthusiasm of the misses, and the cramped interest of doting mamas and wilted companions. Where was Hugh? How had he fared without her?

Had he missed her?

Rubbing the ache from her chest, she swatted aside the annoying questions. She thought entirely too much of the man—of his hands, his smile, his lips. Frustration shredded her patience. Lately, she had spent more time scheming to steal another kiss than pondering the question surrounding her aunt and uncle's disappearance.

— *I don't see him, Fi.* Milton adjusted his cuffs. *He didn't actually say he would attend, though, did he?*

"No." She hadn't been around Hugh long enough to ask. The Duke of August's presence had prevented it. Surely, the coachman had related her plans. "I repeated them often enough."

— *Twelve times, Fi,* Milton chided. *Another time, and the duke would surely have thought you desperate.*

"The duke?" Fiona spat out a leaf. What did she care if Sullied thought her desperate? Hugh's opinion was the only one that mattered. Had he looked for her in the office? Had he wanted to share his experiences with Mr. Higgenbottom?

— *You really are out of practice, Fi.* The crisp green leaves yellowed as Milton stepped into the potted palm. *Subtlety and stealth will win you the title of duchess.*

She resisted the urge to roll her eyes. She wanted a different title, and more important, she wanted the man that went with it.

"Milton."

— *And couldn't you at least try a little harder to control your reaction?* He shook his head. *Fainting,* he huffed. *Such a schoolgirl ploy.*

"That wasn't a ploy. They were dead. Dead and desecrated." Rage had pummeled her the moment she stepped into the museum. The dead hovered near their looted belongings, railing at their impotence.

Then they had spied her and Milton.

They had flown toward her, keening in a dead language, demanding she help them. Their sorrow and pain had overwhelmed her. And Sullied...

Bile exploded on her tongue. Her fainting had freed her of their presence and the man who profited from their misery.

— *I was certain your connivance was a deliberate attempt to gain an embrace.* For an instant, pride lifted Milton's features. *But then I realized it was genuine.* His icy touch sowed goosebumps up her arm. *Perhaps you should consult a physician, Fi. Consumption, when caught early...*

"I am perfectly well, Milton." Just as he knew she found the assault of too many specters unsettling. Fiona shoved aside the fronds and stumbled into a slight opening in the crowd. Even her cousin's base insinuations were better than Milton's endless prattle.

She apologized her way to the foot of the staircase. Indeed, joining Edwina was the perfect solution. Milton would have someone to torment, and she would be left to her thoughts.

"Miss Grey." The Duke of August's immaculate shoulders blocked her path. "This is an unexpected pleasure. Though I must say, I expected you to be in the ballroom dancing and not pacing the entry hall."

Fiona swallowed hard. Her heart dropped to its proper place. Had the man sprung from her thoughts? Do be sensible, Fi. He walked in the front door. Relief shook her knees.

"Your Grace."

A shudder rattled her teeth as he took her raised hand.

Death.

Destruction.

Greed.

His fancy soap had failed to wash the stench from his flesh. Hugh had named him well. The man was definitely sullied.

— *I knew he'd come.* Milton rubbed his hands together. *Well, then, I'll leave you two alone.* He soared to the ceiling then stopped. *And, Fi, if you must faint, at least try to get a kiss out of it. Hmmm?*

"This is, indeed, a surprise." Fiona tugged her hand free and buried it in her skirt. Thank heaven for gloves. Such decay should not touch flesh until three days after death.

Irritation flashed in the duke's eyes. He blinked, and they reflected only herself. Empty eyes. A bankrupt soul.

"Why, Miss Grey, I thought our conversation this afternoon made my choice of entertainment clear." White incisors winked at her. He offered her his arm, cocked his left eyebrow.

Fear soured her mouth. Visions of Red Riding Hood and Grandmother's bed danced inside her skull.

"Indeed, Your Grace." She rested her hand on top of his arm.

His fingers traced the stitching on her gloves.

"It is nice to see you recovered from your earlier...affliction."

Fiona resisted the urge to yank her hand free. Too many late nights with Edgar Allen Poe. Nothing else explained why his touch felt like worms wiggling over her flesh. She locked her gaze on the first-floor landing. The spirits prowling his shadow didn't help. How could Milton envision Sullied for her husband?

"I had feared I would find myself without your stimulating company this evening." The duke's eyes narrowed as he squeezed her hand.

She nodded to a couple lounging in the doorway.

"Cook has a restorative tisane for just such an occasion."

It had been Uncle Andrew's sole basis for hiring her. That, and her high tolerance for the preternatural.

"Do you suffer from such a condition on a regular basis?"

"Oh, no, I am quite fit." She resisted the urge to show him her teeth and focused on the assembled crowd. Where was Hugh? What would he think if he saw her on Sullied's arm? She could hardly feign illness after boasting about her health.

"Perhaps you should dose yourself at breakfast tomorrow."

"Tomorrow?" Fiona stopped, tugged her hand free of his grasp and adjusted her skirt. With luck, someone would step on her train, rip the hem and allow her a graceful retreat to the withdrawing room.

"Yes, I wish to show you my treasures." He smoothed his mustache. "When one feels passionately about Egypt, one can't wait to share in her treasures."

In her treasures. Did he realize his slip? She doubted he even cared. Would he stop educating her if she told him of her disinterest? Not likely. He wanted that necklace.

Enough to kill for it?

He was fit enough. She had felt the play of sinew under her hand, the strength in his grasp. Just as he enjoyed unearthing the dead, he might relish adding to their number. As for scuttling a ship, thanks to his ex-wife's settlement, the Duke of August possessed more than enough money to arrange the deed.

Her allegiance to Uncle Andrew demanded she stay. Hugh would have to understand.

"It is a wonder you can bear to return to England at all."

"No one of any consequence summers in Egypt, Miss Grey."

"Really?" Fiona flicked open her fan. How much stroking would his mammoth pride require before he said something useful? Before she could leave him. "Why is that?"

"The heat, of course." He patted her arm.

"How unfortunate." Did he wear such an expression when he petted his favorite spaniel? Not likely. A dog would run away. Most canines were excellent judges of character.

"The heat, that preserves the past so well, makes the application of my science unbearable six months out of the year."

"I suppose it works out wonderfully well." Fiona's skin tingled in awareness. Hugh. She scanned the ballroom. He stood with his friends and sister near the orchestra. "You may return to England during the height of the season."

"My position requires I socialize, Miss Grey." His disapproval buffeted her. "I find the pleasure I receive from such amusements pales compared to the thrill of the hunt."

Hugh. As if he'd heard her thoughts, he turned in her direction. A smile curved his lips. Wicked lips. Strong, yet tender when pressed against her own. Fiona fanned faster. Delicate tendrils of hair wafted in the breeze, tickled her nape.

"Yet it presents the perfect opportunity to enlighten others to Egypt's glorious past."

"If only that were true." Fiona felt the duke stiffen. "Too often one finds that society believes they are the beginning and end of civilization."

The smile slipped off Hugh's face. He had spied Sullied. Please, God, let him understand.

"I am certain many must share your interests."

He conceded a curt nod then consulted his watch.

"Interest, indeed. But only those who have been expertly educated share my *passion*." He stepped in front of her, blocking her view. "You are looking a bit peaked, my dear."

"I feel perfectly fit, Your Grace." Fiona's fingers itched. If she tightened his prissy neckcloth just a bit, would his ego carry his head away like a hot air balloon's ascension?

"You must accompany me tomorrow. I must infuse the thirst for knowledge into your very marrow." He seized both her hands and tugged her toward the balcony doors. "Only then can you understand that even the most whimsical trifle can impart knowledge."

They cleared the door and stepped outside.

"I'll teach you how to tell the genuine from the forgery."

Clammy air dampened Fiona's cheeks. He was talking about Hugh, condemning him. The truth supplanted the marrow in her bones. A lazy breeze rustled in the nearby trees, whispered through the shrubs. The duke had mistaken inbreeding for well-bred. Her gaze flicked over his well-tailored clothes before settling on his vest. Perhaps it was time for the teacher to become the pupil.

"Your watch bob is not genuine."

"Indeed." He caressed the glistening gold. "However did you discern it?"

"I doubt Imhotep used a jeweler's mark."

"Imhotep?" Sullied stilled as she pointed out the two intertwined initials stamped on the back of the last link.

"That is what this spells, is it not?" Caution chilled her pride. Imhotep. Where had the name come from?

"Yes." He lashed out, wrapping his hands around her upper arms. "How did you know?" Light blazed in his eyes, hypnotic in its fanaticism.

How? The whispers from the darkness under her uncle's desk. The necklace. He *would* kill to possess it. Suddenly, the crowded ballroom didn't seem as safe.

"I'm certain you must have shown it to me."

Pain streaked up her arm as she tried to twist free.

Sullied loomed closer, blocking out everything except him and his obsession.

"And I am equally certain I did not."

"You must have." Her foot collided with his boot. Her toes cracked. Pain gripped her shin. Why couldn't high fashion include a sensible pair of slippers?

"How else would I have known?"

He hauled her to him. Hard sinew crushed her skirt, pressed against her. His breath heated her cheeks.

"How, indeed?"

"I must insist you unhand me, my lord. This is not proper." Fiona stomped her heel onto his toes.

Sullied grunted and lifted her off the ground.

"The proper form of address is your grace."

"Release me, sir." Toes grazed the balcony floor. Her arms squeezed the air from her lungs. Now what was she to do? Da's training never included this.

"You've seen it, haven't you? You've seen the necklace."

"How could I have?" Fiona groaned. Damn the man. How was her knee to strike its target if he continued to turn? "I fear it was lost when the *Sweet Wind* sunk."

"No. No. I do not believe that. You've seen it." His eyes lost focus. "But where?"

"I happen to know my uncle was returning the mummy you gave them to Egypt." For a man so aware of his own dignity, he seemed positively unaware of how silly he looked with a full-grown woman dangling from his hands. She glanced at a disappearing couple. And why hadn't anyone bothered to help? "I am certain it was with the body."

A man's shadow invaded the balcony. The duke shook his head and the silhouette retreated.

"The necklace was not with the mummy."

"It wasn't?" She stopped kicking. Da had said patience was the most underestimated weapon. Patience. Unfortunately, it had also been the one she hadn't bothered to master. *Milton, stop looking down the ladies' bodices and help me.*

"No. I would have been told if it were."

Told? Who would have told him? She glanced over her shoulder. Milton's smoky form was absent. Well, she might as well make the most of her captivity. Hugh would be along soon enough. *He wouldn't desert her.*

"How very odd that you were notified when the body washed ashore."

"Not at all—my name was still on the crate." He smiled down at her. "Naturally, they thought the contents belonged to me."

"So, no one from Grey Shipping told you that it had been recovered?"

"On the contrary." He chuckled. "I told Grey Shipping. The locals thought I had been unearthing dear old dad and selling him to the local medical college. My solicitor tells me he had a bit of difficulty sorting the entire mess out."

"Why didn't you explain to the constables yourself?" Unless his perfect alibi had collapsed. But who would connect him with the sinking? The authorities didn't suspect sabotage.

"My dear, commoners get so bogged down in 'your grace' that they turn incoherent."

"How very trying for you, Your Grace."

"I haven't the patience for long games, Miss Grey." He set her on her feet but kept her close. "Last winter, while working at Saqqara, I discovered a wall of hieroglyphs depicting the *heb-seb*. The illustrations of the rejuvenation ceremony were quite lovely and colorful." He released her right arm to run his knuckles down the side of her face.

"How nice for you." Feeling needled Fiona's hand as the blood flowed. The ivory sticks of her fan pressed against her palm. The delicate work wouldn't knock him out, but it just might stun him enough so she could escape. A broken fan was a small price to pay for freedom.

"Two sticks of dynamite destroyed the obstacle separating me from my desire."

His thumb pressed against her throat. Red tinged Fiona's peripheral vision. Rage evaporated her reply. He was threatening her!

She raised her hand. The fan would stun him. One small push, and he'd fall off the balcony.

"Miss Grey!" Hugh voice severed her concentration. From the corner of her eye, she watched him shake his head slowly from side to side.

Her hand wavered. So, she wouldn't push Sullied off the balcony. Ivory snapped. Surely, Hugh wouldn't deny her the right to whack the arrogance off the duke's face.

"I believe our dance is beginning." Hugh shook his head again and held out his hand.

"You are *de trop* here, Barrett." Sullied's hand slithered around her neck and pinched her nape.

"Release Miss Grey." Hugh ambled closer, his hands behind his back.

Bile burned her throat as the duke tightened his hold. She shoved at his arm. Steel had more give. Was this her reward for mercy? She glanced heavenward. The stars burned silently in the sky.

"You don't learn very quickly do you, Barrett? Miss Grey and I are engaged in a personal conversation."

"Actually, I—ahh." The duke strangled the words from her throat. Her knees bent as she tried to squirm out of the way.

"You don't learn at all, Sullied." Hugh cracked his knuckles.

"Sullied," the duke scoffed. "How childish."

Childish. He was one to talk. They were both posturing like gorillas in a zoological park. Fiona relaxed her shoulders. She should have stuck to the original plan. Well, with a slight modification it might still work.

Muscles coiled around bone, adrenaline heated her skin. Hugh might even help, if he could stop beating his chest long enough.

"Perhaps, but I have the strength of a *man* to enforce my words."

Raising her hand, she pivoted on the ball of her right foot. Her right forearm slammed into the crook of Sullied's arm, collapsing it and freeing her neck. Her left fist smashed dead on his nose. He staggered backward, his torso swayed over the edge of the balcony.

Indecision rooted her as pain sank into her bones. She wouldn't push him over this time, but he had better hurt as much as her hand did.

"Bloody hell!"

Fiona clasped her aching hand to her chest. That was the third brawl she'd been in since setting foot in London. Wasn't England supposed to be a civilized place?

"I think our dance is starting," she said.

"Dance?" Hugh looked from her to Sullied. "She wants to dance." He grabbed her uninjured hand and placed it on his arm. "Do you think you could let me rescue you? Just once. Is that so much to ask?"

"But you did. You distracted him so I might escape." She squeezed his arm.

"I wanted to *level* him." Hugh stroked his chin. "Although I was willing to go further if necessary. America might not be such a bad place to live out the remainder of one's days."

"Thank you." His cheek was smooth under her lips. He smelled of soap and starch.

"Yes, well," He fingered the place she had just kissed. "Next time, let me smash his nose." He escorted her out of the ballroom to the landing.

"What about our dance?"

"We'll dance." He winked and gave her a gentle shove up the stairs. "After you repair some of the damage your brawling wreaked on your most fetching attire."

"Fetching attire?"

"Go and wash his touch from your skin." Hugh pointed to the second-floor landing. "I'll be right here."

CHAPTER 26

"Oh, hello, Kingslea." Montague shuffled out of the ballroom, peered down the stairwell then up it. White powder dusted his lapels. He rubbed his nose. Bloodshot eyes peered from under heavy lids. "I don't suppose you've seen Fiona?"

Bitterness coated Kingslea's tongue. Pent-up rage tasted horrid. He flexed his fingers.

"Aren't you supposed to be looking out for her?"

He could vent it on this pasty-faced excuse for a human being. Granted, Fiona's cousin wasn't Sullied…

"That's what I'm doing." Montague straightened his scrawny shoulders. He winced when his yellowed fingers touched the bridge of his nose. Purple skin rested beneath his eyes.

Again Fiona had beaten him to the punch. Damn woman. She needed a man to protect her from herself. She would have killed Sullied if he hadn't shown up. Not that the pompous lout didn't deserve to die. It was simply that *he* deserved to be the executioner.

"She doesn't need protecting from me."

"Fortune hunters are the bane of all marriageable young ladies." Montague patted his new jacket before finding the snuff box.

Fortune hunters. He polished his fingernails on his sleeve. Had opium loosened the man's survival sense?

"Been looking in the mirror again, eh, Montague?"

"What need have I for an heiress?" He shoved a pinch of snuff up his nose. "I will inherit healthy estates and still have plenty of blunt in the markets."

"Last I heard, The Willows wasn't capable of supporting you or your family in style." Kingslea closed the distance between them, brushed the snuff from Montague's shoulder. The man flinched before retreating a step. "You did beg Fiona's uncle for the money for this season?" He traced the edge of Montague's lapels. "One wonders if Grey's disappearance was fortuitous luck or manmade opportunity."

"The title I shall inherit—"

"Is empty. The entail was broken. The late Lord Heberon left all the 'healthy estates and blunt' to his daughter." Wool wrapped around Kingslea's fingers. Fetid breath washed over his face. "The late Caroline Grey."

"You lie!" Spittle flapped from Montague's thin lips.

"Why would I bother?"

"Because...because you want her for yourself." His eyes rolled wildly in their sockets. "Your title is the empty one. Whoring for your mother's vowels. Wallowing in everyone's dirty linens. Admit it, Kingslea, you only want Fiona to make her pay for that other American. What was her name? Lilith? Lydia?" Montague shoved out of Kingslea's hold.

A small gasp drifted down. Kingslea's fist halted midair. Fiona.

"Lilly." Her white face flashed over the landing above his head. It disappeared just as quickly. His prey sidled across the landing.

Damn the woman. She had deprived him of yet another target.

"Oh, Montague?"

"What?"

"I haven't seen your cousin." Kingslea placed his foot on the bottom step. But he would soon.

CHAPTER 27

Lilly. Fiona quietly shut the withdrawing room door. Who was she? What did she mean to Hugh? Silk slipped off her hands as she milked her fingers. Why did she care? She paused next to the slop pot. Because she cared about Hugh.

— *You did it, didn't you?* Milton shot into the room, scarlet suffusing his spectral form. *You bloodied the duke's nose.*

"I—"

— *Oh, don't bother to deny it. There is blood on your gloves!*

She tucked her gloves around her fingers. Milton's timing was exceptional whenever she didn't want him. "I—"

— *It's because of him, isn't it?* Milton shook his finger. *That Kingston fellow is no good, Fi.*

"That's enough, Milton."

— *You need—*

"I know what I need." Ivory snapped as she shook her fan at him. She had never tolerated his meddling in her life when he was alive. Why was she doing so now? "And it isn't now, nor will it ever be the Duke of August."

— *So you are quite decided on your course.* Milton flew across the room and faced her nose to nose.

"Yes."

— *There is absolutely nothing I can do to change your mind?*

"You will do nothing to harm Hugh, Milton." Fiona set her fists on her hips. Her fingers uncurled, tapping out the mounting adrenaline. "They have priests in London. Good Catholic priests who know how to exorcise restless spirits."

Milton's eyes narrowed to dark slashes in his face.

— *So you've settled on the other one as husband?*

"No." Fiona shook her head. Settled and Hugh had never come close to meeting. In fact, whenever he was near, her emotions and thoughts tumbled together like plateware in an earthquake.

— *I suppose you could do worse. If you wish this Kingston fellow, then I suppose I could be persuaded to help.* Milton drifted back a pace. *Providing you cease this exorcism nonsense.* He shuffled his husband candidates like the queen of hearts in a game of three-card monte.

Fiona pressed her temples. Why was he suddenly cooperative? And why had his support give her hope?

The door eased open. Edwina shoved it all the way, but lingered in the exit. Victory brightened her petulant features, twisted her smile.

"Cousin, dear."

— *If only she were a deer, and I had my hunting rifle.* Milton flicked a ringlet drooping over her shoulder.

"Edwina."

— *Fi, you know I love you and would do anything for you.* He drifted toward the door. *But there are certain fears that don't fade with death.* His back slipped into the wall. *Watching her use the slops is one of them.* With a wink, he disappeared.

Fiona tucked a stray curl into her chignon. She didn't particularly relish such a show, either. After one final glance in the looking glass, she headed for the door.

"I'll leave you in peace."

Silk wheezed. Sweat soured the air as Edwina pulled abreast of her.

"Piers will be positively delighted that I found you, cousin."

"Was I lost?" She glanced toward the stairs. A courting couple lounged in the chairs. A pair of swells observed them from their position on the fourth riser. Where was Hugh? He had said he would wait.

"We are concerned." Edwina snaked her arm around Fiona's and clamped it to her side. "I do hope you haven't filled up your dance card so early in the evening. Several very eligible bachelors have made Mother promise to introduce you to them."

"How nice." Fiona decreased her rate of descent. Perspiration strung incandescent beads across Edwina's forehead. Her cousin would rather they both tumbled to their deaths than release Fiona's arm. What mischief had her relations plotted?

"The Duke of August was most particular in his inquiries."

Fiona shuddered to a stop. She never cared to see that man again. Her cousin glared as she rubbed her arm.

"I have already seen the duke."

"Dear foolish cousin," Edwina clucked. Her bony fingers bit into Fiona's arm. "In England, commoners are always at the disposal of their betters. If the duke wishes your company, you will supply it with a smile."

"I am an American, *dearest* cousin." She forced a smile and slipped her fingers around Edwina's thumb. "I don't have any betters."

She pulled on the thumb. Her captor's cry signaled her release.

"You—"

"Miss Grey?" A sober man bowed in their direction. White paper reclined on a tray of silver. "Miss Fiona Grey?"

"I am she." Her heart slammed into her throat. Was this another threat? Here at a party? Not likely—Mam always said her imagination carried away her sense. But it was a note. From whom?

Hugh. Perhaps he'd had to leave. Then why hadn't he waited? Lilly. The woman's hold on him must be stronger than adventure. The way he had savored her name, like it was clotted cream on fresh scones.

"Fiona, you best not dance with the butler." Edwina knocked the dance card from her hand. "Your scandalous behavior will ruin us all."

Fiona shook the tingles from her hand. Dance with the butler? Edwina's maliciousness had strangled her sense.

"May I help you?"

"Indeed, Miss." The butler controlled his shock. He shoved the tray at her. "This has come for you."

"Thank you." Vellum crinkled under her fingers. To open or not to open?

Edwina sidled closer. Fiona nudged her aside with her elbow. She didn't need an audience, especially one that took pleasure in another's grief.

"Well, what does it say? Who is it from?"

"I haven't read it."

"What are you waiting for?" Edwina reached for the paper.

Fiona danced out of reach. She had better read it. At least then she could destroy it before her cousin paraded it around the ballroom.

She took a deep breath. *Paper can't possibly hurt you, Fi.*

The seal broke with a snap. Shaking fingers opened the first fold. Well, there had been that nasty paper cut a year ago. She opened the paper flat. Black ink flowed across the paper. She blinked as the words swam.

Her knees buckled, and she collapsed against the wall. A dream. She must still be in bed dreaming. Her eyes flew over the words. The message hadn't changed.

Edwina shoved at Fiona's arm.

"Well, what could be so important that they had to interrupt a ball?"

"My aunt and uncle." Fiona handed her the paper. Edwina could parade around the Graham-Russells shouting this news. Hugh. She had to find him, tell him. She spun on her heel. Where was he?

"This cannot be!" Edwina shrieked.

"It is. Aunt Caroline and Uncle Andrew are home." Faces crowded her vision.

"Not at home," Edwina clucked, crinkling the paper in her fist.

"Yes."

"No." She flashed the words at Fiona. "This says they are waiting for you outside in a carriage."

"Outside." Grabbing the crumpled paper back, Fiona smoothed it open and scanned the note. Her cousin was right. They were outside. Indecision rooted her to the landing. Hugh or her family? She headed for the door.

Edwina scampered after her. "Where are you going?"

"To them." She would introduce her uncle to Hugh. They were bound to like each other. "I can't let them stand too long. The note says Aunt Caro's health is still delicate after her ordeal."

"But...but you can't just leave." Edwina pounded the steps after her. "There is a proper etiquette for taking one's leave. And...and Mother is bound to have something to say."

The lady of the house stood at the top of the landing welcoming another guest.

"I'll bid goodbye to our hostess."

Fiona's slippered feet floated across the marble entry. No doubt Uncle Andrew would be amused at her inquiries into his disappearance.

Edwina's mother stepped from behind a potted palm.

"Why, Fiona, you have roses blooming in your cheeks."

Fiona covered her scream with a hiccough. Not even her aunt's sour face could spoil her evening.

"Aunt Annabelle, the most fabulous thing has happened. Uncle Andrew and Aunt Caroline are back."

"Are they?" Confusion pleated the older woman's brow.

"Yes."

"Well, you mustn't keep them waiting." Silk swished as her aunt backed out of the way.

"Mother—"

Fiona paused. Perhaps Aunt Annabelle had a heart after all.

"I need to say my goodbyes."

"Don't bother, dear." Aunt Annabelle's smile curdled. "I'll explain everything to our hostess. Hurry, now. We'll be along as soon as I find Piers and little Melody."

"Thank you, Aunt." Fiona dodged around the sauntering couples. A footman tossed open the door as she approached. She nodded then flew down the stoop. Joy lightened her heart.

A closed carriage waited at the curb. A liveried coachman jumped from his perch and opened the door. Fiona had her foot up before her mind registered the inconsistencies.

One person occupied the carriage. A hand on her bottom shoved her inside. The door slammed shut behind her, nicking her heel. She tumbled forward. Bones ground together as her shoulder collided with the seat. Polished boots reflected her disheveled hair. Piers's reflection joined hers.

"What are you doing here?" Fiona rocked forward. Her bodice slipped down. Her train was caught in the door. Now what was she to do? *Think.* She had bested Piers twice already. Certainly the third time would be no different.

"Securing my future."

Pain exploded across her skull and bile burned her throat as the world faded to black.

CHAPTER 28

"I never knew danger was such an opiate." Kingslea smiled down at his sister as conversation replaced the last strains of the lively country dance.

"Danger?" Fear widened Melody's blue eyes.

"I believe many of your suitors wish to do an injury to my old skin." He nodded toward a cluster of men near the edge of the dance floor. Men had never looked younger, nor had his sister more elegant.

"You are not so old."

"Twelve years older than you." Kingslea sighed under the burden of thirty years.

"That is not so much." A blush stole across her features.

He followed her gaze. Winthrop rocked on his heels. A fissure of unease rent down Kingslea's spine. Impossible. They had nothing in common.

"Tell me, which of your suitors do you prefer?"

They paused as the two couples in front of them stopped to converse.

"Millcock with his two thousand pounds a years? Or perhaps Montbaten's obvious devotion has touched your heart."

"They are splendid companions for riding in the park or a picnic." She nodded at the couples skirting them. "But they are boys. A lady must find a gentleman, one whose age is an attribute. Security and devotion are rare qualities in youth."

Damn. She was looking at Winthrop. And he...

Kingslea pressed his fists against his thighs. His friend was ogling her right back. This was his own fault. He never should have left them alone. He must make an effort to find her someone more suitable.

"Melody, I..."

"There is fondness as well, brother." She smiled up at him.

Fondness. Whatever had gotten into her? His stepmother. Elspeth would have pushed her to consider his friend, and poor Melody would have done anything to please her mother.

"For his money? Or his person?"

"What a beastly question." Tears shimmered in her eyes. "Have you so little regard for me, then?" She raised her chin and blinked away the moisture. "Of course, you do."

"I think the world of you, Mel." He stopped her departure. "I just can't picture you and...and..."

"Winthrop." She sniffed. "He is your friend, I believe."

"Yes," Kingslea agreed. Although a man might have to rethink such a friendship. He couldn't have his friends seducing his young sister. "Perhaps you misinterpreted his offer of friendship."

"Of course, we are friends." Melody sighed patiently. "That is the very best place to start." She pulled her hand away. "I just bet that odious Miss Grey is thinking the very same thing."

Odious? Fiona? Now what maggot had crawled into his sister's brain.

"Miss Grey knows our acquaintance is merely a passing interest."

"No, brother dear. That is what *you* think." She slowed her words as if explaining to an imbecile. "Everyone knows you would be in Siam should she reveal her true interest. I may not have as many years as Miss Grey, but I am a woman grown."

"Miss Grey is hardly upon the shelf."

"Perhaps not." Melody frowned. "But she is certainly close to it. At her age, she is certain to consider every gentleman acquaintance for the title of husband."

He steered her closer to the door. Had Fiona thought of him as husband? The notion was certainly intriguing. He shook his head. What was he thinking?

"Miss Grey's mind is occupied by more pressing concerns than marriage."

"That isn't what she just told me." Edwina sashayed up to them. Her knobby hand clawed at his arm. "Do promise that you won't repeat that."

His skin crawled as her fingers walked up his arm. How could this creature be related to his Fiona?

"Repeat what?"

"Why, marriage, of course." Edwina's eyelashes fluttered in his direction. "Fiona is positively obsessed with it." She snapped open her fan. "Or is it with a title? I guess it doesn't matter." Her hunched shoulders shrugged. "For an American, they positively go hand in glove."

"And with a dowry that size, she could marry the Prince." Melody agreed. "Fortunately, Bertie's vows transcend his fondness for American heiresses."

"I think she is willing to settle for a duke." Edwina eyed him from under her lashes before sliding her glance to the Duke of August.

Kingslea contained his anger. So, that was the chit's game: Warn him away with a little help from past failures. Obviously, Fiona hadn't confided everything in her cousin. Hell, he'd be surprised if Edwina held anyone's confidence.

"She is interested in finding her aunt and uncle."

"Was." Edwina's twisted smile reminded him of his stepmother's cat. Only the tailfeathers sticking out of her mouth were missing.

"Was?" Melody stopped searching the crowd and focused on her cousin.

"Do you know, I have filled up my entire card." Edwina consulted the small white book dangling from her bony wrist. "All but this dance, that is."

Cool air filled Kingslea's lungs. A dance for information. Blackmail. Nothing could be worth twenty minutes in the viper's company.

"I am certain you will be thankful for missing this one dance, come morning."

"Perhaps." Edwina's thin lips puckered before triumph lit her damp face. "Yes, you are quite right. I believe a fresh breath of air would be ever so much better." She clamped her hand around his arm and tugged him toward the balcony.

Prayers for patience pushed against his skull. Any more foolishness and his unwanted companion would take her last breath falling from the balcony. Good Lord. He was almost as bloodthirsty as Fiona. Sighing, he escorted both young ladies out of the crowded ballroom.

"Tell us, Miss Montague, why you believe Miss Grey is no longer interested in finding her aunt and uncle?"

"Why, because Aunt and Uncle have returned."

"The Greys are alive?" Kingslea steadied himself on the balcony railing. Cold leached through his gloves, echoing the chill in his heart. Their adventure was over, and she hadn't bothered to tell him in person. Melody was wrong. Not every woman measured a man in terms of matrimony. Fiona certainly hadn't considered him husband material. More like hired help.

"Yes. I was with her when the butler delivered the news." Edwina turned to Melody. "She couldn't be bothered to say goodbye to our hostess, simply sailed out the door. And to think I may have to call her duchess one day."

Fiona. Duchess. He shook his head. She hated Sullied, had wanted to murder the man. Murder and matrimony. A duchess without the burden of husband. Damnation, a husband hadn't stopped Lilly from seducing him. Bile burned Kingslea's throat. Would fate be so unkind as to allow history to repeat itself?

He shoved away from the balcony. He was master of his fate. They had struck a bargain. If Fiona wanted out, she would tell him to his face.

Alveston and Winthrop stepped onto the balcony as he neared the entrance to the ballroom. Winthrop spied Melody, stumbled a step then righted himself.

"Ah, Kingslea..."

His intention wavered. Apparently, the interest between his sister and friend was mutual. Damnation. He hadn't time to deal with the matter now.

"Watch my sister, Winthrop." He drilled his index finger into his friend's chest. Fortunately, he knew the location of all the man's estates. "If I'm not back in time, I am depending on you to see her safely home."

The baron tucked Melody's hand through his arm and patted her hand. "Of course."

Edwina latched onto Lord Alveston's arm. "Mother will be very content with such a noble escort."

Escort. He stilled.

"Where is Montague?"

"Piers?" Color fled Edwina's cheeks.

"Yes."

"I..." Satin gloves scratched her throat. She moved, hiding behind Alveston. "My brother isn't the most reliable escort."

Montague was gone. Fiona was gone. Unease slithered down Kingslea's spine. Damnation. He had to have mentioned Montague's lack of inheritance. He spun on his heel, shoved aside some young buck sniffing after Melody. Fiona was in trouble.

Where would Montague have taken her? The townhouse? Not bloody likely. Even a halfwit knew that would be the first place searched.

Except this halfwit wouldn't expect his nefarious plans to be exposed.

His knuckles rapped the outside wall. Edwina knew more than she had told. He pivoted and marched back to her.

"Where was she meeting the Greys?"

Alveston arched his eyebrow and moved out of the way, exposing Edwina.

"Wh—where?" Fear shook her.

"Yes. Where?" Kingslea shoved his fists into his pocket. He wouldn't throttle her. Neither would he toss her over the balcony. He was a gentlemen.

"I—" Her normal petulance melted away her earlier alarm. "I don't know."

"I think you do." His hands emerged from his pockets. He was never supposed to inherit the title. So, perhaps he might be forgiven if he forgot to act like a gentleman. "And you will tell me."

"My mother—"

"Isn't here." He stepped closer, forcing her back a step.

"Melody wouldn't—"

She was wasting his time. A commodity Fiona might not have to spare. With every passing second, Montague might very well be pressing his intentions.

"Tell me." His throat closed, making his command barely audible. "Now."

"I don't know where she went." Edwina licked her lips. "All I know is that her aunt and uncle were outside waiting in a carriage."

"A carriage?" A closed carriage, no doubt. Kingslea's mind raced with the possibilities. Fiona would be fine. She was a capable woman. But in a carriage...Montague wouldn't pose much of a problem, but his shadow Oswin would.

"Yes." Curls sprang from Edwina's chignon as she nodded. "Outside."

"Why didn't they come inside?" Confusion creased Winthrop's florid face.

"Overset nerves." Melody shivered and clung more tightly to him. "Imagine surviving a shipwreck."

Kingslea glanced at the couple. He would have a word with his friend after he saw to Fiona's safety.

"Let us hope that imagining is all you ever do, sister."

"I thought you would be happy, my lord." Edwina sidled closer. "Everyone knows your opinion of American heiresses. Helping my poor cousin must have been such a trial."

Not nearly as trying as conversing with her cousin.

"Winthrop."

"I'll see she gets home." He tightened his hold on Melody.

"I'll expect a full accounting in my study tomorrow." He held his friend's gaze. Red stained Winthrop's cheeks. Kingslea spun on his heel and headed for the door.

Alveston fell into step beside him. "Your fascination with Miss Grey is becoming an obsession."

"I don't recall inviting you on this expedition." How large of a lead could Montague have? Twenty minutes? A man could compromise a woman in such an eternity. He should never have left his post at the staircase, never danced with his sister. Duty warred with desire.

He stormed through a knot of gossiping misses. Red tinged his vision. Twenty minutes. Hell, Fiona deserved at least an hour. She deserved to be savored. Her lips enjoyed like a fine wine. And her neck...

He stifled a groan. Perhaps two hours. Definitely two. And then there were her shoulders...

"It *is* possible the Greys have returned without the great Lord Kingslea's assistance."

Alveston's bored drawl scattered his thoughts.

"Houseman would have sent word."

"Houseman?" Alveston stomped across the floor, dodging sets of couples preparing for the next dance. "Perhaps your faithful servant has fallen asleep."

"Houseman sleeps with his eyes open." Kingslea paused at the top of the staircase. "He takes his guard duties seriously."

"Now, listen here, Kingslea." Alveston slipped in front of him and stopped. "We have been friends forever, old man, but siccing your man on her, snooping into her business...Not every woman is as deceitful as Lilly."

Irritation sparked through Kingslea. That made twice in one night some-one had brought up his past. He stepped to the left.

Alveston shadowed him.

"This has nothing to do with Lilly."

"You are following Miss Grey's every move, double-checking to see if she does what she is telling you she is doing."

Somewhere in the house a grandfather clock tolled. He was wasting time. Time Fiona didn't have. He shoved his hand through his hair. Pressure followed his fingers' path across his scalp. He didn't need to convince Alveston, but he might need his friend's help.

"I am guarding her."

Disbelief furrowed Alveston's brow.

"Last evening, that fool Montague sent Fiona home without an escort after he had dismissed the servants and extra footmen. Someone was in the house with her." Anger reared inside him. Heat and bitterness exploded across his palate.

"I see." Alveston preceded him down the stairs. They exchanged a couple gold coins for their hats and canes.

Cynicism in his friend was like salt in the ocean. Too bad they were on dry land. Kingslea shrugged into his greatcoat.

"And that begs the question how her aunt and uncle knew she would be here."

"Servants." Alveston propped his hat on his head and swept the brim with his thumb. "They know everything." He winked at the butler. "As you are wont to remind me."

"Perhaps." Kingslea squeezed through arriving guests. Clammy air brushed his cheeks. Wisps of fog smudged the night. The London Particular was just beginning to form. Gold buttons slipped between his fingers. Boots crunched along the pavement. As his coach wouldn't be returning anytime soon, they would have to walk. He glanced at his friend's glossy boots. Alveston would not be pleased.

A jaunty ditty whistled past Kingslea's lips.

"Admit it. You like the chit."

A cool breeze bathed his face. Fiona was not a chit. A chit was flighty, reckless and annoying. No, his Fiona was dangerous, unpredictable and de-pendable. And the way she looked in the candlelight...

"I'll take your silence for acquiescence."

"Do you not think it odd the Montagues remain at the ball instead of wel-coming the dead back to the earthly plane?"

"That family hasn't an ounce of familial devotion among the lot of them." Alveston kicked at a loose cobblestone. "Besides, the return of the Greys means the end to their profligate ways."

"I'd bet a monkey Montague accompanied her."

"A lady requires an escort."

"And you believe etiquette actually penetrated the man's opium-induced stupor?"

"How's that?" Alveston grimaced as he scraped the heel of his boot against the wrought iron railing.

"Yesterday they stuffed her into a rented hack and sent her home alone." Chilly air wrapped Kingslea's face. A gust tugged at his top hat.

"What has that to do with her aunt and uncle?"

Felt brushed his fingers as his hat tumbled through the air. Where the devil had the breeze come from? He quickened his pace, but the hat continued to roll away from him. The hat or Fiona. Both, so long as they continued to travel in the same direction.

"Refresh my memory. Why are you accompanying me?"

"I never pass up an opportunity to say I told you so."

They rounded the corner. His hat arced through the air and landed in the middle of the street next to a stopped carriage. What the hell was going on here? A pair of horses pawed the air. Swearing filled the night. The team turned, angling across the cobblestones. Another twist, and they were headed right for Kingslea.

"Ham-handed drivers." Alveston sneered. "What is the empire coming to when rubbish like that drives?"

Kingslea ignored the question—he was more interested in what possessed his hat.

"Get 'em under control, man." A round shadow bloomed from the carriage window. "She's not going to sleep all night."

Cold flashed through Kingslea's veins, and blood thundered inside his skull.

"Montague." He rushed forward. Felt crunched under his boot. The carriage rocked. Axles creaked. What had they done to Fiona?

"They were right placid when I got them." Oswin sawed on the reins. "Don't rightly know what got into them, but they spook every bloody step."

Closer. Just a little closer. A whip cracked. The horses plunged forward, straining the traces. The carriage jumped, and Kingslea lunged. The dropped window provided the perfect handhold. Fingers closed around the handle. With a quick tug, the door jerked open, flew out of his grip and banged against the side of the carriage. His foot slipped. For an instant, his legs fluttered behind him like linen on a blustery day.

"What the devil!"

Pain slammed through his legs as he bounced off the pavement. He kicked inside the carriage, slid into a tangle of legs. Silk fell over his cheek. A soft groan rasped from the seat to his left.

"You, there. What do you think you're doing?" Something thumped the bench, nicking his shoulder. "Get out this instant."

Air whooshed out of his lungs as something smashed against his back.

Montague was on his left. Kingslea tossed aside the skirt and lunged. His palm molded around knobby flesh.

"You're the one leaving."

He dragged Montague off the seat by his throat and shoved him toward the door. His victim raised his hand. A cane flashed in the gaslight before smashing against Kingslea's skull. Ringing filled his ear; warmth trickled down his neck. His hold loosened as the horses veered right. Montague tumbled out the door.

"What must a man do to find a brawl in this town?"

"H-hurts."

"Fiona?" Kingslea struggled to his knees as the carriage slowed. Yards of fabric bunched against his legs. Cold fear replaced blazing adrenaline. "Fiona, speak to me. Please."

"Hugh?"

"Yes. It is Hugh." Relief liquefied every muscle. He collapsed against her leg. Warmth caressed his cheek. Her heartbeat drummed in his ear. She was alive. Gloriously alive. "Are you hurt?"

"M-my head." Nimble fingers danced over his face. "They said...my aunt and uncle..."

"Shhh." Her despair tormented him. She should never suffer. Never. He scooped her into his arms. Felt comfort at her acceptance of his offer of solace. "I know all about it."

"Why would they do such a thing?"

"Because..."

"Is she unharmed?" Alveston's voice flooded the interior with the light from the lantern in his hand.

Kingslea winced at the brightness. "She—"

"I'm fine." She nuzzled his chest. Her hold tightened.

"What's going on here?" Lord Robertson stuck his face in the open window. "I say, is that you, Kingslea?"

Foreboding weighted his gut. Damn Alveston and his lamp. The whole ton was bound to find out about this little tête-à-tête.

"Yes."

"Who is that with you?" Another face pressed against the glass. Lady Horsey, the biggest gossip in all of London.

"My fiancé." Kingslea caught the lamp Alveston almost dropped and set it on the hook. He scooted across the floor and stepped down from the carriage.

"Hugh." Fiona shook her head and pressed a gloved hand to her mouth. "You don't..."

He did. Her use of his Christian name sealed both their fates. He smiled as he accepted her trembling hand. She needed to be protected. Without any reliable males nearby, that duty fell to him. He eyed Lady Horsey, Lord Robertson and the two couples who had joined them in the street.

"My lords, ladies, I believe you know my future bride, Fiona Grey."

"Ah, yes." Lord Robertson arched an eyebrow.

The announcement crackled across the couple like fire across a dry prairie.

"Allow me to be the first to wish you felicitations," said Lady Horsey.

A wan smile wavered across Fiona's face before she doubled over and vomited on his boots.

CHAPTER 29

"Bloody hell."

Kingslea paced the worn Persian carpet. Ten steps across. Ten back. His footfalls rattled around the empty bookshelves before being swallowed by the dark hearth. What had he done?

Engaged.

The Marquess of Kingslea was engaged.

To an American.

His head lolled back, taunt muscles corded his neck. The stretch reached down his back.

"There was no other choice."

Liar. He skirted the ottoman and walked to the window. The pressing fog sweated rivulets down the cracked pane. He could have found another excuse. They could have found another excuse.

Fiona was clever.

He rested his forehead against the window. Cold leeched the heat from his thoughts. Very clever, indeed. Cunning enough to land an earl after tossing aside a duke? Doubt joined the melee rattling around his skull.

"Clever enough to make you propose of your own accord?" He shook his head. When had the world stopped making sense?

When he had met Fiona.

"Damnation." He marched to the sideboard. Cut glass bit into his flesh. Brandy sloshed into the nearest sifter. But was it eternal damnation? Marriage?

Did he want it to be?

The nutty aroma teased his nose an instant before the liquid scraped the moisture from his throat. When had the burn faded to tepidness? After his fourth libation? Or was it the fifth? A steady hand reached for the carafe.

Hell. His head was still clear, still ringing with thoughts. Glass scraped wood as he set the carafe down.

Poverty had forced him to water his brandy.

An amber button stared at him from the bottom of his sifter.

"I'd bet the Grey's never watered their brandy." He kicked his chair into position then dropped onto the split-leather seat.

Fiona Gurnsey-Barrett, Sixth Marchioness of Kingslea.

She would grace the title.

She could buy better.

His dinner tossed in his stomach, soured his mouth. She could buy her way out of the scandal. He tossed his glass against the marble fireplace. The shattered crystal sparkled in the dark hearth.

Alveston opened the door. "Celebrating without your friends, I see."

"Go away."

Kingslea's inhospitality rolled off the men's backs. Winthrop lumbered into the library. He tickled the bottles on the side table before selecting one and pouring himself a healthy portion.

"Your announcement will be the talk of the season."

"Don't you mean Fiona's stunning stomach acrobatics?

Alveston grabbed two glasses and a bottle before sauntering across the room.

"That only adds to your reputation." He kicked Kingslea's feet off the ottoman and sat down.

"Which reputation?" He took the glass offered by his friend. "The thief of wives, the despoiler of virgins?"

Winthrop clucked and shoved a chair closer.

"You said it was over with Lilly. That she hadn't left her husband for you."

"And we believe you."

✤ ✤ ✤

"I can't continue like this, Lilly." He ignored the intimate garments scattered around the room and focused on the woman stretched across the bed.

"We have days left before the house party ends." She rose from her pillows, ran her hands over the rumpled coverlet. "Hours to enjoy what should have been ours."

What should have been. Loss pounded his skull.

"You chose to marry him."

She shrugged. The thin strap of her camisole dropped off her white shoulder.

"I would think you, of all people, would find delicious revenge in cuckolding the duke."

The duke. Sullied. Anger rode Kingslea's control. Is that what she thought of him? Their tryst meant only revenge. Only love would corrupt his honor. But did she love him?

"I won't continue to share you."

"I told you, Hugh." Lilly slipped off the bed and strolled toward him. "The duke rarely comes to my bed now that he has his heir and his spare." Her fingers played across his chest, eased his buttons from their holes.

Desire heated his flesh, consumed rational thoughts.

"No." He shoved her caress away. "Either you belong to me or you don't."

"But last night—" Tears dampened her blue eyes.

"Last night will not happen again." His hands closed around her arms, dragging her against him. God help him. He wanted her. Wanted the press of skin. Wanted...

He shoved her away. She stumbled, clutched at the bed rail for support.

"You want me."

Beautiful temptress. He had to resist. "I will only take you if you are mine and mine alone."

"Why must you be so unreasonable?" Honeyed curls cascaded down her back.

"Your answer, Lilly."

"I...I..."

"A marchioness is not a duchess." Kingslea felt his heart split open. Only a fool hopes for the impossible.

"If you loved me..." She flashed her palms at him.

"Love? Love is a lie we tell ourselves to excuse foolish behavior." An excuse he would never use again. He turned on his heel and strode across the room.

"Hugh," she sobbed.

The doorknob was cool to the touch. Tell her goodbye. The words lodged in his throat.

"If you want me, you know where to find me."

✾ ✾ ✾

Had she changed her mind? Was that why she had gotten an annulment? Society had concluded just that.

Alveston cut into his musings.

"We were referring to your ability to turn opportunity to gold."

"Opportunity to gold?" Kingslea swirled his brandy. Had his diversion into history cost him part of this conversation?

"Your engagement, man." Alveston's eyebrows met in a V above his nose.

"The fortune hunter lands an heiress." Kingslea gulped his drink. The alcohol couldn't burn away the bitterness. Is that what everyone saw? Is that what everyone believed?

"Miss Grey wasn't in much condition to protest." Winthrop's adam's apple bobbed under Kingslea's glare. "Don't kill the messenger, old boy."

He was the one whose days were numbered, when Fiona learned about the latest gossip. Kingslea leapt from the chair. He had to talk to her. Explain why he had claimed her as his. Pleasure spiraled through his belly.

226

She was his.

At least for now. How much did she remember? She hadn't seemed particularly lucid on the drive home. Of course, there hadn't been much time to talk before others had joined them.

"Don't you think it odd that her family joined her for the sojourn home because of the attack but not to see their own relatives."

"They weren't too happy about it." Winthrop patted his chest before slipping his hands into his coat pocket and pulling out an apple. "I can tell you. Took it right personally, the shrew did."

"Well, her own cousin was attacked by her brother."

"Not that. The leaving—had a full dance card." Winthrop snorted and crunched into his fruit. Apple bulged in his cheek. "Like I believe that one."

"Her aunt wasn't exactly surprised by the announcement." Alveston raised his glass. "Just the name of the groom."

"So, she knew."

"Plotted it, most like." The whittled apple core plopped against the stone hearth. Winthrop cleaned his fingers on his handkerchief then bent before the fireplace. "Montague doesn't have all the candles lit in his attic."

Humor lifted Kingslea's lips. His friend's desecration of clichés was always welcome.

"She didn't seem overly concerned for Fiona's health. I doubt she would have sent for a doctor if I hadn't ordered the butler to do it."

"What of Heberon? It is his house."

"He's afraid of her." Frustration emerged from the jumble of emotions clawing at his control. How was Fiona faring? What had the doctor said? Why hadn't she bid him good evening? There had been time for her to say something whilst he deposited her on her bed.

"Well, I must say, after seeing Sullied's face, his fear is understandable." Winthrop added a shovelful of coals on the grate.

"Not Fiona." Kingslea snapped open the match safe and chucked one at his friend. Financial wizard, conversational dimwit. His brain never reconciled the two. "Her viperous aunt. Heberon was lurking about when that woman chased me out of Fiona's room. He agreed to watch out for her."

He'd agreed to tell his sister and brother-in-law. Heat licked Kingslea's face. Was there another relative he'd overlooked?

"An imbecile isn't much protection." Alveston had switched to Kingslea's favorite chair. His boots tapped together as he propped his feet up on the ottoman.

"Heberon isn't an imbecile." The defense tripped off Kingslea's lips. Hell. First Fiona, now Heberon. Soon he'd be moving her niece and nephew into his house. His stepmother would be livid. His reflection smiled at him from his empty sifter. "His mind stopped growing before his body."

"You best marry her right away." Winthrop rubbed his pudgy hands together.

Marry Fiona. Blood quickened in Kingslea's veins. He couldn't marry her. He hadn't even proposed.

"I agree." Alveston topped off his brandy then set the bottle on floor. "To special licenses and hasty nuptials."

"Hear, hear." Winthrop drained his own glass.

"You're a bit premature." He set his glass on the desk. Things had gotten away from him this evening. It was time he regained control of his life. "There isn't going to be a wedding."

Sprayed brandy beaded on the cracked leather.

"What!" Anger blinked from Alveston's eyes.

"No wedding."

"Whyever not?" Winthrop collapsed on a couch. More folds creased his forehead. "You're not going to find that much blunt on the market for a while."

"Fiona deserves someone who'll care more for her person than her money."

"And that obviously isn't you," Alveston observed dryly.

"Does this mean you're finished with the adventure?" Winthrop wheezed to his feet and headed for the liquor. "Probably best to send for her father. No reason to involve yourself further. Nasty business, family squabbles."

Send for Fiona's father. Ridiculous. If the man cared an ounce for her, he never would have allowed her to sail to England in the first place. Orange, yellow and red flames danced around the black coals. Kingslea blinked, breaking their mesmerizing spell. *He* would protect Fiona.

"I have no intention of suspending my investigation."

"Nor any intention of doing the sensible thing and marrying money." Winthrop scowled.

"We'll have a long engagement, which will be broken when Fiona returns to America." A sane plan. A rational plan. Fiona would surely agree to it.

"And she agreed to it?"

"I haven't told her," he answered truthfully. But he would. And she would agree. The prospect punctured his earlier buoyancy.

Alveston's snort turned to a cough.

"You may find yourself suspended from a rope."

"Only a condemned man proposes engagement without matrimony." Winthrop agreed gloomily.

✤ ✤ ✤

"Plenty of bed rest." The doctor yawned his prescription.

"Perhaps you should prescribe something," Aunt Annabelle pressed for the third time. "Fiona is restless, the dear."

The latch clicked quietly home behind the doctor and her aunt. Muffled voices drifted through the closed door.

— I wonder if they realize how silly they are being. Milton stroked his chin before his finger swung from digit to digit as he recited the advice. *I mean, really—whatever could the doctor tell her that he hasn't already repeated three times? Plenty of bed rest. No excitement. Keep free of drafts.*

Fiona closed her eyes. The room spun. Her stomach heaved. She opened her eyes.

"I haven't knocked my head so hard since I lassoed Da's new stallion."

— And he dragged you all over the pasture. Milton smiled. *You must have been all of ten.*

"Eleven."

— How do you feel, Fi? He drifted to her side. His cold touch caressed her hand, concern darkened his eyes. *Truly?*

"I feel like Alice, except the pill only enlarged my head." Fiona wiggled farther under the blankets. Bile soured her tongue. "And there is the small matter of my innards wishing to be outards."

— Outards? Is there such a word? A smile teased his lips.

"I would show you, but I don't feel much like moving." Had she really thrown up on Hugh? Embarrassment burned her cheeks. The scene replayed in her mind.

— I am talking about your engagement to a certain gentleman.

She hadn't imagined the rescue or the announcement. Milton's face loomed closer. Why had she acted so brave? Misery would have spared her this argument. At least for a day.

"Milton, I—"

— You certainly took your time about it. He adjusted his cuffs. *Not that I doubted you could bring him up to scratch. I simply didn't think you had realized the depth of your affection for the man. Fiona Kingston. Lady Fiona Kingston. That has a nice ring to it.*

She shook her head and tasted bile. Would Milton ever get Hugh's name correct? Hugh. Strong arms wrapped around her. A soft kiss on her cheek.

"Depth of my affection?"

— I swear, Fi. Milton's legs evaporated into the ether. *If I'd had to find one more eligible bachelor to toss at your head, I would have sent for the priest myself.*

"I thought you wanted me to marry the Duke of August?"

— Good God, no. Smoke drifted away from Milton's torso. *You would have been bored within a month.* He rested his head on her pillow. The firm edge of his form blurred. *I was bored within minutes.*

"What have you done?" Fear diverted her train of thought. "You're fading to nothing, Milton."

— Don't worry, Fi. It was just a hat. He peered at her with one eye. *And don't change the subject.*

"What subject?"

— I pushed you at the duke to make you realize your love for the other one. He closed his eyes. *You are the most contrary woman. I knew if I chose one you'd pick the other.*

"You think I love Hugh."

— Don't you? Milton covered his yawn and snuggled deeper into his pillow. *You always swore you'd never marry a man you didn't love.*

"That's true, but..." Engaged. She was engaged to Hugh.

— Best make it a long engagement. Milton's voice faded. *Your father may very well follow through on his threat to disown you for marrying without him.*

With one last sigh, he dissolved into her bedspread.

Love him.

Did she love Hugh?

The answer rang clearly in her muddled head.

"I love Hugh." Warmth filled Fiona's limbs. A perfect future stretched before her. Their children would have his brown eyes and her even temperament. They would live in London, work at Grey Shipping. Hugh could handle the customers while she worked on the books.

She would have a marriage just like Mam and Da's.

"Just wait until I tell Hugh."

CHAPTER 30

"It is a very pretty ring." Silk swished as Melody joined Kingslea at his desk.
Rubies bracketed an oval diamond nestled in the platinum band.

"It was my mother's." The only piece of jewelry his stepmother hadn't gotten her hands on. The gemstones winked in the candlelight. It was the most precious thing he owned.

Soon, it would belong to Fiona.

Their false betrothal demanded a proper engagement ring. Kingslea tucked it into his vest pocket. If his pockets were deeper, perhaps he would buy her another. He ran his hands down the wool fabric. The shape of the ring comforted as his heart raced.

Would she like it? More important, would he see her tonight? Trepidation knocked an extra beat from his heart. She had confined herself to her room, refused his calls. At least, that was her aunt's tale.

"I wish we shared a mother." Melody's wistfulness tugged him back to the library.

"You would not be nearly the lady you are today without a mother." Kingslea smiled at her. At least, his stepmother had been good for something. Indeed, Melody's need of a lady's guidance was the only reason he tolerated Elspeth.

"But you wouldn't hate me so."

"I don't hate you." He wrapped his arms around her willowy frame. "I never understood you, but I think that is just your feminine nature."

They rocked as she pushed at his shoulder.

"I wouldn't blame you." She stepped out of his embrace and dabbed at her nose with her handkerchief. "If it wasn't for me, you wouldn't debase yourself playing servant to redeem Mother's debts." Red tinged her cheeks. She squared her shoulders, took a ragged breath and plunged onward. "If it weren't for

Mother, you never would have come to London, never would have met Miss Lawson." She waved her crumpled handkerchief at him. "And now you find yourself attached to yet another faithless American. All because of me."

She stuffed her fist in her mouth and spun on her heel.

Shock paralyzed Kingslea. His sister was a lady grown, all right. And like the rest of her ilk, she made absolutely no sense. Lilly, London and Fiona were *his* decisions.

"Mel." He strode to her side. "Look at me. Please."

She sniffed and tossed a glance over her shoulder.

"If it weren't for you, I would have spent all my vacations rattling around Heathmore by myself." Cool linen slicked across his fingers as he plucked his handkerchief from his breast pocket and blotted at her glistening cheeks. "You are the one blessing from my father's second marriage."

"But you rarely spoke or wrote to me after that day."

That day. Lilly's wedding. He had been roaring drunk at nine in the morning. Weeks had past before Alveston and Winthrop had found him. Another month before they had sobered him up.

"Elspeth forbade it. I was a poor influence." He swallowed the bitterness. Among other things. And she had been right, although not for the reasons she recited. He had been too steeped in his own misery to parent a girl of thirteen. Not that he'd tell Mel that. "Besides ladies don't need to know about irrigation, fertilizers or which crop grows best when. Neither should nobility play with the children of tenants nor sup in their kitchens. Alice Jones sends her best, by the by."

"Alice Wells. She married last year." The corners of Melody's mouth lifted then dropped. "You never invited me home for holidays."

Kingslea's legs devoured the distance to the desk. Not invite his sister home. The strongbox clanged shut. What other lies had his stepmother concocted?

"I did. Every year." He dropped the metal box in the bottom drawer of his desk and kicked it shut. "You were always too busy, traveling to this friend or that one. Elspeth gloated in letters full of your improvement. I think she was trying to make clear how useless I had been." He smiled at his sister. "She would have stopped writing if she'd only known how proud I am of your accomplishments."

"Mama always arranged the holidays." Melody smoothed her upswept hair. "We would spend Christmas together at whatever friends' were in her favor. Most times, we'd be so terribly busy with the entertainments that Christmas would catch her quite unprepared."

Swear words slipped out on his breath. Guilt weighed his shoulders. He should have insisted his sister return home. Should have known his stepmother never thought of anyone but herself.

"I'm sorry, Mel. I didn't know." But he would have if he hadn't been so steeped in his own self-pity. "Guess I was useless as a brother."

"Is that why you sent me two gifts, one at the beginning of the holiday and one at the end?" Melody's quick fingers smoothed a knitted throw over the back of the couch.

"No." He cleared his throat. His cheeks burned as he remember Houseman's wife clucking over his choices. "I always found the perfect thing about October. When I gave it to Houseman to deliver his wife would cluck and shake her head. You were too old for dolls, watercolors weren't personal enough. I returned to the shops."

"I thought perhaps you sent them to assuage your guilt."

"Self-pity doesn't allow much room for guilt." Air whistled through his teeth at his sister's stricken look. What wouldn't he give to take the words back?

"I thought you were enjoying your holidays." His gambit fell flat. Well done, old boy. With one careless stroke, his sister's mind returned to her earlier topic of conversation.

"I'll never forget the look on your face when you left that morning." She splayed her fingers across her chest. "I could hear your heart shatter with each peal of the church bell."

He nodded. The noise had been deafening.

"It was a long time ago."

"I won't let it happen again." Melody's small fists landed on her hips.

"It won't."

Determination froze her lips, narrowed her eyes.

"So, you feel nothing for Miss Grey?"

"Fiona?" How had they switched topics? Fiona had little in common with Lilly. A dull ache spread across his temples. Why did everyone insist they were pattern cards of each other?

"She won't play you false." Melody raised her chin, victory chilled her smile. For an instant, his stepmother stood in his sister's slippers. "I've made certain of that."

He blinked, and Melody stared back at him again. His heart settled into its normal rhythm until her words sank in. Were his sister's childish pranks the reason Fiona hadn't been at-home when he called?

"What have you done, pet?"

She opened her mouth.

"Milord." Bunsen bowed. Irritation and discomfort twitched across his face. Something had happened. Nothing short of Judgment Day could bother his butler.

Fiona. Kingslea's heart paused. Had she had a relapse?

"Out with it."

"You have a caller."

A caller? His heart resumed beating. Bunsen would disapprove of Fiona calling without an escort. And Fiona—it probably never occurred to her to take a maid. He glanced at his sister. Grim-faced or not, she would lend an air of propriety to Fiona's presence.

"Show her in."

"It wouldn't be proper."

"I'll be the one to decide what is proper in my own house."

"The *gentleman* insists you meet him in the dining room."

Gentleman. Not Fiona. Unless she disguised herself to get away from her aunt. She possessed a pair of canvas pantaloons, not that they hid her lush curves. She wouldn't dare. She had better not wear them where men might see her.

"The dining room, then." He strode out of the library. He'd burn the damn things, even if he had to personally strip them off her.

"We had considered the servants' entrance." Bunsen conceded as they made their way down the hall. "But milord's dignity is such that it might prove awkward if spied by outsiders."

His dignity. Kingslea stroked his chin. He supposed, as his betrothed, Fiona's behavior would reflect upon him. Not that he cared what others thought.

"Indeed it might."

Bunsen opened the dining room door and stepped aside. Kingslea closed his eyes counted to three then opened them.

There was a man in his dining room. A familiar-looking man. Names swirled inside his skull.

"May I help you, Mister..."

"Gibson, my lord." Bones creaked as the old man bowed. "I am–"

"The Grey's butler. Did Fiona send you? Has Montague returned?" Why hadn't Houseman sent word? Neither Montague nor his lackey had been seen in the last two days.

"I doubt Miss Fi is sensible of anything at the moment." Gibson wrung his hands, like a miser milking a dry goat.

"Is she well?"

"We didn't know where to go. What to do." Wisps of gray hair waved above the man's shiny head. His wild-eyed gaze darted around the room. "We had to do something."

Calm descended over Kingslea. He had faced bullets, irate husbands, determined mamas and jealous lovers. He could handle the distraught butler's dilemma.

"What is the nature of your call, Gibson?"

"Mrs. Worley mentioned your engagement, so naturally, I came here."

Kingslea grabbed a bottle of port from the sideboard and dumped a portion into the nearest cup. The liquid sloshed as he pressed the libation into the butler's hand. It took five seconds for the man to drink it. Another ten for the alcohol to burn away the haze. Impatience tapped Kingslea's boot. Fiona's well-being had better not depend on the snail's progress.

"Well, what is it, man?"

"It was Miss Fi's soup, milord."

Kingslea emptied the rest of the bottle into the man's cup.

"The soup?"

Gibson nodded as he finished the port.

"It came back brown, my lord."

Alcohol stung Kingslea's nose as he leaned close enough to catch the whisper.

"You breeched hundreds of years of social stratification because Fiona made brown soup?"

"Oh, no, sir." Horror contorted the lines in Gibson's face.

"Then what in perdition brings you out?"

"They locked her in her room, they did. Starved her. Mrs Montague took the key. No one in. Fired the tweenie just for asking Miss Fi if she needed more coal." He frowned at his empty cup. "She likes a nice fire, Miss Fi does. They all do. Cook thinks they need the warmth to—"

"Gibson!" Kingslea's control snapped like the crack of a whip. They had imprisoned Fiona. One way or another, they would pay with interest for their audacity. "Your point, man."

"Your coat, my lord." Bunsen held the garment out in front of him.

"Thank you." Kingslea shrugged into his over coat. "Go on."

"They said she weren't going to marry you." Fiona's butler cleared his throat. A measure of calm shone from his eyes. "She is to marry Piers. They'd see to it."

"This is England, by God. They can't force her into marrying anyone." Alveston's outrage echoed off the walls as he shook water from his coat.

"Let alone wed an imminent corpse like Montague." Kingslea acknowledged his friends' entrance with a nod. He had to get to the Greys before Fiona killed someone. This was one prize he refused to be denied.

Montague and Oswin posed little threat, but there were the guards and the police constables to consider. He stabbed his fingers into his gloves.

How did one dispose of two bodies?

"I doubt Miss Grey would say the vows."

"That's where the soup comes in." Gibson nodded.

"Your pistols, milord." Bunsen hefted a wooden box onto the table and lifted the lid.

"Good." Kingslea loaded one revolver and stuffed it into his waistband. His mother's ring rasped against the handle. "What in the name of heaven does soup have to do with anything?"

He passed the remaining pistols and ammunition to his friends.

"The cook made Miss Fi's favorite—chicken broth. It was clear and yellow." Gibson reached for a revolver before shoving his hands into his pockets. "Miss Montague intercepted the delivery. She was about to return it to the kitchen when her mother interrupted."

"Go on." Kingslea bypassed his hat but accepted his cane. With a twist of his wrist a steel blade emerged from the walking stick.

"Where are you going?" Melody stomped into the hall. "Why are you armed?"

"We are going to rescue a reluctant damsel."

"You mustn't." Her slippers snicked across the marble hall. "You'll ruin all our plans!"

"You had something to do with this?" Kingslea roared. His sister knew about the forced marriage. Good God, he had left her at his stepmother's mercy too long.

"I couldn't let you—"

"Melody." Winthrop pinned him with a glare before turning to his sister. "Look at me. Please?"

"I was trying to help." Her lip trembled.

"What do you know about the Montague's plans?"

Melody clamped her jaw shut.

She would tell them what she knew. Kingslea stepped forward. Alveston's fist thumped his chest. His friend shook his head.

"Tell me, love," Winthrop coaxed.

The world had gone mad. Kingslea nodded. This proved it. His sister and his best friend. Fiona and Montague. No doubt tomorrow, the sun would rise in the west.

"It's all because they fought, and Miss Grey is stubborn."

"Yes, Miss Grey is stubborn."

Words clogged Kingslea's throat. Stubborn? Fiona? Headstrong, maybe...

"Now, what's this about a fight?"

"Miss Grey and her cousin had a lover's spat. She told him she could marry anyone she wanted, and she wanted a title bigger than his so he would have to bow down to her." Melody turned to glare at him "Don't you see? That's exactly what she'll get. Your stupid honor forced you to propose. If you go charging into the middle of the wedding, it will be that odious Lilly all over again. What if you don't recover? I don't want to lose my brother again."

Kingslea blinked. His sister had been protecting him. That made two women in less than a fortnight.

"Who told you that Montague and Fiona had a lover's spat?"

"Edwina. She said sometimes love needs help." Melody's jaw jutted forward. "Fiona is bound to think it is romantic. Cousin Piers has arranged the flowers and the registrar to marry them." She turned back to Winthrop. "Which is what the whole argument was about. Cousin Piers wanted her to give up her papist leanings. This will prove his love." His sister's gaze swung again in Kingslea's direction. "She'll forget all about her claim on you."

"She's more likely to kill him."

"At least, you have her gun." Alveston opened the door. His coach waited just beyond the light.

Kingslea shook his head. "You underestimate Fiona's wherewithal."

"I fear Miss Fi will not manage anything in her state." Gibson shuffled down the steps behind them.

"I hardly think they would do her an injury until after the wedding."

"'Twas the laudanum, milord." Gibson moaned. "It made the soup brown."

"Take heart." Alveston drawled. "With that much opiate in her system, she'll not be held liable for her actions if she does kill him."

Not liable for her actions, if she was capable of any action at all. Kingslea flung open the carriage door. Now all he needed was a reason to elude responsibility for his actions.

Winthrop cleared his throat and nudged Kingslea out of the way. Melody marched past. She was halfway into the carriage before his brain reconciled with the sight.

"Where the hell do you think you're going?"

"With you." She scooted to the other side of the bench seat.

"This could be dangerous, Mel."

"It *is* dangerous." She snapped open her fan.

"Listen to me—"

"No." Her profile stood in relief against lace as she pressed her hands over her ears. "I listened to Mother the last time one of those beastly Americans broke your heart. I'm going to stand by your side this time."

"Mel—"

"Either you take me with you, or I'll hire a hansom and follow."

Winthrop struggled to hid his smile.

"It might help to have a lady along. Fiona might need her."

The carriage dipped and groaned as Kingslea climbed aboard. He would take care of Fiona's needs. Alveston coughed up his chuckles. And then he'd deal with the traitors.

"So, what's the plan?" Alveston's conversation gambit died in the oppressive silence.

Kingslea glared at his company. And to think he had actually armed them.

"To stop the wedding, of course." Winthrop answered cheerfully.

"Stop the wedding," Kingslea growled. "I wouldn't dream of it."

"You wouldn't?" Alveston and Winthrop chorused.

"See." Melody snapped her fan shut. "I knew you would come to your senses."

"Indeed, you know how fond I am of role-playing."

"R-role playing?" His sister's fan drooped limply from her wrist.

Kingslea plucked his mother's ring from his pocket and slipped it onto his pinky.

"I wonder if I'll like playing the part of the bridegroom."

CHAPTER 31

"Are you certain the wedding is to take place here?"

Kingslea's gaze roamed over the facade of 118 Piccadilly. Blue and green lights flashed in the ground floor windows. Thumps and bumps pounded against the night. The hair on the back of his neck stood on end. Darkness pressed against him; the air was thick and charged. Behind him, horses stamped and jingled their harnesses. The carriage creaked as, one-by-one, its occupants joined him on the sidewalk.

"Quite so, milord." Gibson smoothed thick straps of hair over his scalp. A smile touched his lips as a crash rattled the windows. "He let all the servants off for the night. Forced us out of the house, he did, locking the door behind us. Threatened to let us go without a character if we came back before noon."

"Everyone is gone, then?"

Everyone except Fiona. Dread tightened Kingslea's muscles. His legs carried him a step closer to the house. A hand on his arm stopped him. His gaze followed the fingers to their owner. Alveston shook his head. Kingslea nodded. A plan was imperative. Fifteen minutes wasn't beyond Fiona's strength. A thump knocked against the air. Ten minutes would be more than adequate.

"Indeed, milord, though not as far as *he* would wish." Gibson nodded toward a cluster of silhouettes huddled near the corner. One broad-shouldered shadow slipped from the crowd and loped toward them.

Houseman. The valet had neither deserted his post nor been dispatched. Kingslea jogged to meet him. So, why hadn't the man reported the danger facing Fiona?

"How many are with you?"

"Twelve or so." The valet dabbed at his forehead. A dark spot glistened on the white linen handkerchief. "They found me in the street." He jerked his head toward the servants. "Muttering and sputtering. Can't make head nor tail of their ranting, but something's afoot, and it involves the lady."

The crowd left their cozy cone of light and slunk across the street. They stopped halfway to them. Conversation rumbled before a two-headed silhouette walked to meet them.

"We number fifteen now," Gibson whispered to the nearest shadow. "A few of the newer hires ran off when the ruckus started."

"At least, Fiona has eluded the laudanum." The knowledge provided little comfort. She was outnumbered.

"Neither is she locked in her room," Alveston added.

"Laudanum? Locks?" Melody's voice rose an octave. "Fiona *wants* to marry Cousin Piers."

"She swallowed it, milord." Certainty rang in Gibson's voice. "They forced it down her. Heard the struggles myself."

"Perhaps she relieved herself of it when they left?" Alveston's suggestion met silence.

"I knocked on the door after those *ladies* left for the ball." The rotund shadow said in a voice reminiscent of wind through reeds. "Silence met me calls and raps. If only I had me keys..."

Gibson shuffled around Houseman and Alveston and stood next to the housekeeper.

"Sounds like there is crockery smashing." Winthrop nodded to the house. "Miss Grey is certainly unhappy about the impending nuptials."

"She's locked in her room, milord." Gibson placed his arm around the housekeeper's shoulders. "We swear it."

"She may have escaped." Alveston glanced over his shoulder. The draperies fluttered. Green light flicked over the cobblestones. "You keep reminding us how resourceful Miss Grey is."

Resourceful, but not invincible. Kingslea eyed the front door. They needed to get inside. Now. The staff would know all the house's weaknesses.

"How do you propose we enter?"

"I know a way." Gibson stepped away from the staff.

The housekeeper stayed his movements.

"You'd be Miss's intended, then."

Irritation flashed through Kingslea. The woman was wasting time. Time Fiona might not have.

"Gibson..."

The butler swayed where he stood, pulled between duty to the staff and to Fiona. A second passed before he shook himself and turned to the woman at his side.

"This is Lord Kingslea, Mary."

"And the others?"

"They are with him." Tired impatience weighted the butler's voice. "Friends of Miss Fi."

Throbbing started in Kingslea's temples. One more minute, and he'd smash the bloody window himself.

"The Pretender returned five minutes past." Mary informed him. "Had the other and wot looked to be a reverend wit' him. That's when the smashing started."

"Ye'd think their kind would remember what a lot of work goes into keeping such a house clean." A slight breeze blew a gaunt woman into their sphere. "And their kind ain't like to help."

"Now, Tizzy, you know they would if they could." The housekeeper caught the slight maid, lashing the wraith to her side before the next breeze carried her away. "'Tis your own mother in there. And she was housekeeper for most of her life, God rest her soul. She'll keep the mess to a minimum but Miss Fiona must be protected."

Kingslea turned back to the house. The racket had reached a fever pitch. The trouncing of piano keys joined the melee. If Fiona was, indeed, locked in her room, then one woman had raised such a ruckus.

"You left a *woman*..." Houseman fisted the front of Gibson's coat. "...behind to defend the lady?"

"Oh, gracious, no." Mary batted Houseman's hands away. "Miss Fi counted six restless spirits."

"Add the one she brought, and that makes seven."

Seven spirits. My companion is dead. Fiona words surfaced in his memory. Preposterous. The dead did not toss aside draperies.

"Shameful, it is." The gaunt woman tsked.

"Now, Tizzy, they were properly engaged."

"Engaged?" Kingslea strode forward. Engaged implied a male spirit. An intimate male spirit. With Fiona at all times.

"How many fiancés has Miss Grey had?" Melody whispered.

"Only the one," Winthrop answered. "Besides your brother, of course."

Kingslea's foot rested on the first riser of the stoop. Blood roared through his veins. Fiona hadn't been at-home when he called, yet she had a man with her every minute of the day. As his wife, she would need to understand there were certain boundaries even dead men shouldn't cross.

He was level with the brass door knocker. How many kicks would it take to open the front door?

Silence rang in his ears Kingslea blinked. Silence.

"Oh, dear," Mary's voice drifted over his shoulder. "It is awfully quiet."

"Think, Mary. The man with the Pretender. He wasn't a priest, was he?" Gibson called up to them from the servants' area. "I heard they can get rid of them."

"No. No, I don't think so." Mary leaned over the railing and peered at her husband. "At least, we never saw a collar."

Curses rolled off Kingslea's tongue, bounced off his grinding teeth. Damn. The silence eliminated both of his options.

"Gibson, I think now would be an opportune moment to present your alternative."

"Indeed, milord." The butler stepped closer to the stoop. The night filled with grinding stone, and then he disappeared.

"I'll be damned." Alveston's teeth flashed in the dim light. "A secret door."

Kingslea nodded. A hidden door, secret passageways and a dead but not gone fiancé. Fate had cast him as the hero in a bloody penny dreadful. He rolled the strain from his shoulders.

"Fiona will undoubtedly be in the library. According to Mrs…"

"Gibson," the housekeeper provided.

"According to Mrs. Gibson, there are only three of them. Houseman, see to Oswin. Winthrop, the right reverend, and Alveston, leave something of Montague for me."

Each of his friends nodded in turn.

"Wot about us, milord," a voice piped up from amongst the staff.

"What about your positions?"

"The Greys look after us. Just as we look after the master." Mrs. Gibson shoved them aside and stood in front. The others nodded. "Ye'll be needing us, milord. The others know us. We'll be quite safe, but Miss Fiona wouldn't forgive us if anything were to happen to you."

Tizzy eased to his left side. "Don't worry, we'll protect you."

"Protect me?" Kingslea blinked at the women. Such a preposterous idea wouldn't happen even in a penny dreadful.

"Oh, yes." A bony arm wrapped around his arm and squeezed. "That one doesn't like you much."

Kingslea struggled against the human bondage. Were the women in the Grey households effected by some sickness? Men protected women, not vice versa.

"I can take care of Montague."

"Of course, you can." Mrs. Gibson's pat thundered up his arm.

"We never doubted it," Tizzy explained, "but Michael…"

"Mitchell?"

"Milton," Tizzy snapped her fingers.

"Yes, that's him." Mrs Gibson poked at Kingslea's bruised arm "Milton is very protective of her."

"And despite his assurances to Miss Fi that he wants her to marry…" Tizzy tsked.

"We don't believe him." Mrs. Gibson shook her head.

"Oh, no," Tizzy seconded. "Not at all."

"You should hear them arguing about it."

"Mrs. Gibson. The Greys left specific instructions that we weren't to talk about such things."

"But he's almost one of them." The housekeeper shook her skirts.

"Yes, indeed," Tizzy agreed.

"I pledge never to tell a soul," Kingslea promised. Who the hell would believe him anyway? Secret passages could be proven, but ghosts? No sane person believed in specters, let alone conversed with them. There was a rational explanation for Fiona's one-sided conversations.

Yet, he had witnessed it himself at their first meeting.

"Where is Gibson?" His question banged off the door.

"Probably stuck in the library," Mrs. Gibson replied.

"What!"

"The passage leads to the library. Mr. Grey complained that it was not a proper escape route, but Miss Caro refused to allow him to tear up any more of her house."

Kingslea sighed. They had returned to kicking in the door. He stepped back. The latch clicked, and the door swung silently open. No one stood in the hall.

"Faulty lock." Alveston's breath misted.

The house was cold, the air thick and heavy. Expectant. Perhaps there *were* ghosts. A shiver rattled up Kingslea's spine. He had no time for such foolishness.

He had a rescue to perform.

Something smashed against the library wall. A fogged mirror hanging on it wobbled.

"I am *not* going to marry you." Fiona's voice echoed into the entry hall. More thumps followed.

She was awake. Specters—he hadn't believed it for a moment.

He threw himself against the library doors. Pain blazed across his shoulder blades, sparked stars in his skull.

Alveston shook his head.

"Always try the doorknob first." The smirk faded as the glass handle refused to turn. "Why the devil would Gibson lock the door behind him?"

"He didn't," the butler's wife whispered. "Their kind must have forgotten to open it."

The flesh under Kingslea's shoulder throbbed. The Greys must be a magnet for superstitious servants.

"On three." Alveston and Houseman nodded. "One." The trio stepped back in the hall. "Two." Muscles coiled around bone. "Three."

They sprang forward as the doors banged open. Kingslea stumbled over piles of tossed books. His foot slipped under an oriental rug. Momentum carried him into the couch. The collision knocked the breath from his lungs.

"Get on with the ceremony."

Montague. He'd know that sniveling anywhere. Kingslea shoved himself upright. Gasps of air burned his lungs. He blinked aside the tears.

"It won't hold up in a court of law." Fiona stood in the midst of the destruction, her back toward them. "I'll get an annulment." She hurled the book in her hand at the chair by the fireplace. "That is, if Da doesn't kill you first."

"Tie that bandage, Oswin."

The top of a head appeared above the plush chair.

"Stand up, man, you're a priest."

Alveston pointed to the matching Queen Anne chairs near the fireplace. A boot rested near the second one. Kingslea nodded. Montague and Oswin. But where was the priest?

"You didn't pay me enough to be stoned to death," a muffled voice protested.

Under the desk.

Kingslea motioned the others forward. Pride and regret waffled through him. Fiona may have held them at bay, but she still needed him to rescue her.

"They are only books," Montague whined. Fiona tossed another book at the chair.

"Thrown by ghostly hands."

Books tumbled off the shelf nearest the desk and pelted the top of the reverend's hiding spot.

Kingslea toed his way through the pile. Shelves break all the time, old man. Nothing preternatural about that.

"Then conduct the ceremony from under the desk, you nodcock."

"Dearly beloved…"

Gardenias teased Kingslea's nostrils. One more step, and he could grab Fiona without getting conked on the head by that tome in her hand.

"Skip that part," Montague ordered.

"Have him say 'man and wife,'" Oswin whispered.

"I'd have to object to that." Kingslea stated as his friends pounced on their appointed targets.

Fiona spun about. He caught her wrist before she chucked the book at his head.

"Hugh?" She blinked at him. Red stained her eyes and right cheek. The torn sleeve of her nightgown fluttered halfway down her arm. What had they done to her?

"Tie them up."

"No!"

Alveston slammed Montague into the wall, cutting short his shout.

"This is my house," he sputtered. "We're already married."

"And gag him."

"I didn't…" Fiona shook her head. A single tear glistened on her chalky cheek.

"I know, love." Kingslea brushed aside the tear and pulled her into his embrace. She clung to him, transmitting her tremors to him. The binding of the book in her hand dug into his ribs. "You were very brave."

"I'll just be going." The reverend plucked at Winthrop's fingers.

"On the contrary," Kingslea corrected him. "You've come to perform a wedding, and you'll do so."

"What!" Fiona shoved out of his arms and scampered to the desk.

"Fiona." Kingslea held out his hand. The hair on his arms stood on end.

"How could you?"

How could he?

"I had planned to give you time, but that seems out of the question now."

"Time?" A silver spike glittered in her fist. "You could give me a million lifetimes, and I would never marry Piers."

Marry Montague? The ordeal had effected her more than he had thought.

"Fiona, put down the letter opener."

"Why?" She focused on her target. "A letter opener is even better than a fountain pen. Da taught us."

"I don't plan to marry a murderess." Kingslea eased closer. Slowly, man. Don't startle her now.

"Marry." She tossed a glance in his direction. "You?"

"Yes." Cold metal burned his fingers as he removed the letter opener from her hand.

"You want to marry me?" She swayed into his arms.

Concern ate at Kingslea. Maybe he should delay the ceremony. Her eyes were overly bright. She must have consumed more laudanum than he thought. Which was precisely why she needed the protection of his life and his name.

"You may begin, Reverend."

"Do you—"

"No. No. Begin at the beginning."

✣ ✣ ✣

Hugh's smile curled Fiona's toes. He was here. Really and truly here. Her hands massaged muscle. Milton had said he would come, but after a week without a visit, she had given up hope. Bile burned her throat as another wave of nausea washed over her.

"Miss Grey actually agreed to marry me."

"Dearly beloved…" The minister ran a finger under his collar, cast a nervous glance around the room and continued.

— *Are you certain this is what you wish, Fi?* Milton's head bobbed next to her shoulder. His defense of her had cost him dear. *I still have a couple good tosses in me.*

"I'm sure." She was marrying Hugh. His warmth caressed her cheek. His strength shored up her quivering muscles. They would be happy together.

"Ah," the minister jumped before locking his wide eyes on her. "Not yet, Miss."

— *It's no problem.* Milton's hair dissipated into the surroundings. His gaze dropped to the book in her hand. *This one looks to be a convincing enough tome.* War and Peace. *Undoubtedly, a treatise on marriage.*

"Do you...?" The reverend cleared his throat.

"Hugh Thomas William Albert Gurnsey-Barrett."

Hugh. Thomas. William. Albert. Tingles raced across Fiona's flesh. They would need four sons. One for each of his names. The floor swayed gently under her feet. They would have his jaw, strong and firm.

"Hugh Thomas William Albert Gurnsey-Barrett take this woman, Fiona Grey, to love, honor and..."

— *Give me that.* Milton's face faded but a hand appeared.

Fiona stepped to the left. The pages in the book fluttered open. A gale would blow her to America. Strong arms wrapped around her waist. Da would like Hugh. Da... Thoughts blurred into chaos.

"...and obey."

"Fiona."

Hugh's voice sliced through her thoughts. They weren't on the *Revere*. They were in Uncle Andrew's library. Then why did she smell the sea? She filled her lungs with warmth. Not the sea—Hugh. He smelled of adventure, just like those crates in the warehouse at G&G Enterprises.

"Now is not the time to catch up on your Russian literature."

It was nice to be married. Already she felt lighter. Fiona stared at her empty fingers. Eight. Nine. Ten. All accounted for. Yet her brain insisted that something was missing. Her hands fluttered in the air before Hugh caught them. She was safe.

Cold metal bumped over her knuckle. Red and white gems twinkled. Her wedding ring.

"It's beautiful."

"In sickness and in health, till death do you part."

"I do," Kingslea answered.

— *I stuck around after death.* Milton face was a mask floating in the air. *He will, too, Fi. I know it.*

"Me, too." Fiona blinked. The walls seem to be creeping towards her.

"Do you, Fiona Grey, promise to love, honor and cherish this man?"

Her eyes closed then stuck. Tired. So tired. She could sleep now. Hugh was here.

— *Hurry, Fi.* Cold washed over her face. *I'm fading fast.*

"Hurry." She willed her eyes open. A slice of the library appeared.

— *Say "I do," Fi.* Milton snapped.

"Yes. I do." Wool cushioned her cheek. Warm breath washed over her. Warm and safe. Hugh. Her eyes fluttered closed.

"Perhaps you should jump to the end, Reverend." Hugh's order drifted to her from a great distance.

A band of strength settled under Fiona's legs, lifting her. She had never imagined love could be like this. Why hadn't Mam ever mentioned the floating?

"I now pronounce you man and wife."

"I object!" A man's voice peeled inside her head. A shriek followed then a thud.

CHAPTER 32

"Man and wife. Man and wife!"

The reverend fumbled with his Bible and extracted a piece of paper. Fiona turned her face to Hugh's. Now the reverend would say it. Now, he would order Hugh to kiss her.

"The ceremony is finished." Hugh's growl rumbled under her hands.

No kiss. Her eyes flew open. Where was her kiss? She blinked her groom into focus. How could she have forgotten how handsome he was? Her hand cupped his smooth jaw while her thumb found a home in his cleft chin. His pulse pounded against her pinky.

"Over my dead body."

Adrenaline chased the haze from her mind. She spun on her heel then staggered backward. Hands settled on her hips, strong but gentle. Excitement hummed in her veins. She would like being married to Hugh. Heaven knew she liked his touch.

"Man and wife. Man and wife." The reverend punctuated the end of his mantra with the slamming of his Bible. Paper crinkled in her ear as he punched Hugh's shoulder. Warmth and pressure left her hip. "My fee has been collected. My services rendered. Put anyone's name for a groom. I'm leaving."

Leaving? She stepped forward and turned her ankle.

"But you haven't finished the ceremony." Fiona kicked at the pile of books. Pain rattled up her shin. They had made a mess. Uncle Andrew would kill her. Uncle Andrew...

She turned back toward the fireplace. A lady in white shimmered between two shabbily dressed gentlemen.

"The ceremony is finished, Fiona." A hand settled on her shoulder. She shrugged it off and stepped closer.

"The hell it is."

Fiona blinked. She knew that voice. Joy and anguish wrestled inside her belly. Uncle Andrew was here. She peered closer at the smaller gentleman. No, not a gentleman at all. *He* was a she. Aunt Caroline. Fiona's eyes roamed to the lady in white. Judging from her clothes, the lady had departed this world some twenty years past. Who was she? A guide to the other side?

"You're not supposed to be dead." Fiona resisted the urge to stamp her foot. They couldn't be dead. She wouldn't allow it. "And who is the other shade?"

Aunt Caroline and Uncle Andrew glanced over their shoulders.

"It's Gibson." Hugh cupped her chin and turned her face to him. "Your uncle's butler." Metal scratched wood seconds before white light stabbed her eyes. Pink shown on Fiona's lids. "How much laudanum have you ingested?"

She wrenched her chin out of his hold. Blessed darkness cloaked her skull.

"Not much. My stomach tends to part ways with most medicinals soon after making their acquaintance." Fiona forced her lids slightly apart. Uncle Andrew, Aunt Caro and the woman were still there. "Mam finds it most vexing."

"A most convenient affliction, in this instance."

"I thought so as well." Especially given Piers's ignorance of it.

"Dearest Fi, perhaps you should come here." Aunt Caro softened her order with a smile.

"Stay here, Fiona." Warmth seeped through her nightgown as Hugh stepped in front of her.

A giggle chugged up her throat. Da would be proud of Hugh's bravery in the face of death. Death? Fiona looked from her husband to her uncle.

"Can you see them?"

"Yes." Hugh nodded. "And until I can determine—"

Fiona darted around him, leapt over the strewn books and landed against her uncle. They staggered a few paces before stopping. The scent of smoke and salt welcomed her. Sea and tobacco. No one else smelled like her uncle.

"You're alive. I knew it." Her feet danced the two steps to her aunt's embrace. "I knew it. Oh, Aunt Caroline. Uncle Andrew. I have so much to tell you."

"We returned as soon as Ronnie told us." Her uncle squeezed her shoulder. A weary smile deepened the lines radiating from his grey eyes.

"I got them, Fi." Uncle Heberon jumped from the gap between the fireplace and the library wall. "Just like you asked. And...and guess what." He bounced on the pads of his feet and pressed his clasped hands to his chest. "I can walk through walls, too."

"You were very brave, brother." Aunt Caro placed a quick kiss on his cheek.

"No." The wail rose from near the chair closest to the fireplace. Hugh's friend shoved Piers. Her cousin crumpled on top of the armchair. His wasted wrist dangled from the arm rest. "You can't be alive. You can't."

"Do shut up, Montague."

"This is my house, sir." Uncle Andrew strode toward Hugh. "Piers, if you don't stop sniveling, that mummy won't be the only thing shipped to Egypt in a coffin."

"So, you've finally decided to accept responsibility for your niece?"

Tension thickened the air. Fiona stumbled forward. This was not how she envisioned introducing Hugh to her uncle. Cotton fabric banded her chest. She glanced over her shoulder. Aunt Caro held Fiona's nightgown. She tugged. Her aunt shook her head.

"Kindly explain your presence in my house, sir." The men stood nose to nose. Fists primed at their sides.

"Hugh." Fiona tugged harder. Seams popped. Her aunt frowned but released the nightgown. Fiona jumped the books and skidded to a halt beside her uncle and husband. She shoved against one then the other. Immovable boulders in the path of progress. She caught her growl with her teeth. Of course, boulders would be easier to reason with.

"Woman, you will kindly cease shoving at me."

"But, Hugh..." She wedged herself between them, facing her husband. Quite a cozy fit, so long as she didn't need to breathe.

"Fiona." Hands clamped onto her shoulders. "You just promised to obey."

Had she? She remember the reverend saying the words but... She plucked at his fingers. Hugh must have promised to obey, too. Not that she would remind him of that. He wouldn't even look at her.

"You needn't sound so happy about that vow of obedience."

"Kindly allow me to speak frankly to your *uncle*, Wife." His gaze dropped briefly to her before resuming his optical battle.

"She is not your wife." Uncle Andrew leaned forward.

"I am, too. I said so." Fiona eased free of her narrowing spot. Confusion filled her sigh. How could God have left men in charge? This entire situation had a rational explanation, but would they listen? No. Her uncle and husband preferred violence to logic. "Actually, I said 'I do.' Not that anyone's listening."

An arm slipped around her shoulders. The scent of roses was added to the air.

"I'm listening, dear," Aunt Caro comforted her.

"Gibson, prepare the carriage." Uncle Andrew dropped his coat onto an overturned chair and rolled up his sleeves. A tattoo of an anchor winked from his muscled forearm. "We'll soon have a body to dispose of."

Body? Fiona groaned. A body meant that someone was dead. One dead fiancé was trying, but add a dead husband...

A shudder rippled through her. She had to stop them, force them to see reason.

"Uncle—"

Aunt Caro tightened her hold on Fiona's shoulders.

"Hush, Fi." Uncle Andrew frowned at the buttons on his vest. "I'll take care of your 'husband.'"

Hugh shrugged out of his jacket, tossed it to Houseman.

"You would have had better luck persuading Montague."

What had happened to the men she loved? Violence and insults had never been part of their nature before.

"Aunt Caro..." she pleaded.

"Dearest, perhaps we should—"

"I knew we should have intervened before this." Gold glittered as Uncle Andrew tossed his watch and fob to his wife. He braced his feet hip-width apart, hunched his shoulders and raised his fists. "Be glad it is I you face. I can assure you my brother would not be so quick to kill you."

"You will wish for your brother's assistance, old man." Hugh mirrored her uncle's stance as they circled each other.

"Caro," Uncle Heberon clutched at his sister's sleeve. "Why does Andy wish to kill Fi's friend? I thought he was helping us."

She patted his hand. "I think, in America, such violence is similar to a firm British handshake." Her aunt winced as flesh pounded flesh.

Fiona closed her eyes then opened them. Blood trickled from Hugh's mouth. How long would this ritual last? And why didn't Hugh defend himself? Her hand dropped to her waist. Helplessness shook her. Aunt Annabelle had taken her lariat.

"Does the mighty Andrew Grey even know the name of his opponent?" Hugh slammed his fist into her uncle's gut.

"I know all your names." Uncle Andrew's fist struck again. "Bounder. Cad."

Hugh answered the assault with a jab of his own.

They circled again. Fiona's brain throbbed inside her skull. This could last all night.

Her wedding night.

She had plans for her husband, and not one of them included nursing him back to health. White waved from the pocket of Hugh's jacket. She marched to Houseman's side and snatched the license.

"That is enough, Uncle Andrew. Hugh." The men exchanged two more blows. "If you do not stop this instant, I will fill in Piers's name in this license."

Both men froze. Fiona shook her head. They surrendered to a white flag but not to reason. She strode to the desk and snatched up the nearest pen.

Hugh dropped his fists to his side.

"He deserves a facer, Fiona." His chin jutted forward. "He left you unprotected."

"Unprotected?" Andrew scoffed. His open arms encompassed the destroyed library. "Look around you, man. Does this look like she's unprotected?"

"I'll grant that she can take care of herself under *most* circumstances." Hugh folded his arms across his chest and glared at him. "But the amount of opiates forced upon her has weakened her. She practically fainted in my arms."

Fiona straightened. Fainted? She had never fainted. *Pride, Fi. What's pride compared to an end to bodily injury?*

"Ha!" Uncle Andrew poked Hugh's chest. "So, you admit it to marrying her while she isn't in possession of all her faculties."

"Someone had to protect her." Hugh poked back.

"And I suppose her dowry of eight million pounds didn't influenced your decision."

"Eight million..." Hugh stepped back.

"In case anyone is interested, I still hold the special license." Air washed over Fiona's face as she brandished the paper. "Whose name shall I write in under *groom*?"

"Mi—oof." Piers rubbed his stomach while Lord Alveston polished his knuckles on his lapel. "Ouch."

"Mine." Hugh looked from her to her uncle before easing closer to the desk.

"Now, see here." Uncle Andrew raced towards her. "I did not expose my wife and children just to see my niece marry some fortune hunter."

"Hugh is not a fortune hunter, Uncle."

"He is, Fi. I was only presumed dead." He reached for the paper. "When Ronnie told us about his interest, I made certain...inquiries."

A muscle ticked in Hugh's jaw. "And did any of your inquiries uncover who tried to kill you?"

"No." A vein throbbed at her uncle's temple.

"The marriage stands." Hugh rapped on the desk.

"Over my dead body." A letter opener flashed in Uncle Andrew's hand.

"And your wife's and children's as well?" Hugh rolled a fountain pen between his thumb and forefinger.

"Are you threatening me and mine?"

"Gentlemen." Aunt Caroline stepped between them. Her hand slid down her husband's arm and retrieved the opener.

Fiona nodded to her. It was time sense and reason were restored.

"I still have the license." Both men lunged across the desk. She danced out of the way. "Now, both of you—sit." She pointed to the overturned chairs. "Please."

Grumbling filled the air as they righted the chairs and complied. Fiona smiled. God had a hand in the minister's mistake. The house was ever so much more pleasant when husbands obeyed. Now when women ruled the world...

"Fiona?"

"How much laudanum did you say she consumed?" Uncle Andrew's question circled in her head.

"Hugh is correct, Uncle. I cannot allow you to endanger Aunt Caro or the children."

"You forget yourself, young lady." He made to rise from his seat, but Aunt Caro sat on his lap. "My brother is counting on me to protect you."

"*I* will protect her." Hugh growled.

"And who will protect Fiona from you?"

"I do not need protection from Hugh." Fiona tapped the pen on the desk. The men hunkered into a glowering silence. "He has been helping me to find you and whoever is responsible for the *Sweet Wind*'s sinking."

"Humph."

"That is very kind of you." Aunt Caroline smiled.

"Unfortunately, our investigation hasn't progressed as far as we would have liked," Hugh grumbled.

"I suppose you offered to assist Fi for completely altruistic motives?" Uncle Andrew leaned forward, but Aunt Caro laid her hand on his chest.

"I have reason to believe that my own venture is related to your misfortunes."

"He stole Captain List's logbook."

"Captain List." Her uncle's eyes narrowed. "But he wasn't at the helm of the *Sweet Wind*?"

"It was his ship." Fiona smoothed the building suspicion. "And he was usually your captain."

"I believe our investigation will proceed much more quickly if we work together."

"You want us to remain dead," Uncle Andrew stated.

"Whoever is responsible thinks they've already gotten away with murder."

"Our reappearing might rattle him."

"Unlikely. You would have to know who it was to rattle. And the risks..." Hugh's voice trailed off, leaving the rest of the sentence to her uncle's imagination.

Fiona resisted the urge to clap. He really was very good, so long as his emotions didn't carry him away.

"And the marriage?" Silence met Uncle Andrew's question.

"It—" She began.

"It will be annulled after we find the culprit."

Fiona choked. Annulled? She sat on the desk. Hugh didn't want her? Didn't love her? She shivered. She hadn't felt this cold since Milton had walked through her.

"You plan to just give her up?"

Hugh cleared his throat and rose to his feet.

"Thanks to the laudanum, she isn't responsible for her actions. The court will see that."

Her mind bent and twisted. Nothing made sense. He had rescued her.

"Our marriage..."

"I could never take advantage of you, Fiona." Hugh's hands were warm mittens around her fingers. "You deserve better than to be haunted by rumors of marrying a fortune hunter."

"You don't want me haunted..." She slapped her hand over her mouth, catching the laughter bubbling up her throat. Tingles raced across her cheek.

"And you'll sign a paper to that affect this very instant?" Uncle Andrew stood, deposited his wife on Hugh's vacated chair and strode toward his desk.

"I hardly think that is necessary." Hugh ducked his head.

Fiona refused to meet his eyes.

He didn't want her. Didn't want to be married to her. And what did she want?

"You have returned. We can all attest to the fact the ceremony was never completed."

Hugh. She wanted Hugh. And no one was going to take him away from her.

"No." She slipped off the desk and fanned herself with the license. Thoughts whirled like a tornado. No man would marry a woman simply for to protect her. He had to love her. He just hadn't admitted it to himself.

"No? Fiona, perhaps you had best sit down." Hugh set his arm around her shoulders, shepherding her towards the chair. "Your cheeks are flushed, and your eyes are glazed—"

"I am fine." She slapped the paper against his chest. "And in possession of all my faculties. Everyone in this room except those strongly biased in your favor will agree to that."

Her aunt nodded slowly. The servants eyed the banter like a ball in a game of lawn tennis.

"Fiona, you have taught me that it is a strong person who can depend on others when they do not feel quite up to task." Hugh stepped in front of her. "Accept this marriage."

She shook her head. He hadn't been listening.

"Your words sparkle like fool's gold yet possess half its worth."

"Fiona Ann Grey!" Her uncle pounded on the desk. "The man is acting honorably."

Patience, Fi. The shipwreck had obviously affected her uncle more than he knew. Why else would he want to kill Hugh one minute and defend him the next.

"What honor is there in pledging before God and family to take a wife knowing in your heart you have no intention of keeping her?"

"You needed protection. I offered it."

"My arm pains me," she countered, stemming the rising hysteria with words. "Will you sever yours for my benefit?"

"Don't be absurd," Hugh glowered.

"Fi, dear."

"Yes, Aunt."

"Look at me, please." Aunt Caro's smile brimmed with understanding. "I know your pride is a bit bruised."

"Pride doesn't excuse her ungrateful behavior." Hugh stalked towards his friends.

"We accept your generous offer of protection, Lord Kingslea."

Tears stung Fiona's eyes. She stumbled into her aunt's embrace.

"Caro," her uncle said, "there *will* be an annulment."

"Yes, dear." Aunt Caro gently turned. Fiona's feet moved. Strange how a broken heart didn't effect movement nearly as much as laudanum. "You sailed to London thinking you were helping your old aunt, and yet you found more than that, didn't you?"

"There will be an annulment!" Panic squeezed the bass notes from her uncle's voice.

"Good, then it is settled."

Fabric rustled. Feet shuffled. They must be near the doorway. Fiona sniffed. Please God, let her be out of the room before she lost complete control.

"Where do you think you are going?"

"I am going to get a doctor." Aunt Caro's voice bounced around the entry hall.

"Oswin may get Piers medical assistance on their way to the docks."

"The docks?" Piers whimpered.

"I have one ship sailing to America and one sailing to Australia. Be on one. Both of you," her uncle commanded.

"Fiona's father lives in America." Hugh words scoured her heart. How could he not want her?

"That's right."

"Australia. We chose Australia." Piers's whine drifted in from the hall.

"Here's the first step, love. Not much farther."

"Caro, where are you taking Fi?"

"Pack at least one trunk." Hugh's order rumbled up the stairs.

Pack? Fiona glanced at her aunt. Why did he want her to pack?

"And just where is my niece going?" Uncle Andrew's voice shook with suppressed violence.

"A *wife* belongs with her *husband*." Hugh answered.

"He's right, dear." Aunt Caro agreed.

"He doesn't want me." Fiona bit her lip. Now she sounded like Piers.

"I'll get the trunk," Uncle Andrew offered.

"No, you and the groom will start putting the library to rights."

Snickers rumbled through the assembled servants.

"But, Caro, we didn't make this mess. Fi, tell your friends to—"

"They're gone." Fiona dried her cheeks on her sleeves. She raised her chin and stared down at her uncle. "Such an expenditure comes with a cost."

"I hardly think—"

"Imagine if there were no gas in the lines." Fiona cleared her throat. She could do this. "The flame goes out. Once the energy has been replenished, it comes back on. Until then..."

"Until then," her uncle finished. "we clean up after their spectral tantrums."

"Would you like to come with us, Melody?" Fiona skimmed over her husband and eyed his sister. Women needed to stick together.

"You mean pack or pick up books?"

"Yes."

"Melody." Hugh shook a stack of books at her. "You will stay."

"I think..." His sister hitched up her skirts and skipped from the library. "...I should get to know my new sister."

"Coward."

"Do you think I should have stayed?" Melody asked, glancing over her shoulder.

"They need to expend all that energy in a more productive manner than fighting." Fiona sighed. Perhaps she shouldn't have invited the girl. She seemed more enemy than ally.

Aunt Caro guided them past the drawing room and ballroom.

"Fiona," she said as they reached the second-floor landing. "Did I ever tell you the story of my marriage to your uncle?"

"No."

"Well, Andrew planned for us to be married for a month. Actually, I think he said fourteen days and six hours." Her aunt winked. "He also counted on the safety net of an annulment..."

CHAPTER 33

It was a nice room, or would have been under different circumstances. The tang of fresh paint mingled with the pungency of paste. Soft cabbage roses crawled up the wallpaper. Whimsical stars cut the dressing table. Who was the lady her husband had in mind when he'd decorated this room? Fiona's sigh fluttered her loose hair.

"I suppose destroying the license would be better than an annulment." She handed him the paper then strolled across the rug. Metal creaked as she lowered her weight onto the green-and-blue coverlet on the brass bed. Everything in this room suited her.

Especially the groom.

"It is for the best." There was scratching as Hugh signed his name to the paper.

Despair anchored her heart to the bottom of her belly. She couldn't give up hope. Not yet. Uncle Andrew's two-week marriage had stretched into nineteen happy years.

Play on his sympathy. Let his strengths shore up your weaknesses. Aunt Caro's advice swirled inside Fiona's skull. When was the last time she had depended upon anyone? Before Brianna's sickness, before the scandal of her birth became a diversion for society's boredom, when even Milton's unfailing support had wavered in the face of overwhelming censure.

Yet she had depended upon Hugh before their introduction.

Hugh's constancy would strengthen in the face of adversity. Her heart fluttered in her breast. Please let Aunt Caro be correct, she prayed. Let Hugh replace her pain for his love.

She filled her lungs, gathered the frayed ends of her courage.

"Don't worry." She traced the rug's pattern with the toe of her slipper. The truth slipped easily from her lips. "I've grown accustomed to scandal."

Hugh's presence pressed against her. He crouched in front of her, arms resting on his knees.

"I promise not to tell a soul you were married in such a fetching dressing gown."

Fiona flicked the soft cotton sleeve. She had forgotten to dress. Not that it mattered.

"I was referring to the annulment."

"I swear I will be the villain in the piece." His hand hovered over her thigh before his fists landed on his knees. "Your uncle rode to the rescue, forcing the dastardly fortune hunter to free his innocent niece."

Fortune hunter. If he knew she had traded her inheritance for him, would he stay? But at what cost to her love? Her foray into gambling ended with her heart. *Sympathy, Fi*. Pride tasted bitter, victory sweet.

"If only others believed it so."

"We'll make them believe." Hugh's knees hit the rug. His hands found hers, his thumb worried her wedding ring.

"You are kind to say so." Heat raced up her arms, melted distracting thoughts. His hands belonged on her. "I know they will feast on my past with relish. Buzzards picking over a fresh carcass."

His fingers circled her wrists. She could taste the flutter of her heart.

"In the end, *you* will have been fortunate to escape *my* scheming."

"I have found you nothing but honest and forthright." His gaze lingered on the blue veins inside her wrists.

The heat spread. Soon she would melt into a puddle of sensation. She bit her lip, snaring her groan.

"A lone voice in a chorus of judges." Fiona leaned against the footboard. The metalwork was ice against her cheek. "Blood will out, you know."

"Blood?" He smiled. His fingers left her wrist to pay homage to her face. His touch tickled her forehead before tucking a lock of hair behind her ear. "You hail from the elite of New York society."

Fiona's heart thudded to a stop. The moment had come. Could she tell him the truth that even the twisted society gossips had failed to match in depravity and infamy? He needed to know. She swallowed the lump in her throat.

"I hail from a gaming hell on Fifth Street."

The words rushed out, deflating her lungs and spirit.

His hands stilled on her shoulders.

"My sire owned Mam, forced her to bear me. And when he couldn't control her..." Tears stung her eyes, choked off the confession. She had to finish. One gulp of air. Two. "When he couldn't, he decided to kill her."

"Your father..." His touch fell away.

"Da is my father." Cold, so cold. Fiona wrapped her arms around her belly. The truth would not be stopped. "My *sire* was called Morgan. I've always known the truth. Polite society learned of it when I was sixteen."

The confession sapped her strength. She rolled onto the bed, tucked her knees against her body. He hadn't understood.

"Milton remained true."

Perhaps an annulment was best.

"Gilly was not so fortunate. They deemed Brianna's sickness God's judgment, punishment for the sins of our parents." Hugh deserved better than her. Tears dampened the cotton, turning the fabric translucent. "Who'd want one such as I muddying their pedigree?"

Metal creaked. The bed dipped. Warmth radiated from the hand on her cheek.

"Who wouldn't?"

"You."

Hugh's thumb caressed her lips. His gaze followed the motion.

"You deserve to be courted. Loved."

A woman's image flashed across Fiona's skull.

"*She* is the reason you refuse your heart, isn't she?"

"Who?"

"The apparition at our wedding." A name whispered across Fiona's memory. "Alice Anne."

"Her name was Lillian." His raw whisper scratched her ears. Hugh flopped onto his back.

"She said she had unfinished business with you."

"My past also possesses a muddying quality." He rubbed the wrinkles from his forehead. "Perhaps you've heard the rumors."

"Most are afraid to speak of you at all." Fiona's fingers crept across the mattress, climbed his arm to rest atop his hand. "Your reputation is most fierce. And your knowledge of others' affairs is frightening."

Hugh squeezed his eyes closed. His adam's apple bobbed twice.

"Lillian married Sullied."

Fiona slipped her fingers against his palm. Lillian had been a fool.

"You love her."

"Yes."

Just as a single bullet shatters glass, his one word broke her heart. He was not free. And she...

Fiona laced her fingers through his, pressed their palms together. She would hold on to whatever he offered.

"I don't wish to be haunted by your former lover."

He tucked her clasped hand next to his heart and rolled to his side. Her body hummed. Only a breath of space separated their bodies.

"And I would prefer if you were not haunted by *your* former lover." His eyes held hers. "He was the companion you referred to that first night we met."

"Yes."

"Is he here?" Hugh's knuckles brushed her cheek before settling under her chin. His heart pounded against her trapped hand. "Now?"

"No. The book battle exhausted him. He's whiling away time in the Nothingness."

"Nothingness." A smile teased Hugh's lips. "That doesn't sound very pleasant."

"It isn't."

He stroked her hair, molded the long tresses to her arm. "And when he returns?"

"He'll complain for at least an hour." Butterflies fluttered in Fiona's stomach. Heaven lay in his touch.

"Here." Hugh frowned at her. His caress stopped. "In your bedroom."

"Yes."

"I would think…" He whisked the ends of her hair over her arm. Pleasure erupted with each sweep. "Given his affection for you, I would think that he wouldn't want to compromise you any further."

Fiona tugged her hand from his grasp. She wanted to touch him. Would her touch give him as much delight as his gave her?

"He's dead." Silky hair slipped between her finger and thumb.

Hugh's eyes followed her strokes. "He's still a man."

"You're a man." She teased the hair at the nape of his neck. "And in my bed."

He eased closer, obliterating the distance between them. Her breasts ached, her thighs tingled. Such a contradiction. Hard and soft. Danger and safety. Man and woman.

"I am your husband." His nose touched hers. His kiss flirted with her lips.

He wanted her. The proof branded her belly. She could have him, but only temporarily. He had unfinished business with Lillian. The memory of her nemesis slowed Fiona's heart. There would be no going back if she accepted his kiss. They must stop here.

"For now."

"Yes." Hugh winced and eased away from her. Cold air filled the gap between them.

Coward. The label was only partially correct. Lillian's presence made it easier to surrender to the fears. Her gaze washed over his battered features. Broken hearts never showed, but the ache was a hundred-fold worse.

"It hurts, doesn't it?"

"Surprisingly so."

"Uncle was a pugilist in his younger days." Her fingers explored his red cheek, skipped over his swollen lip. "Da was forever telling us stories. Mostly how Uncle used to practice on him."

Hugh caught her hand and gave her fingers a quick kiss.

"About your father..."

"Da would approve." Fiona forced the words. Hugh wasn't talking about the fisticuffs when he'd asked her a question. Neither was he talking about them now. "You gave as well as you took. Uncle was holding his chest most tenderly."

"Fiona."

"I am glad he didn't blacken your eyes." She brushed the lock of hair off his forehead. She had to touch him. Wanted to kiss him. Such madness to decide one thing and do another. She rolled closer. "You have the most extraordinary eyes."

"They're brown."

Surely, one kiss wouldn't hurt.

"They're the color of warm cocoa on a dreary day when the fog is so thick it presses the chill into the room." She turned her face to his, brushed her nose against his. Just one.

"We shouldn't."

"I want a taste. To chase away the chill." She pressed her lips to his. His mouth opened. She followed his lead. Tongues touched and parted. His hand stroked her throat, slipped down her neck and cupped her breast. He exchanged his breath for her groan.

Heartbeats knocked against her ears. Her hips moved to an instinctive rhythm while her hands plucked at his shirt buttons. Closer. She wanted closer. Needed the press of his flesh against hers.

"Kingslea." Melody's voice preceded three sharp raps.

Hugh wrenched his mouth away. Red suffused his cheeks. He yanked his hand off Fiona's breast and plowed it through his hair.

"Kingslea? Are you in there?"

"Yes." He flung himself off the bed and paced the carpet.

"Mother's carriage is outside."

His shaky fingers worked on his shirt buttons. "I'll be right down."

"Shall I go with you?" Fiona straightened her dressing gown. Disappointment warred with relief. One kiss. Her body would lie to fulfill its desires.

"No!" He swallowed hard, holding his hands in front of him. "Just stay here and...and use a blanket to keep warm." He threw the coverlet at her.

She caught it and hugged it to her chest. Aunt Caro's plan had certainly worked. But Hugh didn't seem particularly happy about it.

"Are you all right?"

"I could use a stroll in the fog." He smoothed his hair. "A bloody frigid fog."

"Hugh?"

"Go to sleep, Fiona," he tossed over his shoulder as he ran out the door.

"Sleep." She scooted to his still-warm spot. "How can I sleep when I have a steam engine pumping under my skin?"

❊ ❊ ❊

— Good morning, Fi.

Fiona swallowed a groan. Morning already. And late. She rubbed her eyes. The sandman had used her eyes to store his extra sleepy dust.

— Perhaps I should say "Lady Kingslea."

She forced her eyelids apart. Milton's smoky face drifted near her pillow. Light filtered in through her open window. Hugh had not returned to her. She kicked off her blankets and shivered to a stand.

"Fi is just fine."

— Uh-oh. Milton drifted to the fireplace. *Do I smell trouble afoot?*

"It was horrible." And wonderful. Fiona wrapped her arms around her. Their warmth lacked Hugh's touch. How could he not have returned after that kiss? He was supposed to return. Hadn't she changed into her best peignoir for him? Silk slipped around her thighs as she strolled to the fire. Monsieur Worth would certainly be disappointed to have his creation wasted.

— Now, Fi. Milton cleared his throat. His hands fluttered around his face before settling across his wispy chest. *Men have certain needs…*

Hugh's needs? What about her needs? She wouldn't have thrashed around all night if he had simply satisfied the promise of his kiss. "Milton."

— As his wife, it is only natural that Kingslea would look to you to fulfill them.

"Milton."

He spun on his indistinct heel and pointed at her.

— You do wish to have children, don't you?

Children. Fiona coughed a laugh from her throat. Her late fiancé was about to lecture her on intimacy.

"Yes." Should she interrupt? A man's perspective might prove useful.

— I know gently reared young ladies aren't versed in such matters, Fi. Milton rubbed his hands together. *You see, this is why men must be experienced. I know you didn't approve of my visits to Madame Celeste's, but I can assure you on our wedding night—*

"Milton!" Fiona hurled her pillow at him. It sailed through and thumped against the wall. Bawdy houses and prostitutes. She knew about lust. With her mother and sister, she had probably visited more houses of ill repute on errands of mercy than Milton. What she wanted to know about was a man's love.

— Really, Fiona, I hardly think the abuse of my person is justified. He straightened his jacket and tugged on his cuffs. *After all, I didn't keep you up all night.*

"Neither did Hugh."

— He— Milton blinked. *What!*

"He kissed me on the cheek and sent me to bed." Fiona crossed her fingers behind her back. It wasn't such a big lie. Hugh *had* kissed her on the cheek—and the neck and...

She filled her lungs with a cleansing breath. "Alone."

Milton stroked his chin.

— Perhaps, he wanted to give you time to adjust to...

"No."

— You fell asleep, didn't you. Dammit, Fi. A man's ego—

"Milton. I was awake until..." Fiona's gaze darted to the clock on the mantle. "...until just two hours ago. He never came back."

— Well. Milton's brows met in a V over his nose. *I see no reason to make me the object of your tantrum.*

She picked up her spare pillow. Feathers crunched under her fingers.

"I am not having a tantrum."

His gaze lingered on her silk-clad curves. Fiona shifted her weight, resisted the urge to cover herself. This was Milton. Her dead fiancé.

— No man in his right mind would turn away such a deliciously wrapped package unless... Milton tapped his pursed lips.

"Unless?"

— Perhaps your Kingslea has other interests than women.

"Hugh is not a Nancy boy."

— Then you tell me why he turned away... He gestured at her. *...a chance at heaven.*

Heaven. A dull ache stitched her heart. No wonder it had taken her years to find someone to replace Milton.

"One word."

— Lust?

"Annulment."

— Don't tell me you believed that twaddle. Milton shook his head. *It's lust. Pure and simple. Lust is...*

"I know what lust is, Milton." The bed creaked as Fiona sat down. Lust and she were becoming old friends.

— Do you? He peered at her. *Yes, I think you do.*

"It's why I donned my very best peignoir."

— You're going to seduce him. Milton smiled. *Bravo. So, what's the plan?*

Plan? She planned to get Hugh into bed, preferably while neither of them had on any clothes. It was the route to that destination she hadn't figured out.

"I plan to seduce him so he can't give me an annulment."

— Yes, yes. Milton batted away her words. *I mean how are you going to seduce him?*

"Aunt Caro suggested sympathy."

— Sympathy. Milton frowned down at her. *That is not a very good plan.*

Fiona crossed her arms. "Well, it earned me one kiss." And a touch. But it hadn't gotten her that nebulous completion.

— *He kissed you?* Milton sidled closer. *Where?*

"In the bedroom." She hugged the pillow to her chest. They had been in bed with far too many clothes on. What had she done wrong? Milton would know. He was a man, even if he was dead. "Hugh wouldn't like it if he knew you were here."

— *Why not?* He jerked his head up.

"He doesn't think it is proper for me to entertain men in my bedroom, even dead ones."

Crimson tinged his translucent face.

— He *was here?*

"He's my husband."

— *He's jealous.*

"Of what? You can't touch me without causing us both pain."

— *But he doesn't know that, does he?* A wicked smile twisted Milton's face. *Your husband is jealous. Which is so much better than sympathy. Now, how do we turn it to our advantage?*

Jealousy. Misgivings peppered Fiona's determination. Milton's plan could come back to haunt her.

"We can't. Hugh can't see you."

— *Yes.* He nodded. *That might be a problem...or a benefit. Seems that your husband has ideas about me watching you bathe and dress.*

Bathe and dress. Hugh hadn't mentioned anything specific. Fiona smoothed the carpet with her bare feet. What could Milton be thinking? Unless...

"You haven't watched me, have you?"

— *No, of course not.* He turned to face the fire. *But if he's thinking I would do such a thing then he must be thinking of doing so himself.*

"That makes no sense."

— *It makes perfect sense to a man.* Milton dashed to the end of the bed and poked at the coverlet. *Give me your robe.*

"Why?" Fiona shoved off the bed and strode to the wardrobe. The robe lay puddled on the floor. She shook out the wrinkles and held it out to him.

It took two tries for him to hold onto it.

— *No man with a beating heart would refuse you in that.*

Fiona glanced in the full-length mirror. The nightgown was nice, but it fit her no more tightly than one of her ball gowns. There was no more skin exposed.

"Why?"

— *Men are not complicated, Fi.* He waited for her by the door connecting her room to Hugh's. *See woman. Want woman. Very simple. Now, open the door.*

The brass handle felt cool in her palm. She twisted, and the door sprang open. Hugh's scent drifted into her room.

"What has that to do with my robe?"

— *I am going to put it in his room.* Milton winked at her before zooming across the room, heading for the big bed squatting in the center.

"What! Milton, no!"

He draped it across the coverlet then rushed back to her.

— *You can thank me later.* He slipped through the door and grinned at her.

"Only because I can't kill you all over again." Fiona milked her fingers. Why had she listened to him? Aunt Caro's plan would have worked eventually. She should have been patient. "Go get it back Milton."

— *Imagine it, Fi. Your prince will wake up with you bending over him.* Milton licked his lips. *Just brush a kiss across his lips, and you'll be under him in seconds flat. Before he even wakes, any chance of annulment will be erased. I'm brilliant, positively brilliant.*

Lust and love warred within her breast. Mam always said mornings were the best. Yet, she also declared honesty to be the best policy.

"I don't know." Cool marble slid under her fingers as she dusted her mantle. "It seems a bit underhanded."

— *You love him, don't you?*

"Yes."

He grabbed her and spun her toward the connecting door. His cold touch burned her shoulders.

— *Then for his own good, you must take advantage of him.*

For *his* own good. Fiona straightened her shoulders and reached for the doorknob.

"All right."

— *Make sure he knows I took your robe, and that I saw you dressed like that.*

Fiona nodded, counted to ten and opened the connecting door.

CHAPTER 34

Empty. Her footsteps echoed off the water-stained ceiling. Half a dozen Fionas stared back at her from the cracked looking glass. Worn, decrepit and tired. The room and its furnishings had given everything they had to those who'd come before. Just like their current owner.

"Oh, Hugh." She pressed her hand to her chest. Her heart slowed as it tumbled deeper in love.

— *Good God!* Milton drifted through the wall. His eyes widened as they noted the peeling wallpaper, the cracked wardrobe door, and the shattered mirror. *What man in his right mind would turn away a fortune to live in such squalor?*

"Hugh would." Fiona rebuffed his scowl with a smile. The contrast between her newly refurbished room and her husband's shabby one stoked the embers simmering in her belly. "He offers the best to everyone else, leaving nothing for himself."

— *He's destitute, Fi,* Milton scoffed, poking at a bowl of standing water on the windowsill. *Putting on a good show until he snags an heiress.*

"Milton." Fiona shook her head. She had forgotten how consumed with appearances he had been. How could anyone not see the truth? Hugh's armor might be tarnished, but his heart was solid gold. She would tell him as soon as she finished kissing him.

— *Listen, Fi, you don't wish to be tied to a man who treats his possessions so abysmally. It may very well reflect on how he will treat you.*

"You forget, Milton. The rest of the house shows signs of recent repair. Proof that Hugh didn't allow the neglect to spread." Snippets of gossip replayed in her mind. No doubt, his stepmother and late brother were responsible for allowing the decay. "Hugh needs someone to take care of him."

— He needs *a plasterer, a chimney sweep and a glazier.* Milton surveyed the wainscoting near the window. *A carpenter wouldn't hurt, either.*

Fiona strolled to the bed and scooped up her robe. The embroidered silk chilled her shoulders. Her husband's scent teased her. Hugh's bed. Twisted sheets and bunched coverlets. How like her own. Had he lain awake thinking of her? Had he dreamt of caressing her? Her fingertips trickled down his pillow and over his sheets.

"His bed is cold."

— You could warm it up for him.

Fiona turned the suggestion over in her head. Milton proposed a sojourn in purgatory. Embraced by Hugh's scent but not his arms nor his heat. With one last glance at the bed, she turned her attention to the washstand.

"I don't know when he'll return."

— Well, I hope the maid returns soon. Milton flicked at a stack of papers under a chipped washbowl. *This place is a mess.*

"Grey Shipping" flashed in the fluttering pile. Porcelain scratched marble as she plucked the pile of papers free. Cramped numbers marched in columns down the page. Why would Hugh have invoices in his bedroom?

— Fi. Now is not the time to work.

"Hmmm?" Smelt's Emporium. Johnson's Dry Goods. Banks. Kelly. Jones. She sifted through the papers. Another for Smelt's and Johnson's. A scrap of paper slipped free.

— I know you favor those novels where the master of the house and the beautiful housemaid live happily every after but... Milton stepped into the papers. *I doubt your Kingslea has fantasies about seducing the servants.*

Fiona blinked. Seducing servants. The only person Hugh had better seduce was his wife.

Movement caught her eye. She stared at the folded paper flickering like a moth's wing on the washstand.

"What's that?"

— Don't look at me. You dropped it.

She unfolded the paper. "Your performance has been most disappointing thus far. Perhaps your marked interest in Miss Grey can be of use. Escort her to the function of her choice for the nights of June first and second. Give the guards and servants the night off."

Fiona glared at the note. At least, now she knew why Hugh had taken the invoices home.

— How would he know about Kingslea's performance. Milton wagged a finger at her, *Or should I say lack thereof?*

"The writer of this note holds Hugh's stepmother's vowels. He is responsible for sending him on those dangerous errands." Fiona set the note on top of the invoices. He was also responsible for their meeting, and for that, she would ask her uncle to spare his life.

— Seems that Kingston fellow isn't as reliable as we thought, Fi.

Back to Kingston. Milton's displays of annoyance were becoming a nuisance. Hugh had been correct. His errands and the *Sweet Wind*'s sinking were related. But why hadn't he told her?

"Do you know what this means?"

— Yes. Milton nodded.

Fiona hugged the stack to her chest. Paper crinkled, echoing the pleasure crackling through her. Hugh loved her. Why else would he marry her when he knew who was responsible for everything?

— It means the blackguard hasn't finished pilfering items from your uncle.

Not yet, but soon his larcenous deeds would end. Hugh must have something planned. But what? Fiona's speculations spilled into words.

"I think the papers should be enough evidence, but I suppose catching him in the act is best."

— Perhaps the annulment is for the best, Fi.

"Annulment? Oh, no, this deserves a reward. A big reward."

— Civilized societies don't reward thieves. Milton crossed his arms and glared at her.

"Of course not." Fiona glared back. Milton hadn't always been so slow to catch on. Had he left part of himself on the other side? "But we do reward heroes. And I think discovering who tried to kill Uncle Andrew and Aunt Caro is very heroic."

— He knows?

"Yes."

— Why didn't he say?

"Because then he wouldn't have to marry me." Fiona strode across the room. Hugh had used her uncle's ignorance of his assassin against him.

— So, where does the annulment fit in his plans?

Leave it to Milton to discover the one piece that didn't fit her theory.

"He's always thinking of others. The annulment gives me a way out of the marriage. We've never actually spoken of love, and Aunt Caro and Uncle Andrew's return last night was a bit of a shock."

— I don't think he knows he knows, Milton stated.

"He has the proof." Fiona waved the papers at him.

— Where are you going?

"To let him know that I know and that I love him."

— That's a big chance, Fi. If he doesn't know and you tell him, what's to stop him from returning you to your family? Milton reached for the papers. *Perhaps you should wait one more night. I know you'll seduce him tonight.*

"You forget. Tomorrow is the first, and Melinda, Cedric and Uncle Ronnie are still in the house."

— Just one more night.

"He loves me, Milton. I know he does." Fiona kicked the connecting door shut behind her and marched to the wardrobe. Her selection was limited. A pink morning dress or a blue walking one? Blue. Hugh said it matched her eyes.

— I hope so.

"Now, shoo, Milton." She swatted away her doubts. Hugh had to love her. "I need to dress."

— Shoo, Milton? What am I—a fly in your pudding? He mumbled as he drifted toward the door. He was halfway in the wall before he jerked about. *Who is it, Fi? Who shall feel the wrath of Milton Davis?*

"You'll find out when I talk to Aunt Caro and Uncle Andrew."

— But...

"Goodbye, Milton."

✤ ✤ ✤

"How much did you lose, Mother?" Melody's strained voice rustled the ferns squatting in the entry.

Fiona paused on the last step. Her new sister-in-law and stepmother-in-law were in the dining room. Should she interrupt or should she look for Hugh? Her growling stomach decided the question.

"Ten thousand." Plates chinked together. "It was a particularly dreadful evening."

Fiona winced. Dreadful for whom? Not for *her*. It was Hugh who would have to redeem the woman's debts.

"Pounds?" Melody screeched, "Oh, Mother, how could you?"

Hugh's butler slipped through the open dining room doors. Anger stamped his features. He started when he spied her. Fiona shook her head. She didn't wish to intrude. Yet.

"Do stop overreacting, Melody." The dowager Lady Kingslea selected a slice of toast from the rack and tossed it on her plate. She added a dollop of preserves before sauntering to her place at the head of the table. "These debts are a trifle compared to the dowry that American will bring."

Fiona felt Bunsen stiffen. Ten thousand pounds was more than most dowries. Certainly more than what she had brought to her marriage to Hugh. How were they to find the money?

"I don't think we should count on Fiona's dowry." Melody poured a cup of tea then joined her mother at the table.

"Of course we should. Whyever would your half-brother consider marrying so far beneath him if not for the money?"

Fiona's breath caught in her throat. Melody knew about Hugh's plans for an annulment. If she told her mother, Lady Kingslea was bound to tell the rest of society.

"I am certain Kingslea has his reasons."

"*We* are his reason. It is his duty to us and to his title to realize the largest marriage settlement he can. Lillian Lawson brought one million pounds to her marriage. Despite the shame your brother has brought to the title, the Marquess of Kingslea is certainly worth as much."

Shame? Kingslea? Fiona's palm touched polished walnut. That beastly woman had shamed the title more than Hugh ever could. She shoved against the door. It refused to budge. Bunsen rested his hand on hers. She looked at the butler, who shook his head. Apparently, Lady Kingslea's abuse was not new.

"He'll marry the chit." She gloated. "Then you and I will be a credit to Monsieur Worth. We needn't socialize with my dreadful sister or her shabby offspring. And your brother can take his dowdy little wife and his gauche manners to rusticate in the country. Forever."

Gauche manners. Fiona flicked her anger out of her fingertips. My lady's abuse of Hugh stopped today. She smoothed the bodice of her blue morning gown and nodded to the butler. The door swung soundlessly open.

"Mother, I—" Concern creased Melody's brow.

"You need not worry about sharing Aunt Annabelle's company." Fiona nodded to her sister-in-law. Obviously, the girl took after Hugh's father.

"You—" Lady Kingslea's half-eaten toast tumbled out of her hand and splatted onto the tablecloth. Bunsen rushed forward and scooped up the bread.

Fiona sauntered to the sideboard. It was best if the butler stayed. She could gain his approval and warn the staff at the change in management with one interview.

"My aunt and cousins are off on an *extended* holiday."

"My dear." Lady Kingslea daubed her napkin to her lips. "If one wishes to be a proper marchioness, one mustn't call before established hours and never in one's morning dress." She rested her napkin on the table and stood. "There are so many little subtle graces. Perhaps we will hire a tutor to instruct you."

Instruction. Fiona whacked an egg-laden spoon against her plate. Melody jumped as the noise shot across the room. Bunsen cleared his throat discreetly. Someone was about to learn a lesson, but there would be no tutor involved.

She smiled sweetly at her new mother-in-law. "Do you think so?"

"I would train you myself..." Lady Kingslea's soft hands pinched the last piece of toast from the rack. "...but duty must come before family."

Fiona selected a knife from the drawer. Light sparked off the blade as she twirled it.

"Would that be duty to oneself or the crown?"

"As a peeress—" Lady Kingslea began.

Lady Kingslea. Fiona selected a fork. *She* was Lady Kingslea now. It was time the household learned of it.

"As a peeress, *I* shall always place my family before my own pleasures." Fiona sauntered to the end of the table. Bunsen rushed ahead of her and cleared Hugh's stepmother's recently vacated place.

"Naturally, but with a married daughter, one has certain social obligations."

Fiona nodded as the butler held out the chair.

"I speak of your gaming, madam."

Color fled from around Elspeth Gurnsey-Barrett's tightly pursed lips. Her glare poured over Fiona's head.

"You should address me as Marchioness." Toast jumped as she slammed her plate onto the table. "Or my lady. Never—"

"I believe that title belongs to Hugh's wife." Fiona speared a forkful of eggs. Revenge, not eggs, was best served cold. "Which would be me."

"You—"

"*You* may address *me* as Lady Kingslea." Fiona added another bite of scrambled eggs to her fork. Her teeth scraped off the food. Creamy eggs dissolved on her tongue. Hugh's cook really was quite good. "Or my lady."

Elspeth's eyes widened in her chalky face. "He married you!"

Fiona swallowed. Blast. She had forgotten her tea.

"Last night." She couldn't very well get up and get a cup. Her new mother-in-law would steal her seat back. "By special license."

Bunsen smiled as he lowered a cup and saucer by her hand. Steam danced above the tea. Milk, lemon and sugar joined her at the end of the table.

"It was very romantic." Melody added before gulping her own tea.

"You knew," Elspeth hissed.

"We had to have witnesses. And you were otherwise engaged. Ten thousand pounds." Fiona picked up her knife. Undoubtedly, the staff kept it honed to razor sharpness. She sliced off a pat of butter. Elspeth cared more for her reputation than her person. "You should count yourself fortunate you already possess a wardrobe for the season."

"One needs to live up to one's station." The Dowager Marchioness of Kingslea sniffed before taking the seat next to Fiona.

"Actually, Da says one must live according to one's means." Fiona smiled over the rim of her cup. As Milton was wont to remind her, a reputation depended more on appearances than on actions. "You have no means of support other than Hugh's generosity, do you?"

"My late husband's son knows his duty"

Late husband's son. Fiona sipped her tea. She would need more sugar to wash down the bitterness. Elspeth might deny Hugh a relationship, but she would not deprive him of his rightful title.

"I believe we both depend on his lordship's kindness for the clothes on our backs."

"I am certain your father made certain…" Wrinkles appeared in her mother-in-law's powdered brow. "…stipulations in the marriage contracts."

"No contracts. No stipulations."

"So, Kingslea gets everything?" Elspeth licked her lips.

"Hugh gets me. Nothing else."

Elspeth blinked. Once. Then twice.

"I don't believe I heard you correctly."

"I wed without my father's permission, knowing as I did so that I was disinherited." Fiona smiled as the news stilled Melody's fidgeting. "Eight million pounds gone with just two words. *I do.*"

She held out her hand. Her wedding ring sparkled in the morning light.

Elspeth slumped in her chair. "Surely…"

"Hugh was relieved. Marriage contracts are such a bother."

"He knew." Red seeped into Elspeth's pale face.

"Of course. Love is so romantic."

"That fool." Silverware jumped and plates crashed together as she banged her fists on the table. "How I wish he had died—"

"That is enough." Fiona shoved out of her seat. She raked the knife off the tablecloth and faced Hugh's stepmother. The woman was denser than a three hundred-year-old redwood. "I am mistress of this household."

"You." Elspeth scoffed. "You are nothing but a—"

"A peeress." Fiona leaned closer. "And this is my home now. If you wish to reside here, you will obey a few simple but nonnegotiable rules. First, you will cease maligning Hugh's good name. Second—"

Tears stung her eyes as the woman's palm connected with her cheek.

"How dare you!"

Fiona worked the tingles from her jaw. Sea-crusted sailors had better manners than this woman.

"Your gaming will cease. It has already cost you next year's wardrobe. If you cannot manage to stop wagering then you will cease socializing."

"I most certainly will not." Elspeth raised her hand again.

Fiona raised hers to block the blow. The knife winked from her fist.

Tan fingers closed around Elspeth's lace cuff.

"I think it is a most excellent idea." Her husband stood at her elbow. His left eyebrow arched as he gazed at the knife. "Whyever didn't I think of it before?"

"Because you enjoy your adventures so much." Fiona placed a kiss on his smooth cheek. Lime-scented soap teased her senses. Maybe tomorrow she could watch him shave. Maybe tomorrow she would awake in his bed. She fell into her seat as her knees buckled. "I trust you slept well."

Hugh twisted as Elspeth jerked free of his grip.

"Tell me that penniless nobody in not mistress of my house!" she spat.

"As my wife, Fiona is mistress of this house."

"I'll not stand for it." The dowager stamped her foot, kicked free of her chair. "I won't." Skirt in hand, she stormed across the carpet.

"Melody," Hugh's voice softened as he addressed his sister, "perhaps you should take your mother to her room."

"Certainly." Melody glanced at him before rushing after her mother. The door snicked shut.

A dimple flashed in Hugh's left cheek as the corner of his mouth lifted.

"Are you always so agreeable in the morning?"

"I will not stand by and listen to her haranguing."

"No, of course not." His knuckles swept the sting from her cheek. "But perhaps you could take her to task in a room where there aren't so many knives."

Fiona set the knife on the table and eased closer to her husband. Slowly—she didn't want to lose his touch.

"A knife won't wound her where she is most protected."

Her hands tested the softness of his morning coat. Temptation pulsed beneath her hands.

He cupped the back of her head.

"I doubt she cares as much for Melody as she does her reputation."

Butterfly kisses flitted across her forehead.

"Precisely." Fiona nuzzled his cheek, inhaled his scent. She would know him in the dark. Please, God, let her know him in the dark.

He kissed her temple. She turned her head. And in the light. Another kiss. Her cheek this time. Just a little closer.

"I did warn you that I have experience with rumors."

"Yes." He pressed his answer into the tender skin near her mouth. "You did."

He would kiss her mouth now. Anticipation effervesced in her veins. Her lips parted.

"I thought we were to meet in the library."

Fiona's heart slammed against her ribs. Hugh cleared his throat and retreated to the sideboard. Her hands fell to her sides. Empty. And cold. So cold. First last night, now this morning. Her uncle really had to work on his timing. She took a deep breath, slapped on a smile and turned to greet the newcomers.

"Have you eaten, Uncle?"

"Hours ago." Uncle Andrew consulted the gold watch tucked in his worn shopkeeper's vest. "Are you just now waking, Fi?"

"Yes." Fiona resumed her seat. She set her fork across her congealed eggs. Was Milton correct? Did Hugh really not know what he had discovered?

"I could use a cup of tea." The scent of roses followed Aunt Caro into the room. Questions blazed in her eyes as she looked from Fiona to Hugh then back again. Fiona shook her head. Aunt Caro sighed.

"Perhaps tonight," she whispered, kissing Fiona's cheek and squeezing her hand.

Fiona added another spoonful of sugar to her tea. Tonight. There would be no tonight if she revealed the villain. Yet, how could she not?

"Caro." Uncle Andrew's frown encompassed them both.

"Hmmm?" Her aunt smiled and took Melody's place at the table. "That marmalade looks delicious."

"Would you like a slice?" Fiona offered as Bunsen appeared with a new rack of toast. Her aunt nodded and selected a square. The men took their seat, bracketing the women.

"We were just about to plot our next course of action." Hugh frowned then glared at the two slices of lemon he'd just squeezed into his tea.

"What have you learned?" Aunt Caro place a quick kiss on her husband's cheek and snatched his saucer. She placed a spoonful of marmalade on the plate when he reached for it.

"Not much," Hugh swallowed his tea with a grimace. Bunsen cleared his throat and offered a fresh cup. Hugh's chest grew as he inhaled the unadulterated brew. The butler cleared away the lemon and half-full cup.

Hugh didn't know. The truth weighted Fiona's heart. Duty demanded she tell.

And what of the duty to her heart?

Rubies winked in her ring. Did one actually have to sign the annulment or was it granted without the parties' explicit permission? The answer would determine the length of time she had to seduce her husband.

"You are too modest, Hugh."

His brow furrowed. He met her eyes for the first time since her uncle had interrupted their kiss.

"I have reason to believe there will be another break-in at your house tomorrow."

"I see no reason to wait that long." Fiona swirled her tea. She would give anything to have Brianna's gift, to see the future. To know that she and Hugh would remain together forever. "We must consider the safety of Melinda, Cedric and Uncle Ronnie."

"You know, don't you?" Uncle Andrew propped his elbows on the tale.

"Hugh found it." Fiona rested her hand atop her husband's.

"I did?" He stared at her hand before turning his own over and closing his fingers around it.

"You did."

"Well?" Uncle Andrew glared at their clasped hands. "Who is it?"

"Mr. Bartholomew." Fiona watched her family's reaction as the silence exploded. Hugh nodded slowly. Aunt Caro's brow furrowed as she stirred her tea. Red suffused her uncle's face.

"Nonsense." China rattled as he pounded on the table. "I'd stake my life on his innocence."

"He almost took it and Aunt Caro's once." Fiona sighed. This couldn't be easy for him. She had just accused his trusted friend of twenty years of attempted murder, and that wasn't the end of it.

"Why?" Aunt Caro asked gently, lacing her fingers between her husband's.

"Money. He's been stealing little by little." Fiona tugged the invoices from her pocket. She set the duplicate invoices side-by-side. "Undoubtedly, the originals went to the merchants for payment. The copy and its tallied amount was delivered to you for entry into your ledger. The difference went into Mr. Bartholomew's pockets."

"How long?" Uncle Andrew plowed his fingers through his hair.

"I don't know for sure, but the forging of invoices appears to be a recent development." Hugh squeezed her hand and offered her a reassuring smile. "Hugh was blackmailed into stealing your ledger, or at least attempting to."

"The captain's log?"

"Look at the numbers—the handwriting is the same." Fiona passed Hugh the note and an invoice in Mr. Bartholomew's handwriting. "Uncle's original ledger was in a captain's log."

"The thefts were blamed on the wagoneers." Uncle Andrew sagged in his seat. His head lolled to the left.

"What would he do with the items?" Hugh's question distracted her from her uncle's misery.

"Sell them."

Admiration flashed in her husband's eyes. "But not as himself."

"He needed someone else."

"Hancock."

Fiona turned to stare at her uncle.

"I should have known when he accused Hancock. The man is as honest as sweat on a coachman's brow. I thought he was having a streak of bad luck, but Bartholomew found silver plate in his coat. I started watching more closely."

"And you hired his son."

"Black." Her uncle nodded. "No wonder the man's a pariah. Bartholomew must have noticed you on your guard."

Hugh rubbed a star-shaped scar on his hand.

"Noticed. Hell, I flat out told him something wasn't right."

"You couldn't have known, dear."

"But he was too greedy to give up the money."

"By changing the invoices," Fiona added, "he didn't have to worry about selling the merchandise or sharing the profits with a partner."

"Why sink the *Sweet Wind*," Aunt Caro asked. "It seems his latest plan is fairly well foolproof."

"The books would tell. How could the same merchandise keep coming in yet offer lower returns? It couldn't."

"I guess we needed *your* work-related talents over your mother's."

"Bartholomew." Uncle Andrew rubbed his forehead. "I can't believe it."

Hugh snapped his fingers. "That was his suit you gave me, wasn't it?"

Fiona nodded. "And I found an IOU with your stepmother's initials for five hundred pounds."

"I'll kill him." Uncle Andrew's chair clattered to the ground as he stood. He snapped open his watch and glared at the face. "He should be at work by now."

"If he's as wily as we think, he won't be at work." Hugh rose to his feet and scratched his chin.

"Why the hell not!" Her uncle marched around the table and roared at him.

Fiona winced. She had better tell the rest before they came to blows.

"I don't suppose you've met the special auditor Da hired, Mr. Bookbuttons."

Hugh bowed.

"Damnation."

"There is another way." Hugh crossed his arms. "I have a meeting with him tonight. On the docks. He mustn't have realized I had the other note." He pulled a piece of paper from his pocket and handed it to her uncle.

"'Your performance has been disappointing. Bring the key to her house to the Landed Whale tonight at eight. Escort Miss Grey to the entertainment of her choice on the first of June.'" Her uncle paced the room "The Landed Whale? I believe that is in Wapping."

Fiona's tongue stuck to the roof of her dry mouth. She, too, recognized the name.

"That's where Captain List was murdered."

Uncle Andrew ignored her. "Are your friends available this evening?"

"Of course." Kingslea smiled.

Fiona rubbed her eyes. White splashed on her lids. They were going to trap Mr. Bartholomew. Mr. Bartholomew who'd murdered one man and attempted two more murders. They would need help. Her help.

"I'm glad I packed my lasso."

Hugh rounded on her. "You are not going."

"Don't argue, Fiona," her uncle snapped at the same time.

Fiona held her ground. "But—"

"No." Hugh stopped a foot from her. "Absolutely not."

Her uncle nodded. "It is too dangerous."

"I am more than capable of taking care of myself." Fiona glared at her husband and uncle in turn. "You know I am."

"Fiona and I will keep each other company." Roses accompanied the light touch on her shoulder. "Perhaps we'll even roll bandages."

Betrayal punched Fiona in the gut. "Aunt Caro!"

"It is for the best, my dear."

"Roll bandages?" Disbelief colored her uncle's words.

"We would only distract them, dear." Her aunt guided Fiona back to the table. "And if they are distracted, they might get hurt. You wouldn't want that, would you?"

She sank onto the chair. Arguments died half-formed. Her aunt's reasoning made sense.

"No, I suppose not."

"Of course not." Wool swished as she shook out her skirts. "Now, you men go plan and plot in the other room. I don't want to worry any more than I have to."

"Now, *I'm* worried." Her uncle remained in his spot. The men exchanged glances.

"Fiona." Hugh walked to her side. "Do you agree to stay with your aunt?"

Her heart screamed no, but without an ally, there was little she could do.

"Yes. I'll keep her company."

Hugh didn't budge.

Fiona clenched her hands together in her lap, lest she grab him and beg him not to go.

"Kingslea."

Her husband nodded. "The library."

Her heart cringed as he walked away. He could be hurt. Or killed. She glared at her aunt.

"I can't believe you're letting them go by themselves."

"Who said I was doing that?" Aunt Caro selected another piece of toast and spread marmalade across the golden surface.

"You just sent them out of the room."

"Isn't your delightful fiancé around, dear?"

"Milton?"

— *I'm here. Not that you noticed.* He drifted closer to the table. *Too busy trying to kiss that Kingston fellow to worry about your beloved fiancé.*

"Ghosts are very useful in discovering secrets. Listening where there doesn't seem to be any ears." Aunt Caro took a bite of toast.

— *Very clever, your aunt.* He rubbed his hands together than dashed across the room. *The library it is. I'll let you know what I discover, Fi.*

"He's gone."

Her aunt swallowed her bite. "I take it last night did not go as planned."

"No. Hugh is too honorable." Fiona picked up a piece of toast. But they had come close. So very close.

"Most vexing, isn't it? But there may be a way around such an unhappy circumstance."

"How?"

A wicked smile curved her aunt's lips. "It has been my experience that men find adventure very...stimulating."

"Stimulating." Sweet strawberries exploded across Fiona's tongue. Hugh certainly enjoyed his adventures, but he never said they were stimulating.

"Yes, even their iron control often crumbles in the face of more immediate...pleasures."

"How does that help?" Excitement coursed through Fiona. Her aunt was talking seduction. Hugh's seduction.

"I believe women of easy virtue inhabit the docks."

"The Landed Whale is a tavern, not a brothel."

"There is always the dark carriage that carries you home." Aunt Caro raised her teacup as if to toast her idea. "And I have just the outfit for the occasion."

CHAPTER 35

He lusted after his wife.

Not exactly unique in the history of man, but how many had promised to give the woman up? Kingslea's groan rippled across his pint. Bits of debris bobbed on the piss-colored ale. Maybe if he wasn't sitting in a pub reeking of sex, lewd suggestions and bawdy laughter. Maybe if her kiss goodbye hadn't tasted of raspberry jam and chocolate. Maybe if he was sane or possessed an ounce of control. He leaned back in his chair. None of this would have happened if she had simply kept her lips to herself.

That bloody kiss.

Kingslea throttled his coarse mug. White tipped his knuckles. A simple press of her lips to his shouldn't have decimated his control.

Yet, it had.

He shifted in his seat, trying to ease the constriction of his trousers. Would the vile stuff wipe the taste of her from his mouth? He raised the cup. What about the feel of her in his arms, her soft groans in his ear?

Damnation.

He abandoned his cup and plowed his fingers through his hair. Pressure raced across his scalp.

Where the devil was Bartholomew?

His leg bounced in irritation. A bleary-eyed drunk blinked at him before nodding off to drool on the scratched table. The clerk had better put in an appearance soon. Kingslea cracked his knuckles then dipped his head to the left then right. Tension released his shoulders. He was tired of this infernal waiting.

Leather cushioned his fingers. His fingers bumped over the embossed letters on the front. *Captain's Journal.* An innocuous book. A mundane name. Yet, inside was a story of betrayal and murder.

Numbers and names winked as he thumbed through the pages. The smoke-choked air stirred with the movement. The final chapter would be written in the musty tomes kept by bewigged judges. Bartholomew would spend the last of his days festering in prison.

That is, if Grey didn't kill the man. Kingslea's gaze slid to the back of the room. Fiona's uncle slouched over his pint of bitter while Winthrop guffawed bawdy jokes to his nearest neighbors.

"I'll kill him if he doesn't show up soon."

"Lord A will be off with the ladybird in another tick or so." Houseman rammed his chair into Kingslea's back and scratched his ankle.

Ladybird. Prostitute. Sex. Hell. Kingslea took a swallow of his beer. It tasted worse than it looked and hadn't done a bit to relieve the ache. He had never wanted a woman more than he wanted Fiona.

And he had promised to give her up.

Catch Bartholomew, and his marriage ended. Yet if the larcenous clerk never showed up, Fiona would go home with him tonight. Home. The townhouse had never been home. It had always been Elspeth's house.

Or had been until this morning.

Fiona had sent his stepmother packing. Fiona had defended him, protected him. She must care for him a little. Perhaps... His heart pumped the idea into his brain.

Perhaps he would court her.

Could one court one's wife?

Houseman rammed his seat against Kingslea's. The collision rattled his teeth. Bartholomew had arrived. Adrenaline pumped through him. He tugged his watch from his pocket. Feral eyes noted the gold. Murmurs crashed around the room. Fifteen minutes ago, he would have welcomed the challenge. Fifteen minutes ago, the clerk was a half-hour late.

The air stirred as the newcomer waded through the crowd. A grizzled salt staggered to the bar. Grey ducked his head, his nose disappeared into his cup. What was the man drinking for? He had a wife to go home to. A willing woman who'd...

Kingslea blinked as recognition skittered across his skull.

Bosson.

Where was Bartholomew?

The seaman grabbed his mug and plunged back into the throng. A spot cleared for him near the darkened hall. He gulped his beer then wiped his damp chin on his sleeve. His beady eyes worked their way around the room. They paused on Kingslea before moving on.

Kingslea adjusted the cuff of his suit. Bosson hadn't recognized him as the drinking sailor from the dock. He pinched the brim of his top hat. Of course, the man wasn't exceptionally bright. A knife winked in his hands as he cleaned his fingernails.

They planned to kill him.

Kingslea swallowed his amusement. Better men had tried and failed. Their attempt tonight would be no different, even without his four friends at his back. He tugged his hat lower over his forehead. Bartholomew should have hired more men.

Bartholomew.

Where the devil was the man? Didn't murderers and thieves have any sense of decency?

Houseman went rigid at his back. *About bloody time.* Expectation weighted the air. Kingslea's muscles quivered. He ran his fingers down the book's spine and shifted in his seat. He must not be recognized too soon. Something brushed his elbow. His company stilled.

"I see you had no problem finding the place." An umbrella slapped the table. Beads of water rolled across the lopsided surface and plopped on the floor. "And you have the book."

Gloved hands reached for the journal. Kingslea looked up. Confusion clouded Bartholomew's brown eyes. An instant later, it was gone.

"You!"

Kingslea shoved to his feet. The book dangled from his fingers.

"Perhaps we should finish our business outside."

"I have nothing to say to you."

Houseman's shadow loomed across the table. His beefy hand engulfed the clerk's scrawny arm.

"'Ere now. He asked polite-like."

"Unhand me." Bartholomew struggled against the restraint.

"Ye had best stop afore me knife slips."

The clerk froze.

"As to our business…"

"I have no business with the likes of you." Hatred blazed in Bartholomew's eyes.

"I believe you are correct." Kingslea opened the book. "According to this book, your business is with the magistrates."

The clerk's adam's apple bobbed. Color drained from his face.

"The magistrates won't listen to a silly little chit and her lover."

"I think they will listen to me." Grey roped his arm around his former employee's shoulders and propelled him toward the door.

Bartholomew's eyes narrowed. He swallowed twice. A second later, surprised calm replaced his malevolence.

"Mr. Grey, I am so happy to see you alive. I…"

"Stubble it, Bartholomew." As they cleared the door, Grey shoved the man. He staggered into the street.

Kingslea strode after the criminal. He was liable to run. To his surprise, Bartholomew found his feet and turned to face his accusers.

"Mr. Grey, I…" Bartholomew's eyes flew to the door. His smug smile slid from his face when Lord Alveston stepped onto the walk.

"Don't bother looking for your accomplice." Alveston cleaned his hands on a handkerchief. "Winthrop has acquired a new audience. Too bad your lackey is unconscious, I believe he would find Winthrop's jokes quite amusing."

Grey advanced upon Bartholomew. "Tell me why I shouldn't kill you."

The clerk stood his ground.

"You already have blood on your hands. What's one more dead body?"

Grey raised his fists. "The Duke of August died almost twenty years ago."

Duke of August. No wonder Fiona had wanted to meet the man. But twenty years ago, Sullied wouldn't have been duke. What had Grey kept from them? Kingslea glanced at his friend. Alveston shrugged and lit a cigarette.

"Duke!" Bartholomew spat. Spittle flew from his mouth. "I'm talking about my wife. My wife."

"Your wife?" Grey's fists dropped. "I had no hand—"

"Kind Mr. Grey. Wonderful Mr. Grey." Bartholomew simpered. "Let's take care of the widows of our sailors. But when my wife fell ill, where was your generosity?" With madness in his eyes, he lunged at Grey.

Fiona's uncle batted away his hands and shoved him back across the road.

"My personal ship was at your disposal. Ready to carry you and your wife to Italy, just as the doctors—"

"Butchers. All of them." Bartholomew lunged again. Madness gave him strength, but still he was not match for Grey. "You never paid me enough to hire the best. Not like you and your kind used. If you had given me what was my due, my Bess would still be alive."

Grey caught Bartholomew on his next attack. He pinned one of the clerk's arms behind his back, the other he clasped around the wrist.

"I sent my personal physician to look after her."

"You should have died." Bartholomew's legs collapsed. The fight left him, leaving behind a husk of a man. "You deserve to die."

Kingslea started as a mob emerged from the narrow alley next to the Landed Whale. Alveston flicked aside his cigarette. Winthrop was to warn them if anyone came to Bartholomew's assistance. Nothing short of death would have kept his friend from his duty.

Death.

Kingslea raised his fists. He couldn't very well punish the blubbering Bartholomew, but the hearty and hale group in front of him was another matter.

"Take him away." A woman's voice slipped into the street. Fiona's Aunt Caro. Unease itched down Kingslea's spine. "For the night. We'll make arrangements for his care in the morning."

"Aye, mum." A half-dozen police constables swarmed around the clerk as Winthrop dragged the unconscious Bosson out the door.

"Did I miss everything?"

"It's over." Kingslea sighed. Over. His marriage was over.

"I did everything he asked, didn't I?" Grey's hesitated.

Something was amiss. Something. The missing information swam just beyond the fringe of thought.

"Yes." Caro laid her head against her husband's chest. "His grief has turned to sickness. We'll see he is well taken care of."

"You never do listen, do you?" Grey's voice firmed. "I distinctly told you to remain home."

Home. Rolling bandages. With Fiona. Fear iced Kingslea's blood. If her aunt was here then Fiona could not be far away. His gaze flew frantically around the street.

"I didn't wish to leave my home and flee with you to some far-off place with more lax laws."

"Bloody hell!"

A woman's shadow slipped into the next alley. Kingslea skidded around the corner. Smashed crates and empty casks climbed the walls. Nothing stirred. Had he imagined her? God knew, he'd been dreaming of her all night. Gardenias perfumed the air. She was here.

"Fiona?" His question bounced back at him. Broken glass crunched under his boot heel. "Answer me." Silence. Two more steps. "I know you're here."

"Hugh."

Her caress trickled down his arm. His heart raced. The shunting of blood to other parts of his body muddied his thoughts.

"Fiona. What in the name of all that is holy are you doing here?"

"I want you."

Want you. Her words pulverized his control. He knew want. He wanted her. His feet carried him closer. Her breasts brushed his chest. His hand found her shoulder. Her pulse raced against the pad of his thumb. Logic made a foray into the haze of pleasure.

"We are in the middle of an alley."

"Do you want me?" Her lips pressed the question into his neck. Heated breath slipped down his back.

"I—" Thought snapped and fizzled. His fingers played with the buttons at her throat. The first one came undone.

"Make love to me." Her hands slipped down his chest. Pressure cut across his back. Buttons rained to the ground. Busy hands pushed open his vest, tugged his shirt free of his trousers.

Honor made one last attempt at control.

"I can't." He slid the second and third button free. Her creamy flesh glowed in the dark. Last night's encounter on her bed fed his mind. Passion ignited an inferno in his blood. She was more beautiful than he'd dare imagine.

"Your body wants mine." She stroked his turgid length through his trousers. Nimble fingers undid his buttons to grasp him, stroke the hard flesh.

Sweat beaded his forehead. One more touch, and he would be spent. He gently removed her grasp and placed her hand on his shoulder.

"I want you." God, how he wanted her. Needed her. He kissed her forehead. Her jaw.

"Then take me."

She was his wife. She was his.

"I think..." Fabric bunched against his arm as he raised her skirt.

"Don't think. Just feel." She placed his free hand inside her open blouse. Her breast fit perfectly in his palm. She fit him perfectly. His thumb teased her pebbled nipple. "And taste."

Her mouth found his. Her tongue slipped against his. Raspberry. Chocolate. Heat. His blood surged.

"God, Fiona." His hand slipped under her hem, lifted her up over him. Smooth skin welcomed his touch.

"You're not wearing any drawers," he panted. His finger slipped through a nest of curls. Silken folds caressed him. Wet and hot. She was ready for him. He wrapped her leg around his waist. His manhood nudged her opening.

"Love me," she whispered. Her hips moved. Her breath caught. She slid down his length. Full. Complete. Perfect.

"Yes." His thumb circled her, stroked the liquid pleasure from her body before he gave himself over to the abyss. Her tight flesh convulsed, milking his seed from him. "Yes, I do. I do love you."

"I love you," she panted before crying her ecstasy into his mouth.

Seconds passed. An eternity. His body calmed. Sounds filtered in. Rats scurrying, bawdy laughter. Reason pressed against him. What had he done?

Fiona chuckled before she nipped his ear. "You're mine now."

"Fiona. Kingslea." Grey's voice cut through Kingslea's lingering pleasure, rent the cocoon of gardenias enveloping him. "Dammit, man, where have you gone?"

"Let them talk, dear."

Fiona's tongue traced patterns on his neck. "I guess we should return to the others."

Kingslea released her leg. Her skirt tumbled into place. Her shaking fingers fumbled with her buttons. He tucked his shirt into his closed pants. He had just made love to his wife. Man and wife had consummated their union an alley. Contradictory emotions tussled inside his skull. Joy. Despair. Contentment. Worry.

"Talk? He's liable to kill her." Grey's growl was closer. Kingslea finished straightening his attire. "What possessed you, Caro? Sneaking off."

Possessed. Fiona had possessed him. His words returned to him. I love you. Clarity in the confusion. Light in the darkness. Kingslea glanced over his shoulder. His wife's attire was in order. His wife.

"What the hell have I done?"

CHAPTER 36

What had he done?

Hugh's words tormented Fiona as she placed her foot on the carriage step. A warm hand closed around her elbow. Hugh's grim face frowned down at her. An ache started in her stomach, dropped to the apex of her thighs and quivered down her legs. What had *she* done?

She'd trapped Hugh into a marriage he didn't want.

Tears pricked her eyes and needled her nose. Why had she listened to Aunt Caro? Despite her parentage, Fiona Grey was no gambler. Hindsight battered her sanity. She'd lost Milton because of a bet, and now she'd lost Hugh because of another one. If only she'd been a bit more patient.

She could have made him love her.

She could have had more than just one night with him.

"Well, that's settled." Uncle Andrew's voice pelted her back.

"Yes." The carriage dipped and swayed. Her legs trembled. She collapsed on the seat. The scent of tobacco wafted from the leather squabs.

"We'll stop off at the townhouse, Kingslea." A figure appeared in the doorway. "I had the lawyers draw up the papers this morning. Don't worry, Fi. You'll be out of this marriage soon."

"No."

Fiona's heart stopped. Had she said that or...

"Pardon." Confusion thickened Uncle Andrew's voice.

"No. No annulment." Kingslea leapt into the carriage and slammed the door shut.

"Where the hell do you think you taking my niece?" Her uncle's red face appeared in the window.

Kingslea pounded his fists against the roof. "Houseman. Drive on."

"'Bout bloody time." The coachman's words drifted down from the box.

Hope bloomed in Fiona's chest. No annulment. Could he really mean it?

"Don't you dare touch that whip." The door latch rattled. Kingslea held it closed. "Dammit, Fiona, get out of there."

Her hand settled on the door latch on her side of the coach.

"Stay." Hugh's voice filled the coach. "Please."

The coach lurched forward. Her uncle's curses chased after them.

Stay and chance her heart being rejected or leave with it badly broken? She returned her hands to her lap. Wretched hope. Hugh probably wanted to discuss another way to end the marriage now that they had consummated it.

"Fiona, I—" Hugh cleared his throat.

"I know what you are planning to say." Divorce? Fiona shuddered. They would find another way.

"You do?" He grasped her hands in his.

"I won't allow you to stay in this marriage simply because of honor." She took a shaky breath but couldn't bring herself to pull away from his touch. "I seduced you. I knew what I was doing."

"Fiona—"

"And I'll lie. If you say, we did anything then I'll say we didn't and–"

"*Fiona.*"

"And I will hire a hundred doctors to swear that I am untouched. I—"

"Bloody hell, wife." His hands settled on her shoulders. "Do you ever stop chattering?"

"I'll not bind you to a marriage you don't want."

"The marriage—"

"Will be annulled."

Kingslea's gently shook her. "Kindly allow me to finish my sentences."

"I know what you are going to say."

"Then you know I need you."

Fiona stopped mid-nod. "You need me?"

"Yes." He clasped her hands, opened her fists and placed a kiss in each palm. "I was a fool. I believed I was staying with you because *you* needed help. You needed me to protect you, to help you find your uncle. I was lying to myself. And was pretty good at it." He leaned forward. The carriage lamplight washed over his smile. "I had convinced myself it was true until tonight."

"Until the alley?" Could he really mean it? She leaned forward. The tip of her nose touched his.

"Until I realized that I love you."

Happiness exploded within her. Hugh loved her. Her gamble had paid off. She launched off the bench and tossed her arms around his neck. Arms closed around her. Strong arms. Hugh's arms.

"You love me."

"I know you don't *need* me to protect you or take care of you." He settled her on his lap. "You could even have found your uncle on your own. But if you would just give us a chance, maybe you'll find I can be of some small service to you as a husband."

Cold air filled the interior. Fiona glared at the spirit forming across from her.

"Can we exorcize Lillian?"

"Lillian isn't dead." His hand kneaded her hip.

Fiona smiled. Well, that's all right, then. She could ignore other spirits.

"You are wrong about one thing."

"Only one?" Hugh fingered the buttons on her bodice.

"I do need you." Desire drummed in Fiona's veins. "You have my heart." She settled her mouth on his. Kissing was such a wonderful invention. Hugh left her mouth to nibble on her ear.

— *Uh, Fi.*

"Go away, Milton."

"Yes, go away, Milton." Hugh pressed the words into her neck.

Fiona opened her eyes. Lillian's wasn't the only spirit in need of a priest.

Milton adjusted his cuffs. He examined his fingernails a few times then cleared his throat.

— *It's time for me to leave, Fi.*

"You're leaving?"

Hugh tightened his hold on her.

"No, I'm staying." He placed a kiss on her forehead. "I thought we had this settled."

"*Milton* is leaving." Loss settled in her stomach. He was leaving. After two years. Fiona blinked. There were no tears in her eyes.

"Good." She felt her husband smile. "I mean, rest in peace." She jabbed her elbow into his stomach.

"Ouch."

— *My job is done.* Milton cleared his throat. *I make a pretty good Cupid, not that I'd want his job.* He tapped his hat onto his head and sniffed. *Now, no moaning or weeping. I can rest in peace now, though you shouldn't tell him that. Tell him I'll be back if he makes you cry. I've gotten pretty good at tossing books.*

"I'll miss you." She would, but his leaving wouldn't devastate her as it had before. Fiona clutched Hugh's hand.

— *Of course, you will. You loved me.* Milton brushed at his cheek. *And who wouldn't.* He fleshed himself out.

Fiona's heart skipped a beat. This was the young man she had loved not so very long ago. Loved. Past tense. Just like Milton. She tossed her arms around him. He wasn't his normal cold self.

"I can see him." Hugh's whisper filled the carriage.

"And you'll see a lot more of me if you don't treat her right." Milton shook his fist at him.

"She'll be my queen."

Fiona let go of the past. Her back rested against the future. Her husband. Hugh.

"I'll be satisfied with being your wife."

"Be happy, Fi." Milton's voice lingered as he faded away.

"I will."

"Is he gone?"

"Yes." She sniffed the tears back. Milton was gone, this time for good. She would see him again, but she didn't need him anymore. Her heart filled. She had been blessed to love and be loved by two special men.

"It's alright to cry, love." Hugh tucked her head beneath his chin. "I'll be here."

She and Hugh were alive. She had spent two years grieving for a life stolen. She refused to waste a second more.

"I love you, Hugh."

"And I love you." He kissed her head. "I have the rest of my life to show you how much."

Fiona turned her head to catch his next kiss. "Why don't you start now?"

CHAPTER 37

*"I guess your uncle arrived before us." Hugh tucked a loose strand of hair be-*hind her ear as they pulled up in front of the house. Light glowed from all the windows.

"Houseman did circle the park twice." Fiona pulled up her bodice then placed a kiss on her husband's chin. He really was amazing. And he was hers. Uncle would just have to understand.

"Three times." Hugh slid her off his lap, opened the door and climbed out.

"Get your hands off my daughter, you blackguard."

Da! Joy warred with trepidation. She had hoped to convince Uncle Andrew of her happiness before telling Da.

"Sir, I—" Something slammed against the coach.

Fiona winced. If she were a gambler, she would have bet that something was her husband.

"Fiona. Out. Now."

She poked her head out. Da usually reserved that tone of voice for her sister Gilly. Her knees shook as she stepped to the ground. However did her sister stand it?

Mam slipped out the front door. Aunt Caro and Uncle Andrew followed.

"Everett."

"My dear..." Da kept his pistol trained on Hugh. "...I'll allow you to stay. A wife cannot be compelled to testify against her husband even in drizzly England, but I insist you remove your daughter from the streets."

Fiona stepped in front of her husband. She had to make Da see reason.

"I'm not going."

"Dearest—"

"Mam—"

"Fiona." Hugh set his hands on her shoulders. "I think I should speak with your father."

"But..." Fiona stared at her husband. He didn't understand what Da was capable of.

"I'll be all right."

Poor Hugh. She should have warned him about her father's wartime duties.

"Do you promise not to kill him, Da?"

"Agreed."

"As you wish." Fiona turned in her husband's embrace. Her whip was out of the question. As was her lasso. Something thumped against her thigh. She smiled, fished it out of her pocket and pressed it into her husband's hand. At least he wasn't completely defenseless.

❋ ❋ ❋

Kingslea shook his head. His wife had given him a fountain pen. Did she really think he would harm her father? Rubbing his bruised shoulder, he stared at the broad-shouldered, white-haired man.

"Do all Americans proffer their introductions over the barrel of a pistol?"

"Only those educated in England."

Fiona's father was educated here? He seemed a little too wild, too American.

"Touché."

"I'll give you a choice."

Kingslea straightened. He should have known this was coming. "No. No choice. We are staying married."

Grey would have to use that gun if he really wanted the marriage over. Something told Kingless the man knew it and was willing to accept the terms.

Grey arched a white eyebrow.

"Two million pounds has a way of changing a man's mind."

"Keep it. Fiona stays my wife."

"Three million."

He counted to ten. His father-in-law's bribery was beginning to grate.

"Keep it."

"When you married without my permission, Fiona was cut off. No pots of money waiting for you."

Kingslea leaned against the carriage. Fiona had given up everything to marry him? And he had repaid her with talk of an annulment. Was a lifetime long enough to make it up to her?

"Then keep your money. If you disown Fiona, you'll be the one poorer for it."

Grey folded his arms across his chest, the gun still casually held in his hand.

"And do you know about the ghost sharing your bed?"

290

"Milton?" Hugh watched the deviltry fade from his father-in-law's face. "He's gone."

"Gone. Of course, he's gone. The fool was killed in a carriage race two years ago."

"No. Gone as in no longer a spirit on this plane." Confusion knit Grey's brow. "He bid her goodbye in the carriage then left. Poof. I suppose I should have thanked him."

"Thanked him? For what? Ruining my brother's library?" Fury vibrated Everett Grey's frame. "Accompanying my daughter on this harebrained adventure? She never would have come if he hadn't goaded her into it."

"You mean you didn't know?"

"Came back from the Continent to find Jonathon running the company and a note from Fiona saying she'd hied off to England."

Kingslea rubbed the scar on his hand. He had been afraid this evening's events hadn't been an aberration in his wife's character.

"All this time, she led me to believe you sent her here."

"Offended your sensibilities, eh. What lousy father would allow his daughter to junket off to England with nothing but a ghostly companion?"

"Milton certainly put the opportunity to good use. He handpicked another groom."

"Good God." Grey took a step backward. "Milton choose you?"

"No. He choose someone else."

"Well, that's all right, then."

"I am determined to stay married to your daughter."

"And I suppose she loves you."

"I believe so."

"Thought as much when she gave you the fountain pen."

"You saw?"

"I see too much." Grey stuffed the gun in his waistband. "The white hair proves it. That's why I promised not to kill you. I was hoping to nick you. Guess that's out now."

Nick him? The man talked of shooting another with a chilling casualness.

"I'm relieved to hear it."

"Has she told you everything, then?" Grey strolled down the steps, rolled a cigarette and lit it.

"I know about Milton and her sire."

He nodded. "What about Gran?"

The hair on Kingslea's neck stood up. Fiona had mentioned Gran, but from the way Grey spoke her name, he had a feeling Gran was also dead.

"I take it she's deceased."

"Wouldn't know it by the way the woman interferes." Grey rubbed the back of his neck. "Can't go for a peaceful drive unless Grimsree's around. Who'd have thought I'd actually welcome the presence of the Grim Reaper."

"The Grim Reaper?" Kingslea's stomach lurched. Joking. The man must be joking. Nick him. Grim Reaper. The whole thing was too fantastic.

"An old family friend." His father-in-law flicked his cigarette onto the sidewalk and ground it out. "Don't worry, he's Aidan's cross to bear now." A smile twisted his lips. "He'll be jealous that you managed to send Milton to the hereafter. Hell, *I'm* jealous."

"Who—Grimsree or Aidan?"

"Both." Grey offered Kingslea a piece of rolling paper. Kingslea took it and a generous pinch of tobacco.

"If one daughter has a dead fiancé for a companion and the other Death, I shudder to think what accompanies the third one."

"Brianna has a cat."

He rolled his cigarette. A cat. How perfectly mundane. At least one of Fiona's sisters could visit.

"That doesn't sound too bad. Several of our tenants have them."

Grey grinned and struck a match against the bottom of his boot. Sulfur stung the air.

"Portent climbed out of her grave to return to Brianna."

Smoke choked Kingslea. He coughed. Tears blurred his vision.

"Perhaps she wasn't dead."

"Oh, she was dead, all right." Grey held up two fingers. "Two days dead. I should know. I was with the man who ran her over." He blew a cloud of smoke. "She left her more affectionate nature on the other side. And she was just plain mean *before* the accident."

"Perhaps--" Logic refused to accept his explanation.

"Very, very dead."

Kingslea tossed his cigarette away. Milton wasn't so bad. Not bad at all.

"Nothing you've said has changed anything. I love your daughter."

"I suppose you'll keep her fat with babies and lock her up."

"I think she enjoys working at Grey Shipping. I know I certainly do."

"So, I've missed another wedding." A face appeared in the townhouse's window. Andrew Grey. Fiona's father waved him out. "But I suppose I could endure another reception."

"We were not churched."

"Were you married in a brothel?"

"A...!" Kingslea shook his head. His father-in-law's sense of humor knew no bounds. "Lud, no. We were married in your brother's library."

"Then that is something you have over your brother-in-law."

Grey was serious. One of his daughters had married in a brothel. Elspeth would be appalled. Kingslea rubbed his hands together. He was going to like his new family.

"I think Fiona might like a priest to say the words."

"She probably will. She's learned how effective such social gatherings can be to a business. Have you always been in shipping?"

"No, I only started two days ago."

Grey stroked his chin. "You're not in shipping. I doubt you're the coachman or groom. Ah, well, your occupation doesn't matter." He elbowed Kingslea. "I'd take a tailor over these fancy nobs you have over here. Useless, the lot of them."

"Milord."

Kingslea winced as his butler lumbered onto the stoop.

"The dowager marchioness is preparing to depart."

"Hellfire." Grey stumbled backward. "You're one of them."

"Tell Elspeth Houseman will take her to the station."

"Very good, milord." His butler bowed and left.

"I can't believe that you're…"

"The titles are—"

"There's more than one?"

Fiona skipped down the steps. "He's a marquis and an earl ."

"Fiona, I can handle this." Kingslea gritted his teeth. His wife's rescue was threatening to undo all his work.

"Uncle Andrew has persuaded Hugh to sit in Parliament, more votes to his side. And—"

Fiona's father scowled at him. "You mean he hasn't even fulfilled his responsibility that comes with his titles."

"He found the discrepancies, Da. He found proof that Mr. Bartholomew has been embezzling for nine months."

"Bartholomew?" Grey grudgingly allowed respect to dilute his surly expression. "He's that drab fellow that looks like a buzzard."

"Vulture."

"Hmm." Grey nodded. "Yes, that's more accurate. I'll have Andrew's lawyer draw up the settlements. Can't have my daughter living in a leaky house."

"I can assure you, sir—"

"I almost lost one daughter to consumption." He offered his hand. "I'll not chance losing another on account of pride."

"Da, we don't want your money." Fiona slipped her arm around Hugh's waist. "We want your blessing."

"You'll get the money because it is your birthright and because you worked for it. As for the other…"

Fiona went still at Kingslea's side. "Mam has already given hers."

"And I suppose Gran has threatened me with a frying pan if I withhold mine."

"No."

"I only want you happy, Fiona." Grey cupped his daughter's cheek. "An old man's selfishness wanted me to be there to share your day with you."

"You can. Mam is reserving the church. Aunt Caro knows a priest and…"

"And I'll telegraph your sister."

"I love you, Da."

"I'll take care of her, sir." Kingslea shook his father-in-law's hand.

"Of course, you will." Grey walked up the stoop. "Our family is littered with dead people who'll haunt you if you don't."

END

ABOUT THE AUTHOR

LINDA ANDREWS lives with her husband and three children in Phoenix, Arizona. When she announced to her family that her paranormal romance was to be published, her sister pronounced, "What else would she write? She's never been normal."

All kidding aside, writing has become a surprising passion. Just how did a scientist start to write paranormal romances? What other option is there when you're married to a romantic man and live in a haunted house?

ÆBOUT THE ÆRTIST

CAROL WEBB is a two-time finalist in the Golden Heart Contest of Romance Writers of America and has won and placed in numerous other writing contests. She loves writing about ordinary people who find themselves thrust into extraordinary circumstances. Between writing, she currently owns and operates, Firebird Web Designs, a company that specializes in doing web sites, promotional video trailers website optimization.

Made in the USA
Charleston, SC
24 November 2012